⪼A MODERN GRAPHIC RETELLING OF *THE SECRET GARDEN*⪻

The Secret Garden
on 81st Street

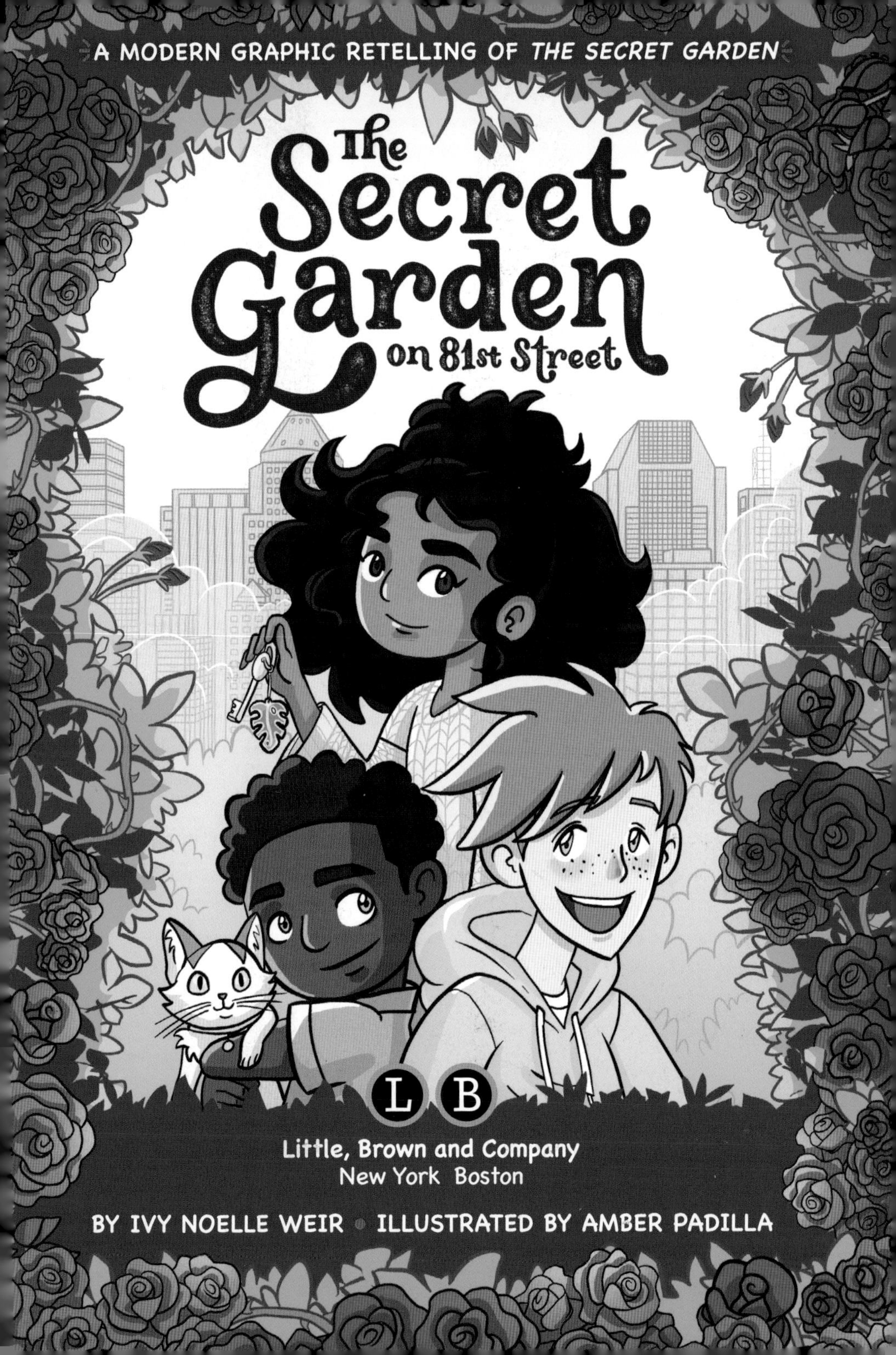
A MODERN GRAPHIC RETELLING OF *THE SECRET GARDEN*
The Secret Garden on 81st Street
LB
Little, Brown and Company
New York Boston
BY IVY NOELLE WEIR • ILLUSTRATED BY AMBER PADILLA

About This Book

This book was edited by Rachel Poloski and designed by Ching N. Chan. The production was supervised by Bernadette Flinn, and the production editor was Lindsay Walter-Greaney. The text was set in Chalkboard, and the display type is Creative Vintage.

Little, Brown and Company
Hachette Book Group
1290 Avenue of the Americas, New York, NY 10104
Visit us at LBYR.com

First Edition: September 2021

Little, Brown and Company is a division of Hachette Book Group, Inc.
The Little, Brown name and logo are trademarks of Hachette Book Group, Inc.

The publisher is not responsible for websites (or their content) that are not owned by the publisher.

Library of Congress Cataloging-in-Publication Data
Names: Weir, Ivy Noelle, author. | Padilla, Amber, artist.
| Burnett, Frances Hodgson, 1849-1924. Secret garden.
Title: The secret garden on 81st street : a modern retelling of
The secret garden / story by Ivy Noelle Weir ; art by Amber Padilla.
Description: First edition. | New York : Little, Brown and Company, 2021.
| Summary: "Entitled loner Mary Lennox moves to her uncle's house in New York when her parents pass and makes friends for the first time, who help her restore her uncle's abandoned rooftop garden, teaching her to grieve and grow." —Provided by publisher.
Identifiers: LCCN 2020019856 (print) | LCCN 2020019857 (ebook)
| ISBN 9780316459655 (hardcover) | ISBN 9780316459709 (paperback)
| ISBN 9780316459686 (ebook) | ISBN 9780316459693 (ebook other)
Subjects: LCSH: Graphic novels. | CYAC: Graphic novels.
| Grief—Fiction. | Gardens—Fiction. | Friendship—Fiction.
Classification: LCC PZ7.7.W399 Se 2021 (print)
| LCC PZ7.7.W399 (ebook) | DDC 741.5/973—dc23
LC record available at https://lccn.loc.gov/2020019856

ISBNs: 978-0-316-45965-5 (hardcover), 978-0-316-45970-9 (paperback),
978-0-316-45968-6 (ebook), 978-0-316-45967-9 (ebook), 978-0-316-45966-2 (ebook)

PRINTED IN CHINA

1010

Hardcover: 10 9 8 7 6 5 4 3 2 1

Paperback: 10 9 8 7 6 5 4 3 2 1

For my mom, who taught me that sometimes the best place to find peace is digging in the dirt. –Weir

To my grandma Marcella, who gave me a little plot of land in our backyard so I could plant wildflowers and make my own Secret Garden. –Padilla

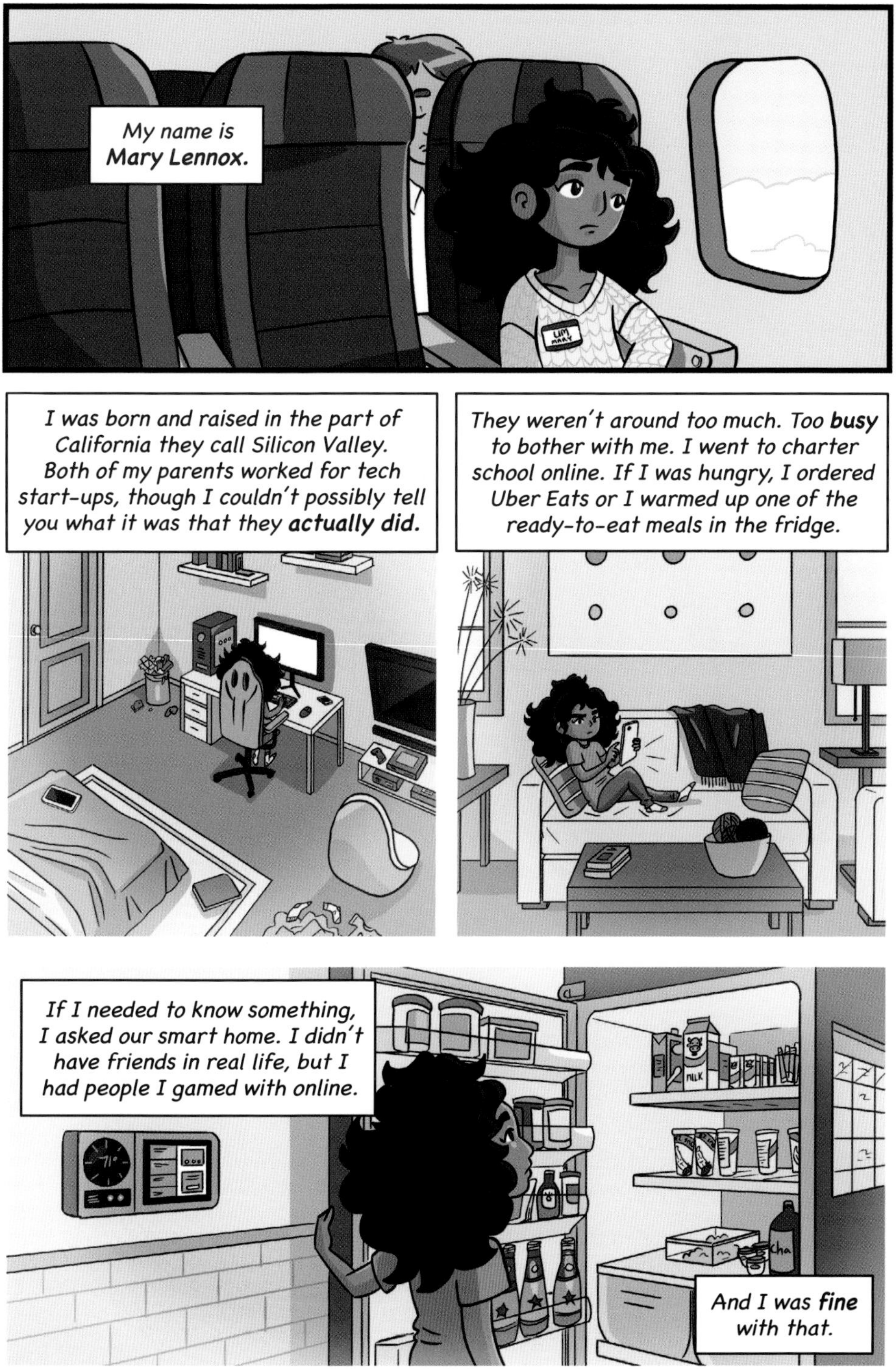
My name is Mary Lennox.
I was born and raised in the part of California they call Silicon Valley. Both of my parents worked for tech start-ups, though I couldn't possibly tell you what it was that they actually did.
They weren't around too much. Too busy to bother with me. I went to charter school online. If I was hungry, I ordered Uber Eats or I warmed up one of the ready-to-eat meals in the fridge.
If I needed to know something, I asked our smart home. I didn't have friends in real life, but I had people I gamed with online.
And I was fine with that.

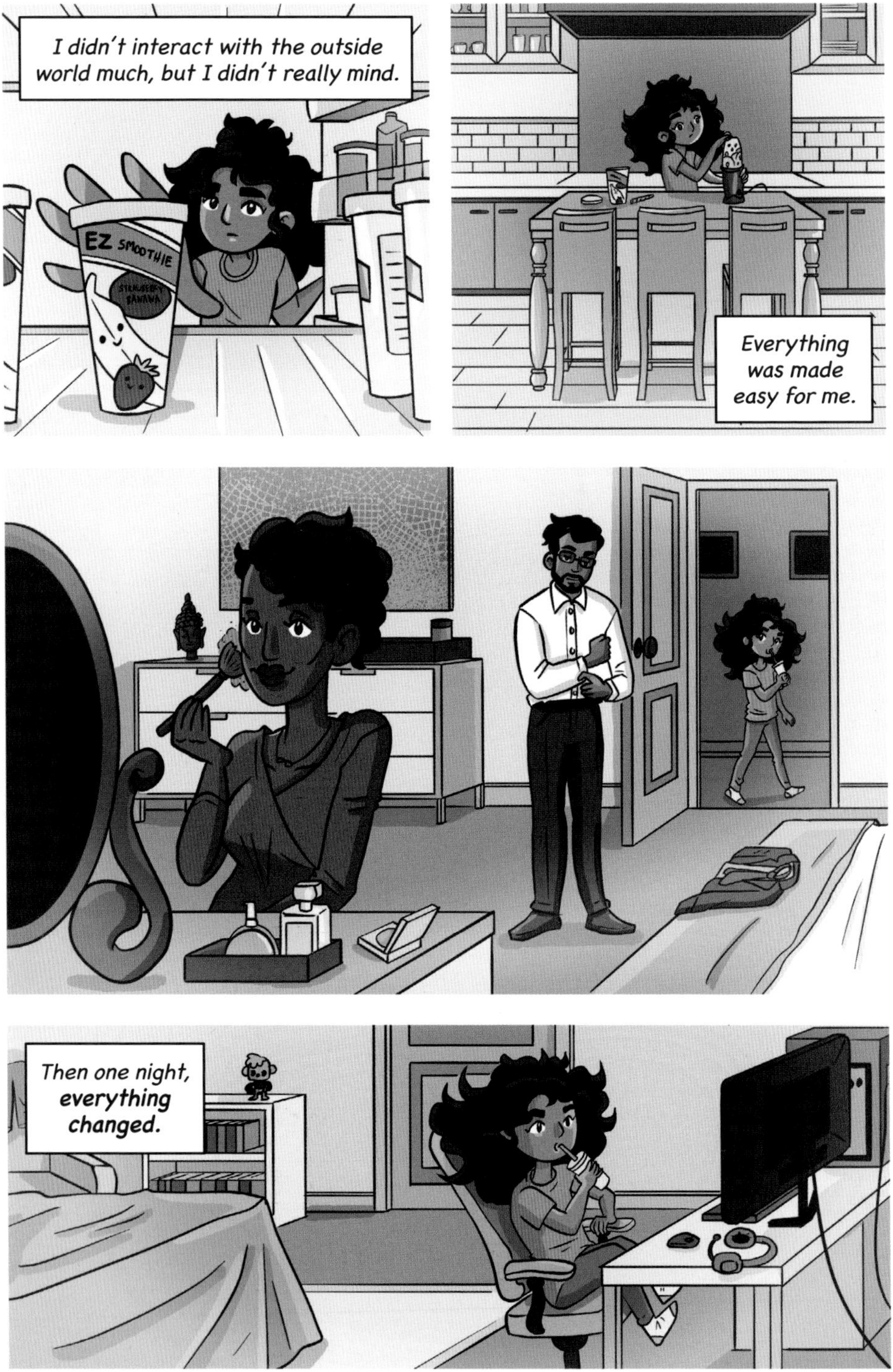
I didn't interact with the outside world much, but I didn't really mind.
EZ SMOOTHIE
Everything was made easy for me.
Then one night, **everything changed.**

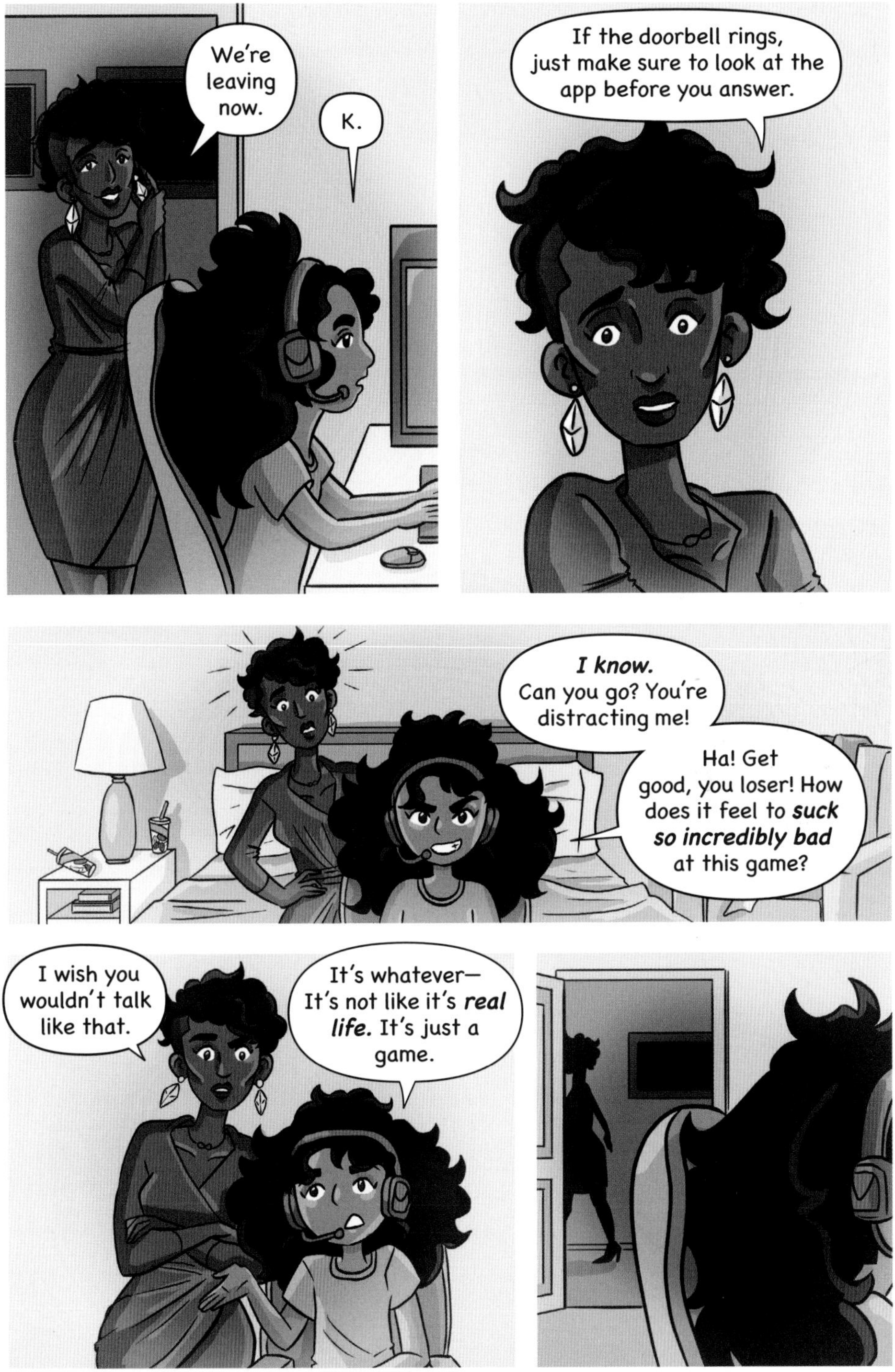
We're leaving now.
K.
If the doorbell rings, just make sure to look at the app before you answer.
I know. Can you go? You're distracting me!
Ha! Get good, you loser! How does it feel to *suck so incredibly bad* at this game?
I wish you wouldn't talk like that.
It's whatever— It's not like it's *real life.* It's just a game.

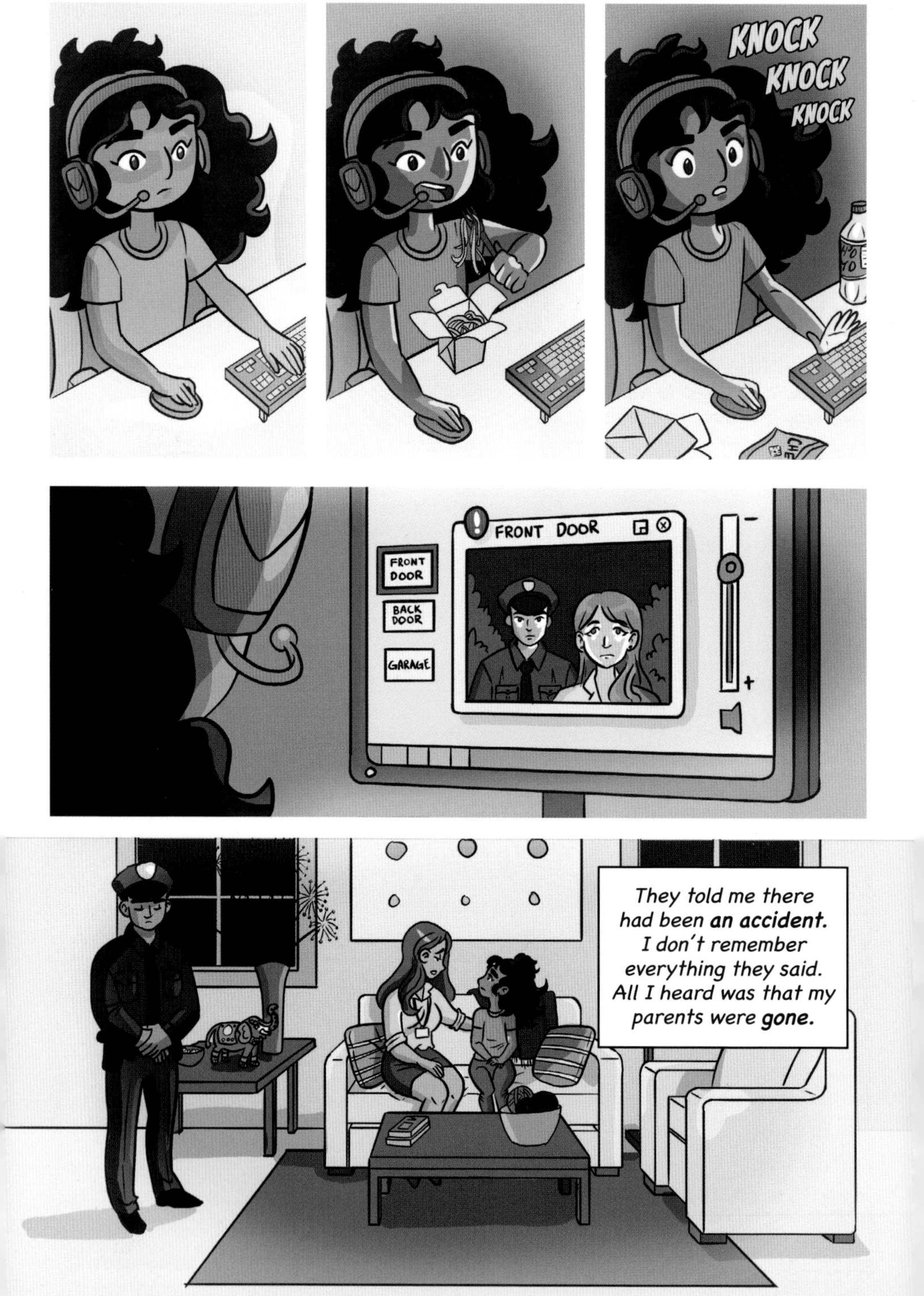
KNOCK
KNOCK
KNOCK
FRONT DOOR
FRONT DOOR
BACK DOOR
GARAGE
They told me there had been **an accident.** I don't remember everything they said. All I heard was that my parents were **gone.**

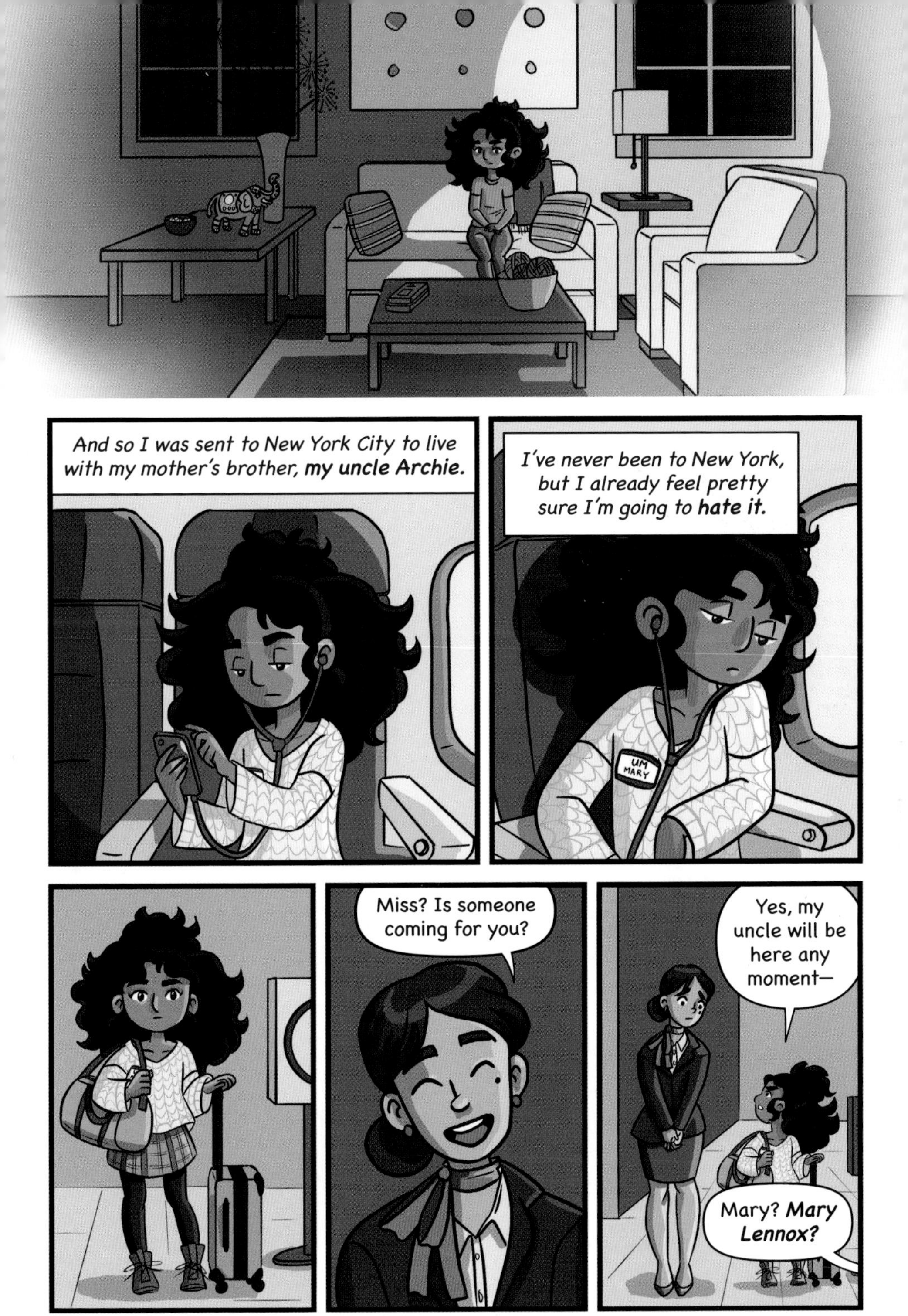
And so I was sent to New York City to live with my mother's brother, **my uncle Archie.**
I've never been to New York, but I already feel pretty sure I'm going to **hate it.**
UM
MARY
Miss? Is someone coming for you?
Yes, my uncle will be here any moment—
Mary? **Mary Lennox?**

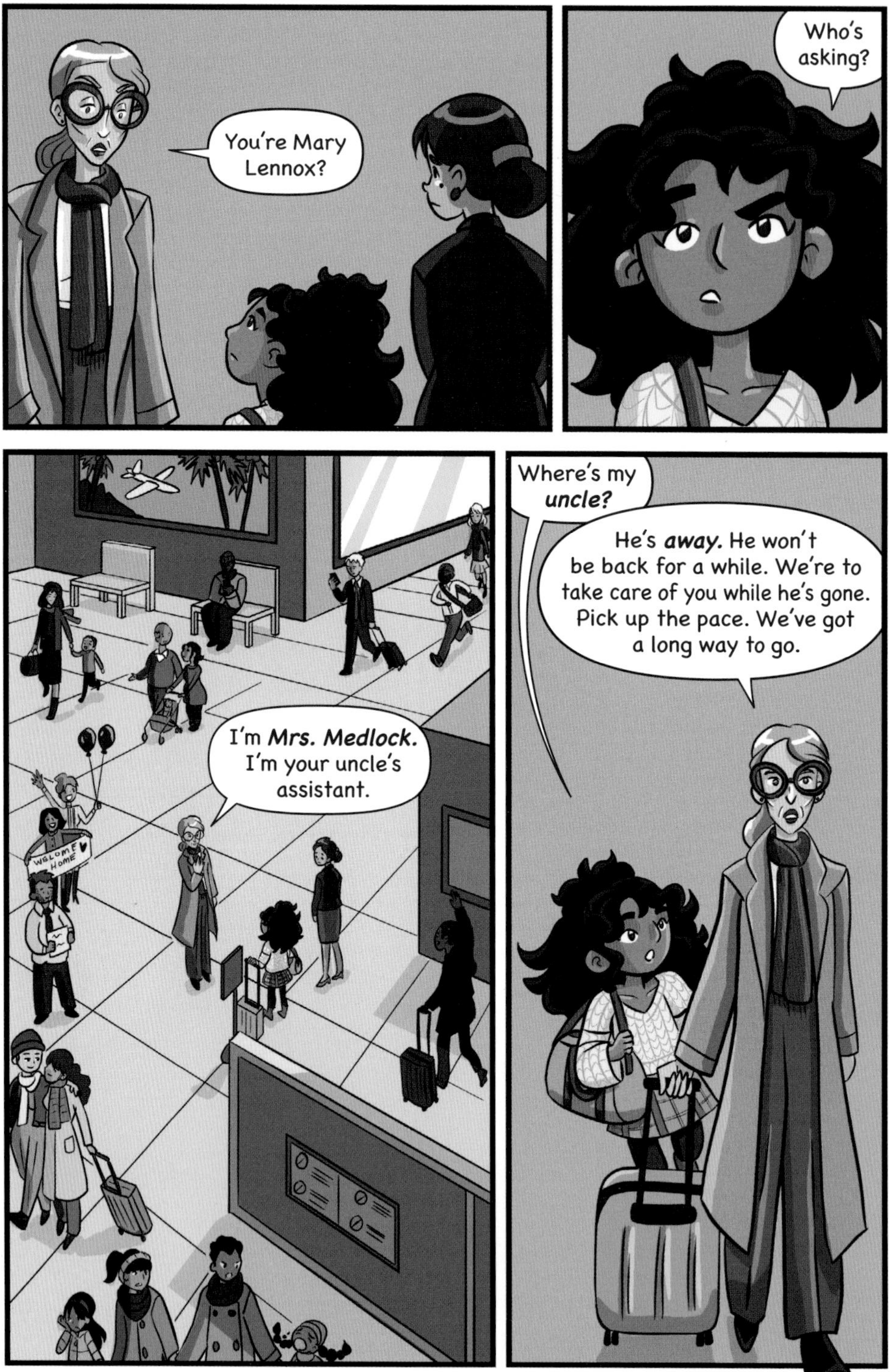
You're Mary Lennox?
Who's asking?
I'm **Mrs. Medlock.** I'm your uncle's assistant.
Where's my **uncle?**
He's **away.** He won't be back for a while. We're to take care of you while he's gone. Pick up the pace. We've got a long way to go.

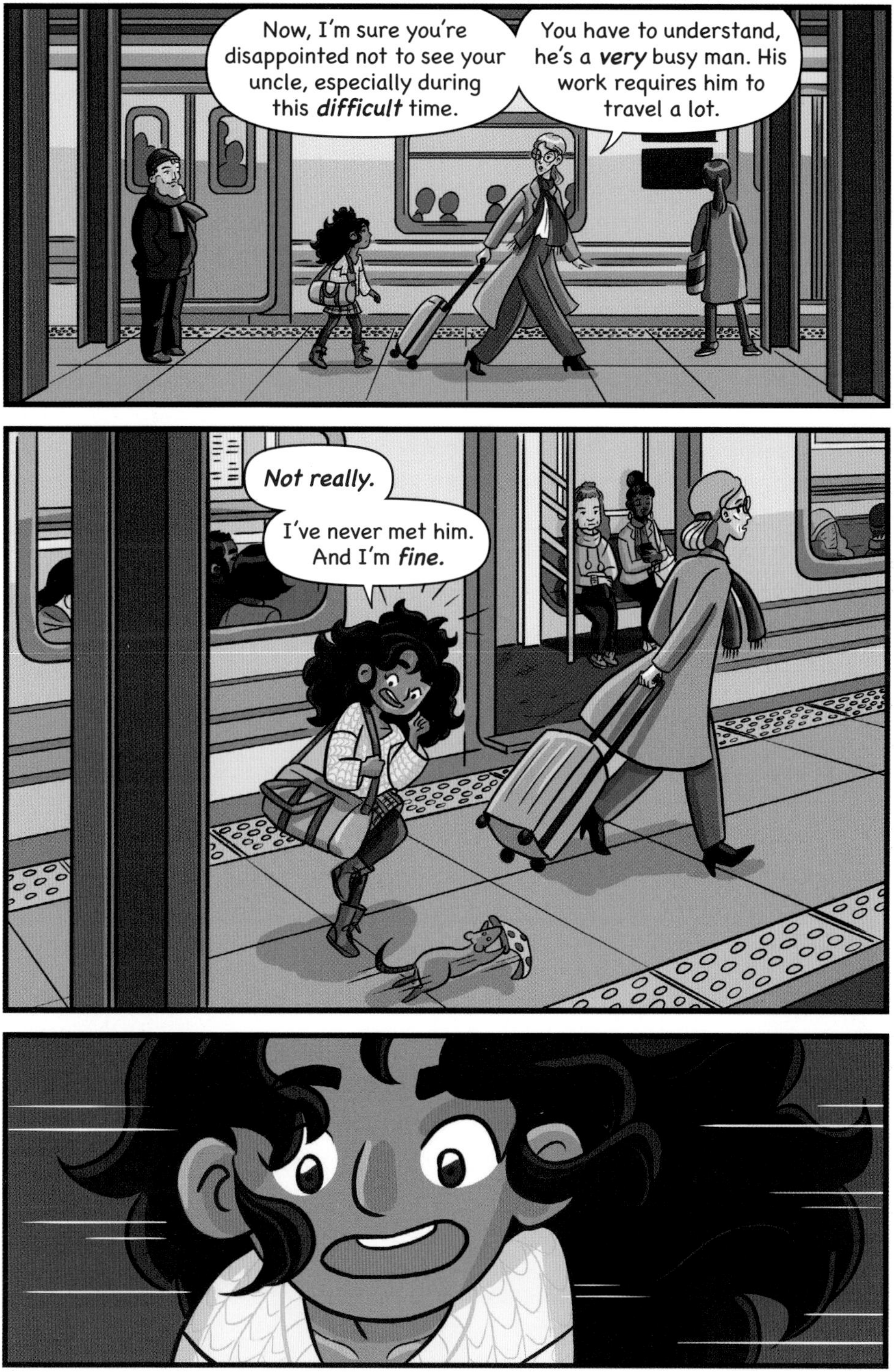
Now, I'm sure you're disappointed not to see your uncle, especially during this *difficult* time.
You have to understand, he's a *very* busy man. His work requires him to travel a lot.
Not really.
I've never met him. And I'm ***fine.***

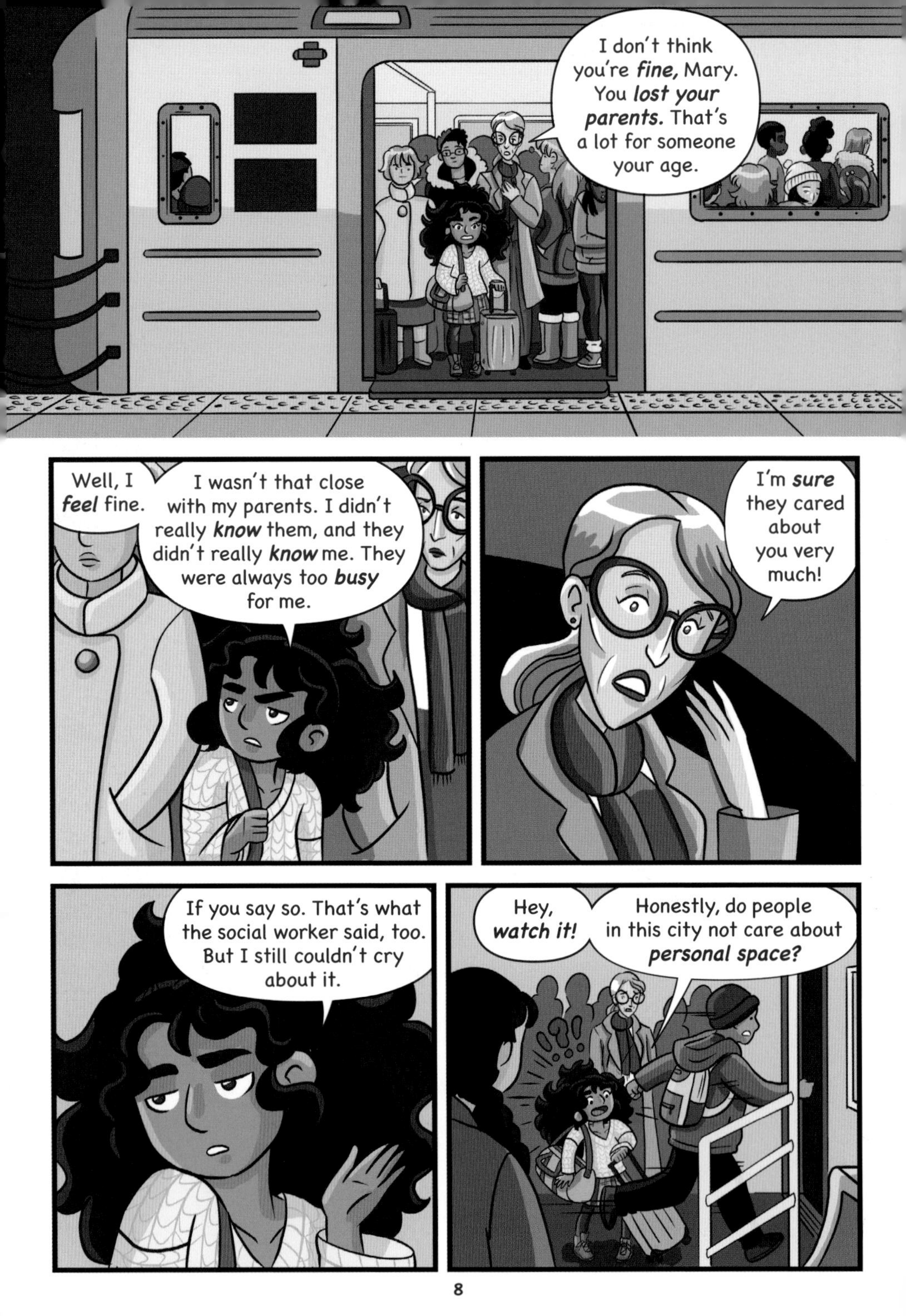
I don't think you're *fine,* Mary. You *lost your parents.* That's a lot for someone your age.
Well, I *feel* fine.
I wasn't that close with my parents. I didn't really *know* them, and they didn't really *know* me. They were always too *busy* for me.
I'm *sure* they cared about you very much!
If you say so. That's what the social worker said, too. But I still couldn't cry about it.
Hey, *watch it!*
Honestly, do people in this city not care about *personal space?*

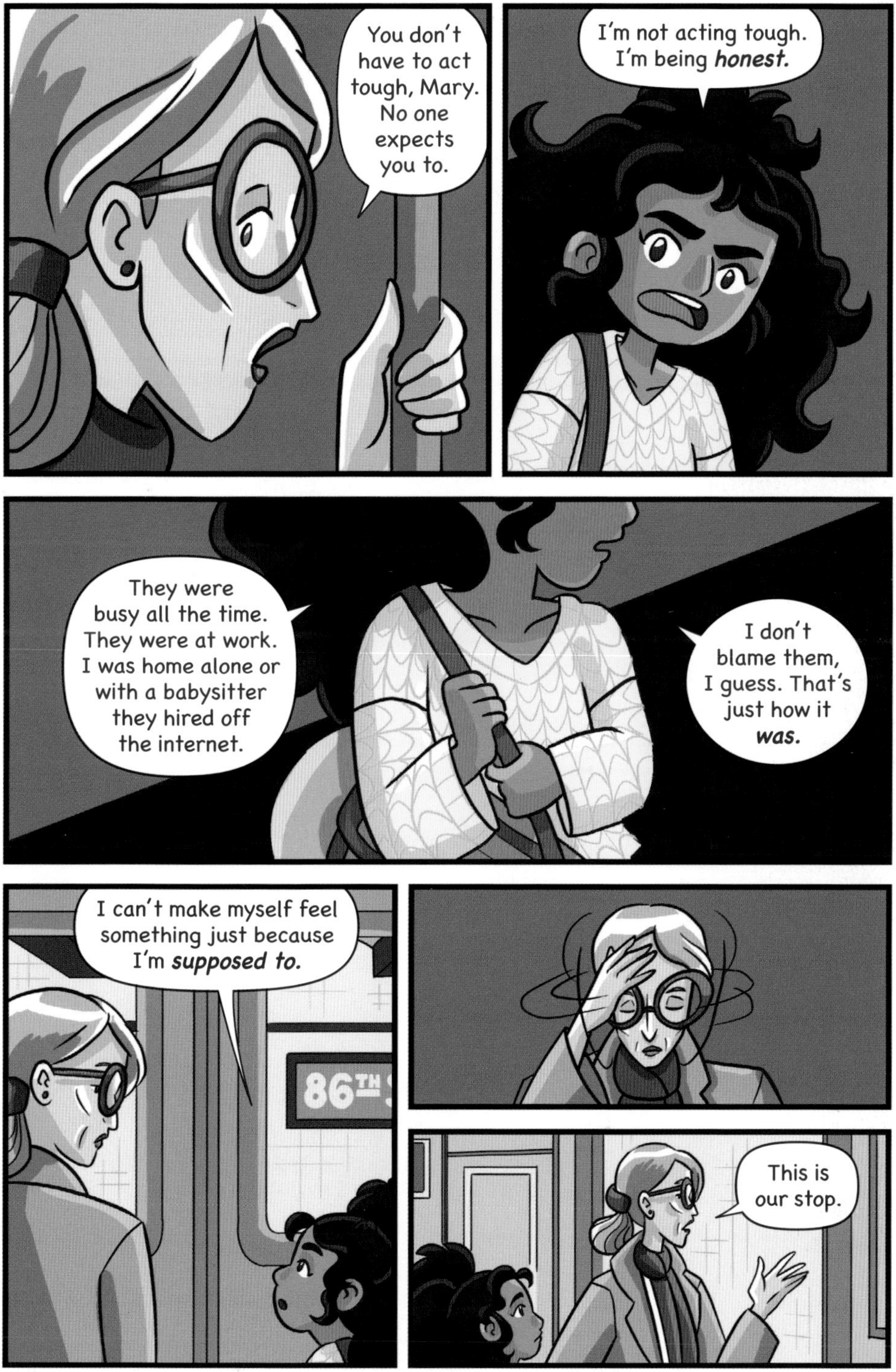
You don't have to act tough, Mary. No one expects you to.
I'm not acting tough. I'm being ***honest.***
They were busy all the time. They were at work. I was home alone or with a babysitter they hired off the internet.
I don't blame them, I guess. That's just how it ***was.***
I can't make myself feel something just because I'm ***supposed to.***
86TH
This is our stop.

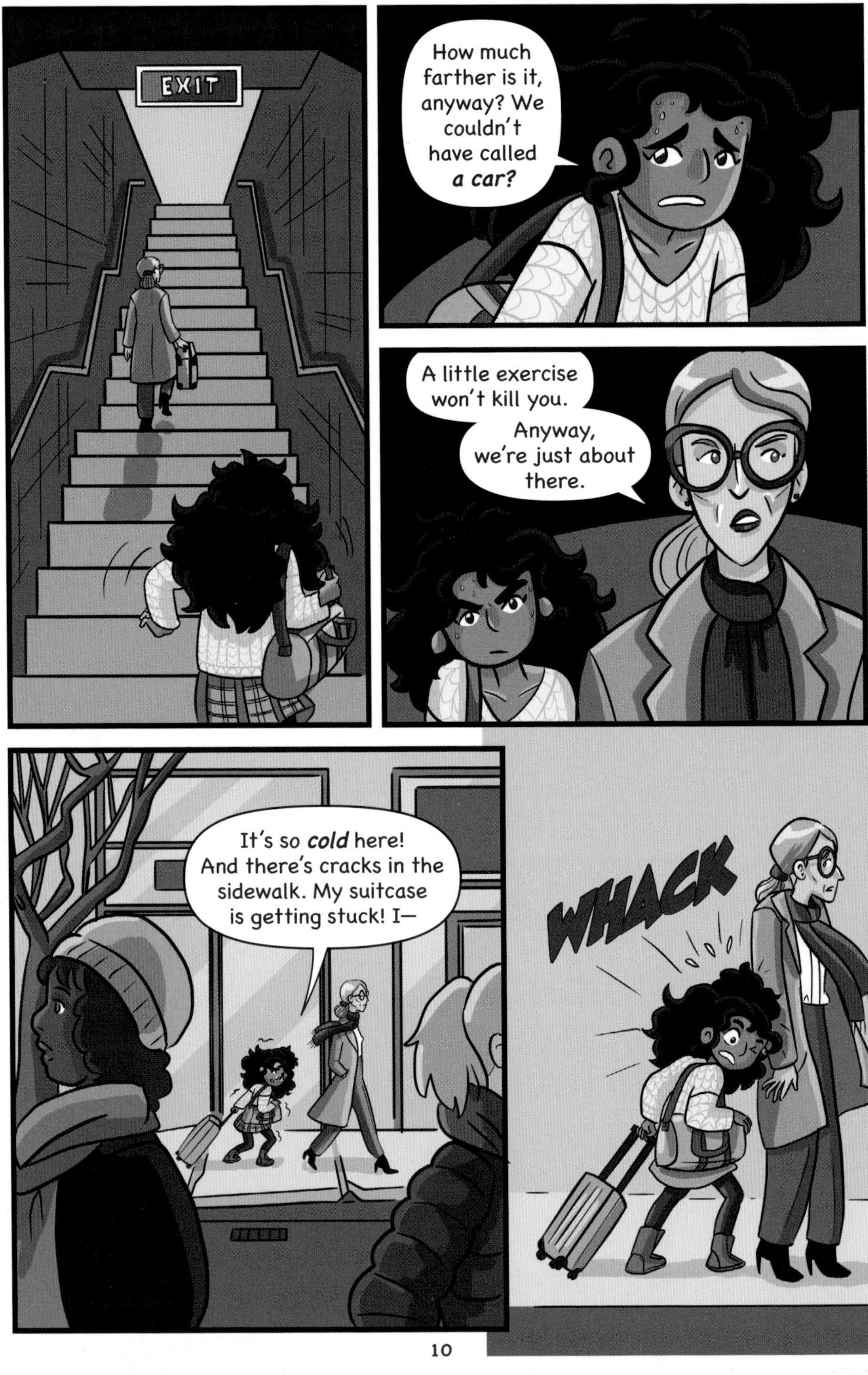
EXIT
How much farther is it, anyway? We couldn't have called *a car?*
A little exercise won't kill you.
Anyway, we're just about there.
It's so *cold* here! And there's cracks in the sidewalk. My suitcase is getting stuck! I—
WHACK

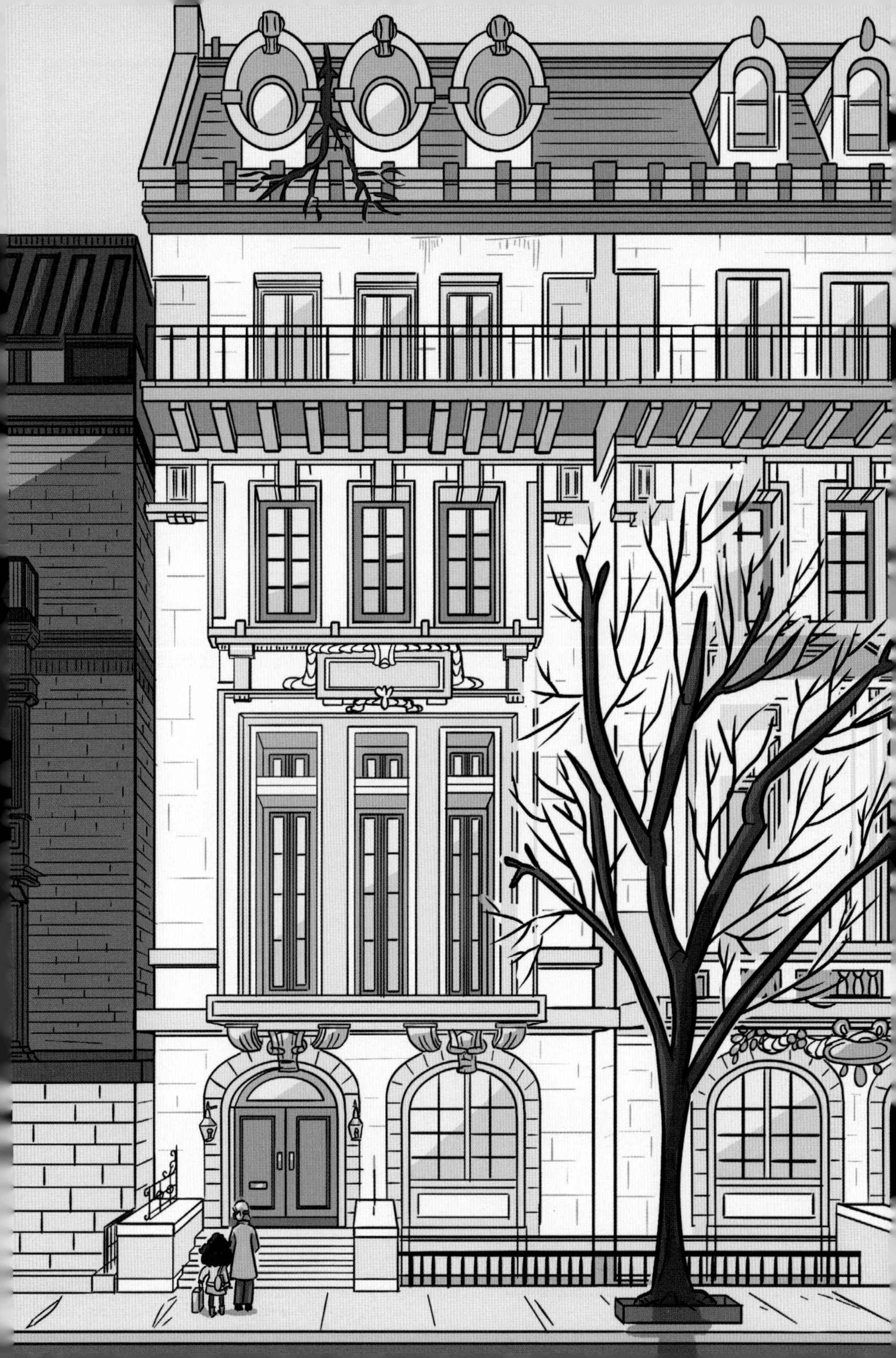

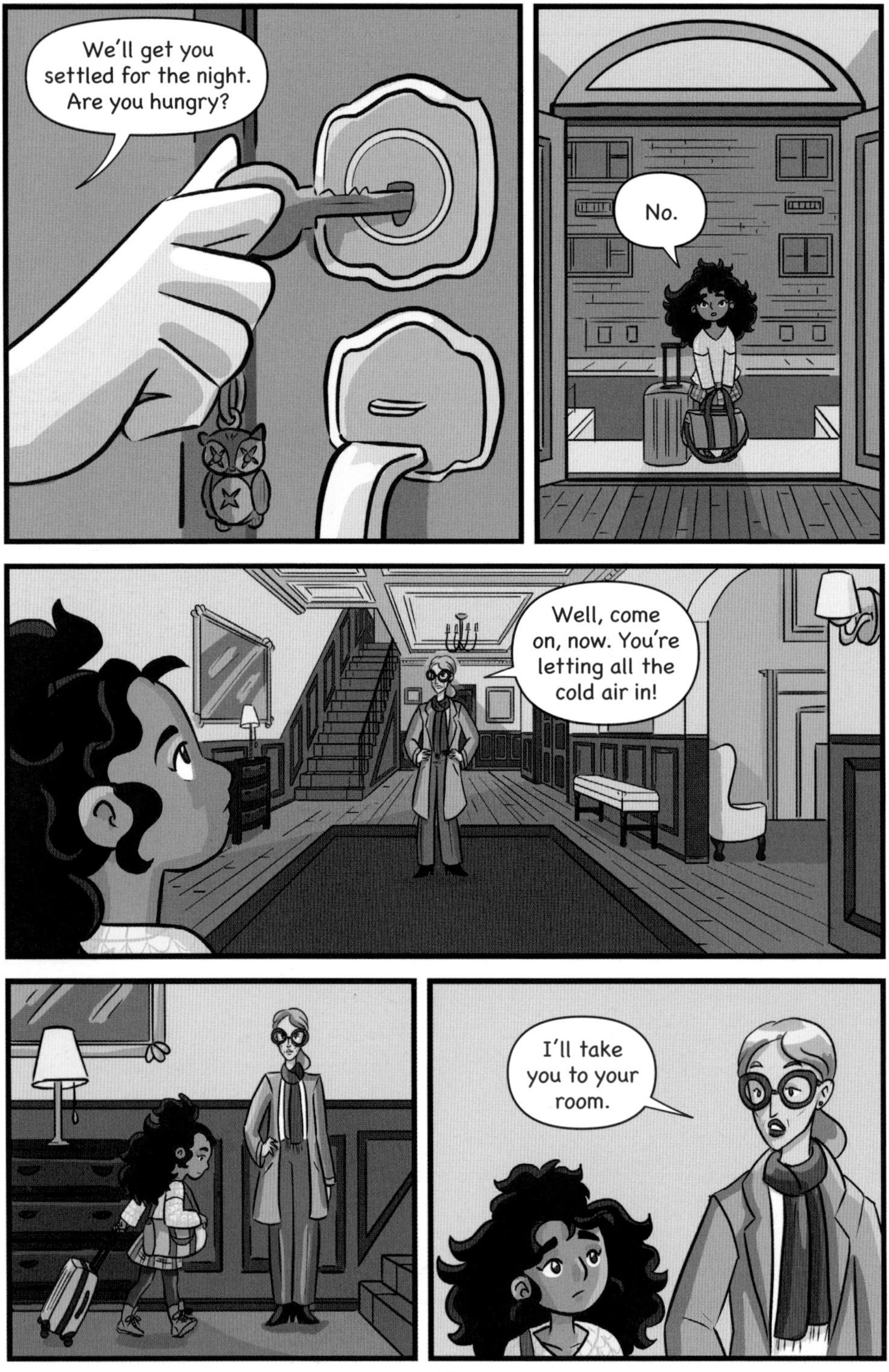
We'll get you settled for the night. Are you hungry?
No.
Well, come on, now. You're letting all the cold air in!
I'll take you to your room.

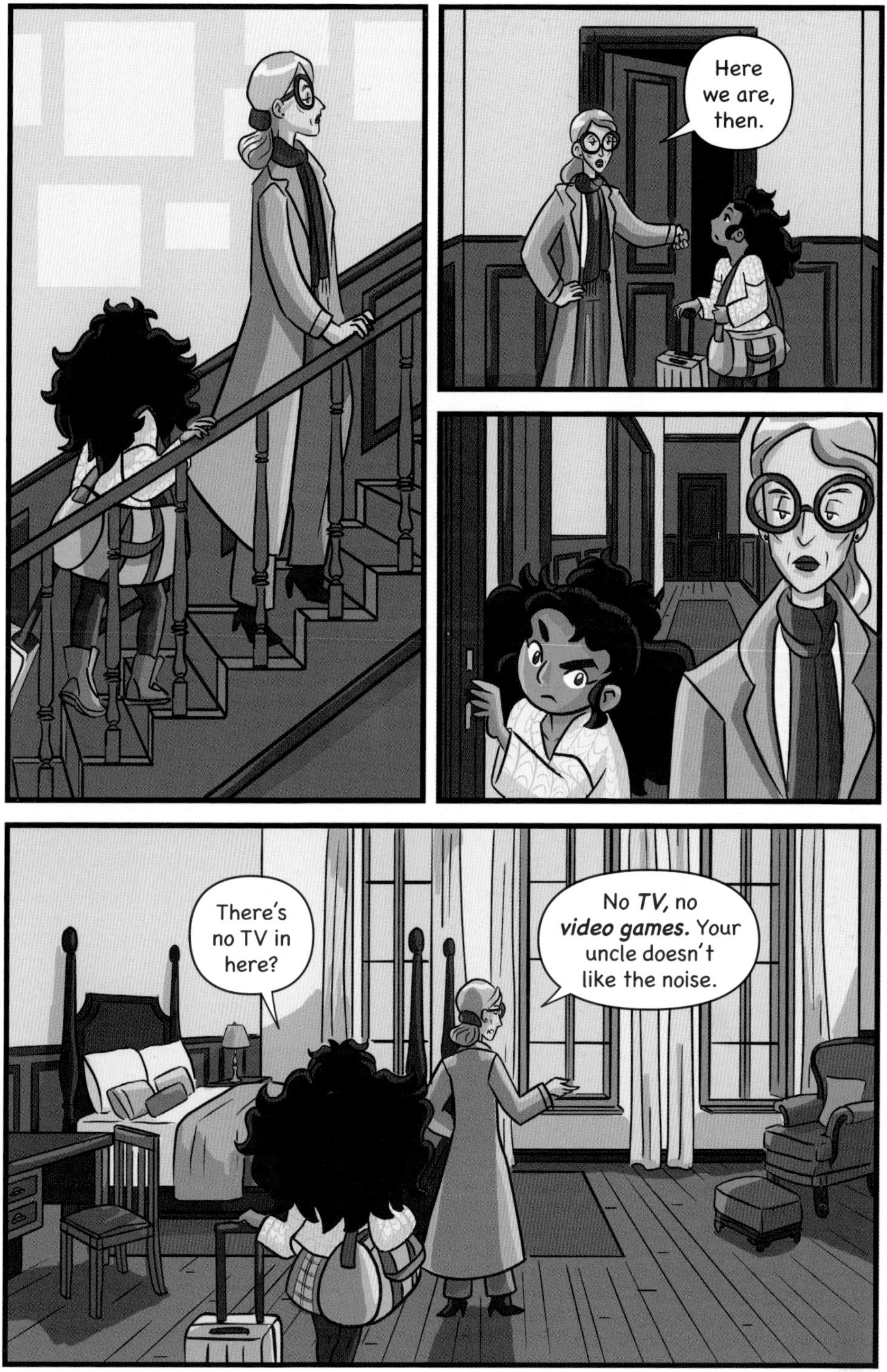
Here we are, then.
There's no TV in here?
No *TV*, no ***video games.*** Your uncle doesn't like the noise.

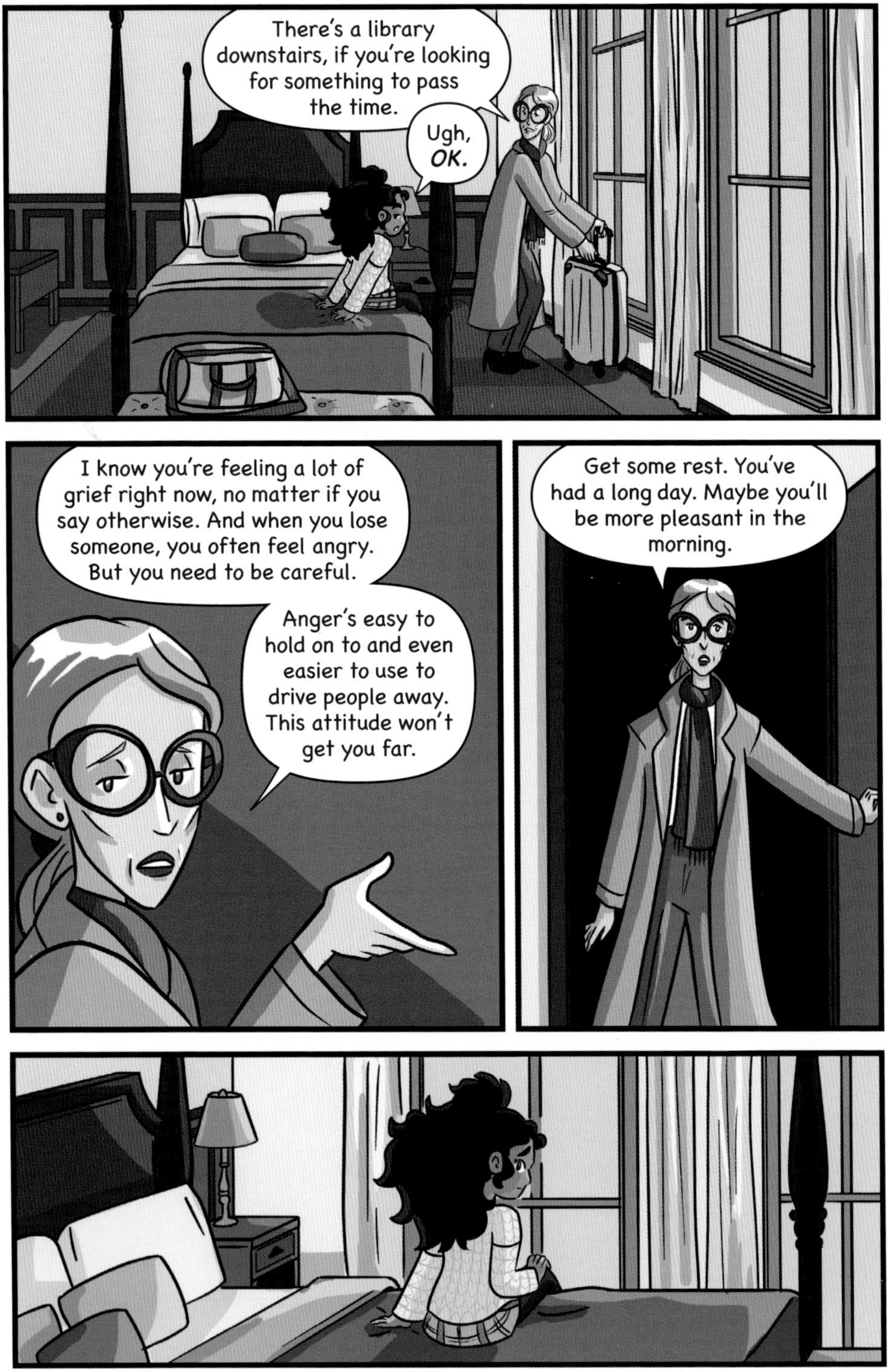
There's a library downstairs, if you're looking for something to pass the time.
Ugh, *OK.*
I know you're feeling a lot of grief right now, no matter if you say otherwise. And when you lose someone, you often feel angry. But you need to be careful.
Anger's easy to hold on to and even easier to use to drive people away. This attitude won't get you far.
Get some rest. You've had a long day. Maybe you'll be more pleasant in the morning.

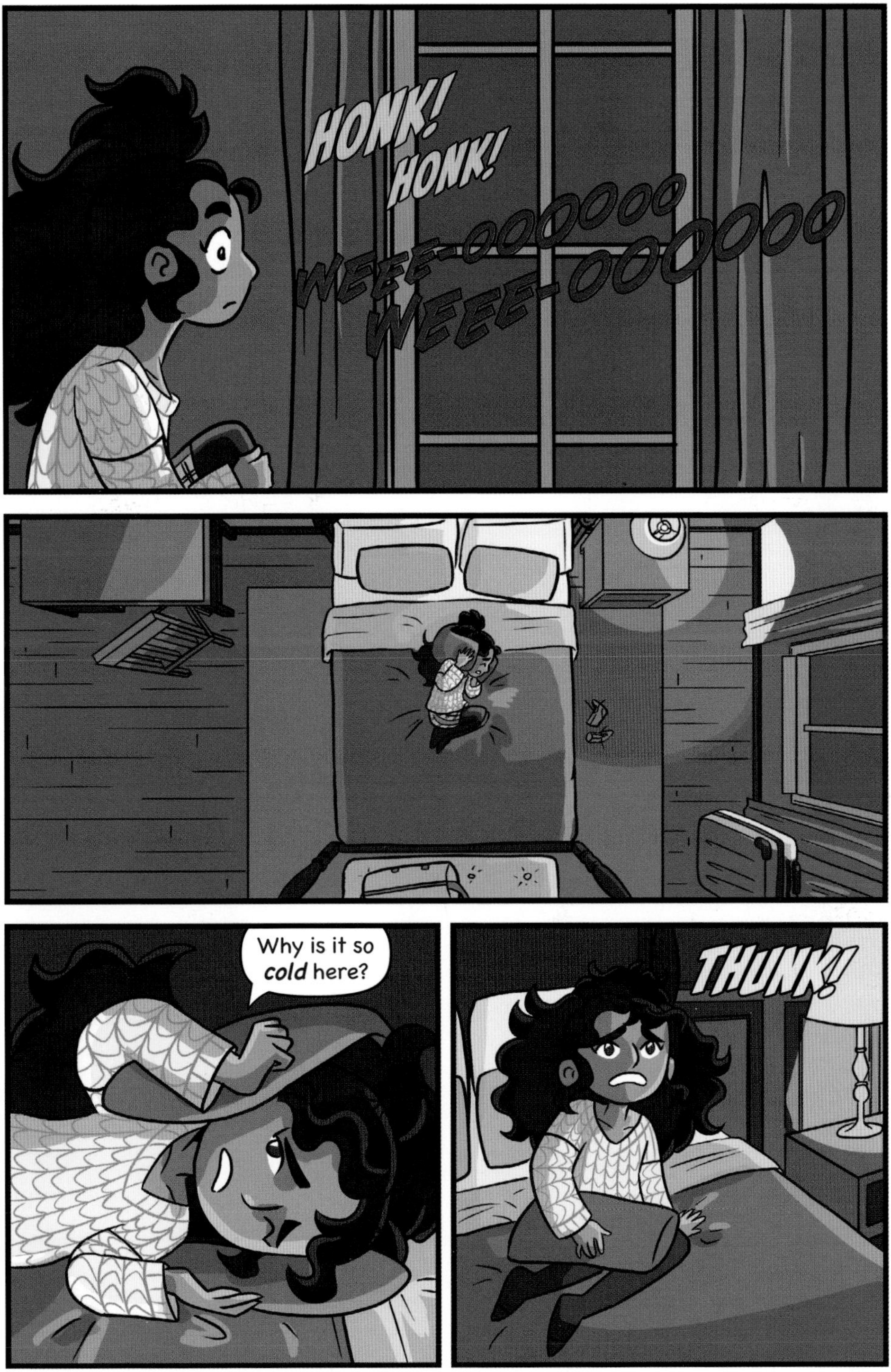
HONK! HONK!
WEEE-OOOOOO
WEEE-OOOOOOO
Why is it so *cold* here?
THUNK!

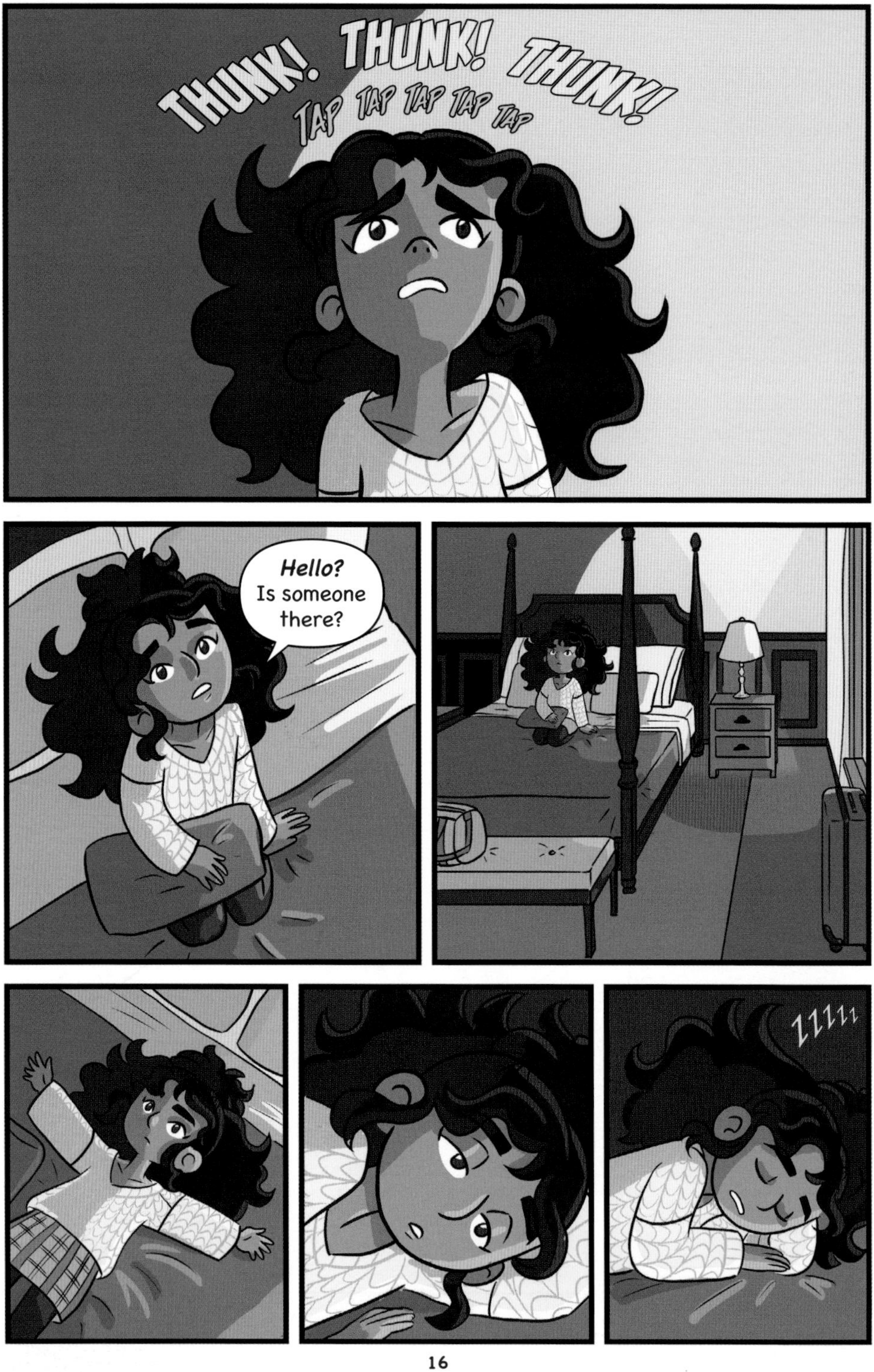
THUNK! THUNK! THUNK!
TAP TAP TAP TAP TAP
Hello? Is someone there?
ZZZZZ

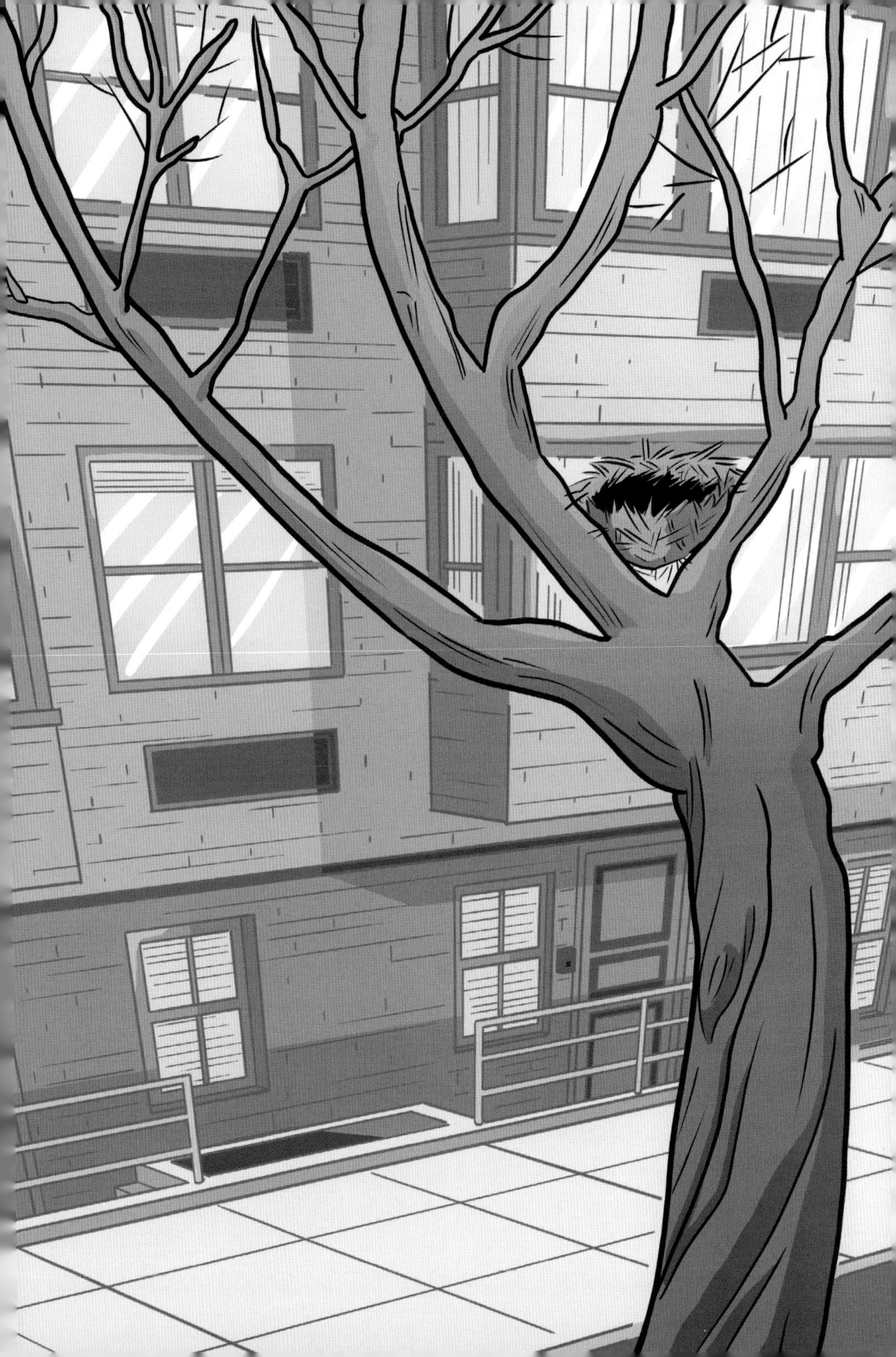

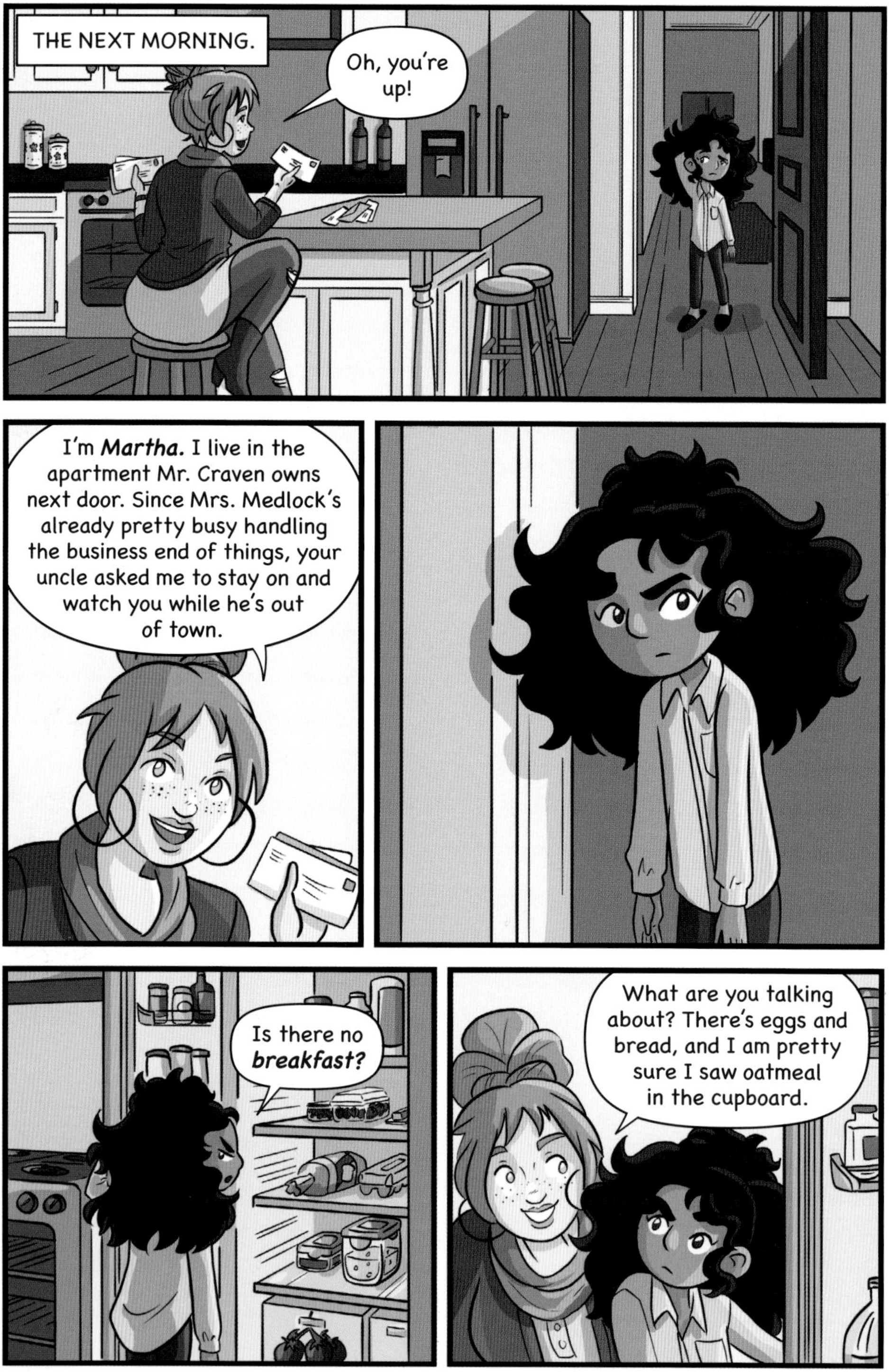

THE NEXT MORNING.
Oh, you're up!
I'm *Martha.* I live in the apartment Mr. Craven owns next door. Since Mrs. Medlock's already pretty busy handling the business end of things, your uncle asked me to stay on and watch you while he's out of town.
Is there no *breakfast?*
What are you talking about? There's eggs and bread, and I am pretty sure I saw oatmeal in the cupboard.

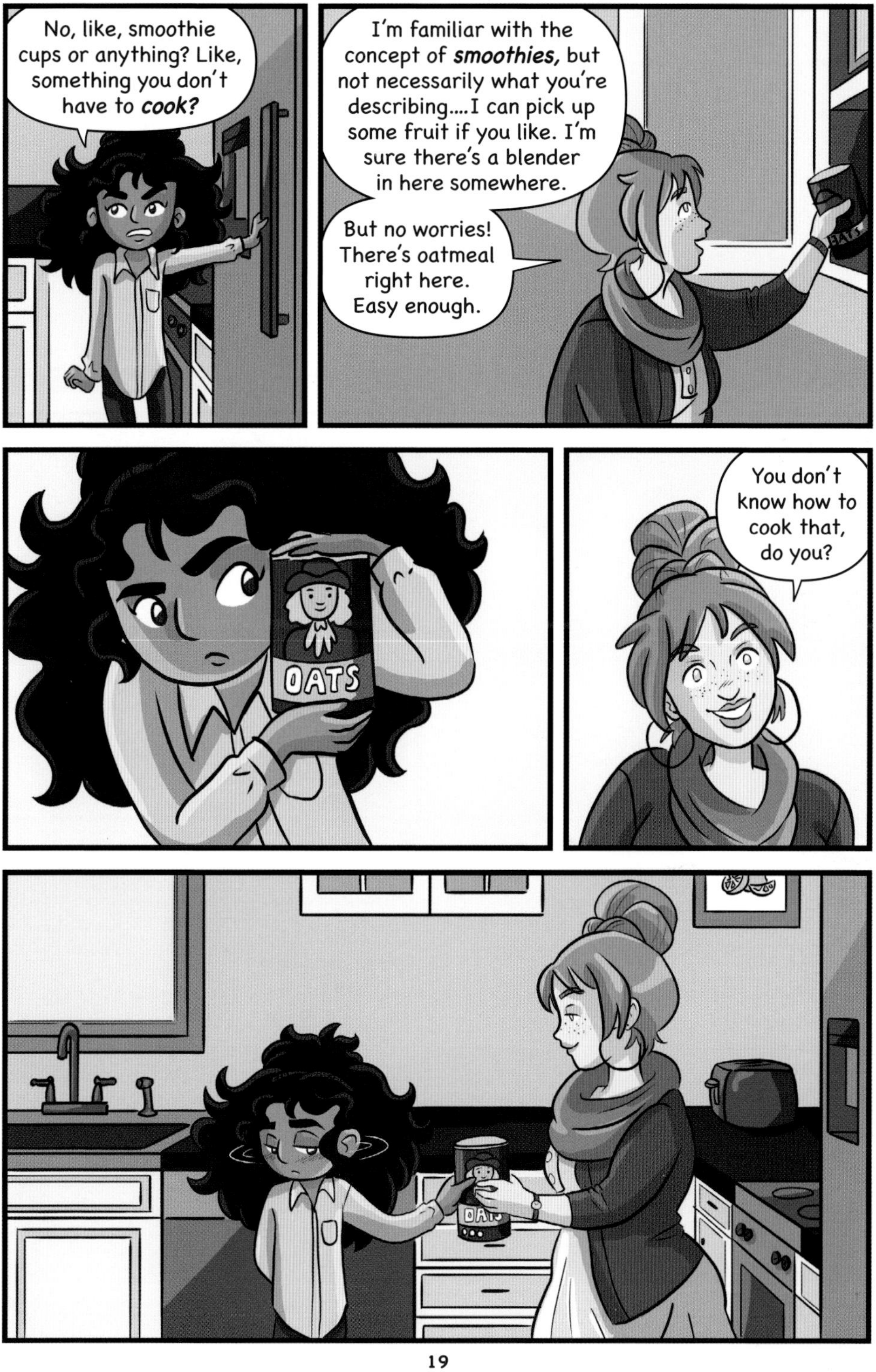
No, like, smoothie cups or anything? Like, something you don't have to *cook?*
I'm familiar with the concept of *smoothies,* but not necessarily what you're describing....I can pick up some fruit if you like. I'm sure there's a blender in here somewhere.
But no worries! There's oatmeal right here. Easy enough.
OATS
You don't know how to cook that, do you?
OATS

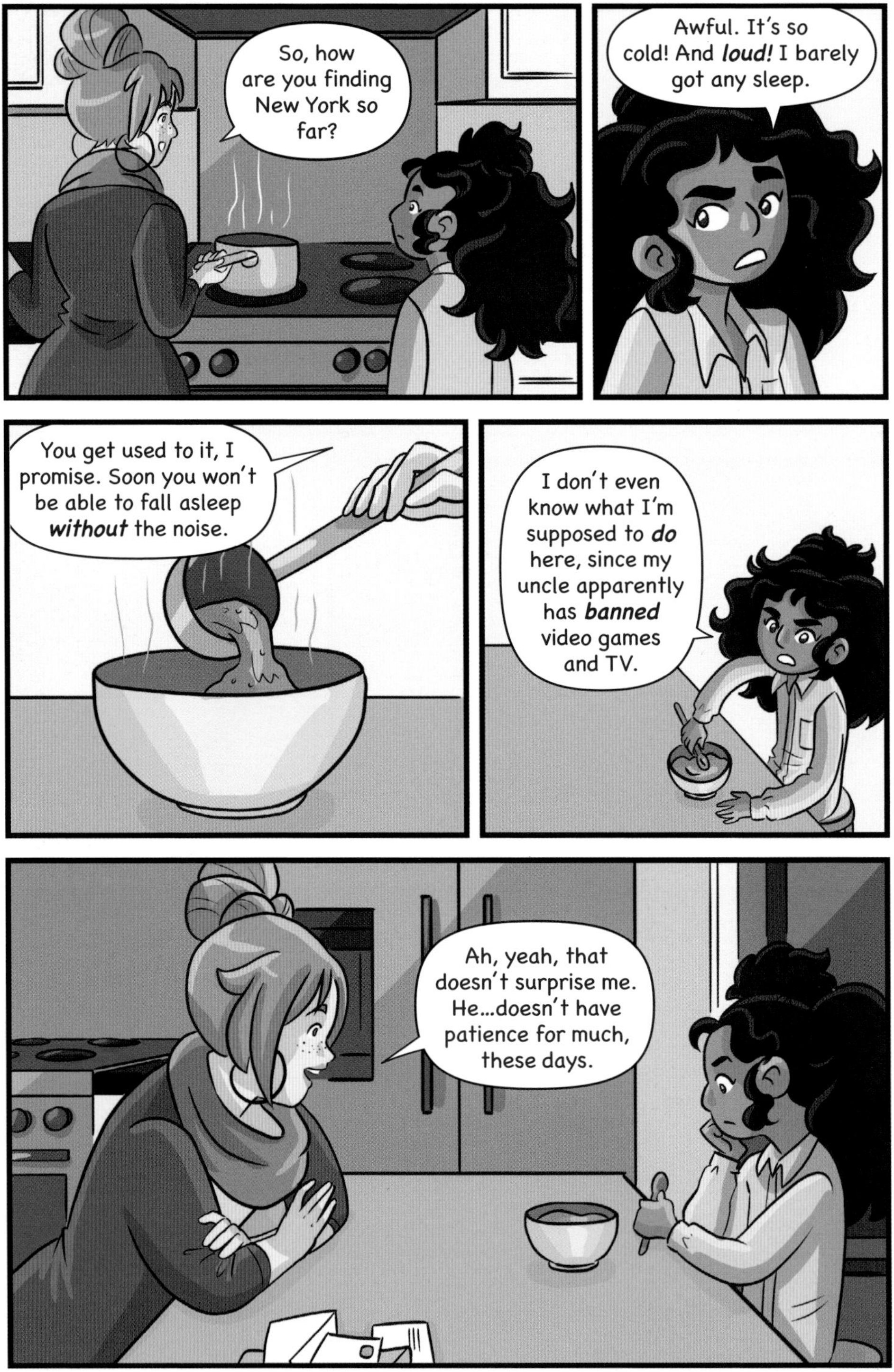
So, how are you finding New York so far?
Awful. It's so cold! And *loud!* I barely got any sleep.
You get used to it, I promise. Soon you won't be able to fall asleep ***without*** the noise.
I don't even know what I'm supposed to ***do*** here, since my uncle apparently has ***banned*** video games and TV.
Ah, yeah, that doesn't surprise me. He...doesn't have patience for much, these days.

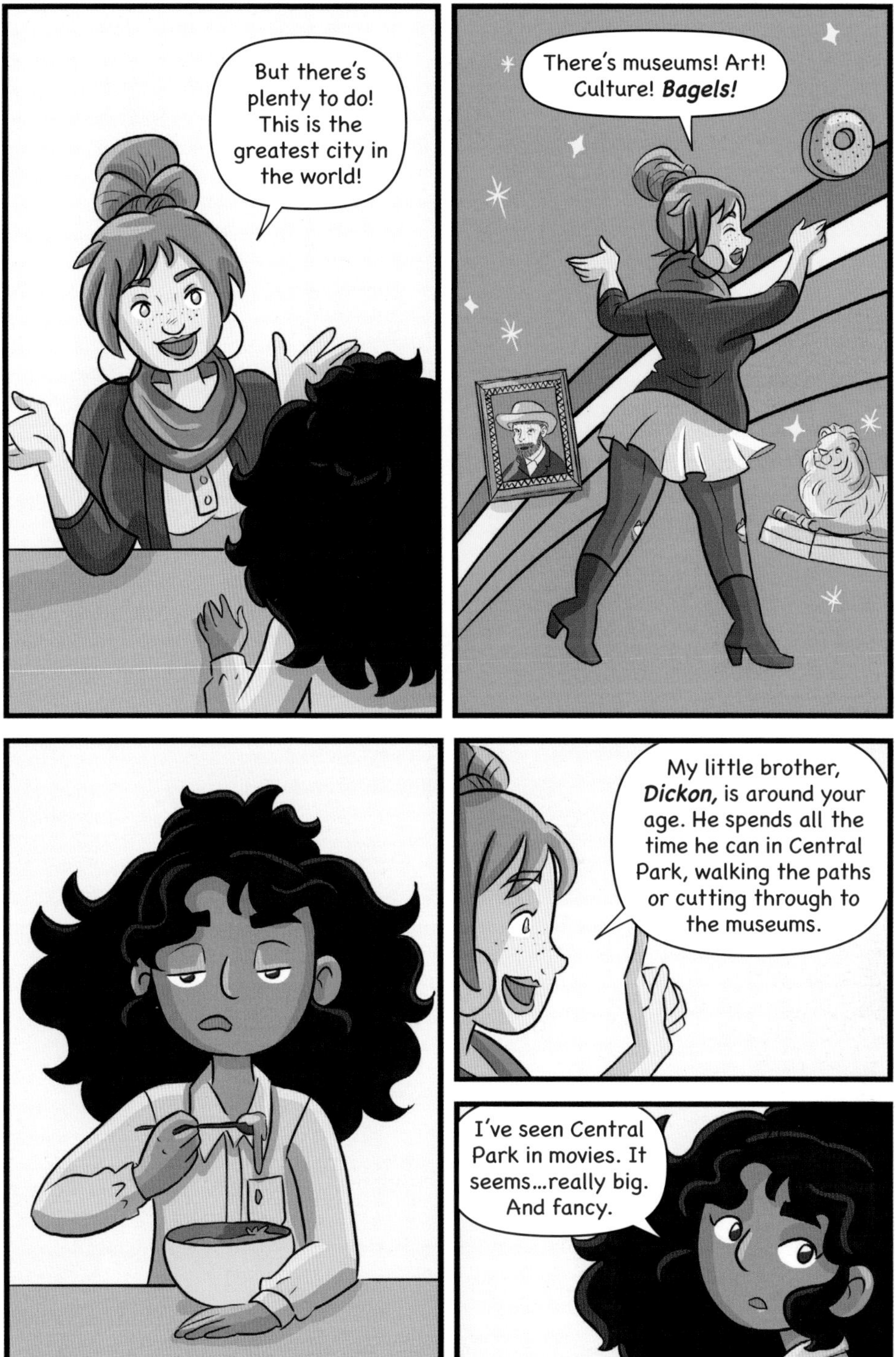
But there's plenty to do! This is the greatest city in the world!
There's museums! Art! Culture! **Bagels!**
My little brother, **Dickon,** is around your age. He spends all the time he can in Central Park, walking the paths or cutting through to the museums.
I've seen Central Park in movies. It seems...really big. And fancy.

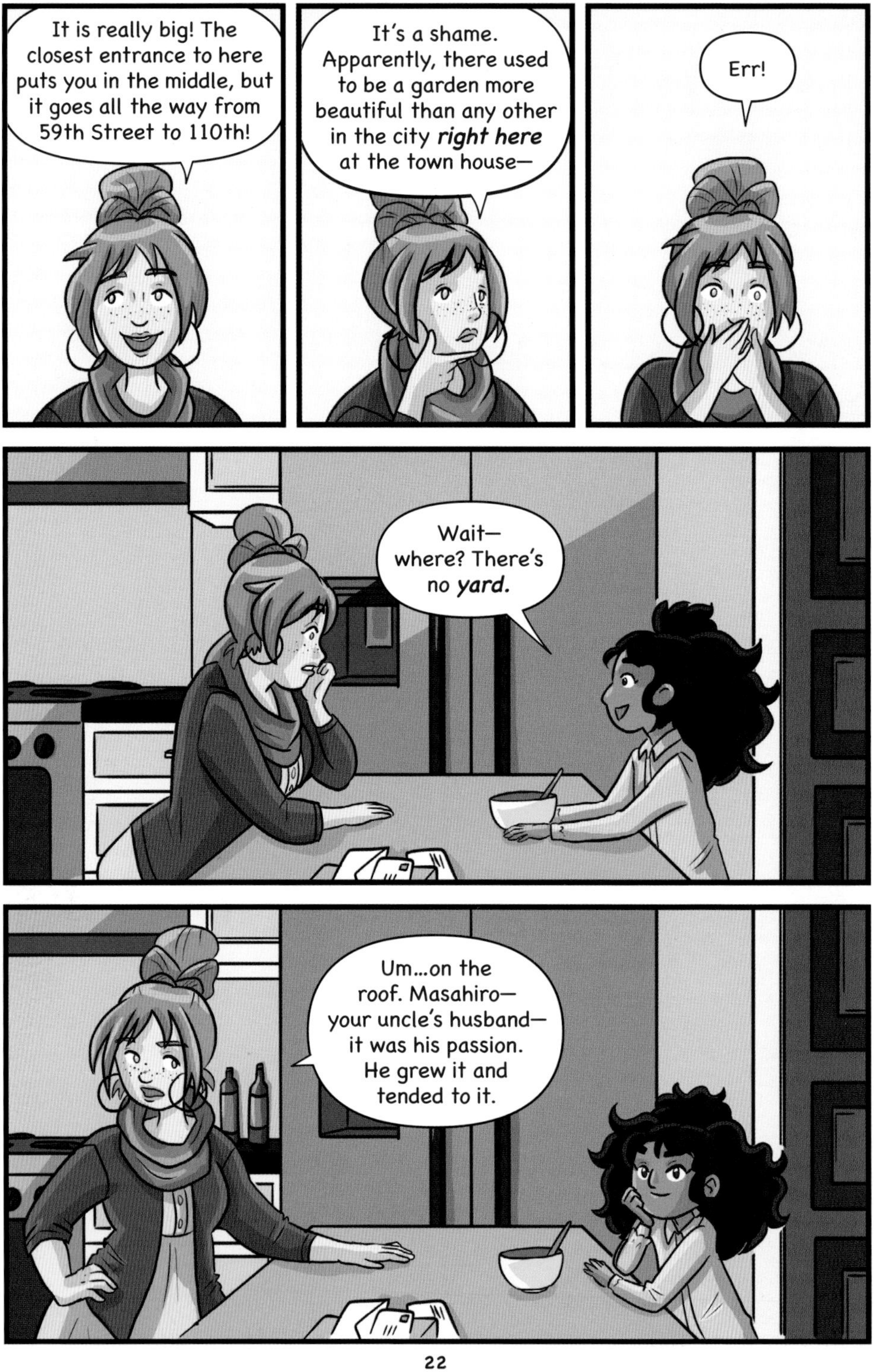
It is really big! The closest entrance to here puts you in the middle, but it goes all the way from 59th Street to 110th!
It's a shame. Apparently, there used to be a garden more beautiful than any other in the city *right here* at the town house—
Err!
Wait— where? There's no *yard.*
Um...on the roof. Masahiro— your uncle's husband— it was his passion. He grew it and tended to it.

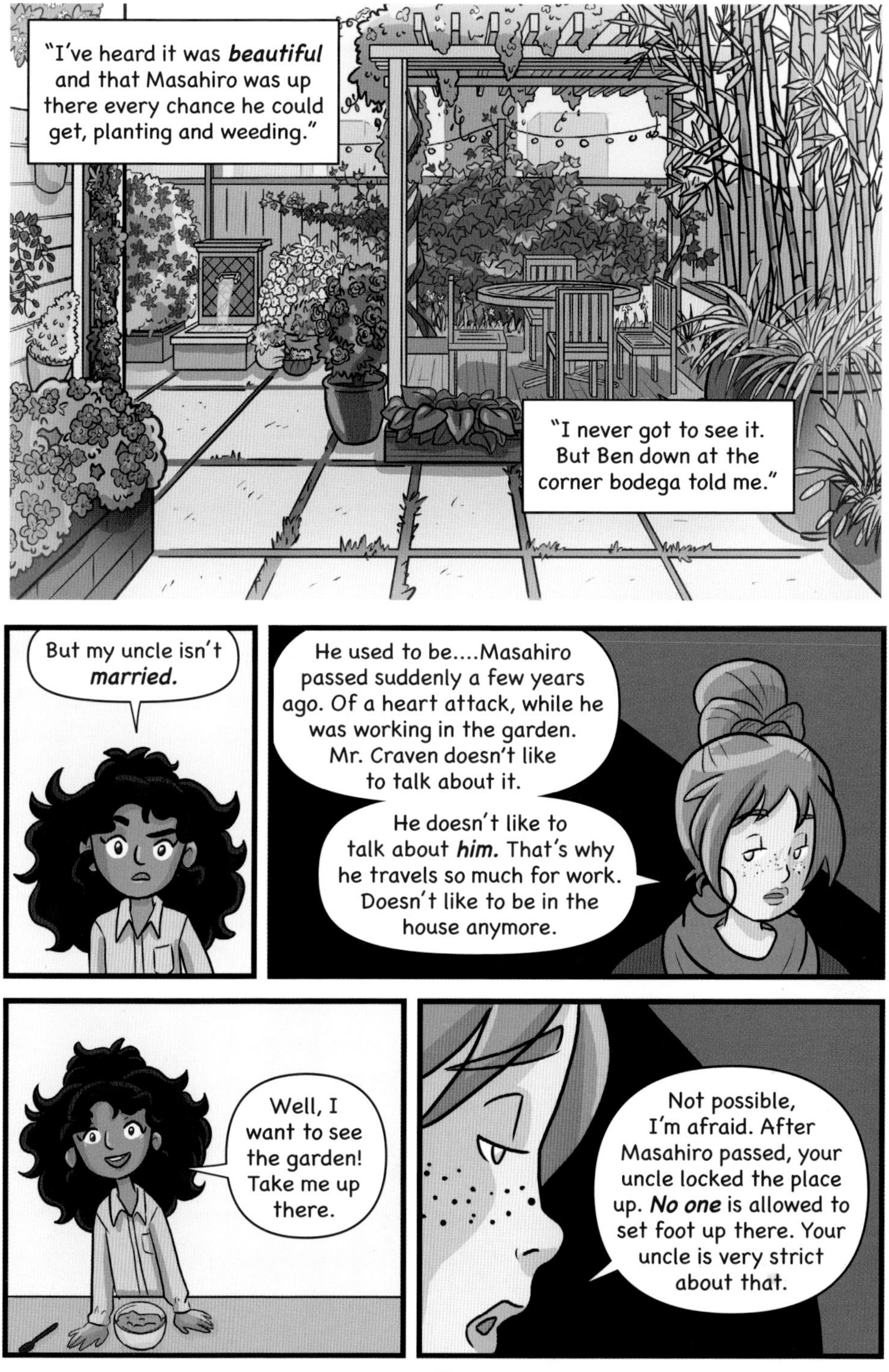
"I've heard it was ***beautiful*** and that Masahiro was up there every chance he could get, planting and weeding."
"I never got to see it. But Ben down at the corner bodega told me."
But my uncle isn't ***married.***
He used to be....Masahiro passed suddenly a few years ago. Of a heart attack, while he was working in the garden. Mr. Craven doesn't like to talk about it.
He doesn't like to talk about ***him.*** That's why he travels so much for work. Doesn't like to be in the house anymore.
Well, I want to see the garden! Take me up there.
Not possible, I'm afraid. After Masahiro passed, your uncle locked the place up. ***No one*** is allowed to set foot up there. Your uncle is very strict about that.

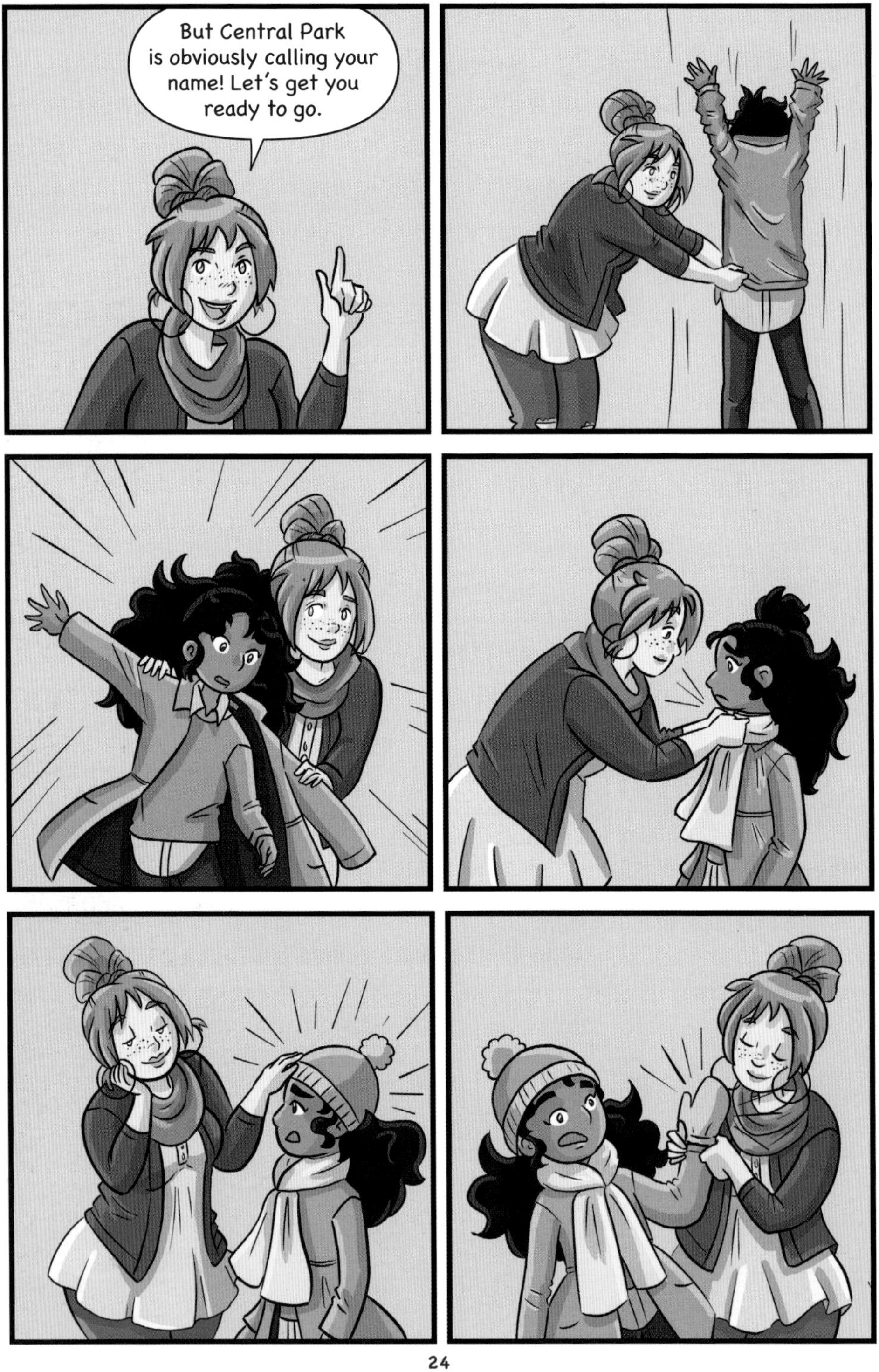
But Central Park is obviously calling your name! Let's get you ready to go.

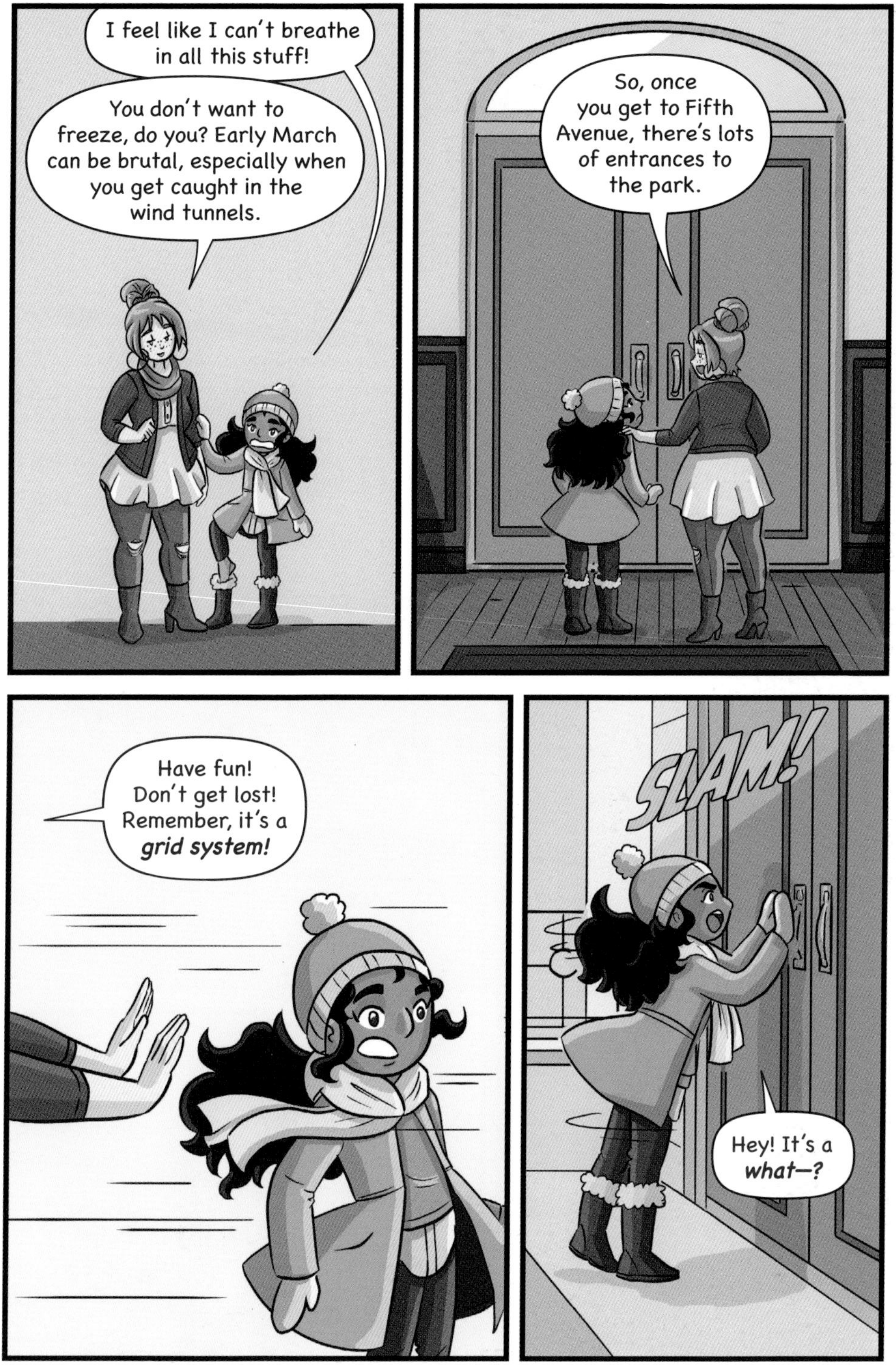
I feel like I can't breathe in all this stuff!
You don't want to freeze, do you? Early March can be brutal, especially when you get caught in the wind tunnels.
So, once you get to Fifth Avenue, there's lots of entrances to the park.
Have fun! Don't get lost! Remember, it's a *grid system!*
SLAM!
Hey! It's a *what—?*

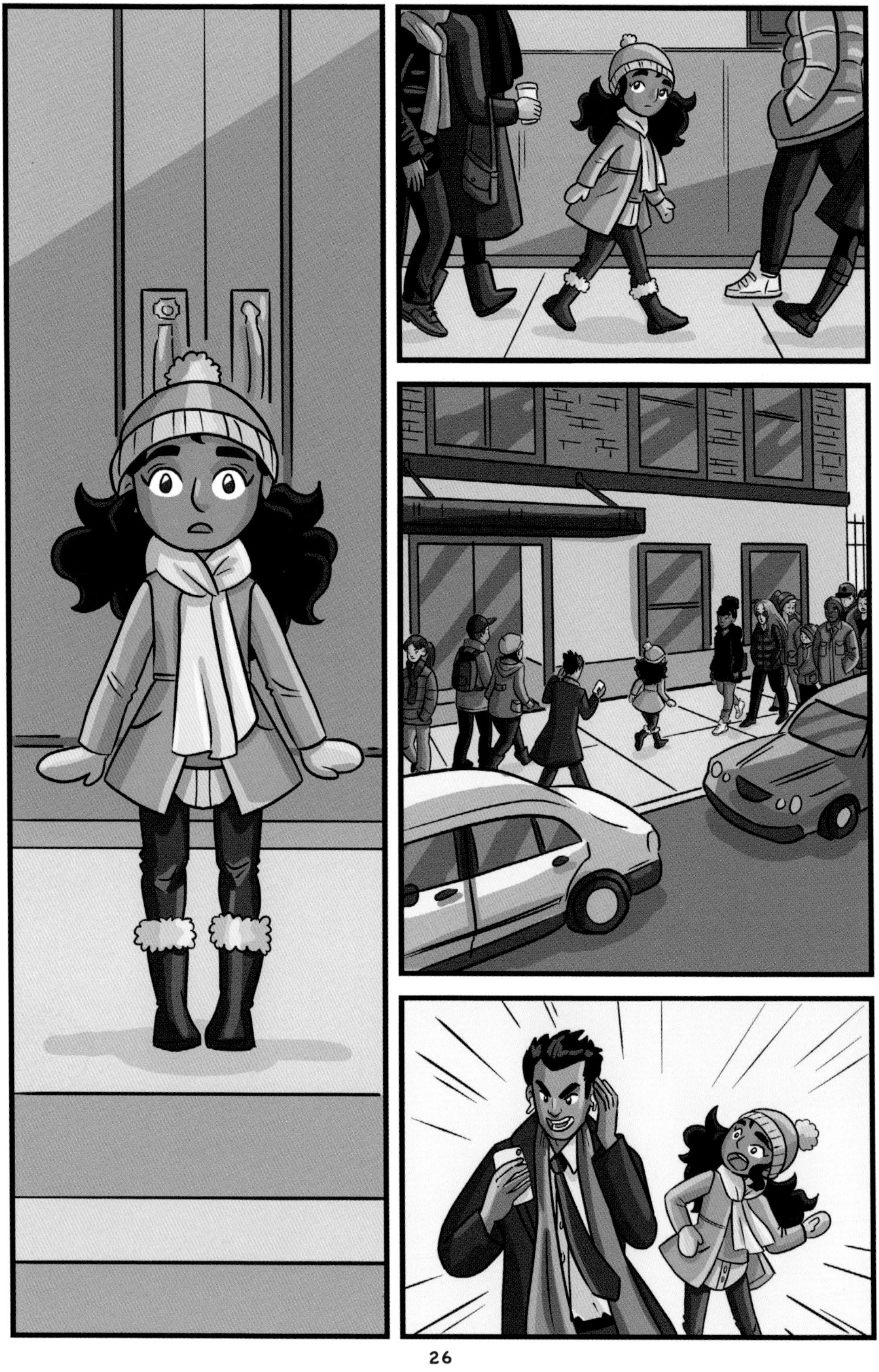

SHOPS AT
5th Ave

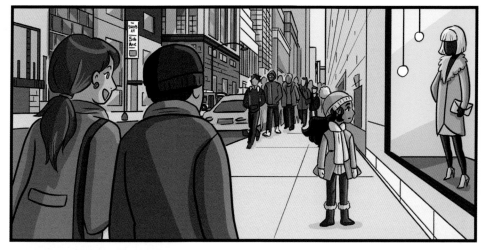

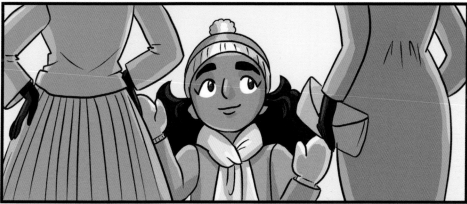

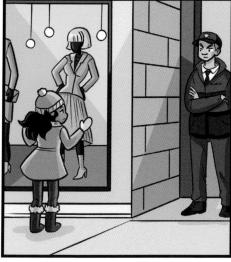

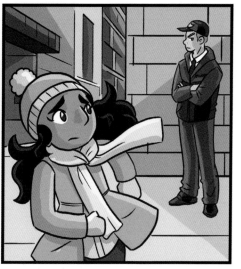

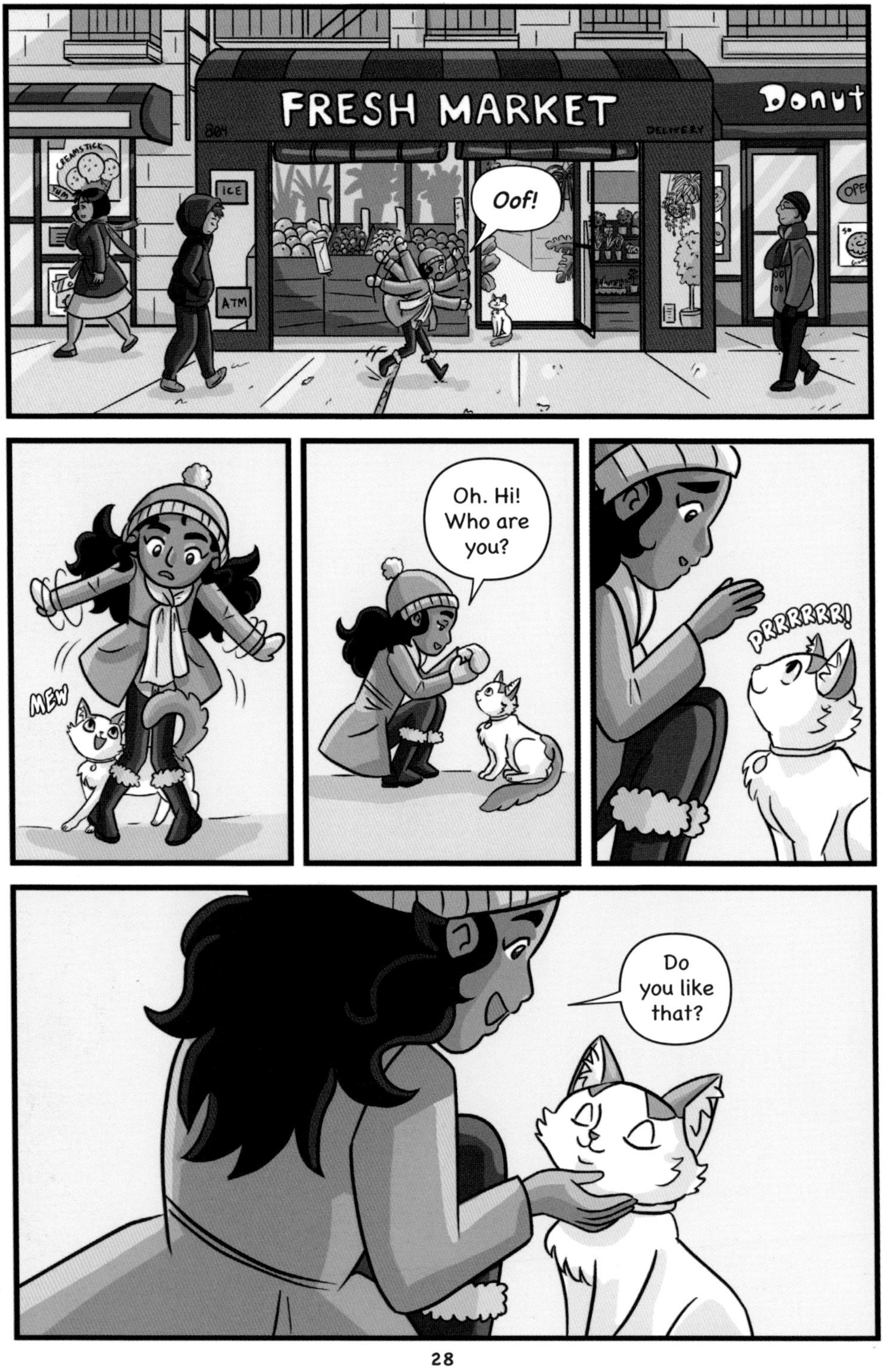
FRESH MARKET
Donut
ICE
ATM
CREAMSTICK
Oof!
MEW
Oh. Hi! Who are you?
PRRRRRR!
Do you like that?

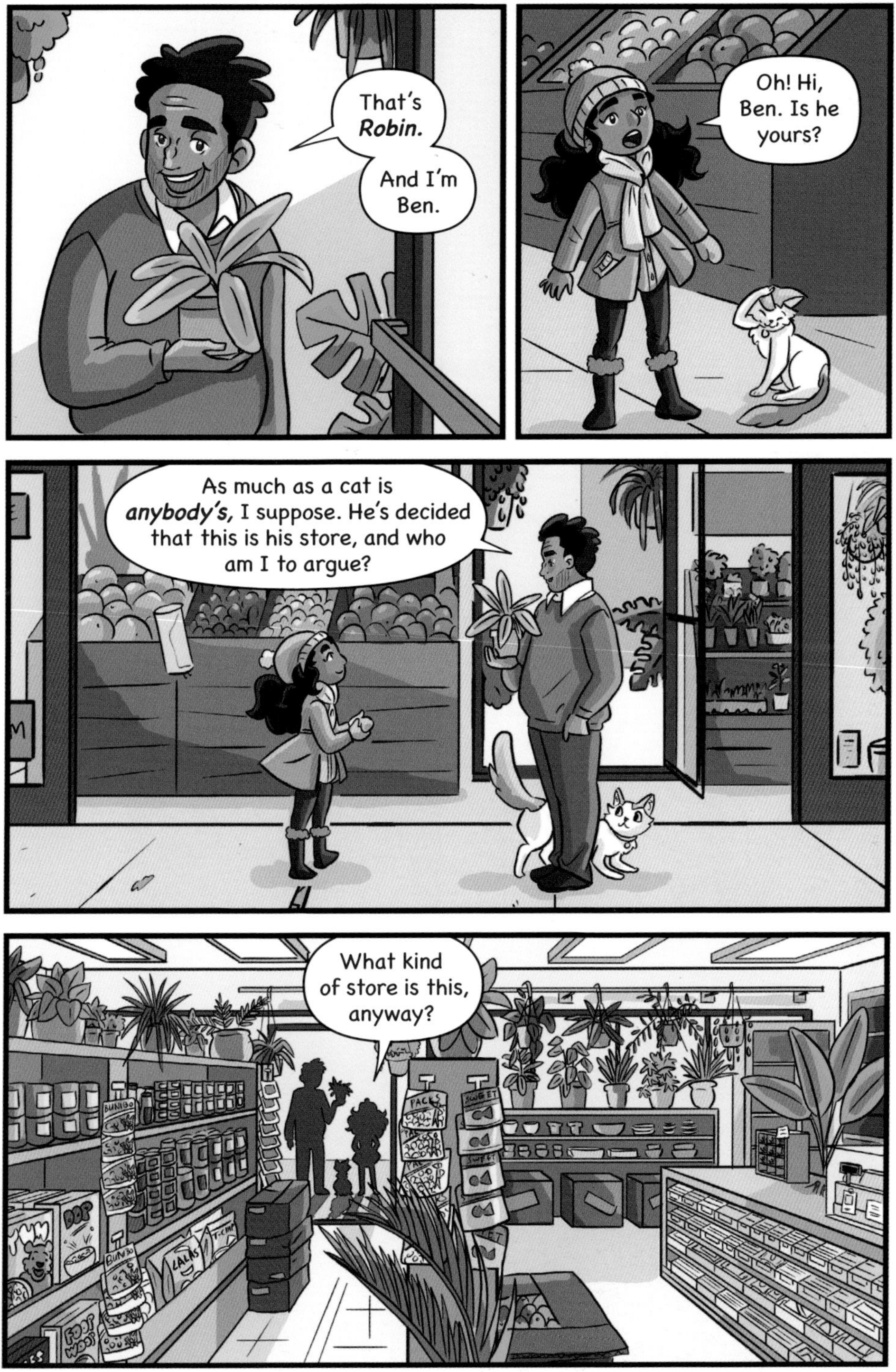
That's ***Robin.***
And I'm Ben.
Oh! Hi, Ben. Is he yours?
As much as a cat is ***anybody's,*** I suppose. He's decided that this is his store, and who am I to argue?
What kind of store is this, anyway?

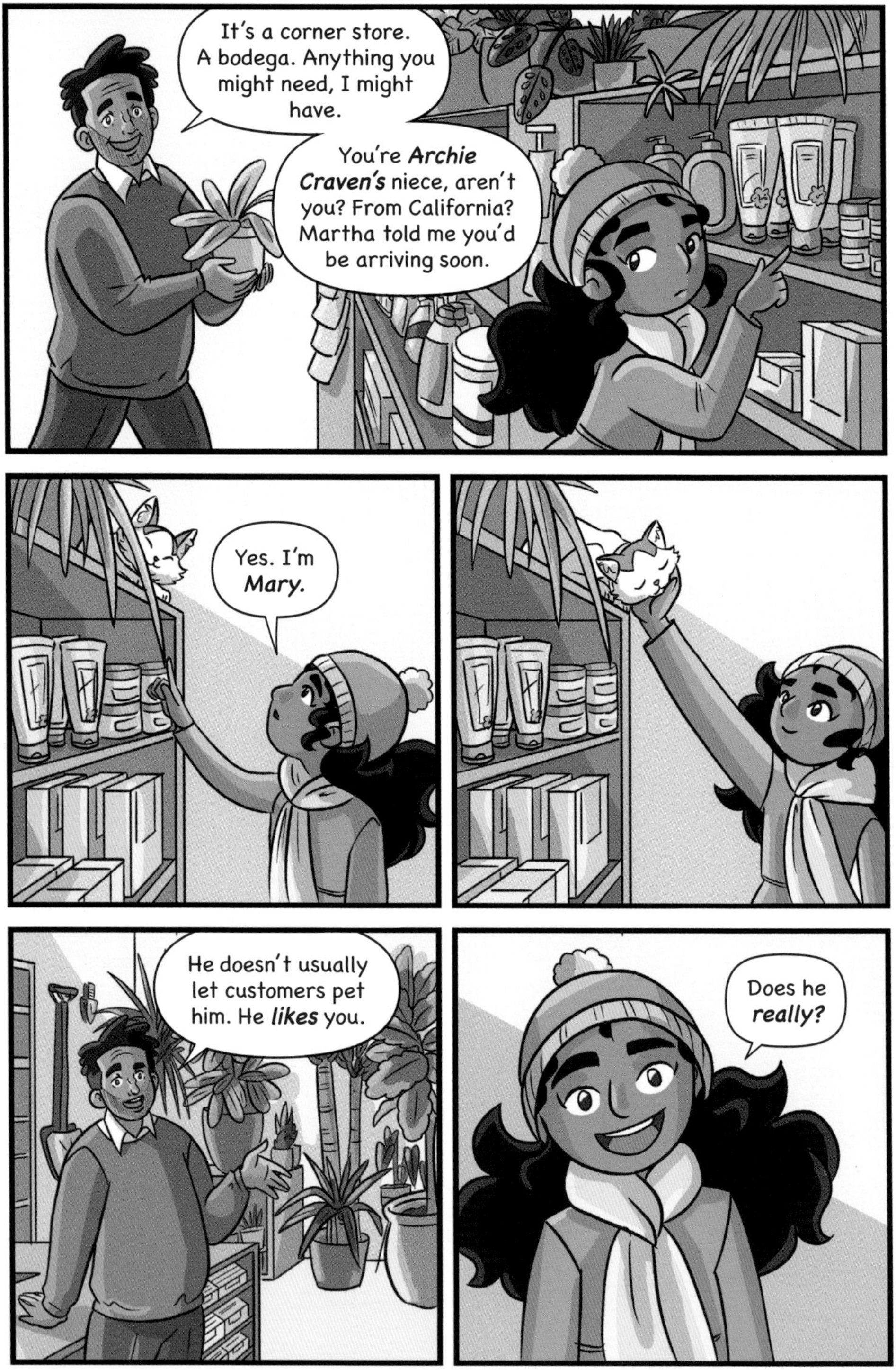

It's a corner store. A bodega. Anything you might need, I might have.
You're *Archie Craven's* niece, aren't you? From California? Martha told me you'd be arriving soon.
Yes. I'm *Mary.*
He doesn't usually let customers pet him. He *likes* you.
Does he *really?*

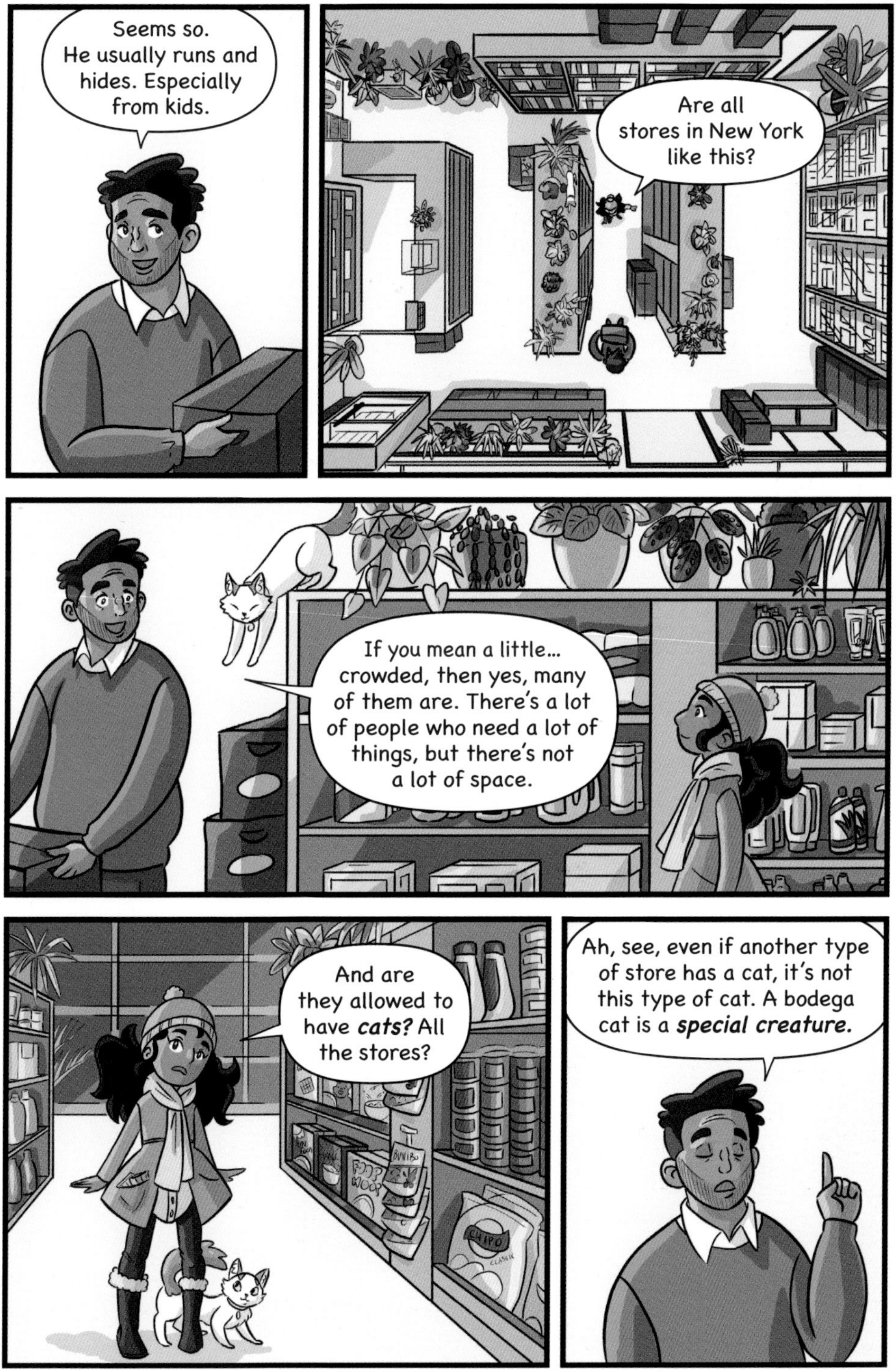
Seems so. He usually runs and hides. Especially from kids.
Are all stores in New York like this?
If you mean a little... crowded, then yes, many of them are. There's a lot of people who need a lot of things, but there's not a lot of space.
And are they allowed to have *cats?* All the stores?
Ah, see, even if another type of store has a cat, it's not this type of cat. A bodega cat is a ***special creature.***

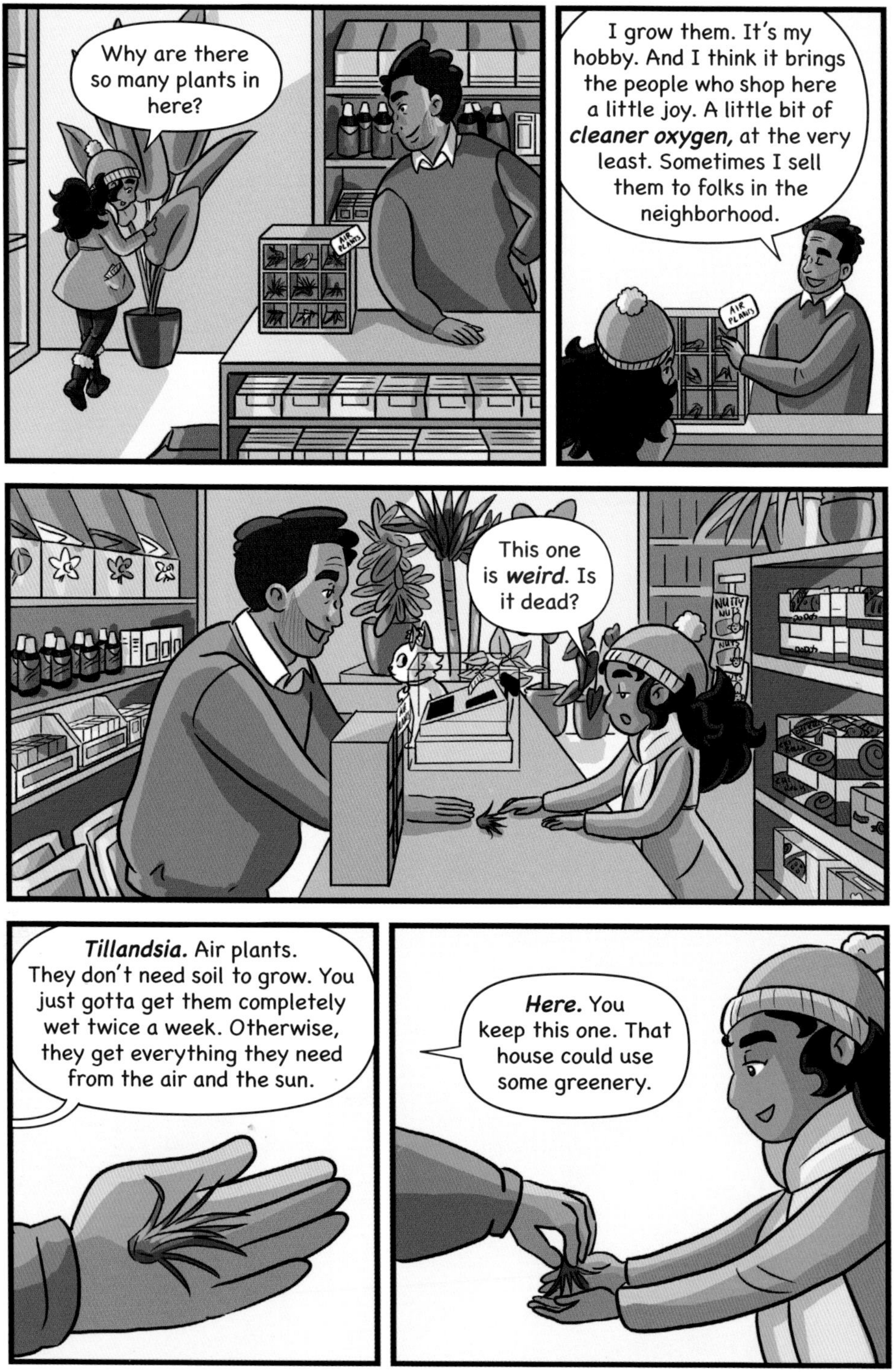
Why are there so many plants in here?
I grow them. It's my hobby. And I think it brings the people who shop here a little joy. A little bit of ***cleaner oxygen,*** at the very least. Sometimes I sell them to folks in the neighborhood.
AIR PLANTS
This one is ***weird***. Is it dead?
NUTTY NUTS
Tillandsia. Air plants. They don't need soil to grow. You just gotta get them completely wet twice a week. Otherwise, they get everything they need from the air and the sun.
Here. You keep this one. That house could use some greenery.

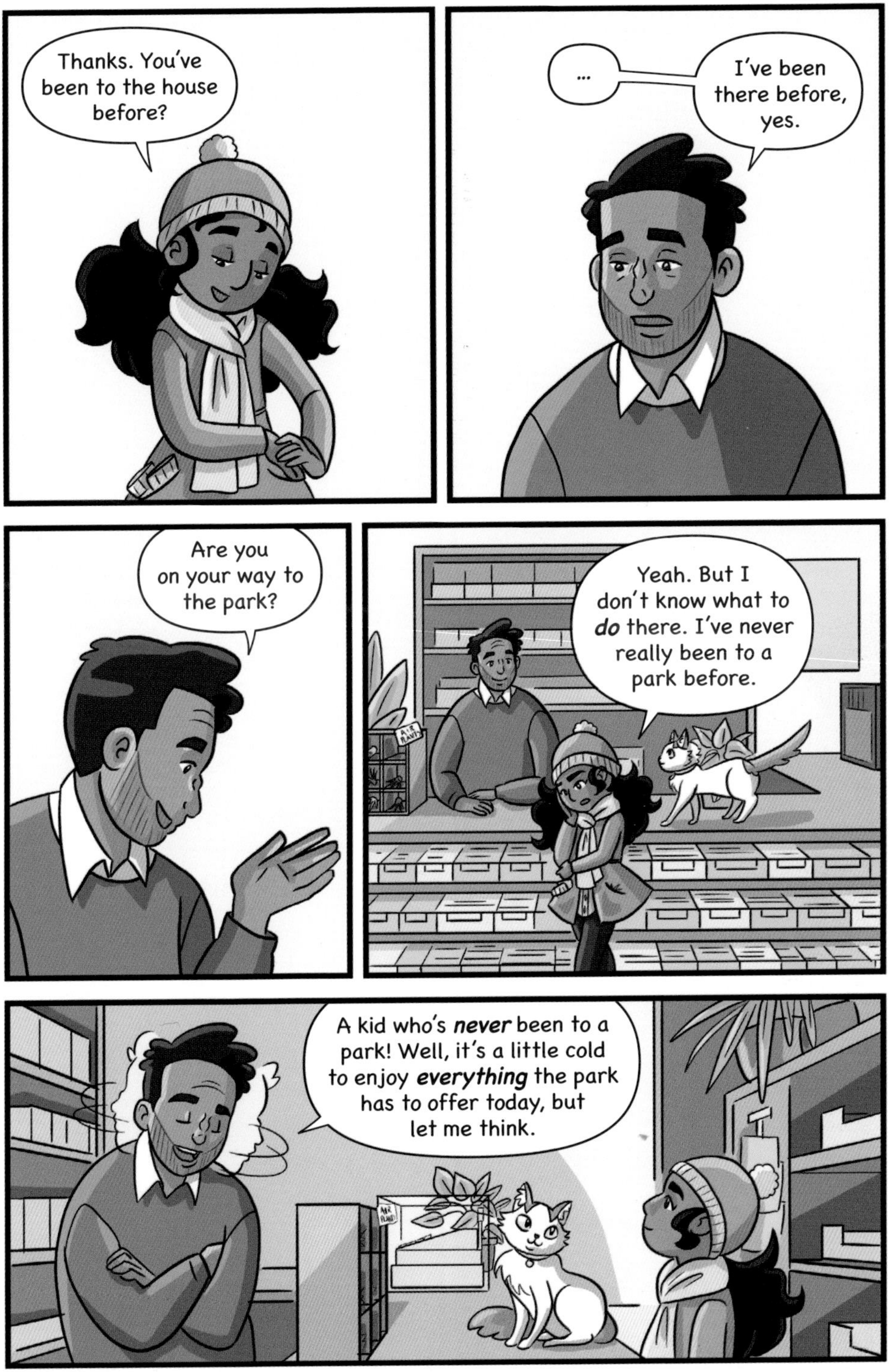
Thanks. You've been to the house before?
...
I've been there before, yes.
Are you on your way to the park?
Yeah. But I don't know what to *do* there. I've never really been to a park before.
A kid who's ***never*** been to a park! Well, it's a little cold to enjoy ***everything*** the park has to offer today, but let me think.

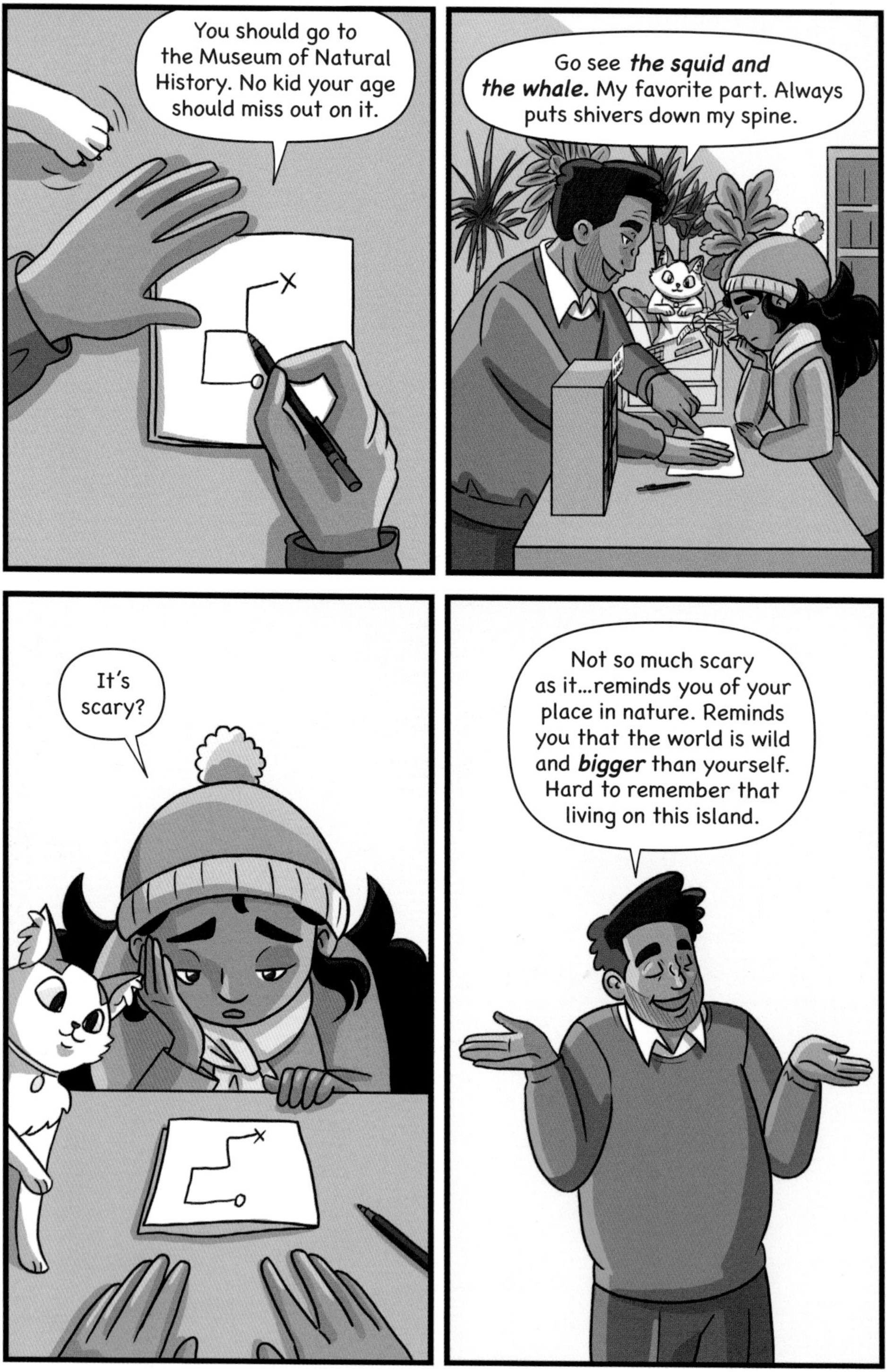
You should go to the Museum of Natural History. No kid your age should miss out on it.
Go see ***the squid and the whale.*** My favorite part. Always puts shivers down my spine.
It's scary?
Not so much scary as it...reminds you of your place in nature. Reminds you that the world is wild and ***bigger*** than yourself. Hard to remember that living on this island.

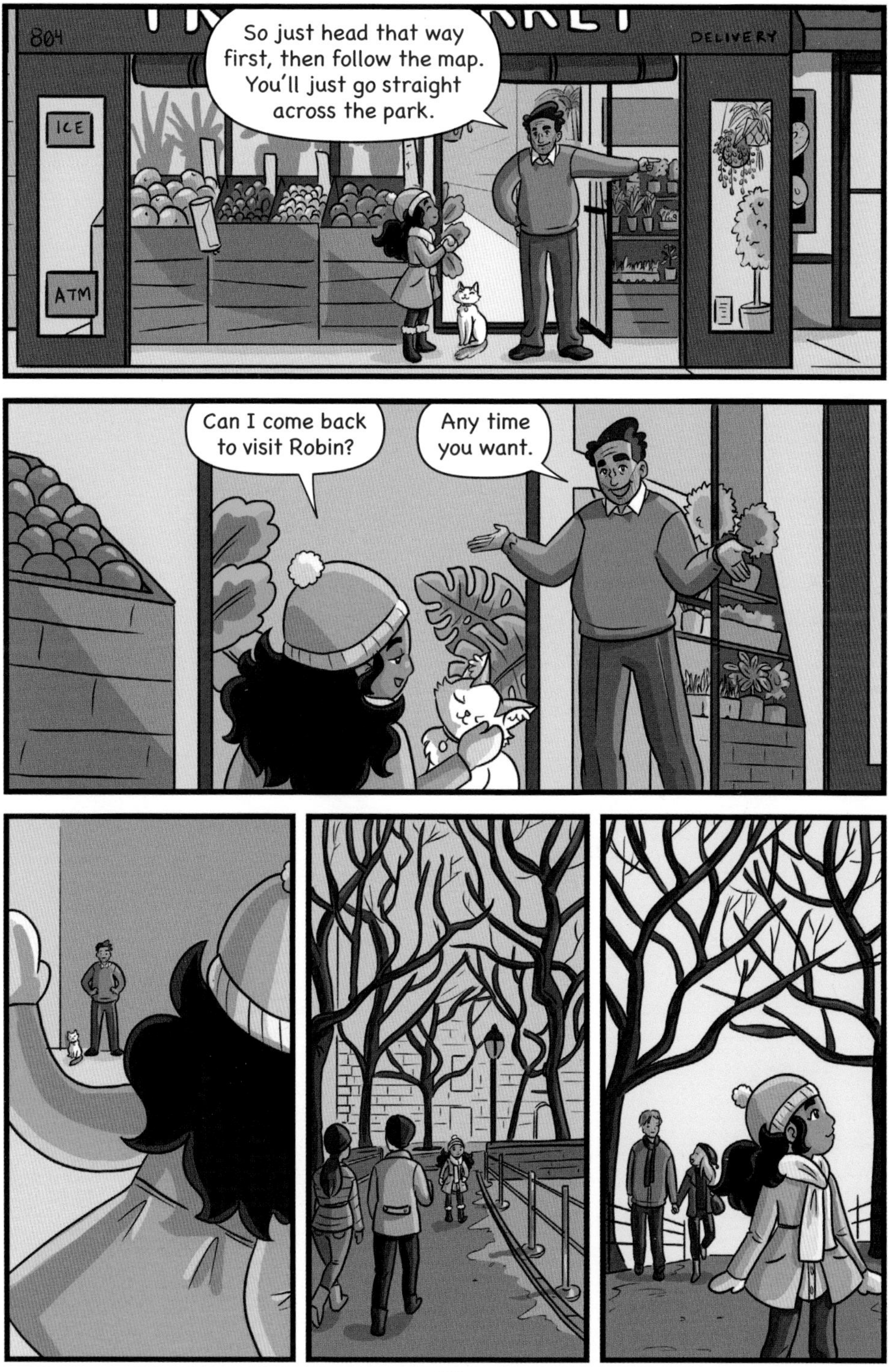
804
DELIVERY
ICE
ATM
So just head that way first, then follow the map. You'll just go straight across the park.
Can I come back to visit Robin?
Any time you want.

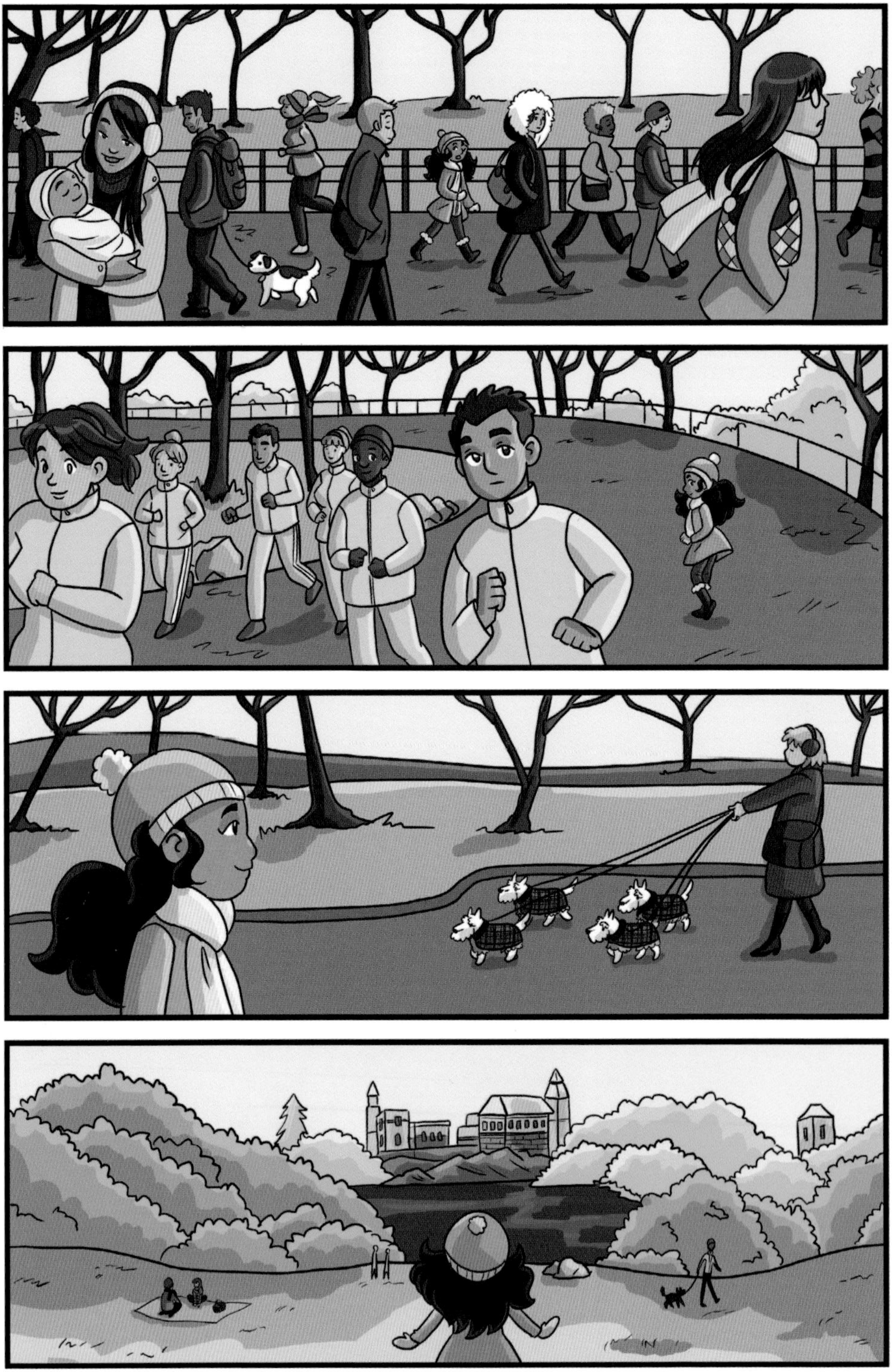

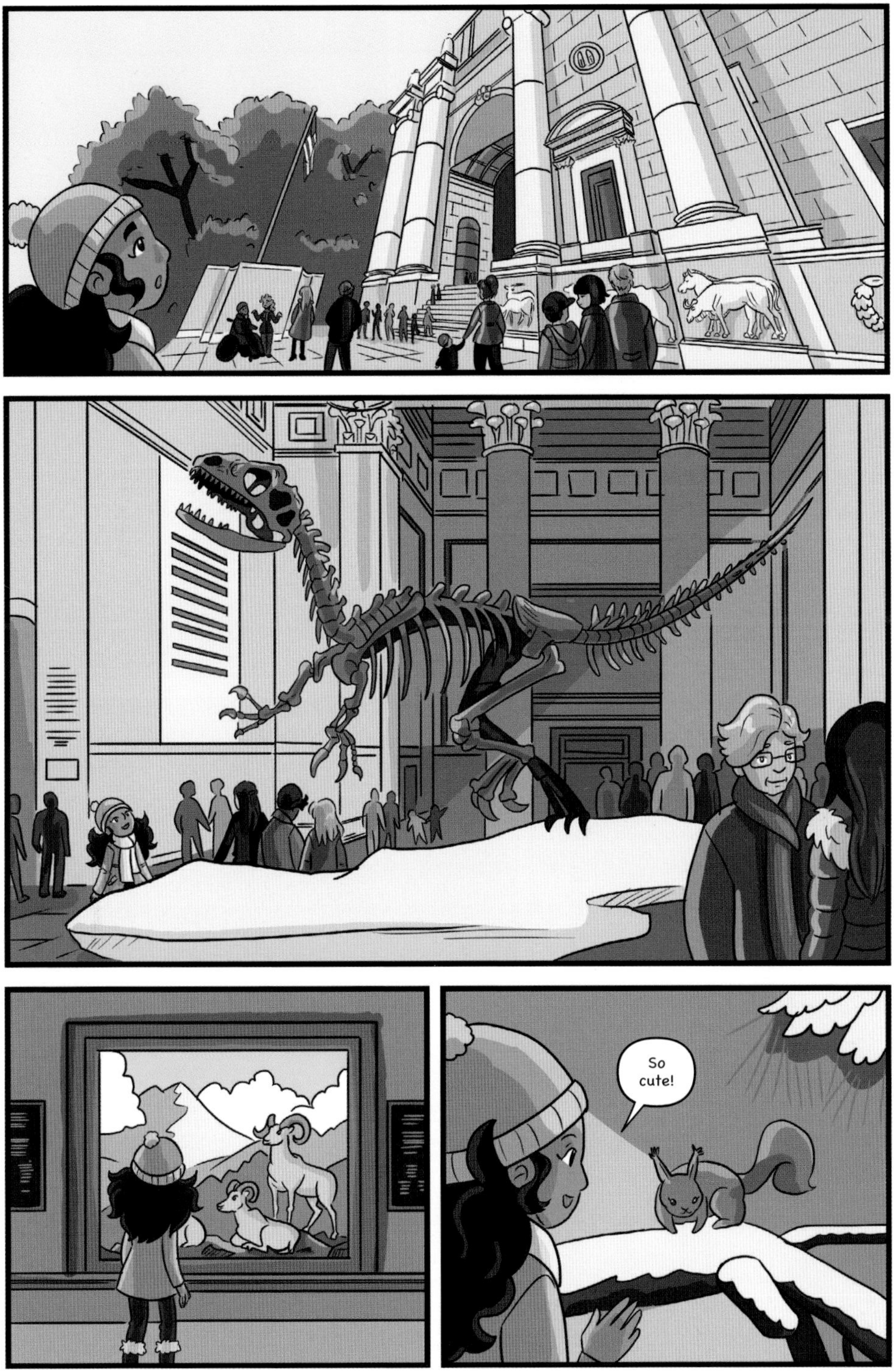
So cute!

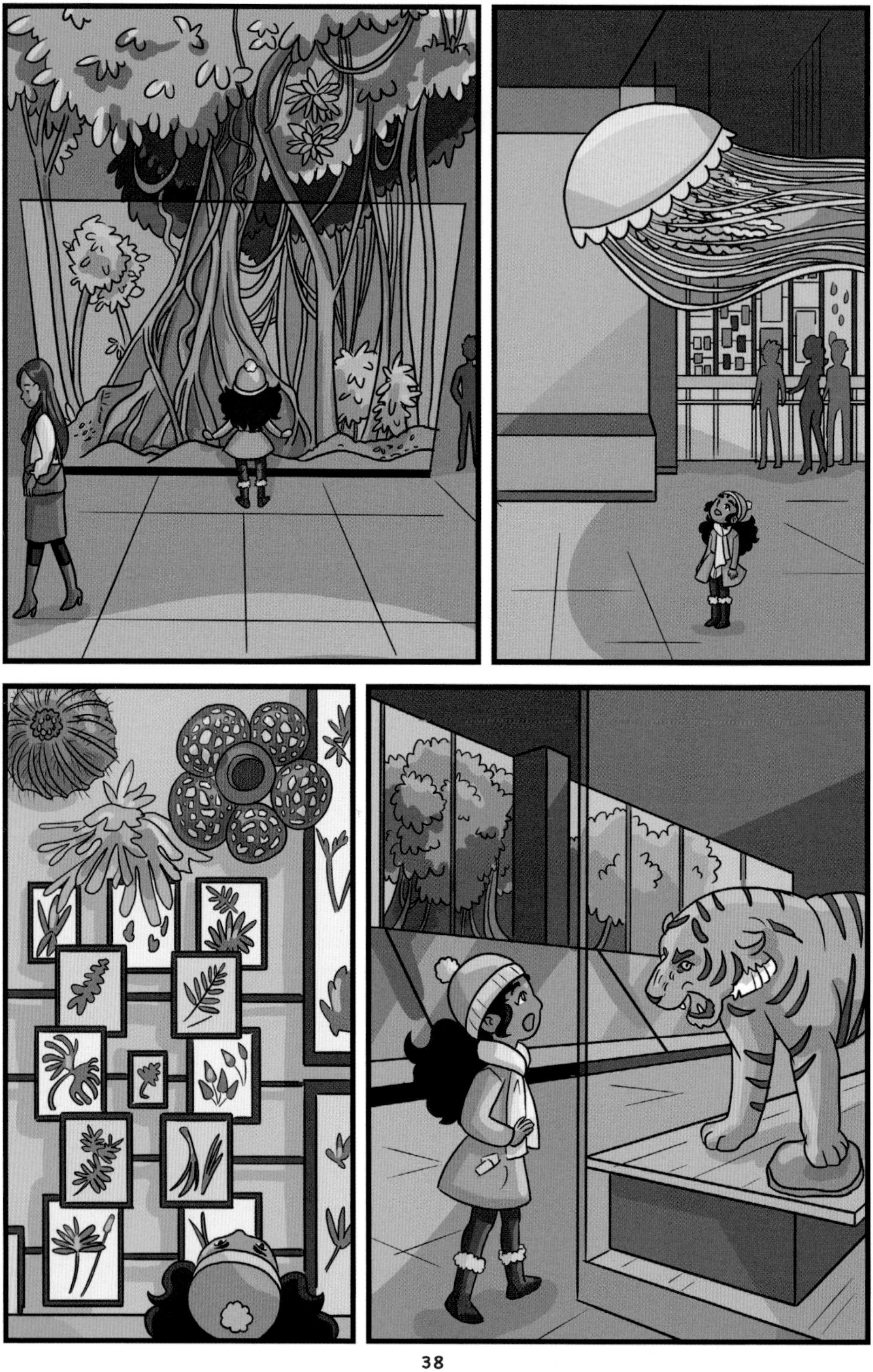

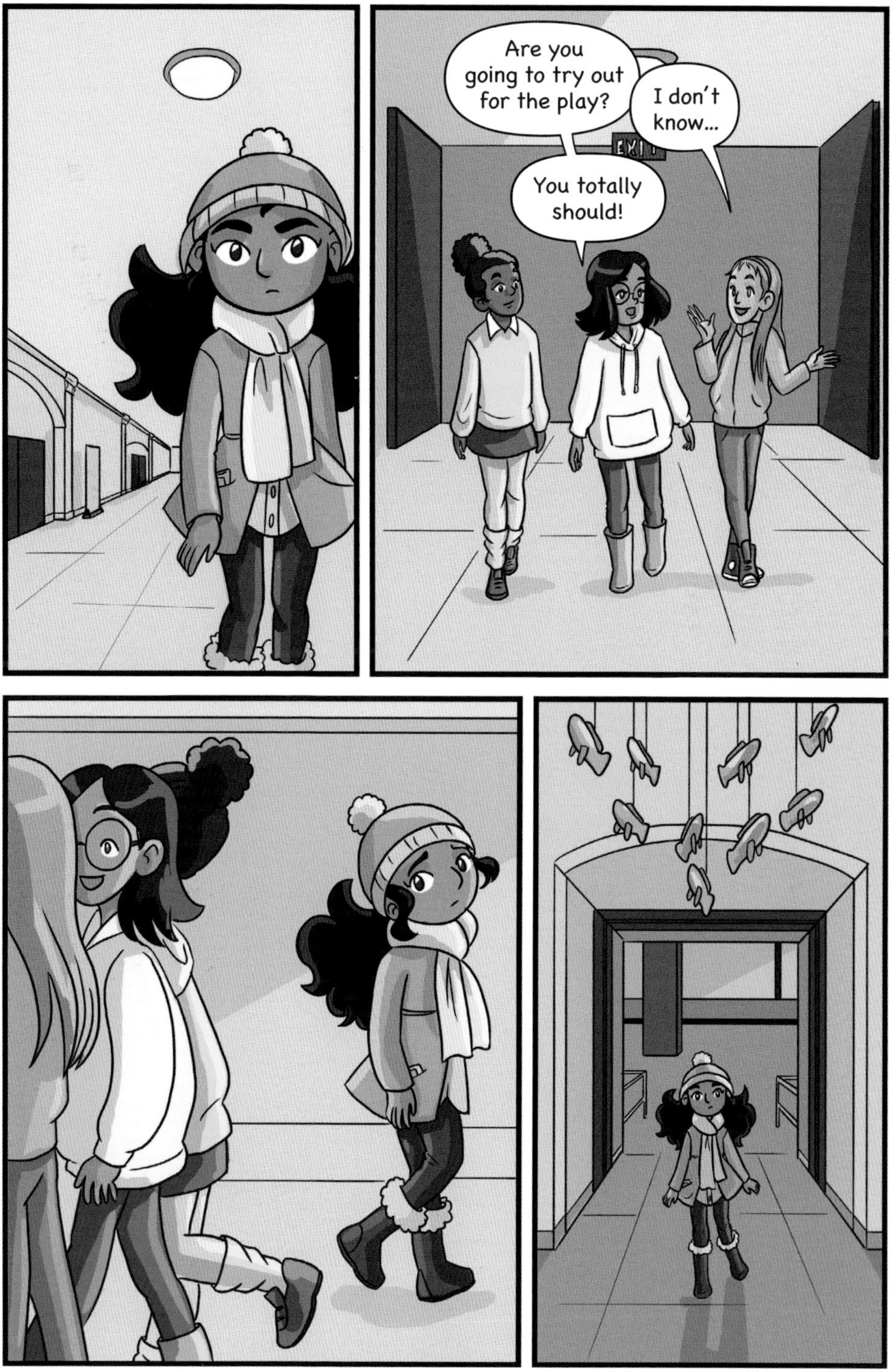
Are you going to try out for the play?
I don't know...
You totally should!
EXIT

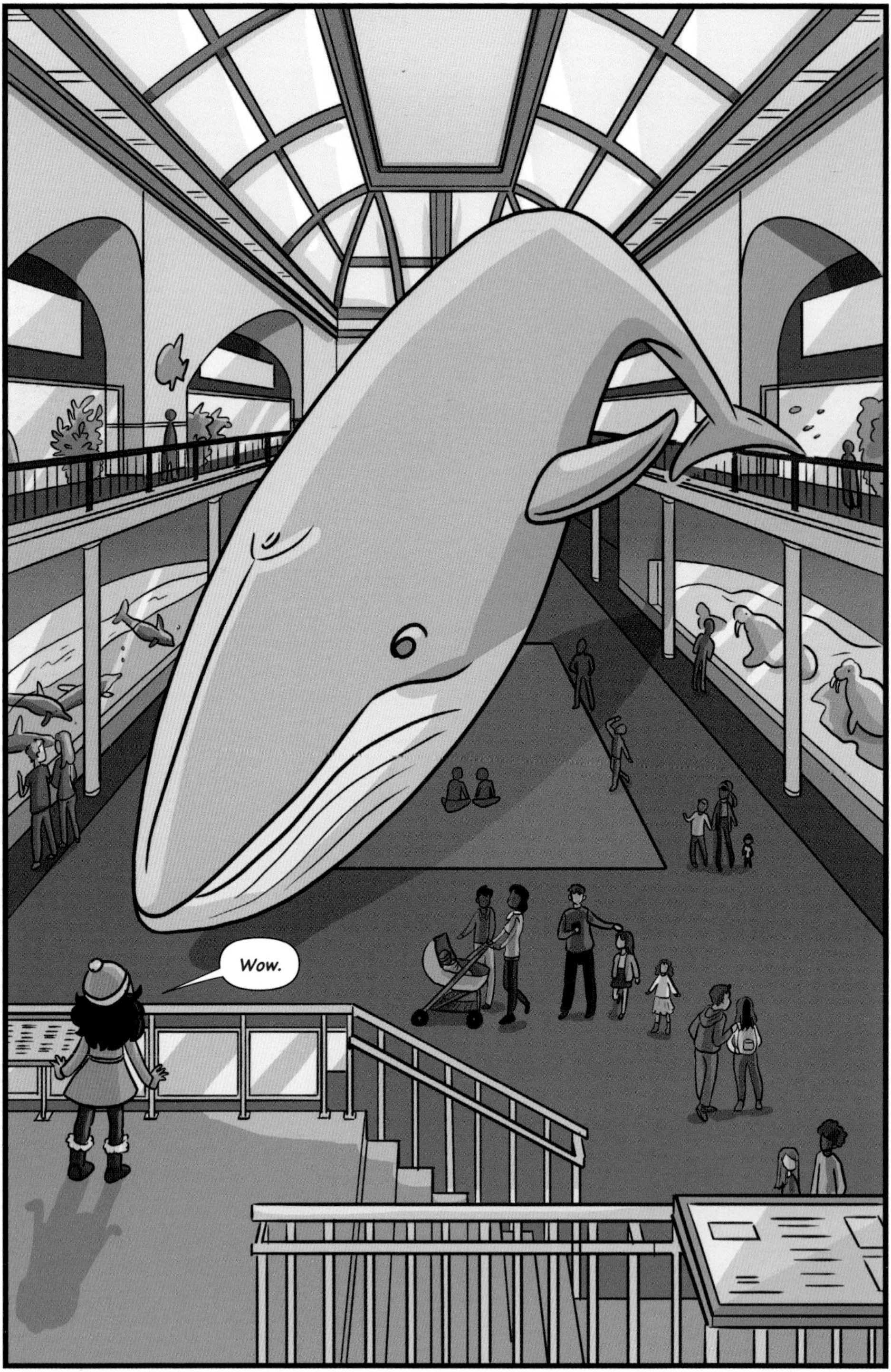
Wow.

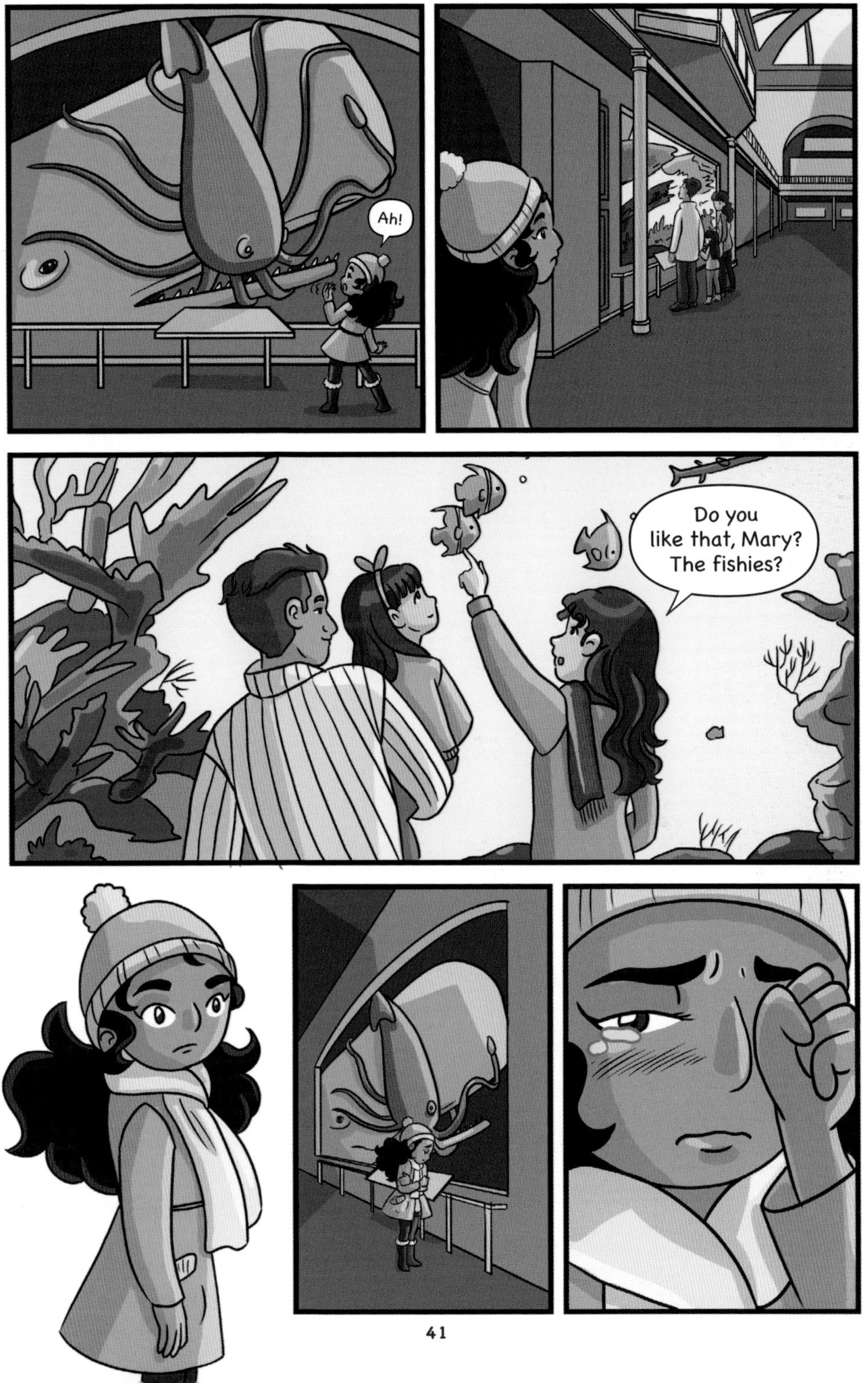
Ah!
Do you like that, Mary? The fishies?

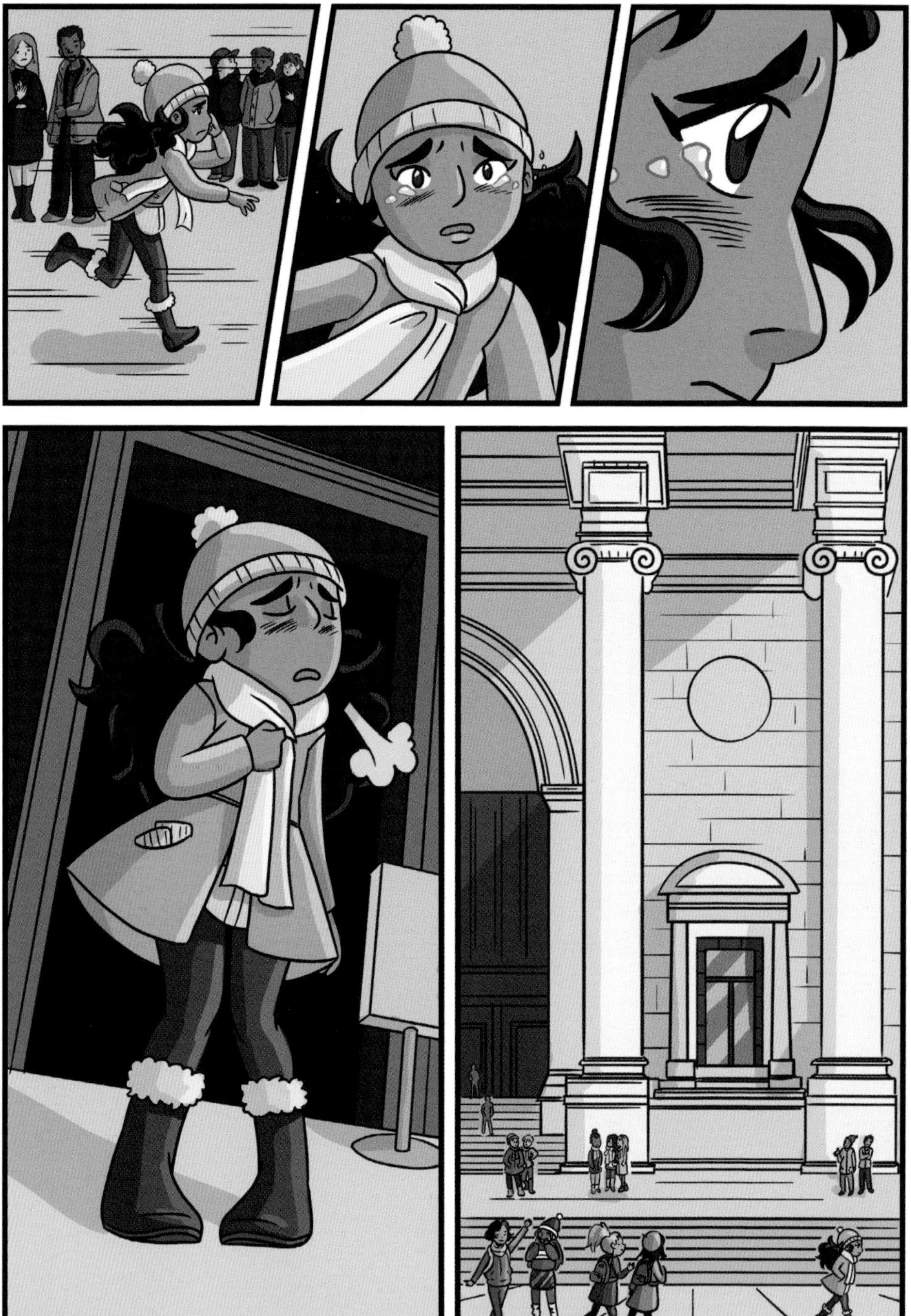

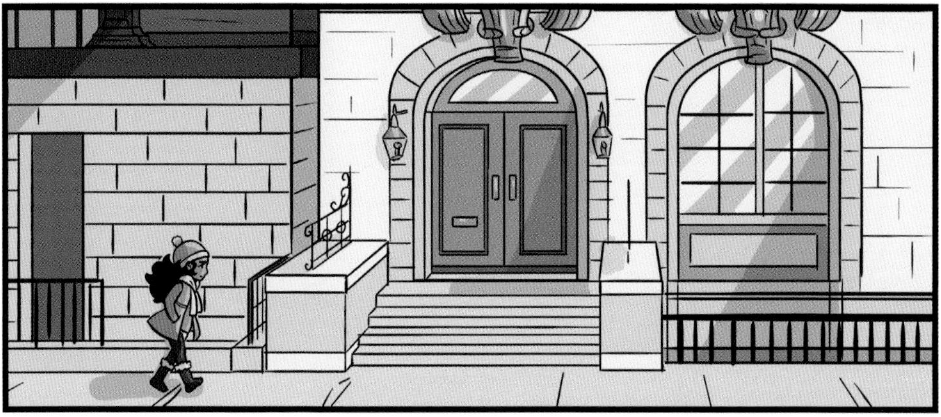

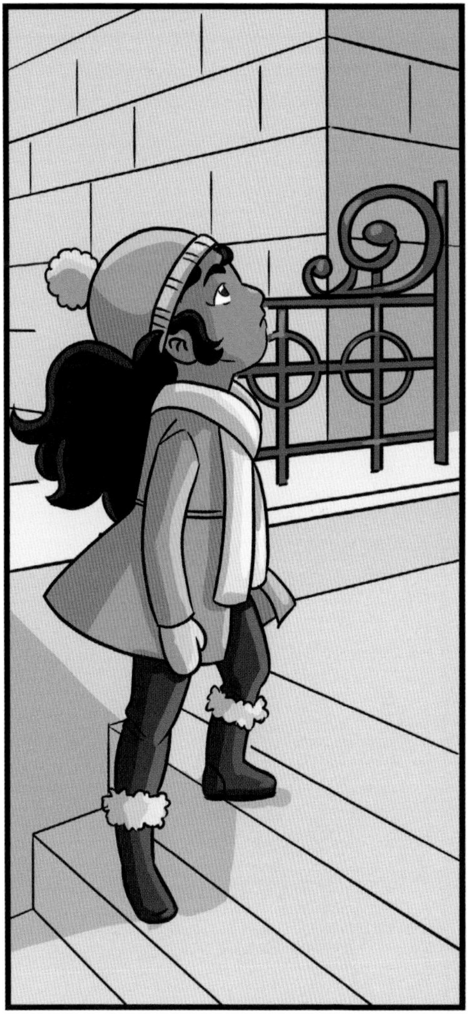

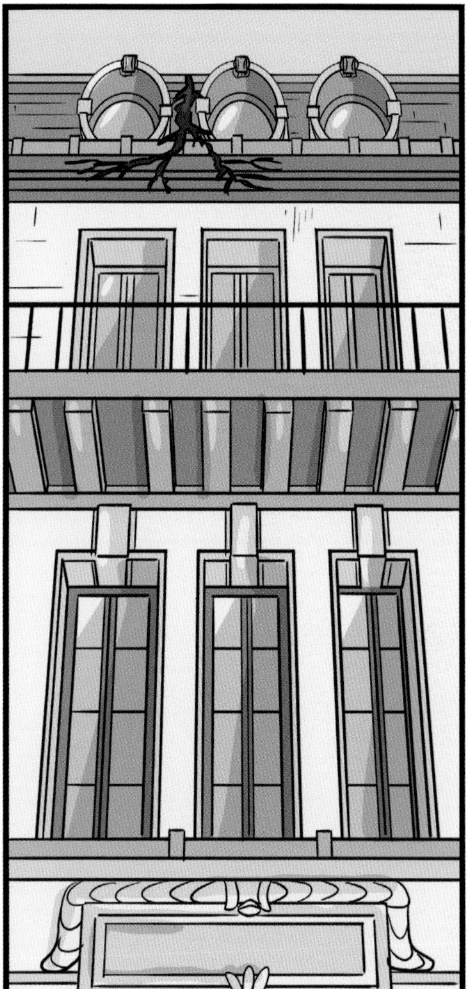

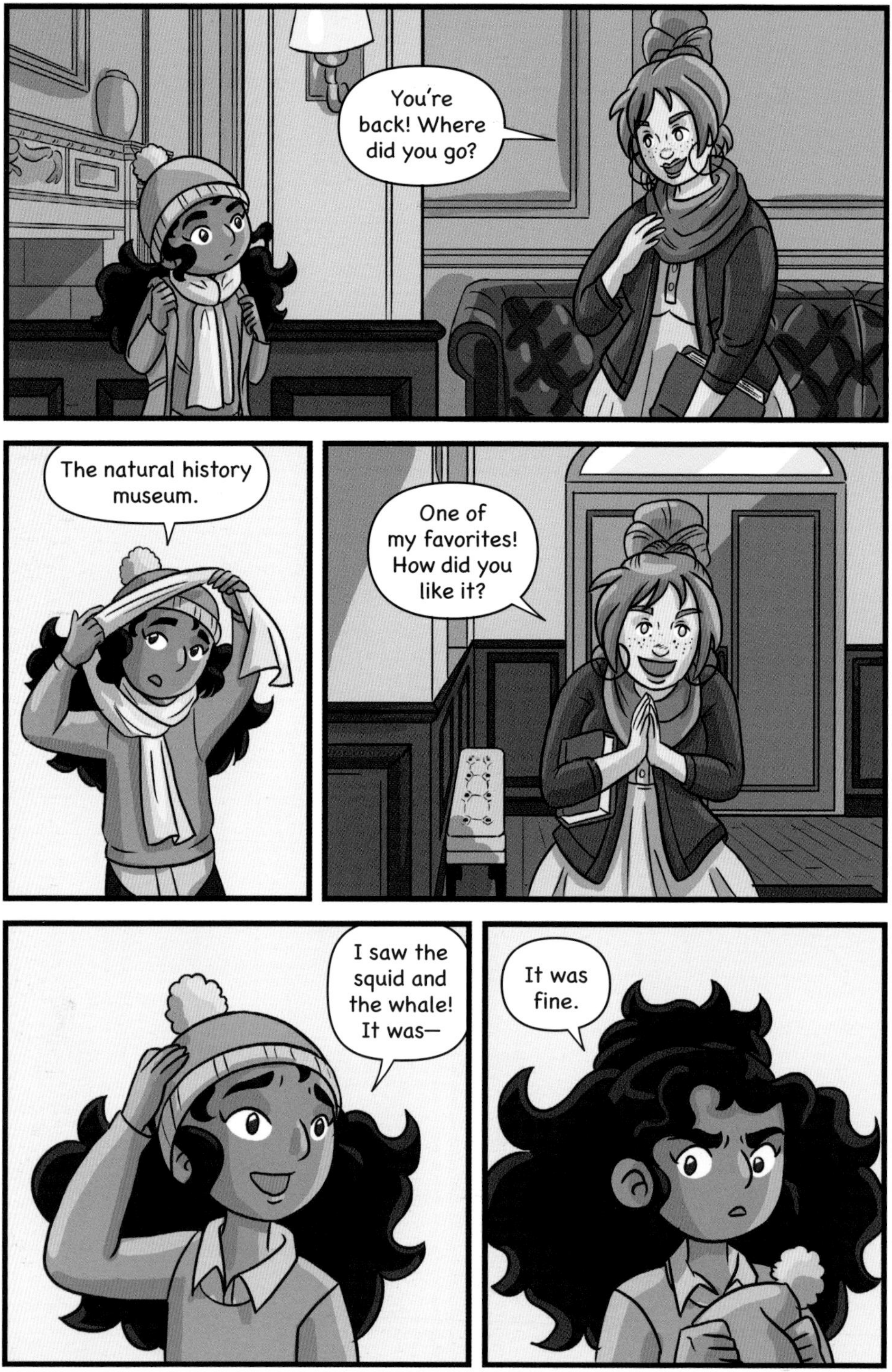
You're back! Where did you go?
The natural history museum.
One of my favorites! How did you like it?
I saw the squid and the whale! It was—
It was fine.

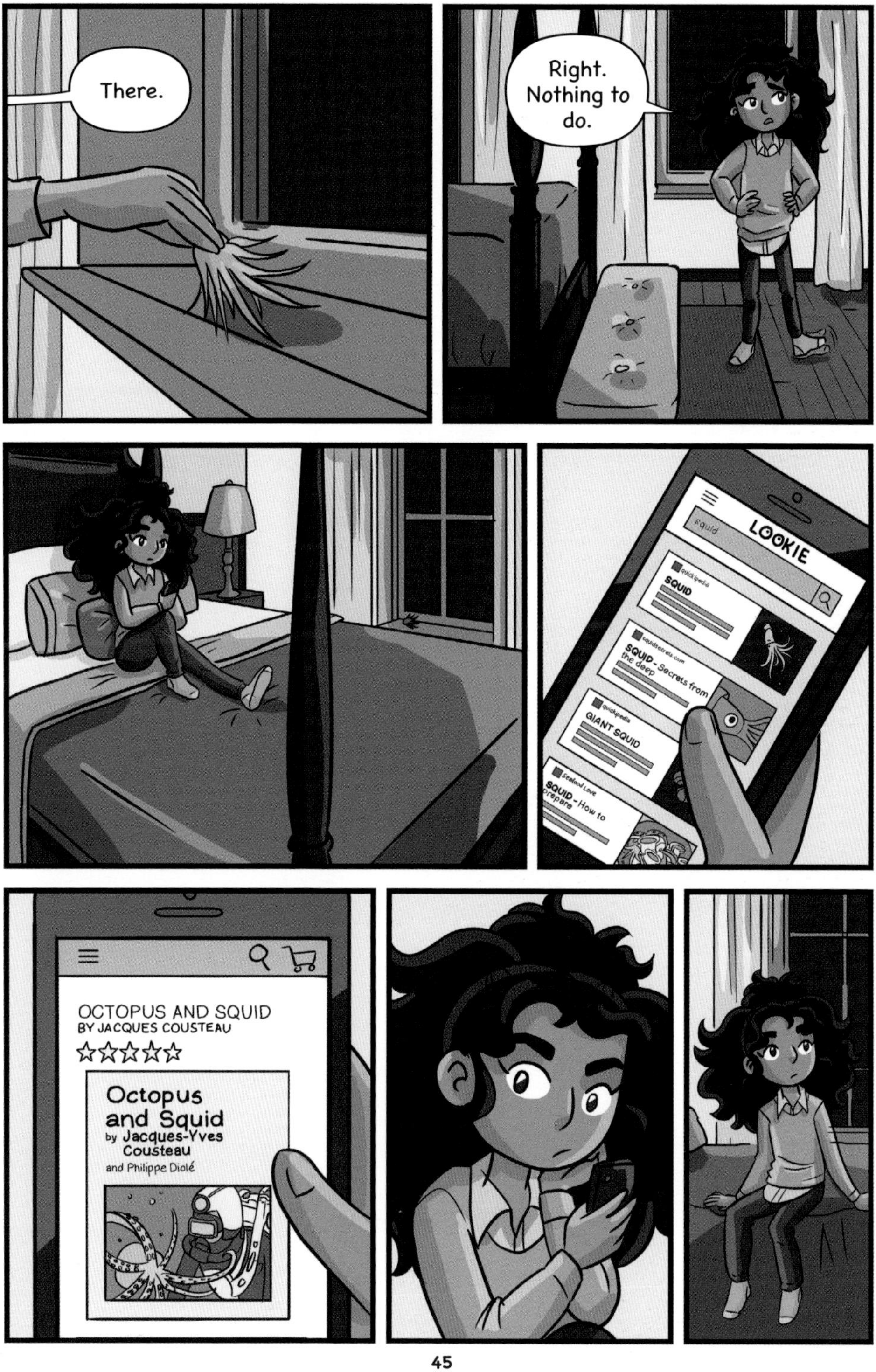
There.
Right. Nothing to do.
squid
LOOKIE
quickipedia
SQUID
squidsecrets.com
SQUID - Secrets from the deep
quickipedia
GIANT SQUID
Seafood Love
SQUID - How to prepare
OCTOPUS AND SQUID
BY JACQUES COUSTEAU
Octopus and Squid
by Jacques-Yves Cousteau
and Philippe Diolé

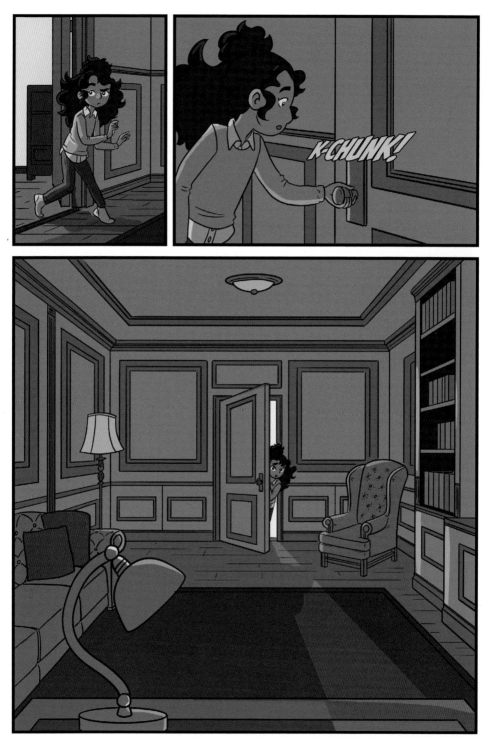

K-CHUNK!

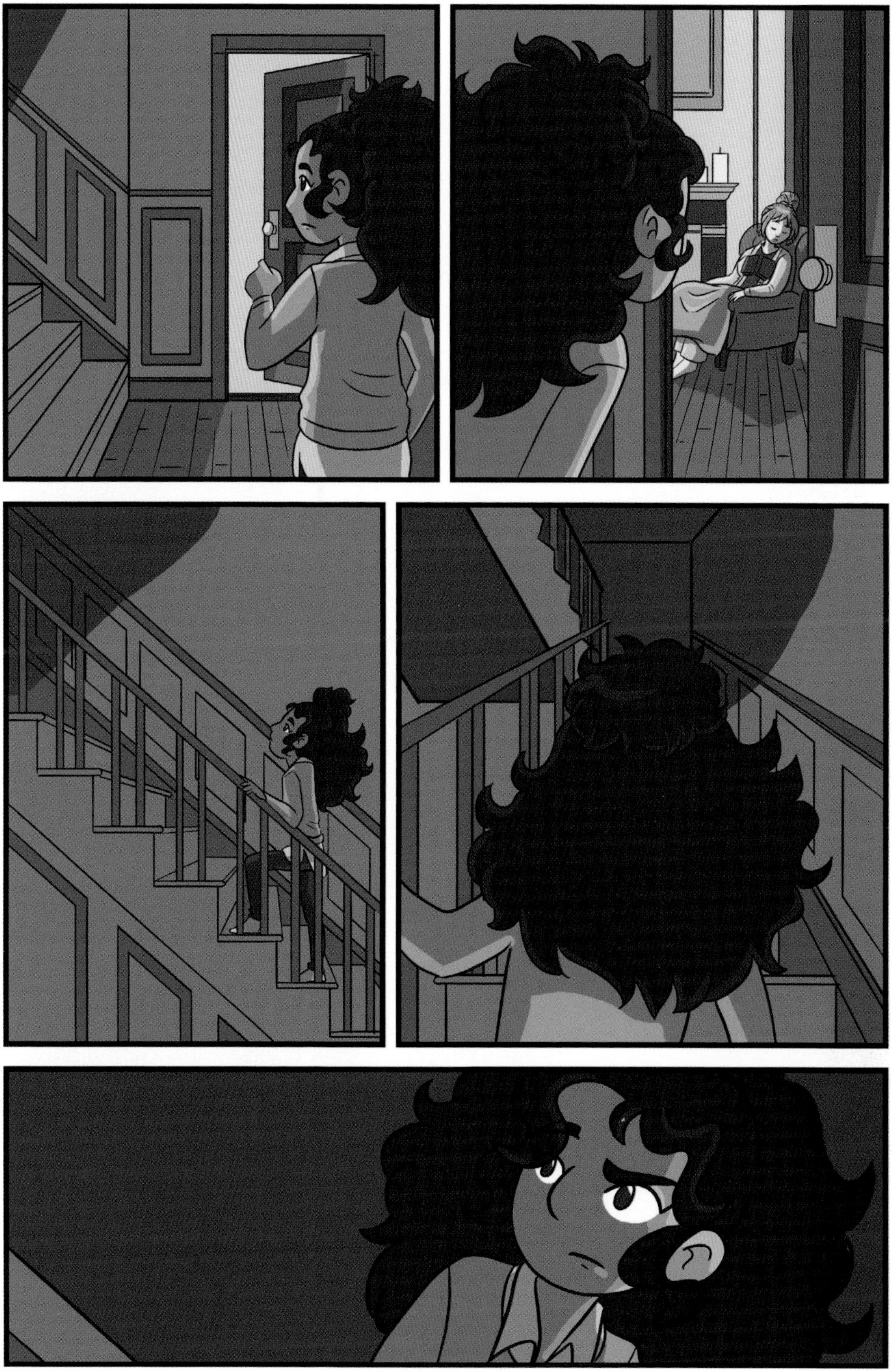

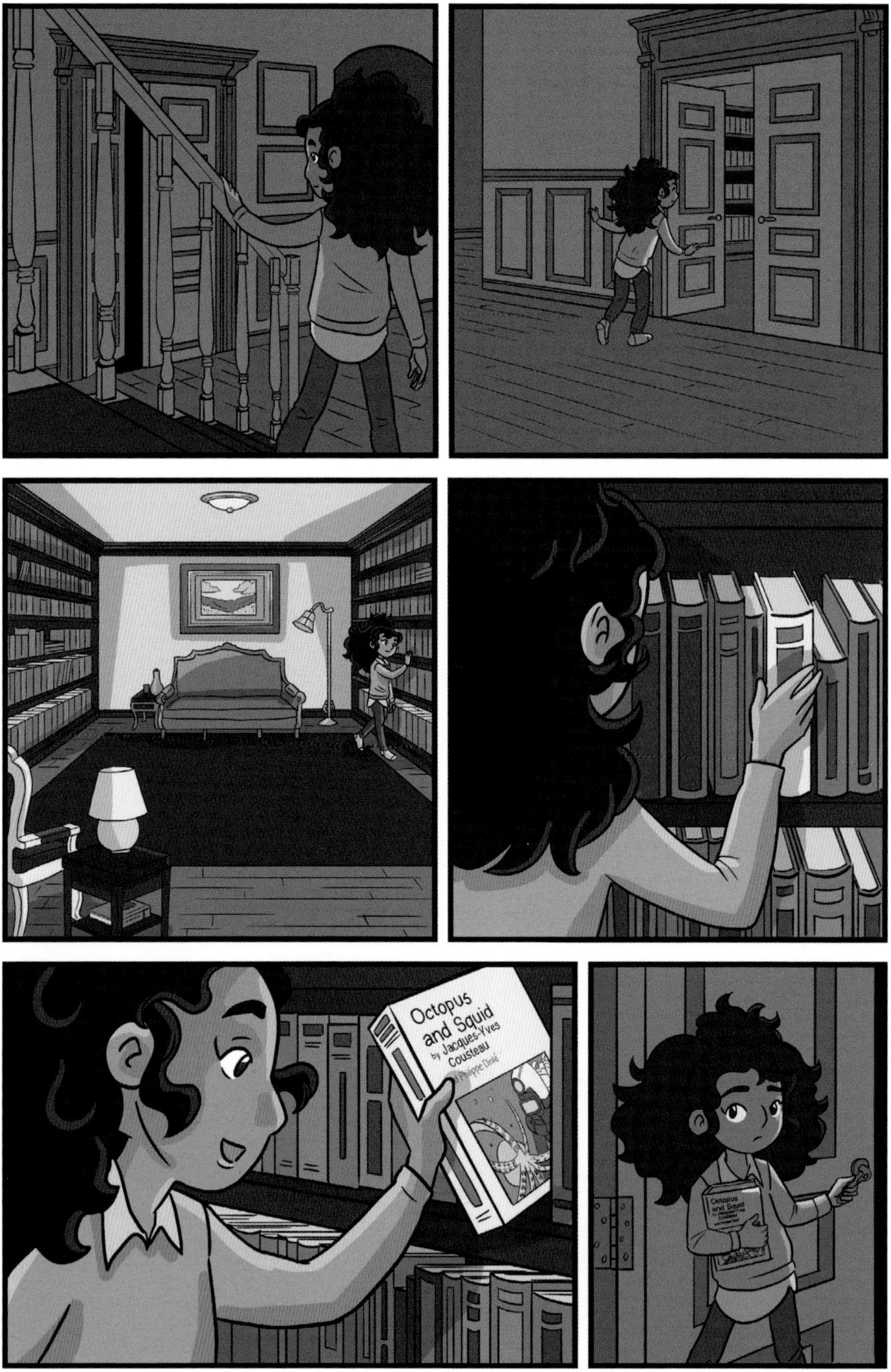
Octopus and Squid
by Jacques-Yves Cousteau

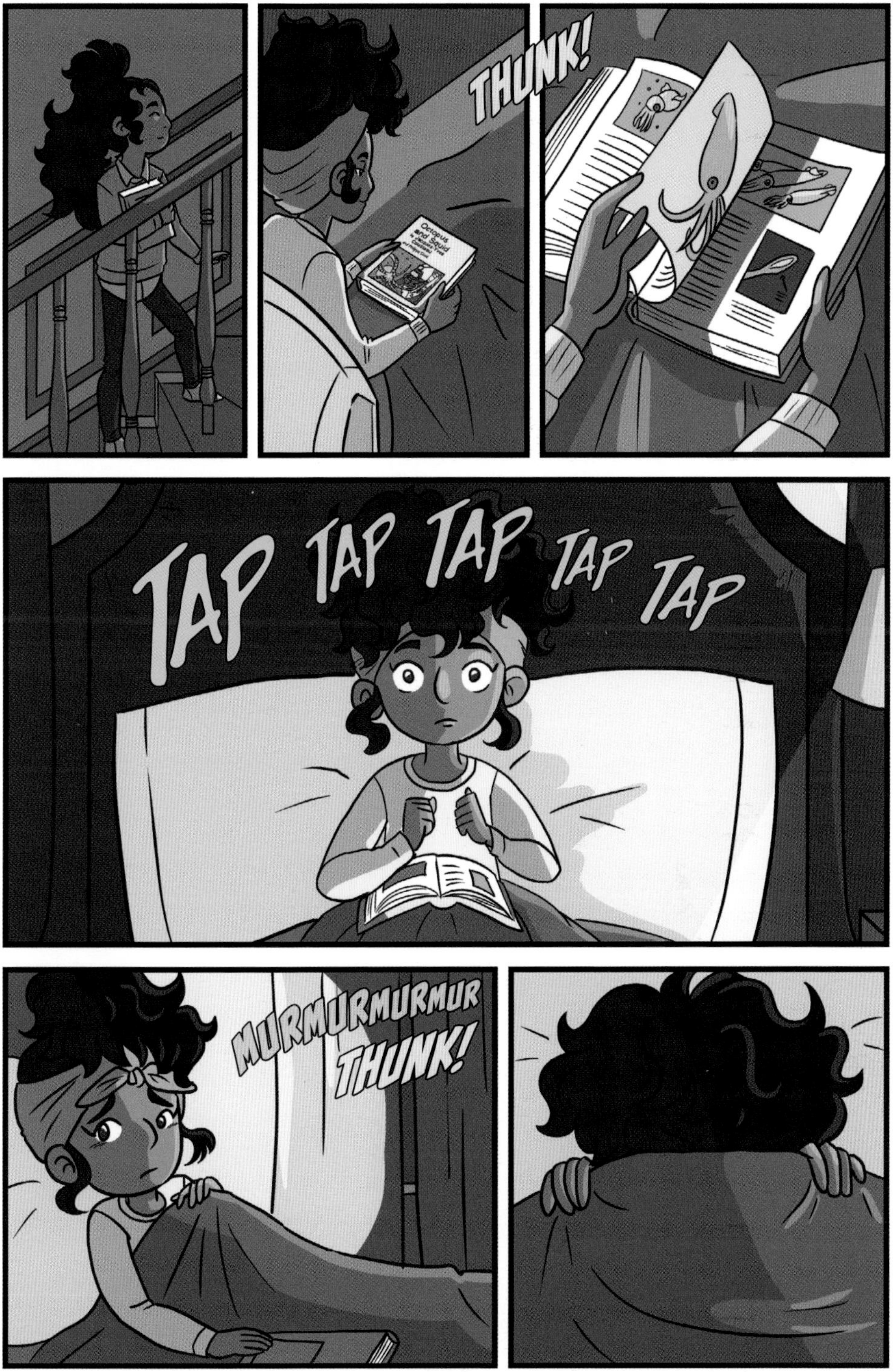
THUNK!
Octopus and Squid
TAP TAP TAP TAP TAP
MURMURMURMUR
THUNK!

Medlock

eMAIL

INBOX | Starred | Sent | Drafts | Spam

NEW MESSAGE

TO: archibald_craven@craveninc.com

FROM: medlock_cravenhousehold@craveninc.com

SUBJECT: Mary's Arrival

Archie,

Your niece has arrived safely and is settling in. The girl's gone through a terrible ordeal, one that you are, of course, yourself familiar with, but it hasn't done much for what I suspect is an already poor attitude. She turns her nose up at most of the food that's offered and gives most answers in one-word replies. Still, Martha tries her best. You know how she is: relentlessly cheerful.

Have you given any thought to Mary's plans for school in the fall? If you are still considering boarding schools, I can begin to gather information to have ready when you return.

Best regards,
Constance

SEND

Household finance

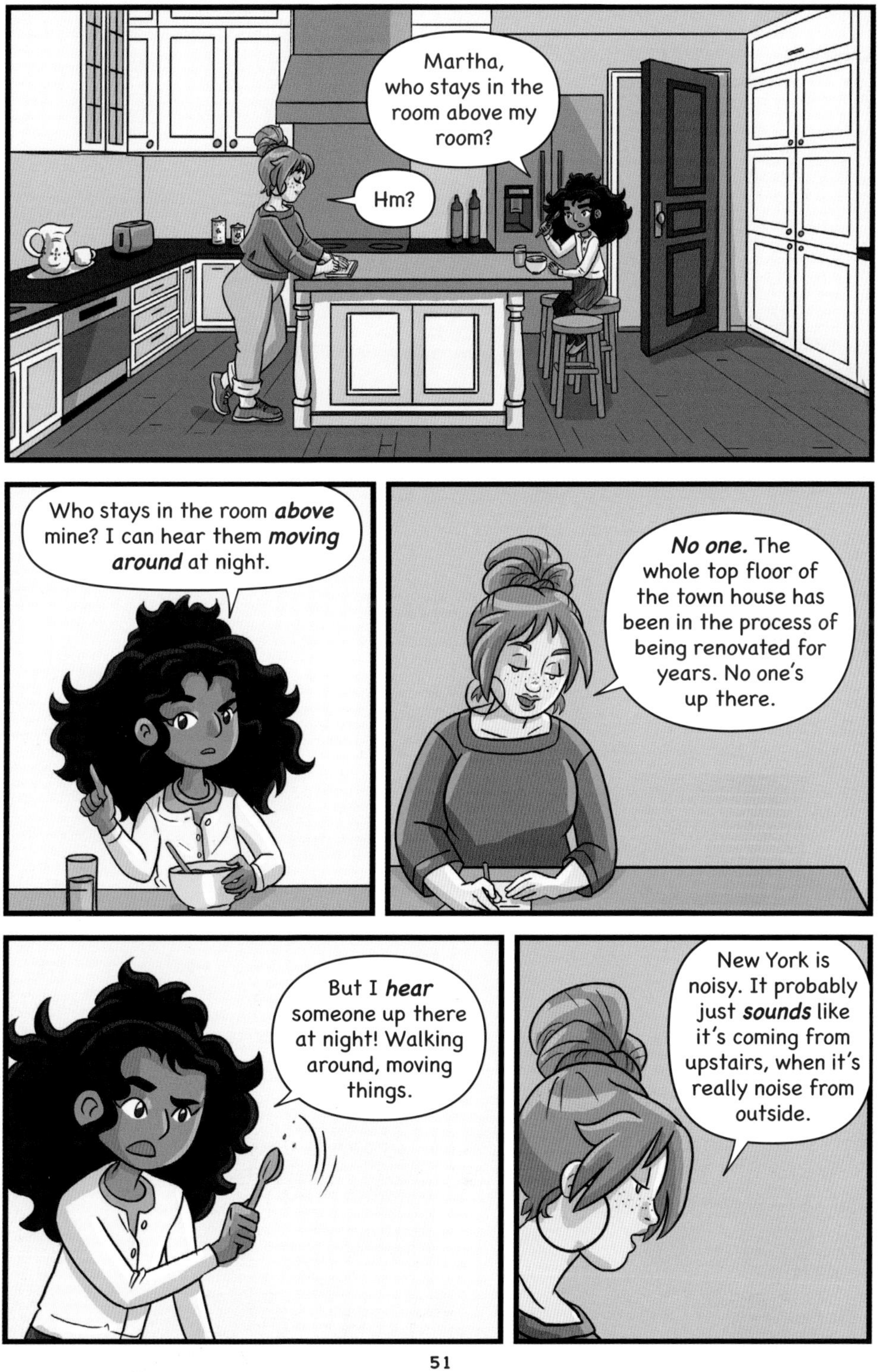
Martha, who stays in the room above my room?
Hm?
Who stays in the room *above* mine? I can hear them *moving around* at night.
No one. The whole top floor of the town house has been in the process of being renovated for years. No one's up there.
But I *hear* someone up there at night! Walking around, moving things.
New York is noisy. It probably just *sounds* like it's coming from upstairs, when it's really noise from outside.

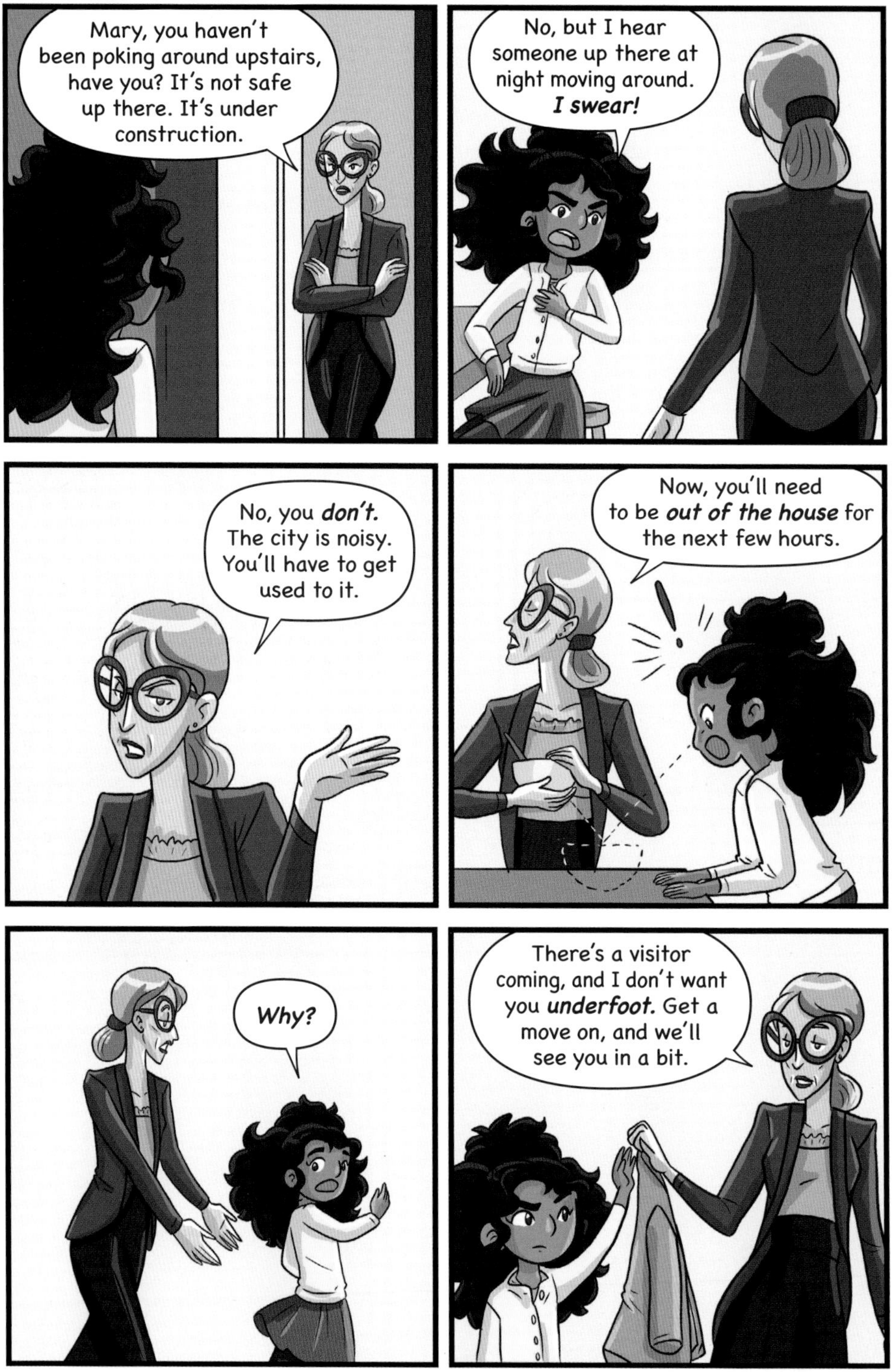

Mary, you haven't been poking around upstairs, have you? It's not safe up there. It's under construction.
No, but I hear someone up there at night moving around. *I swear!*
No, you *don't.* The city is noisy. You'll have to get used to it.
Now, you'll need to be *out of the house* for the next few hours.
!
Why?
There's a visitor coming, and I don't want you *underfoot.* Get a move on, and we'll see you in a bit.

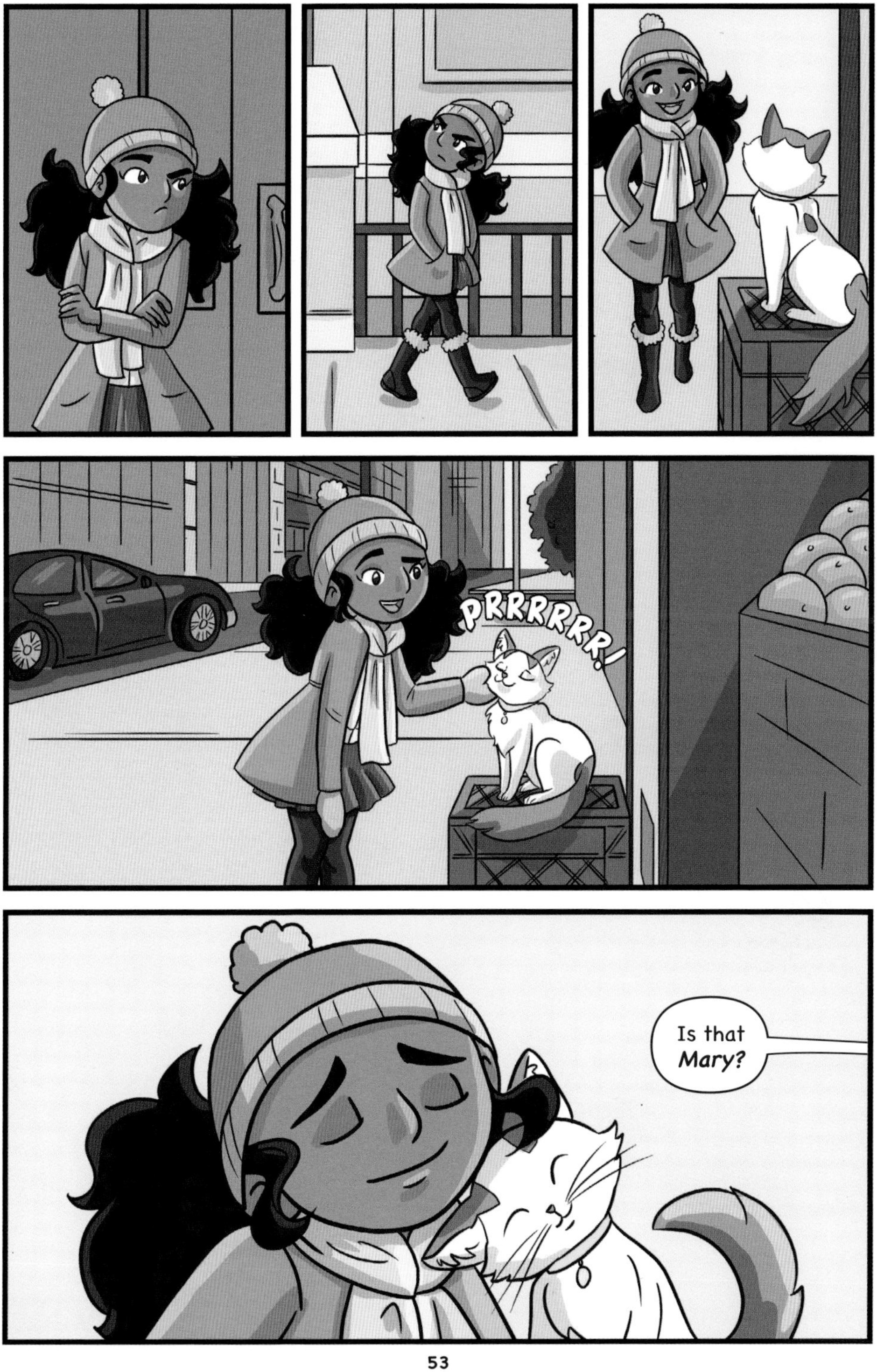
PRRRRRRR!
Is that Mary?

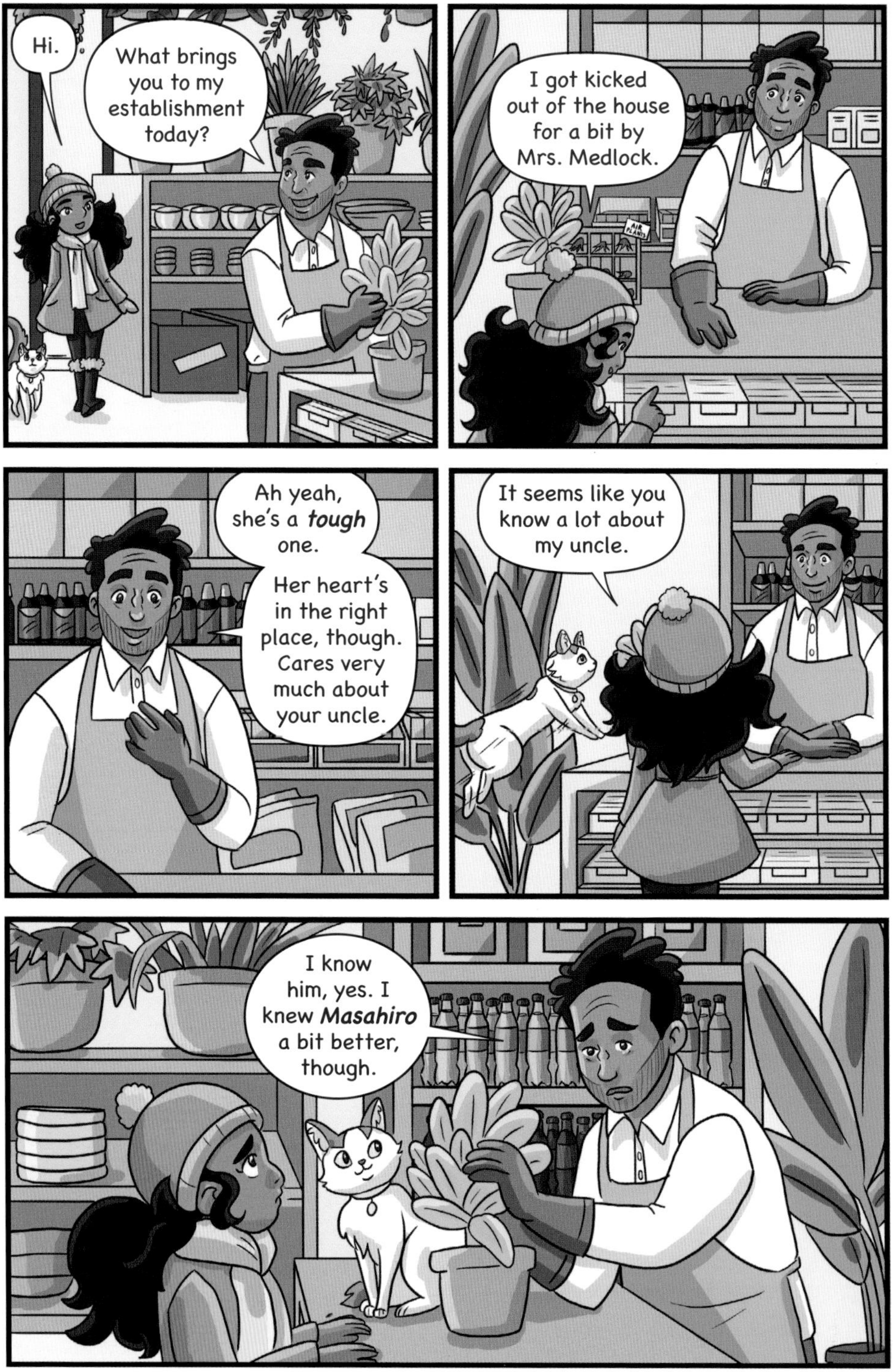
Hi.
What brings you to my establishment today?
I got kicked out of the house for a bit by Mrs. Medlock.
Ah yeah, she's a *tough* one.
Her heart's in the right place, though. Cares very much about your uncle.
It seems like you know a lot about my uncle.
I know him, yes. I knew *Masahiro* a bit better, though.

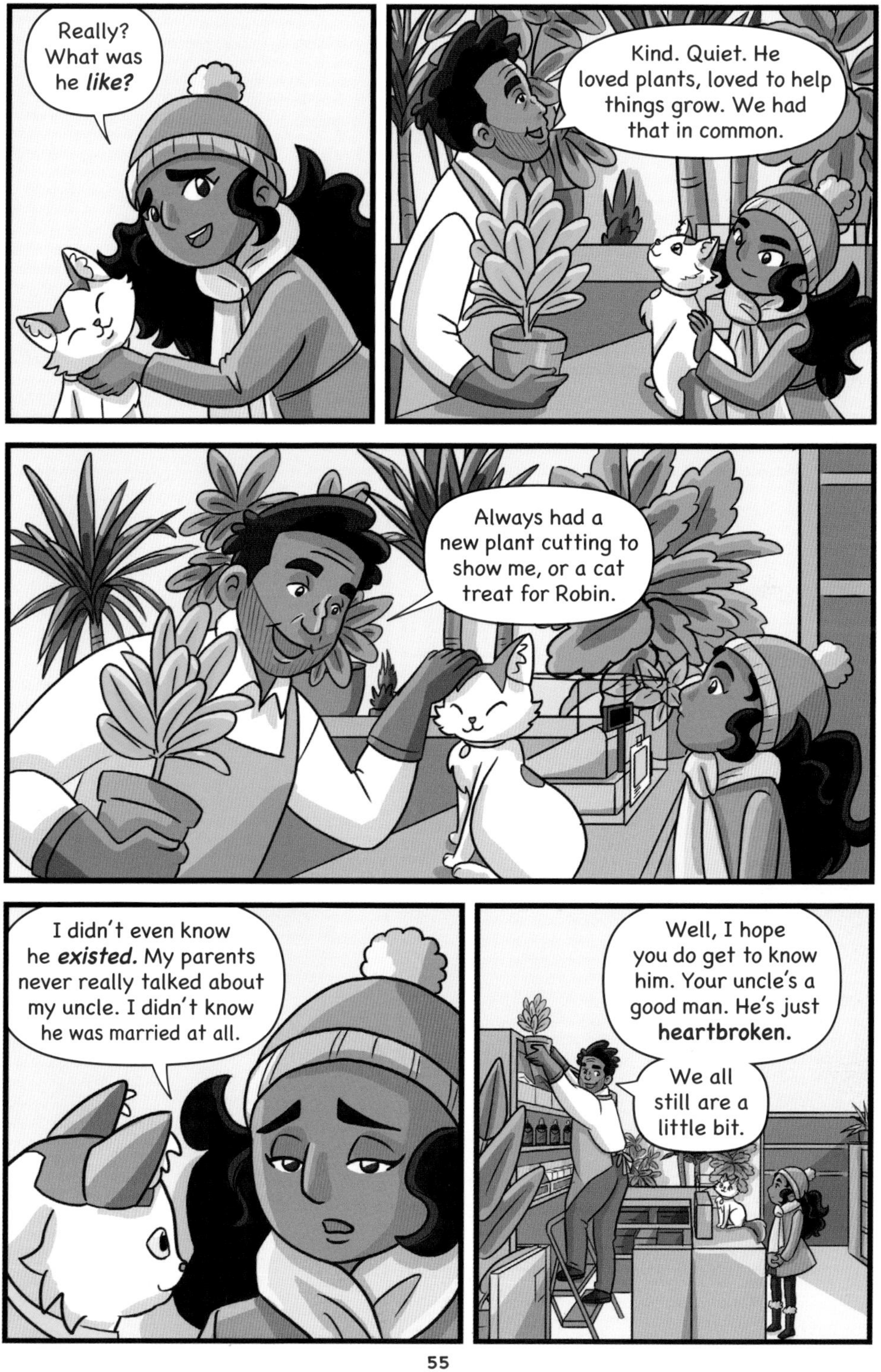
Really? What was he *like?*
Kind. Quiet. He loved plants, loved to help things grow. We had that in common.
Always had a new plant cutting to show me, or a cat treat for Robin.
I didn't even know he *existed.* My parents never really talked about my uncle. I didn't know he was married at all.
Well, I hope you do get to know him. Your uncle's a good man. He's just **heartbroken.**
We all still are a little bit.

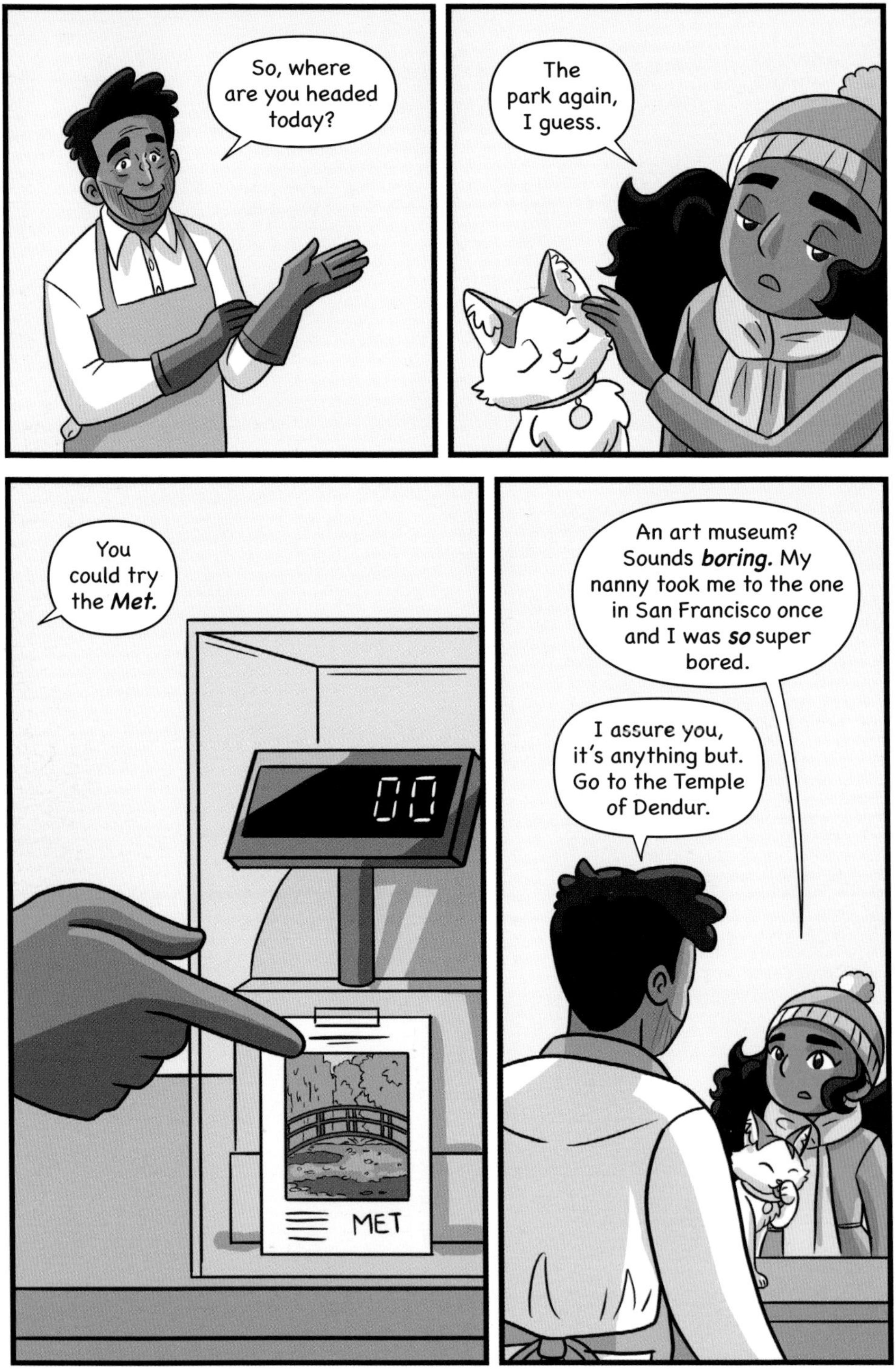
So, where are you headed today?
The park again, I guess.
You could try the ***Met.***
00
MET
An art museum? Sounds ***boring.*** My nanny took me to the one in San Francisco once and I was ***so*** super bored.
I assure you, it's anything but. Go to the Temple of Dendur.

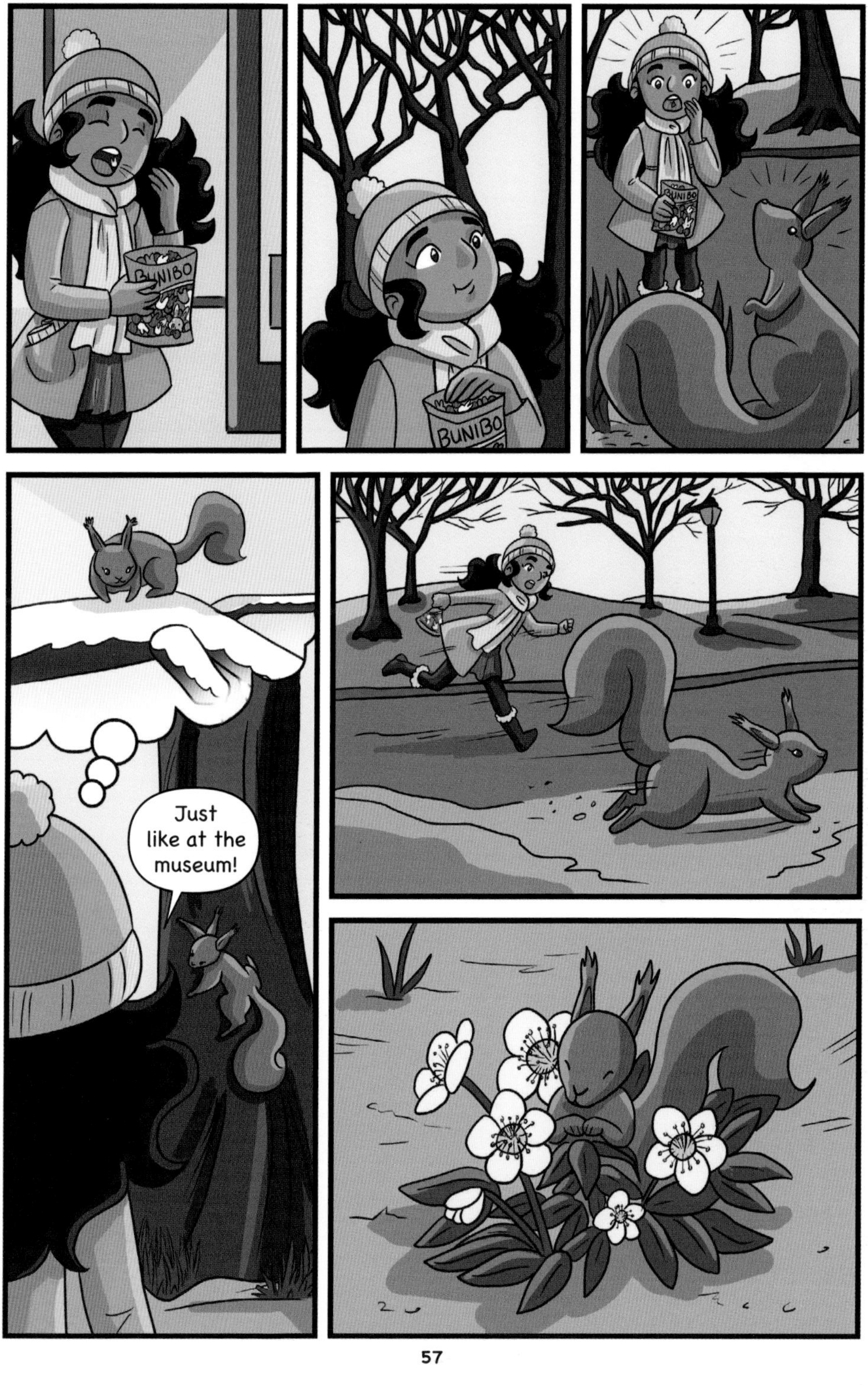
BUNIBO
BUNIBO
BUNIBO
Just like at the museum!

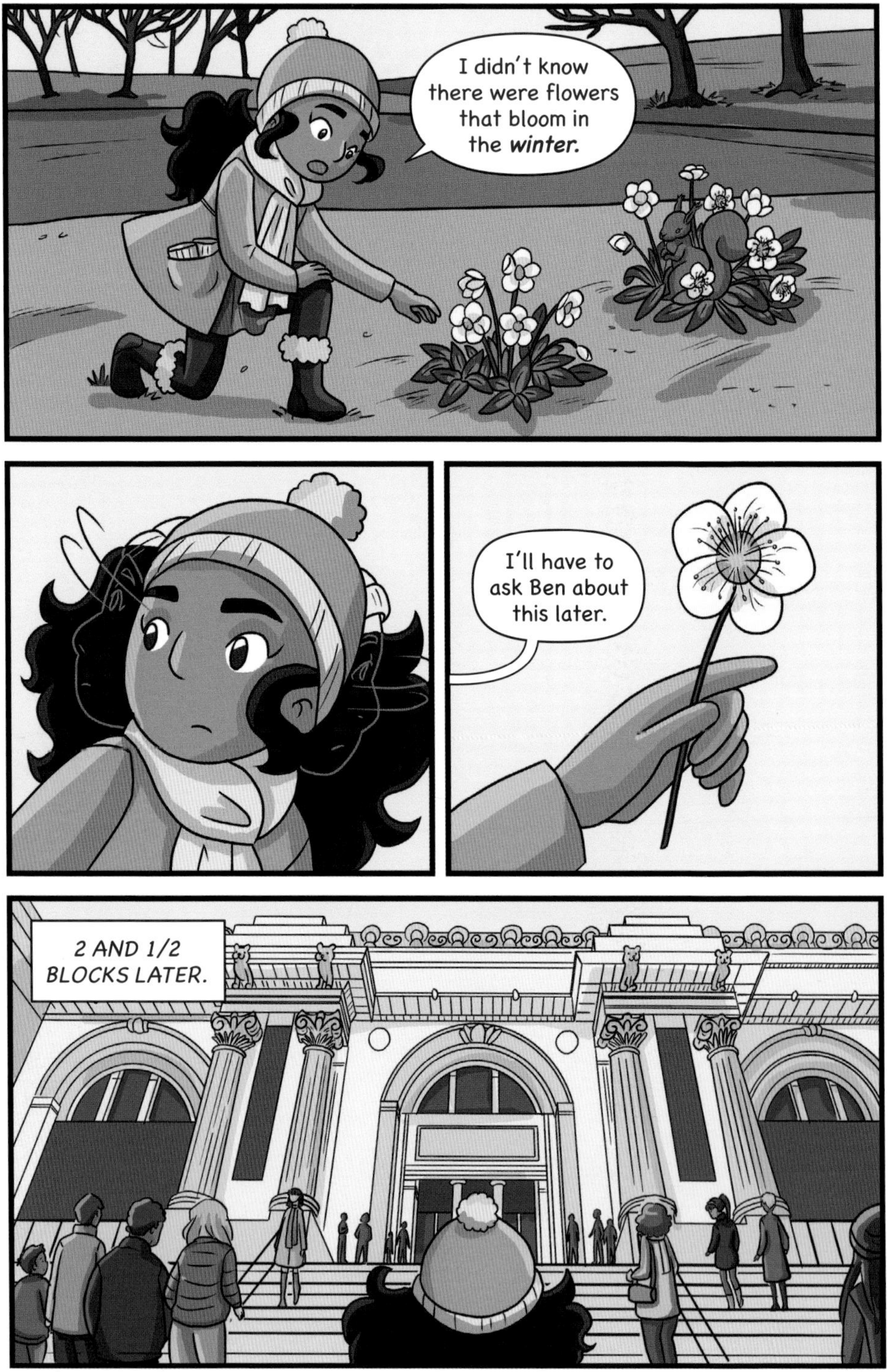
I didn't know there were flowers that bloom in the *winter.*
I'll have to ask Ben about this later.
2 AND 1/2 BLOCKS LATER.

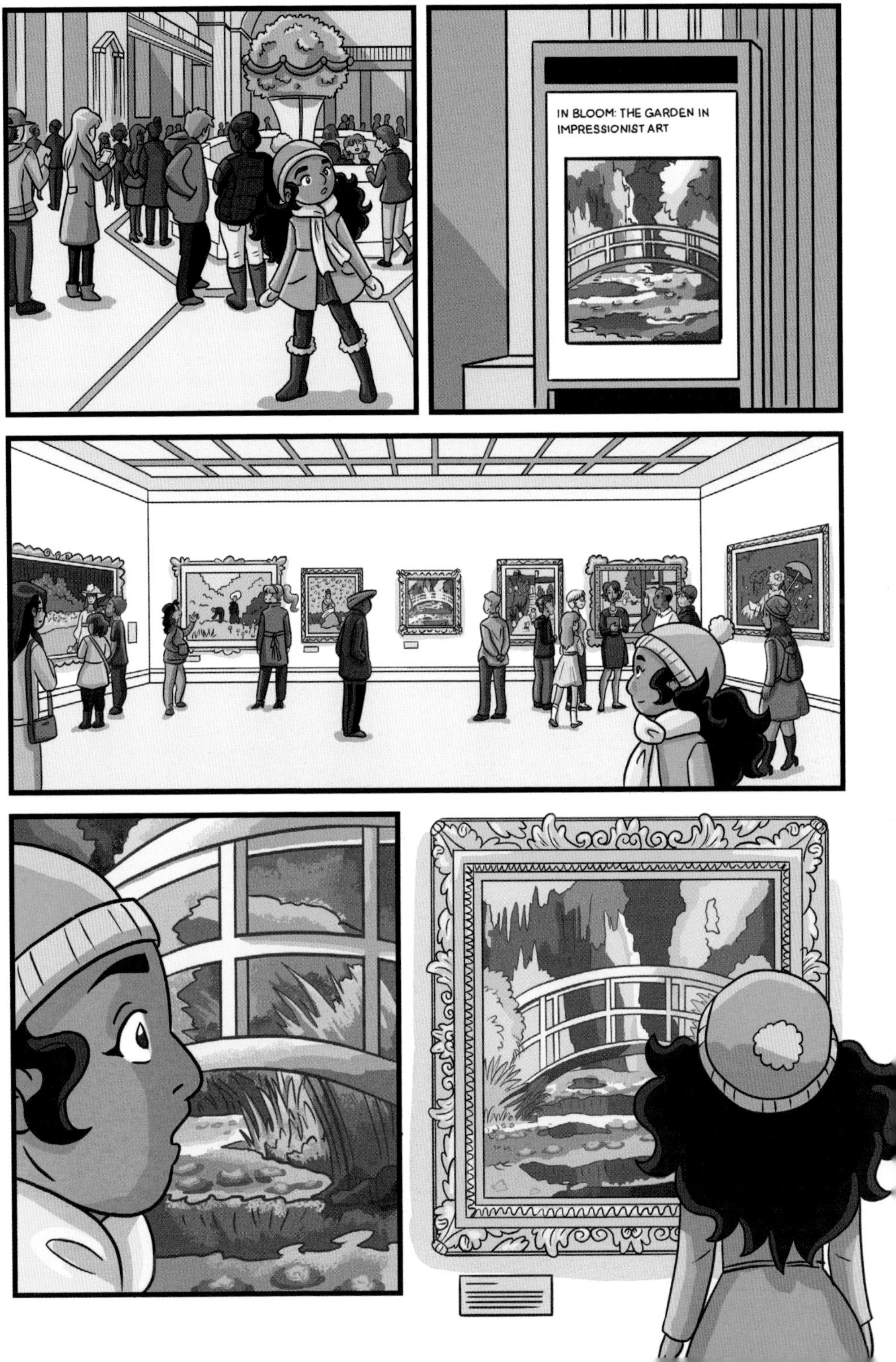
IN BLOOM: THE GARDEN IN
IMPRESSIONIST ART

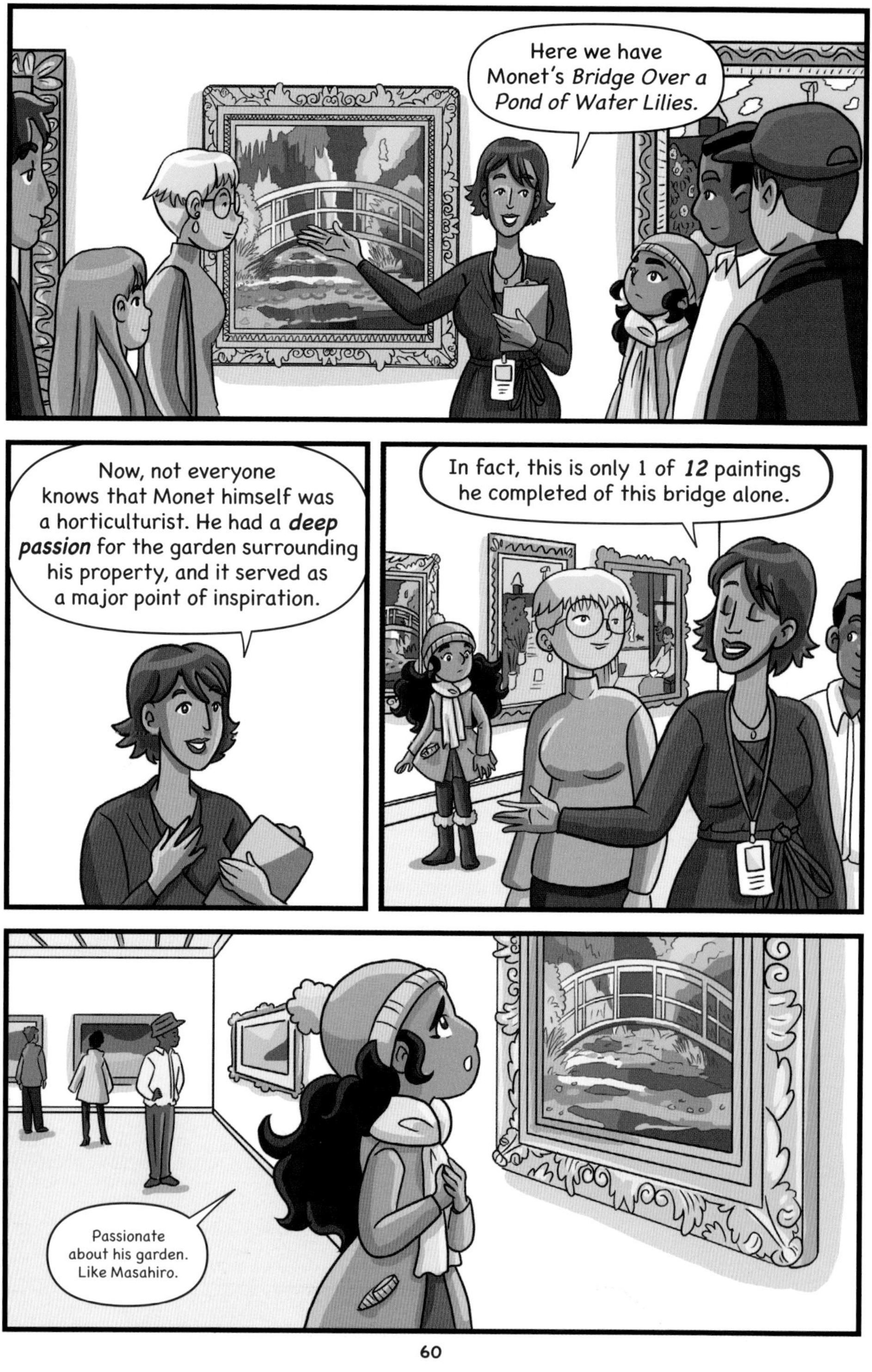
Here we have Monet's *Bridge Over a Pond of Water Lilies.*
Now, not everyone knows that Monet himself was a horticulturist. He had a ***deep passion*** for the garden surrounding his property, and it served as a major point of inspiration.
In fact, this is only 1 of ***12*** paintings he completed of this bridge alone.
Passionate about his garden. Like Masahiro.

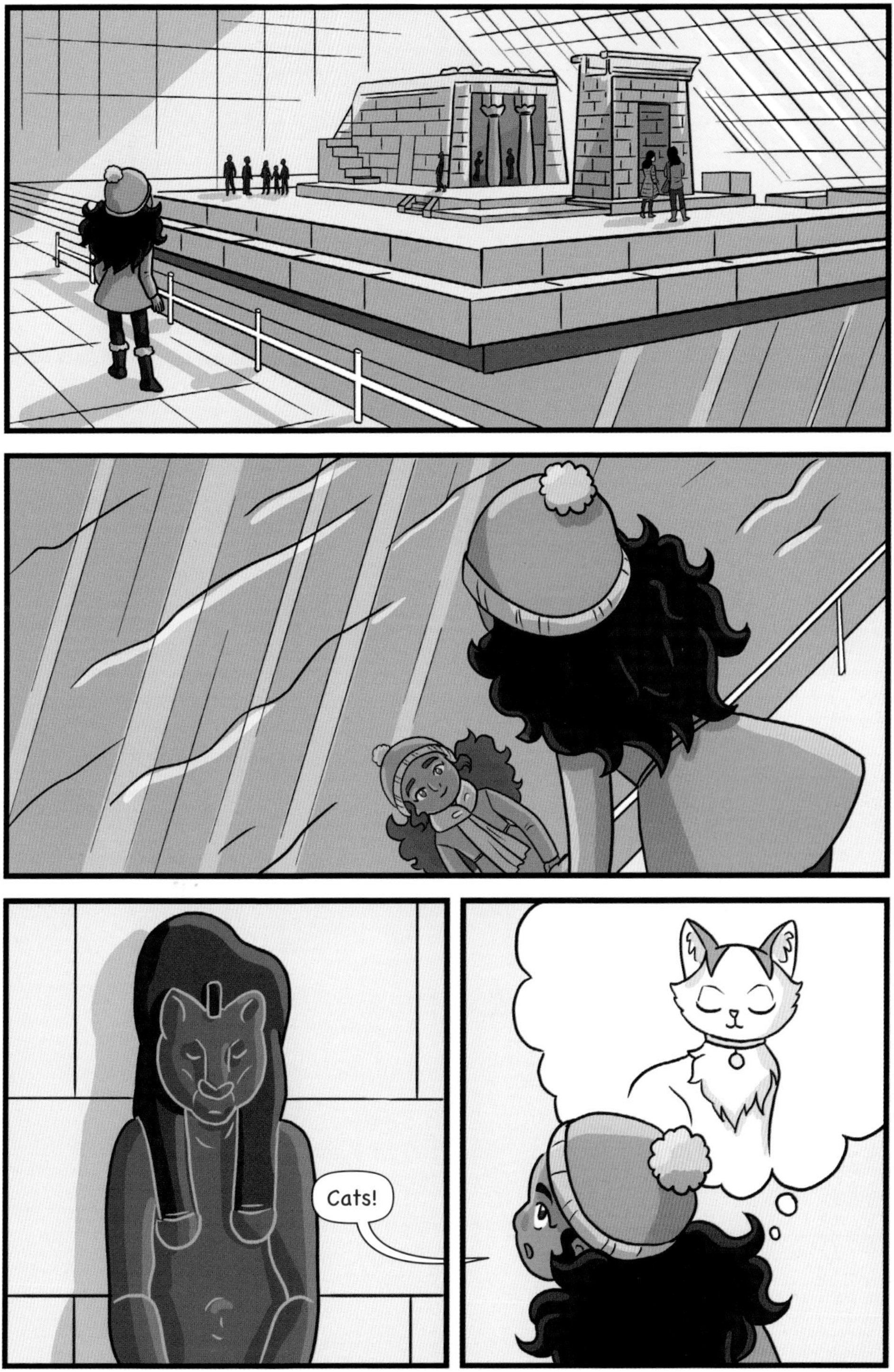
Cats!

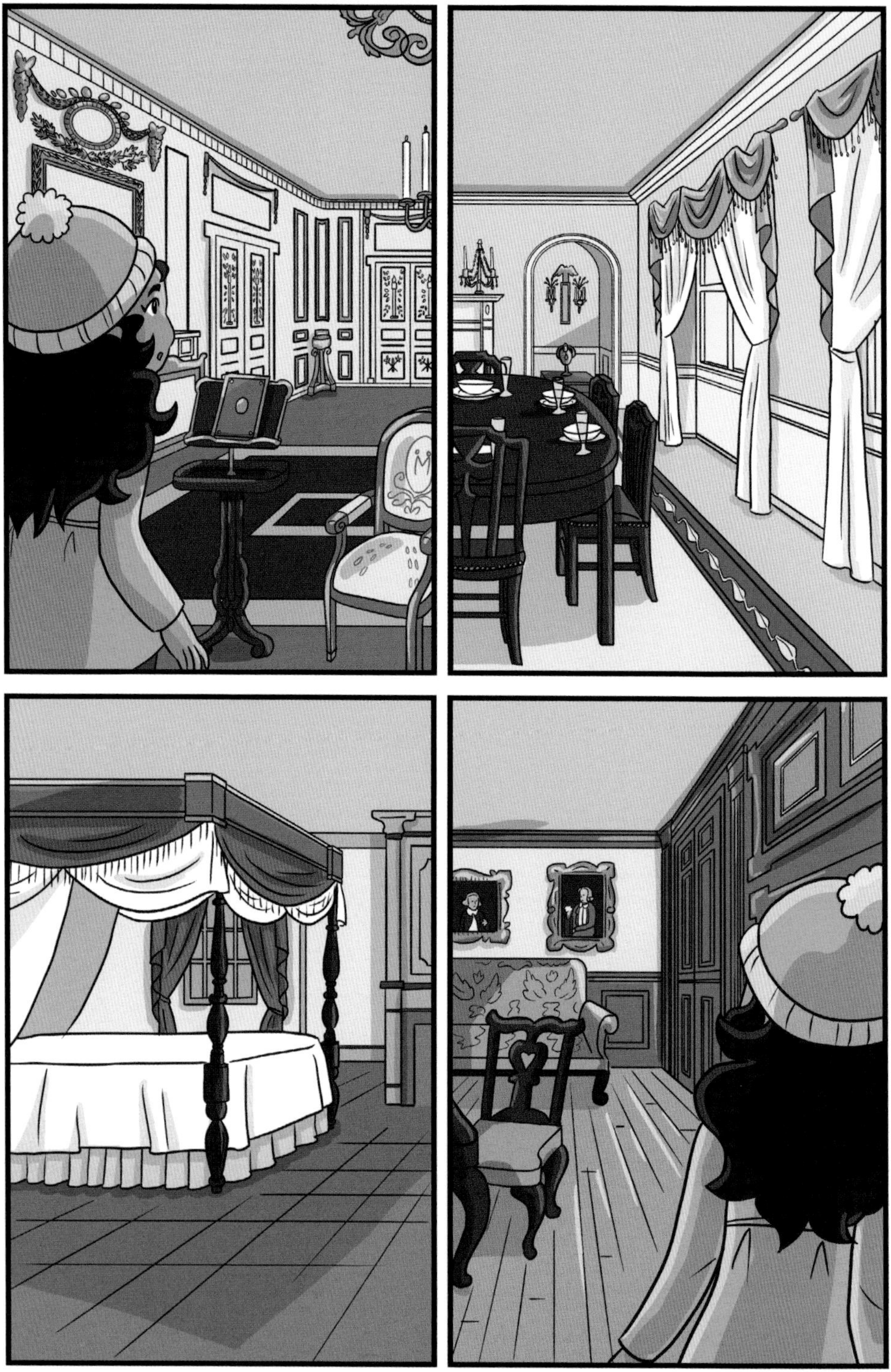

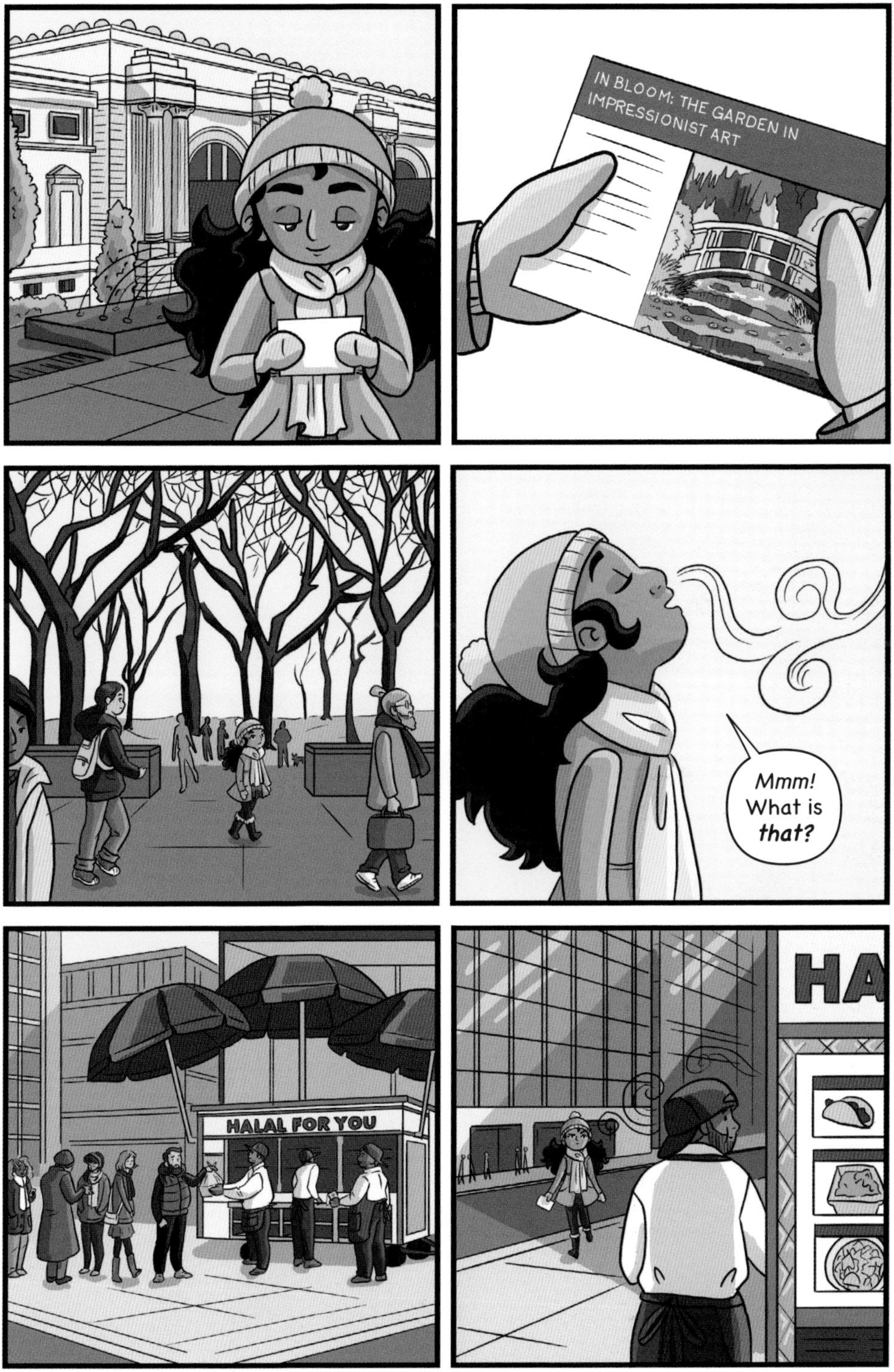
IN BLOOM: THE GARDEN IN IMPRESSIONIST ART
Mmm! What is *that?*
HALAL FOR YOU
HA

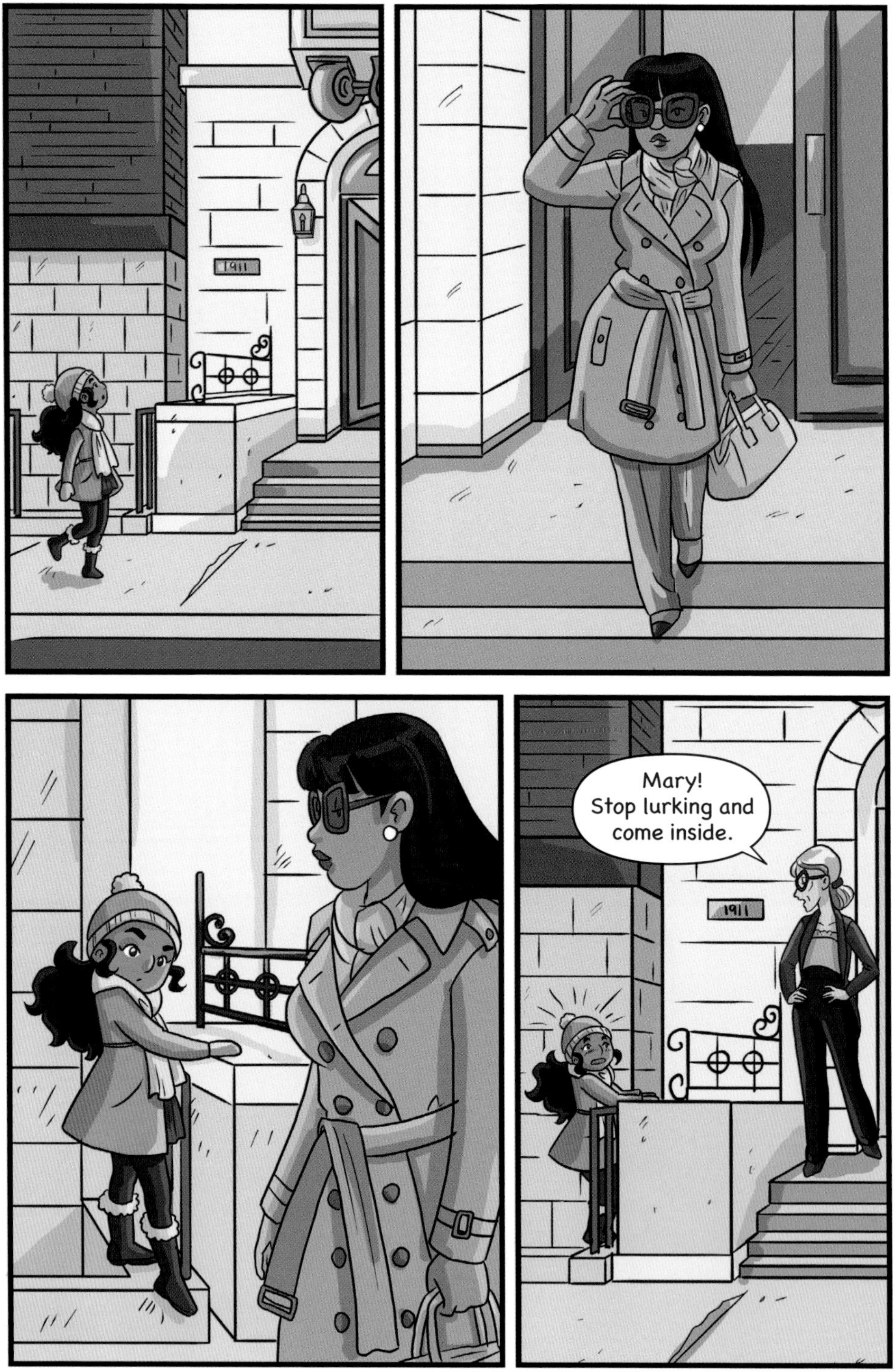
1911
1911
Mary!
Stop lurking and
come inside.

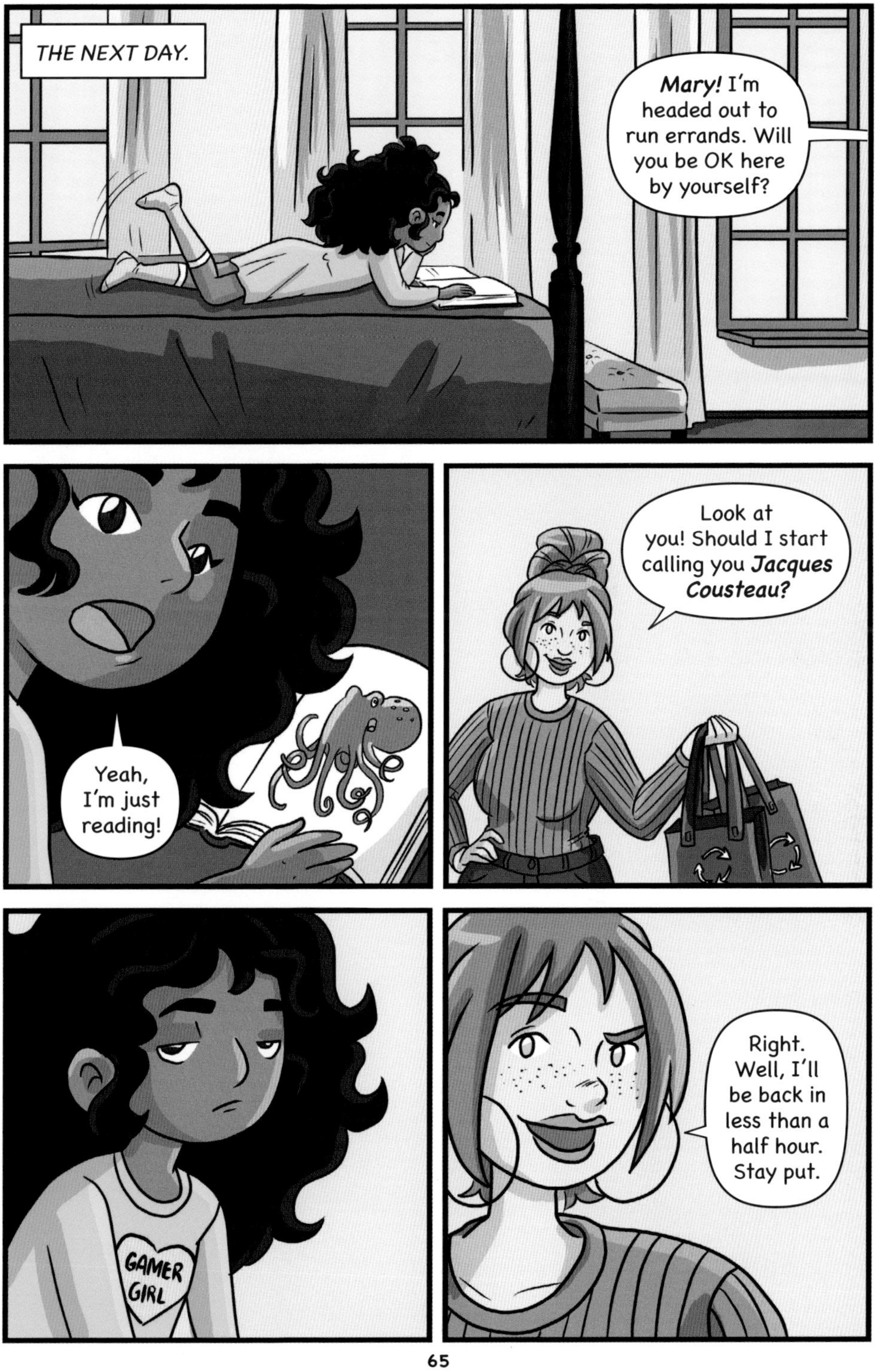
THE NEXT DAY.
Mary! I'm headed out to run errands. Will you be OK here by yourself?
Yeah, I'm just reading!
Look at you! Should I start calling you *Jacques Cousteau?*
GAMER GIRL
Right. Well, I'll be back in less than a half hour. Stay put.

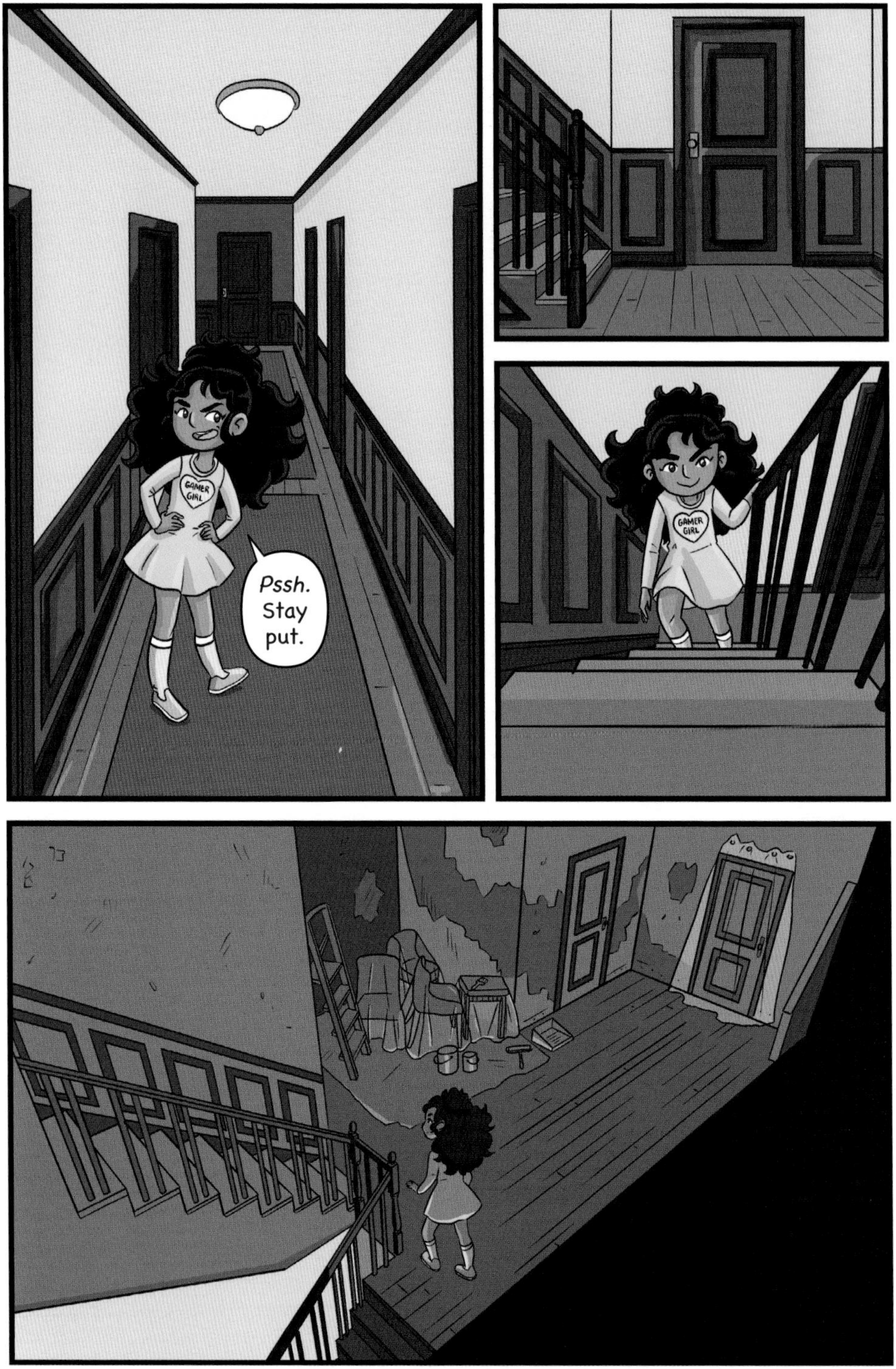
GAMER GIRL
Pssh. Stay put.
GAMER GIRL

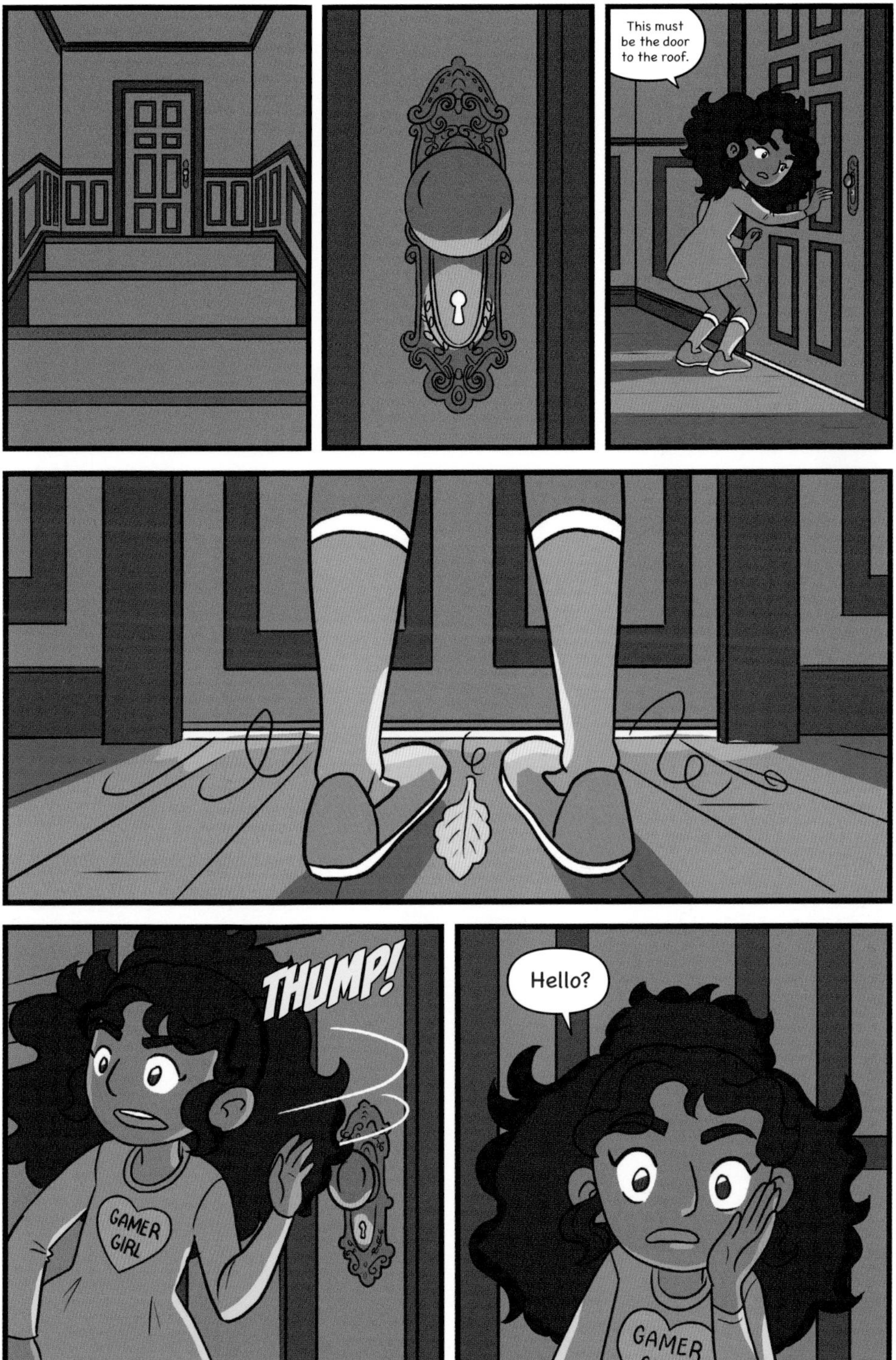
This must be the door to the roof.
THUMP!
GAMER GIRL
Hello?

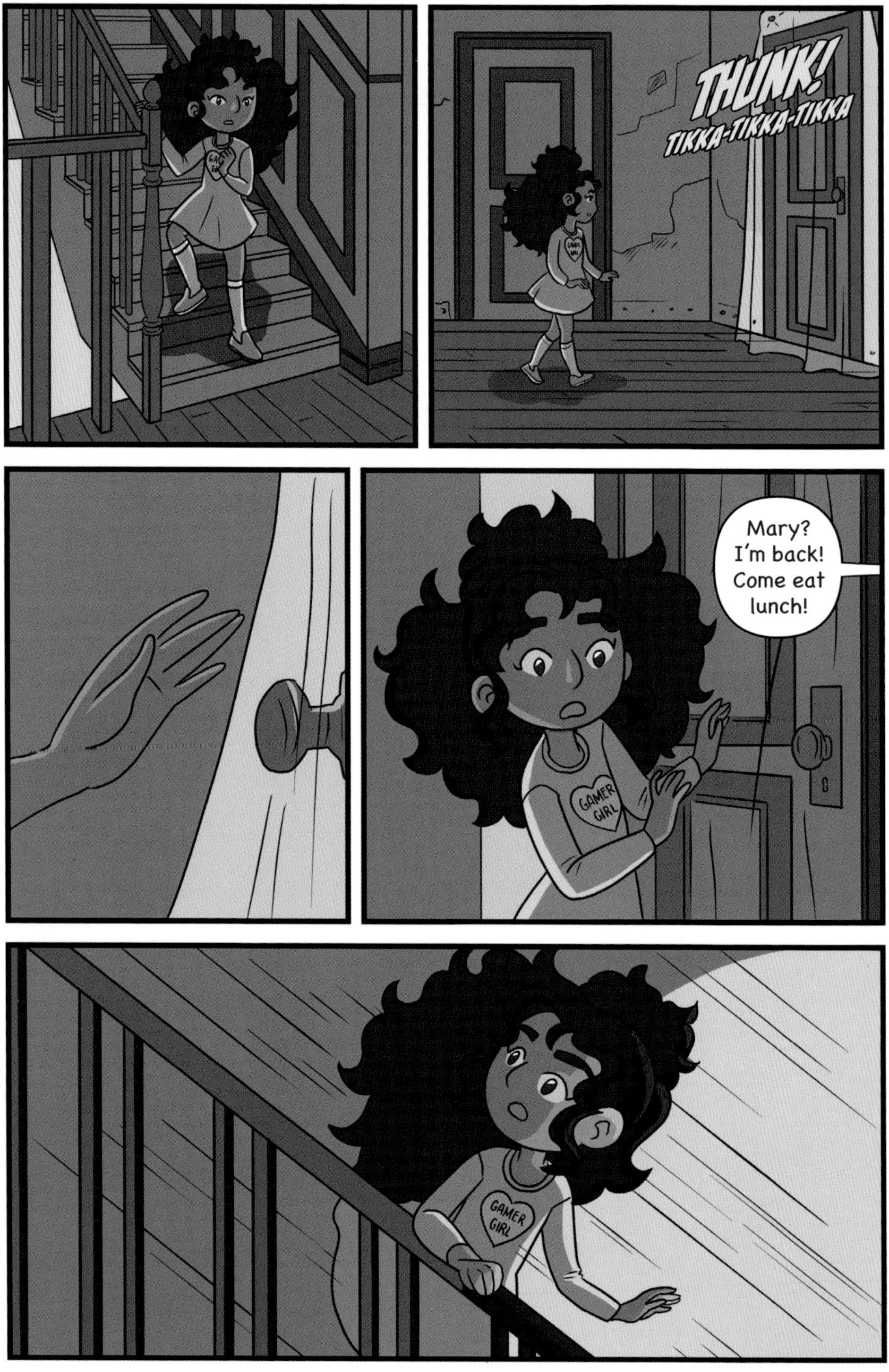
GAMER GIRL
THUNK!
TIKKA-TIKKA-TIKKA
Mary? I'm back! Come eat lunch!
GAMER GIRL
GAMER GIRL

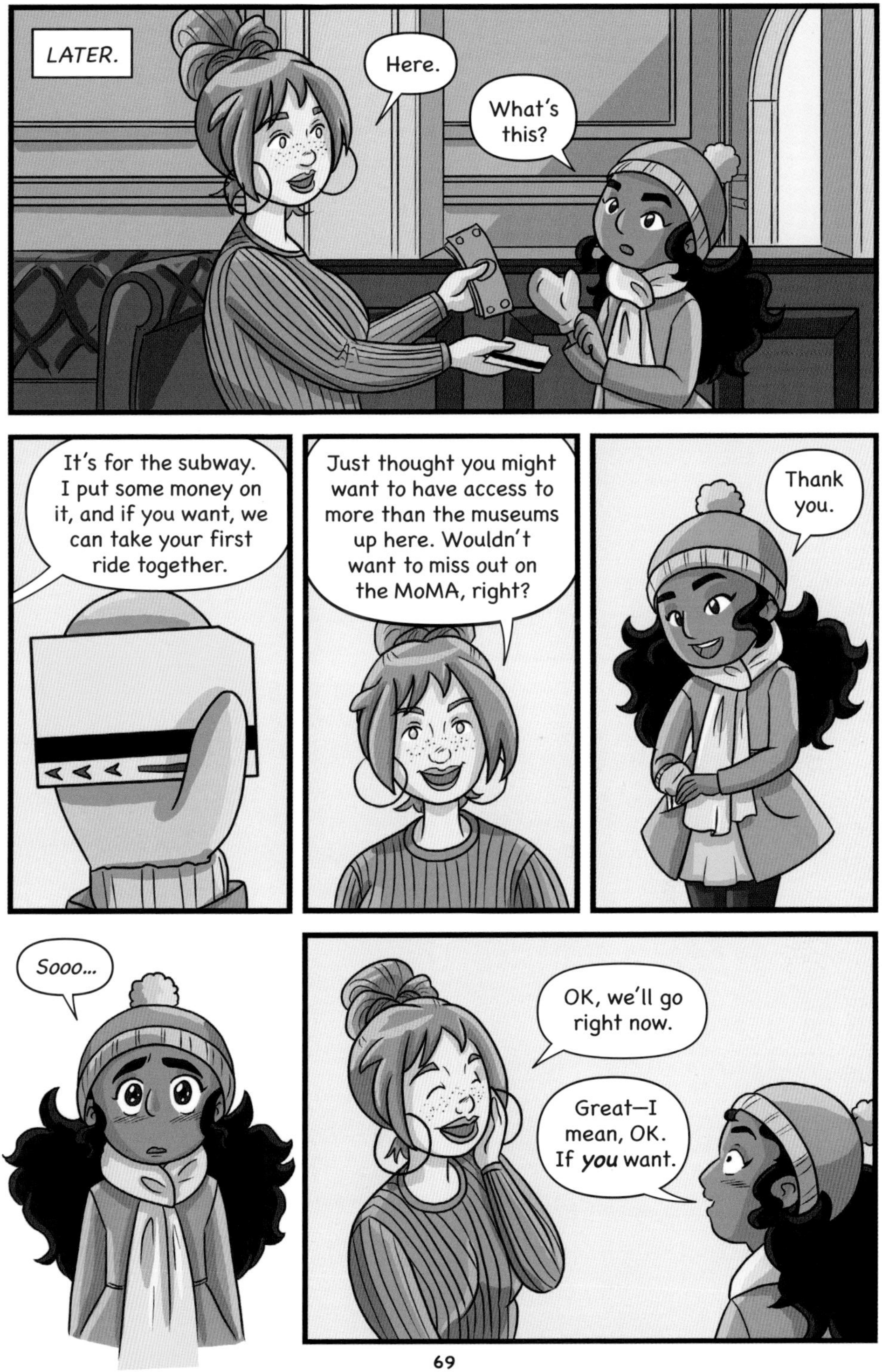
LATER.
Here.
What's this?
It's for the subway. I put some money on it, and if you want, we can take your first ride together.
Just thought you might want to have access to more than the museums up here. Wouldn't want to miss out on the MoMA, right?
Thank you.
Sooo...
OK, we'll go right now.
Great—I mean, OK. If *you* want.

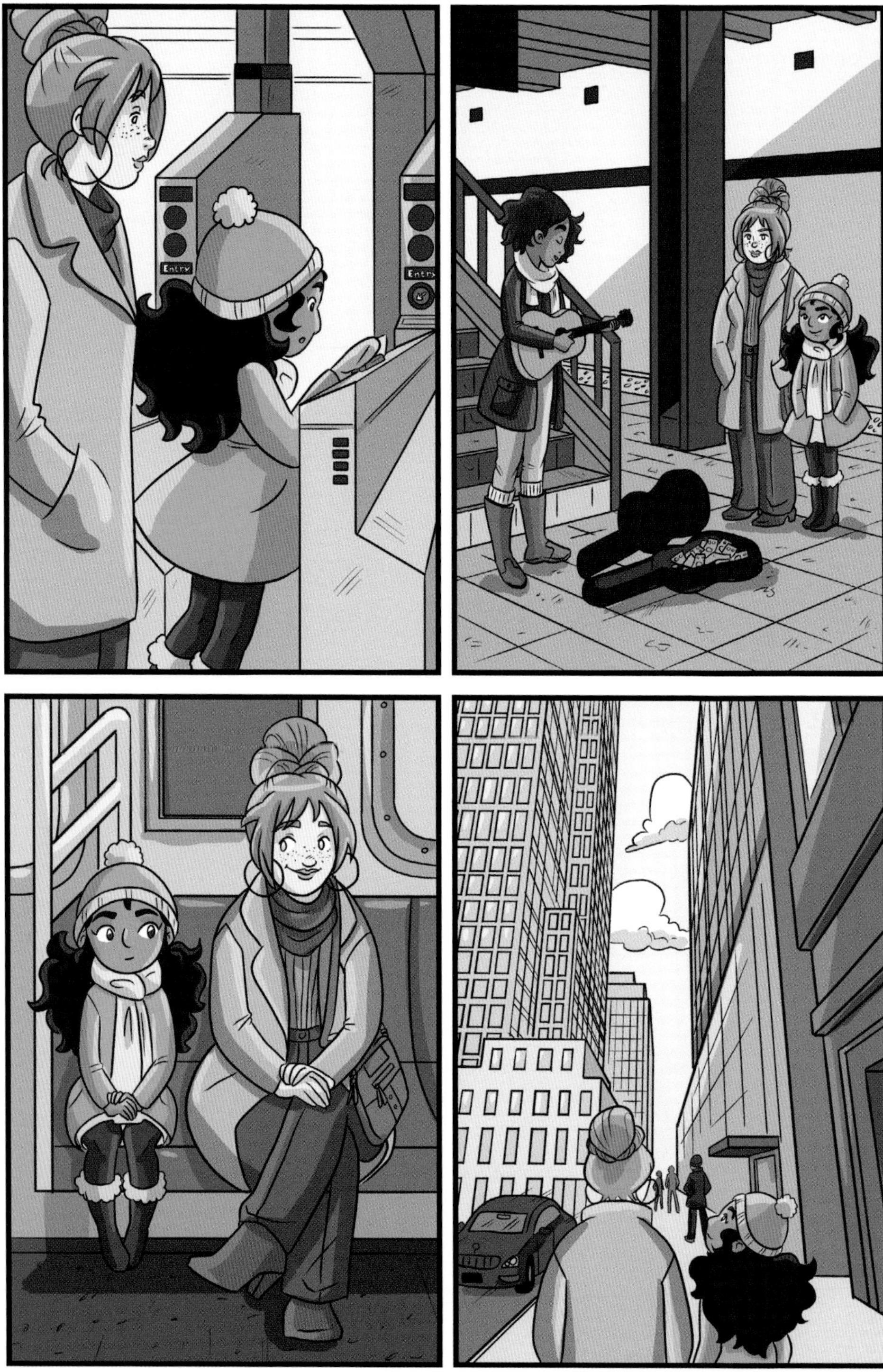
Entry
Entry

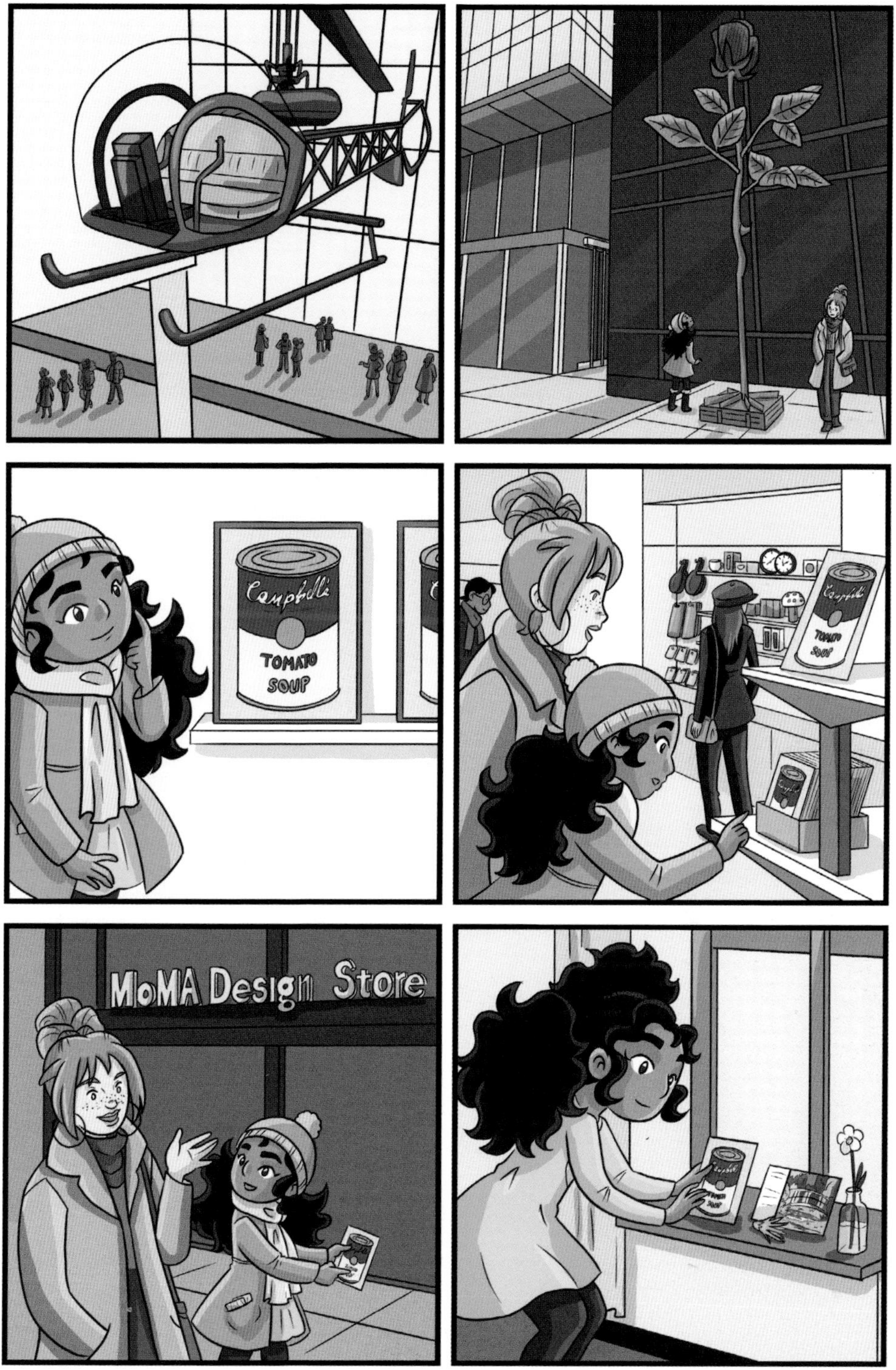
Campbell's
TOMATO SOUP
MoMA Design Store

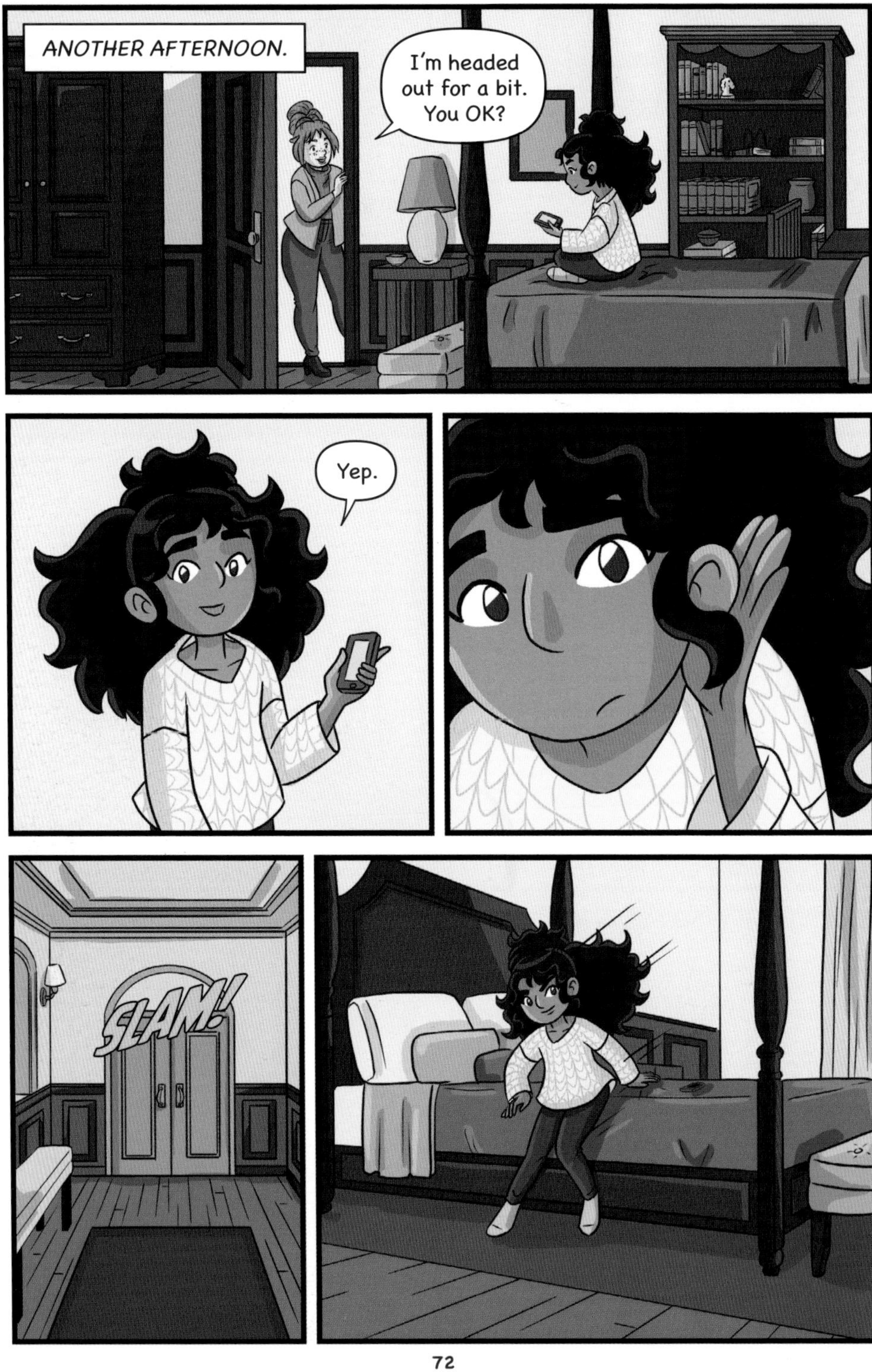
ANOTHER AFTERNOON.
I'm headed out for a bit. You OK?
Yep.
SLAM!

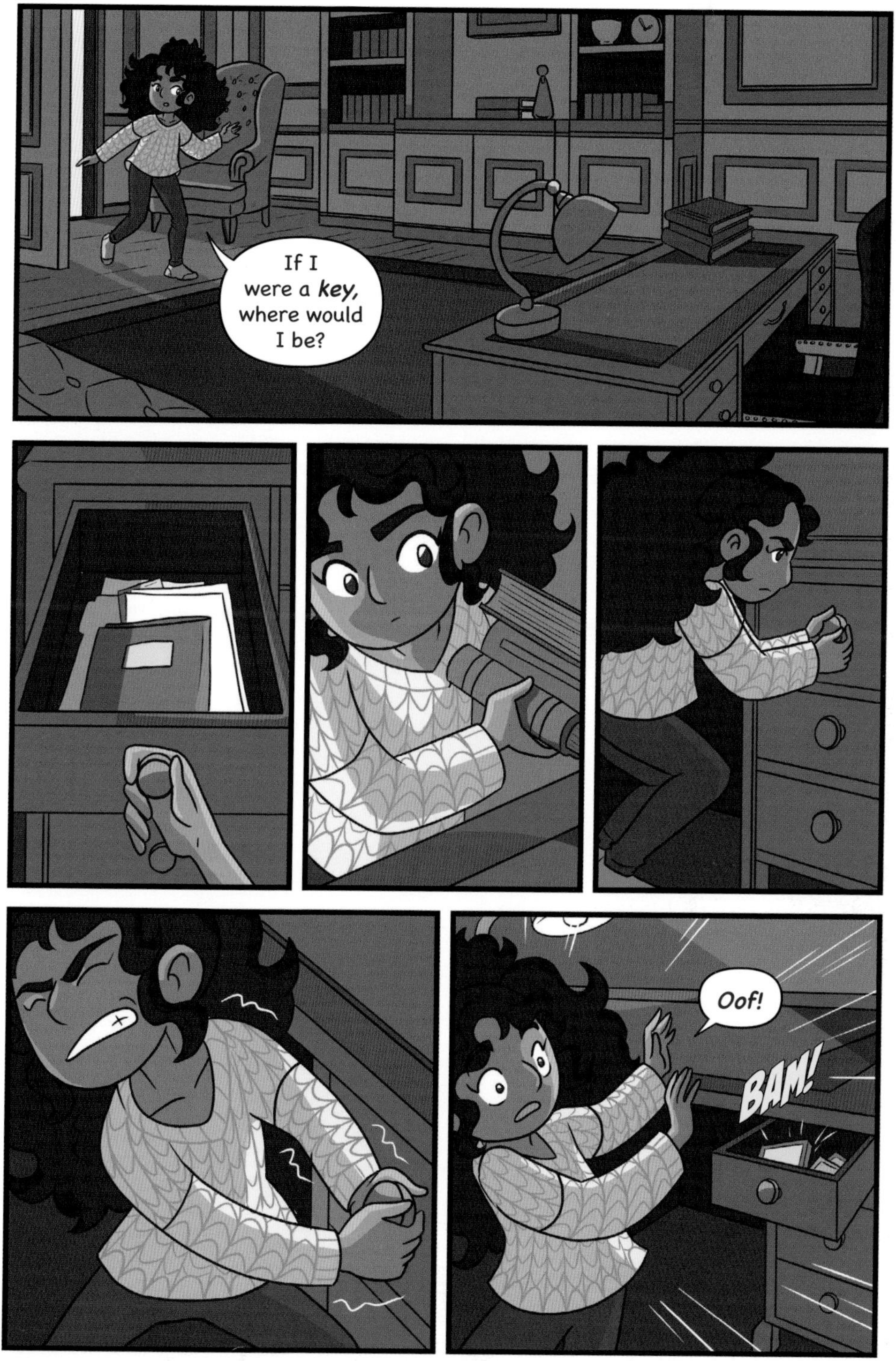
If I were a *key,* where would I be?
Oof!
BAM!

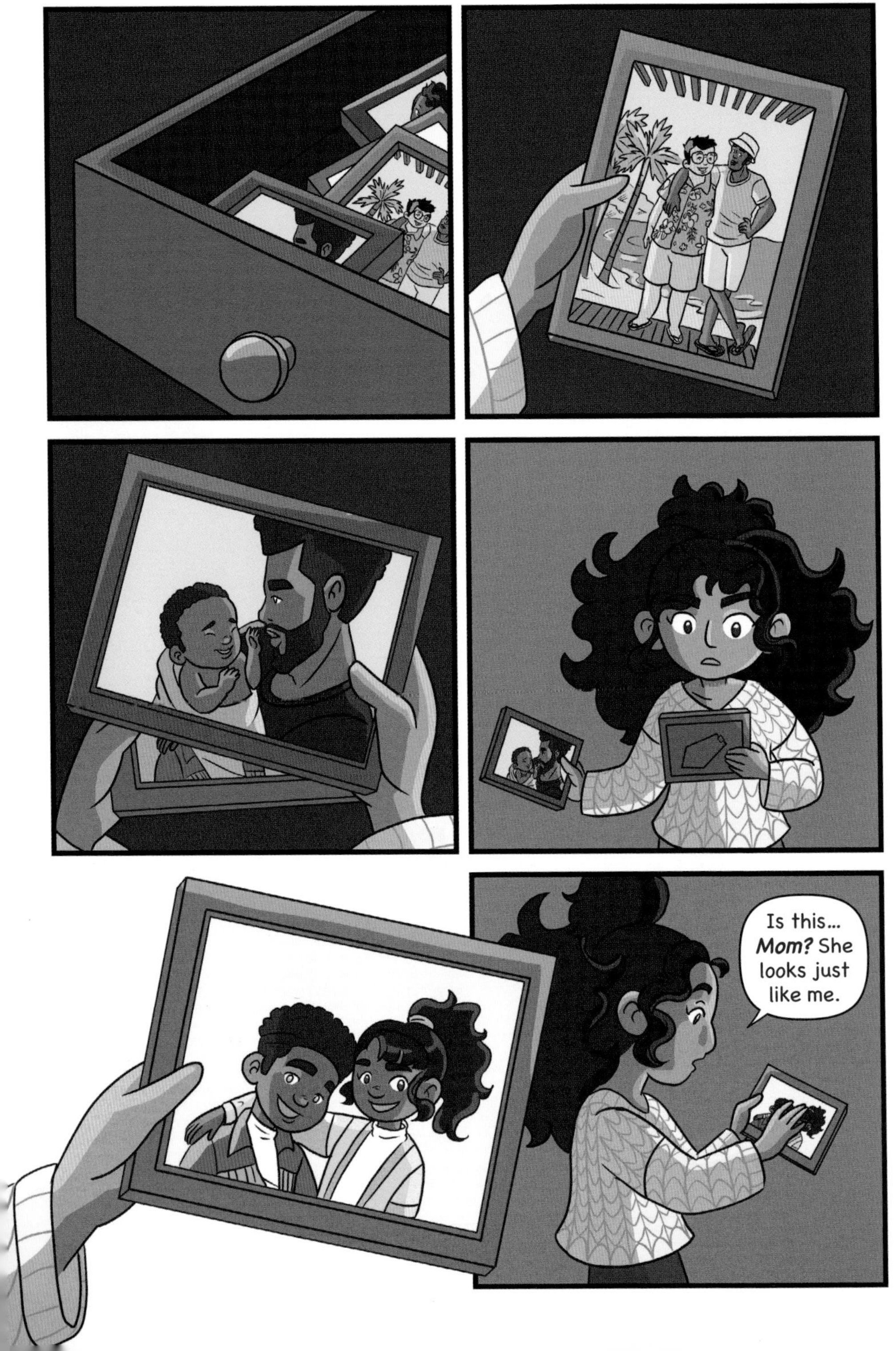
Is this... *Mom?* She looks just like me.

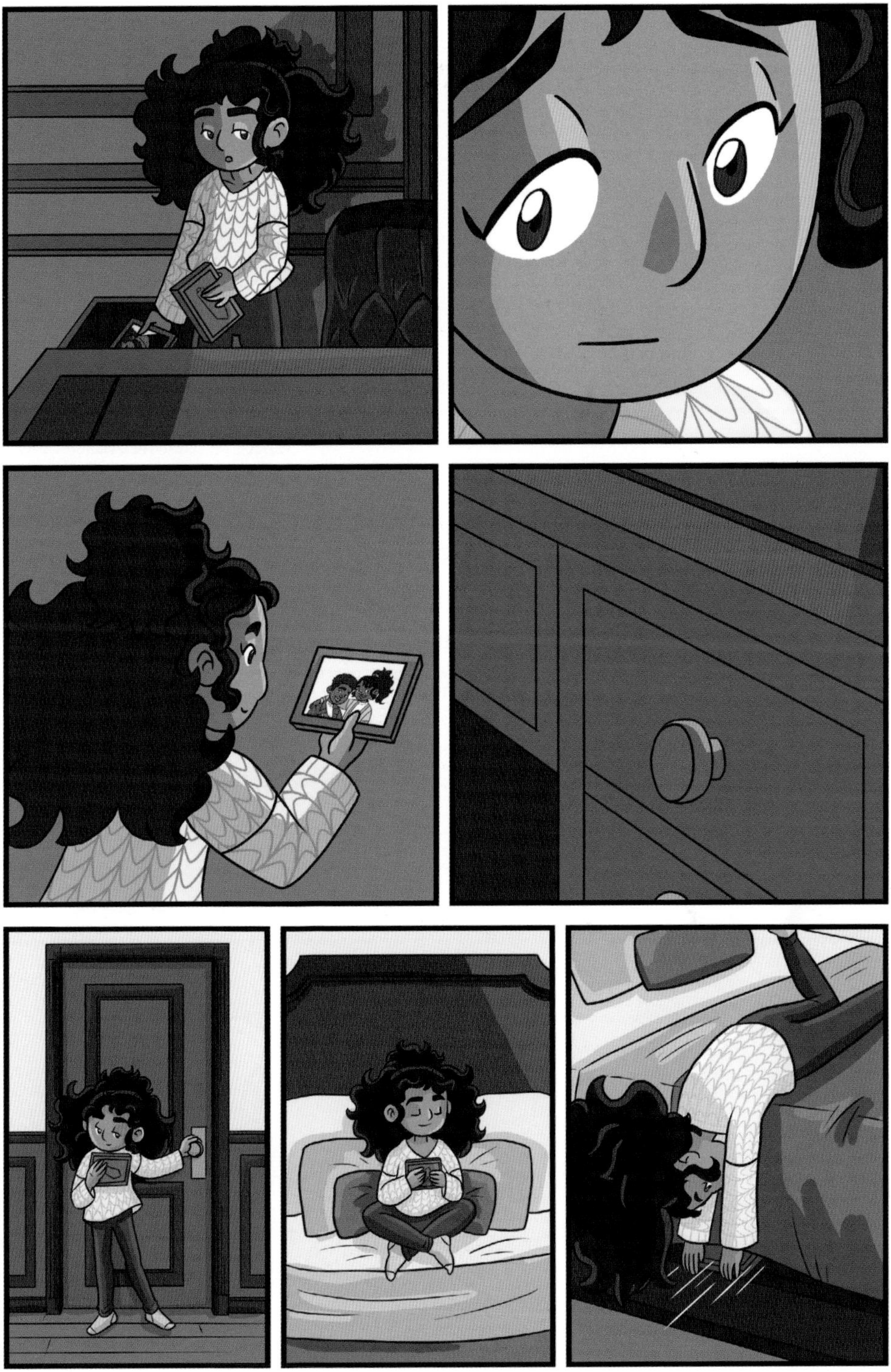

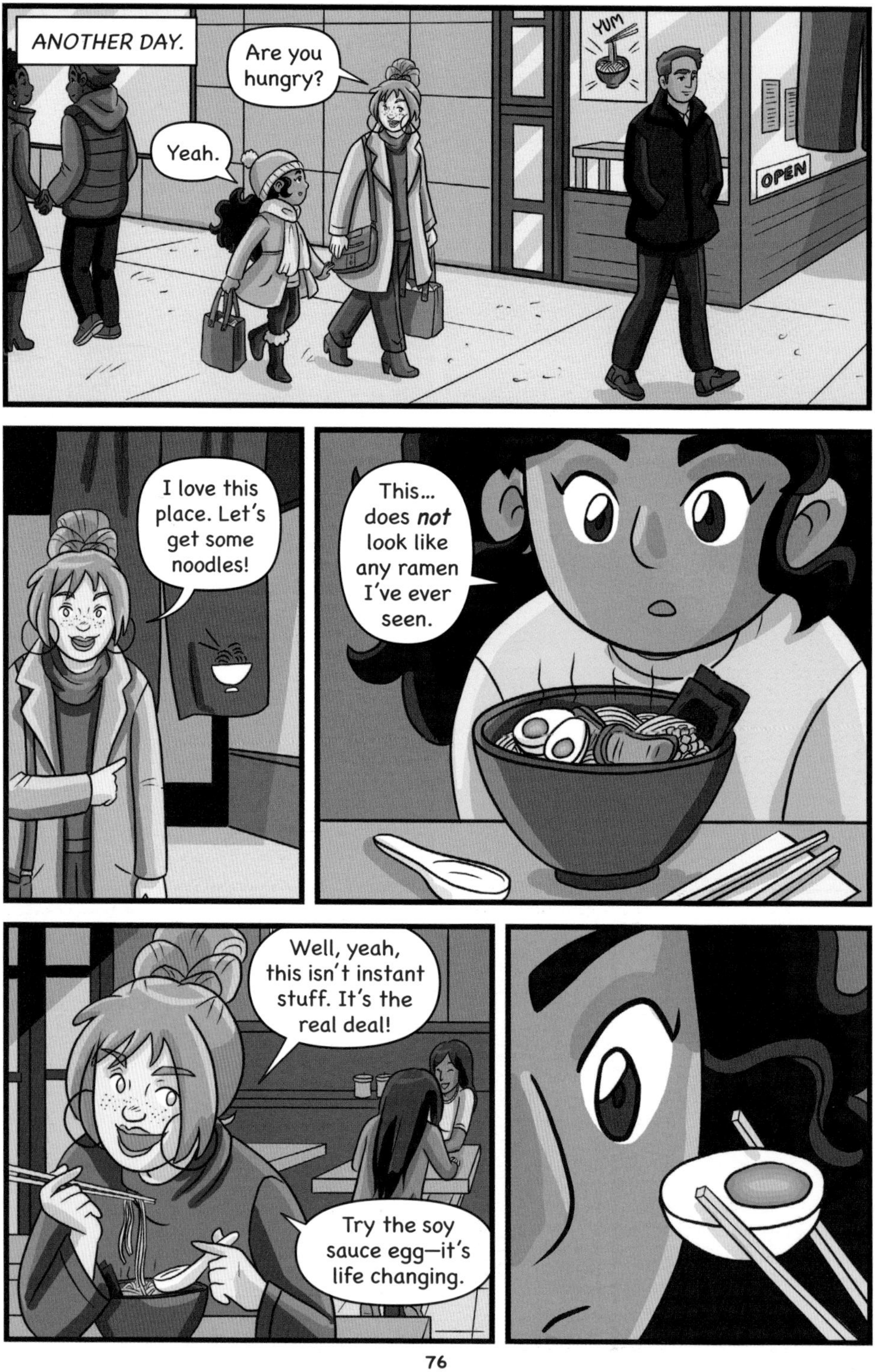

ANOTHER DAY.
Are you hungry?
Yeah.
YUM
OPEN
I love this place. Let's get some noodles!
This... does ***not*** look like any ramen I've ever seen.
Well, yeah, this isn't instant stuff. It's the real deal!
Try the soy sauce egg—it's life changing.

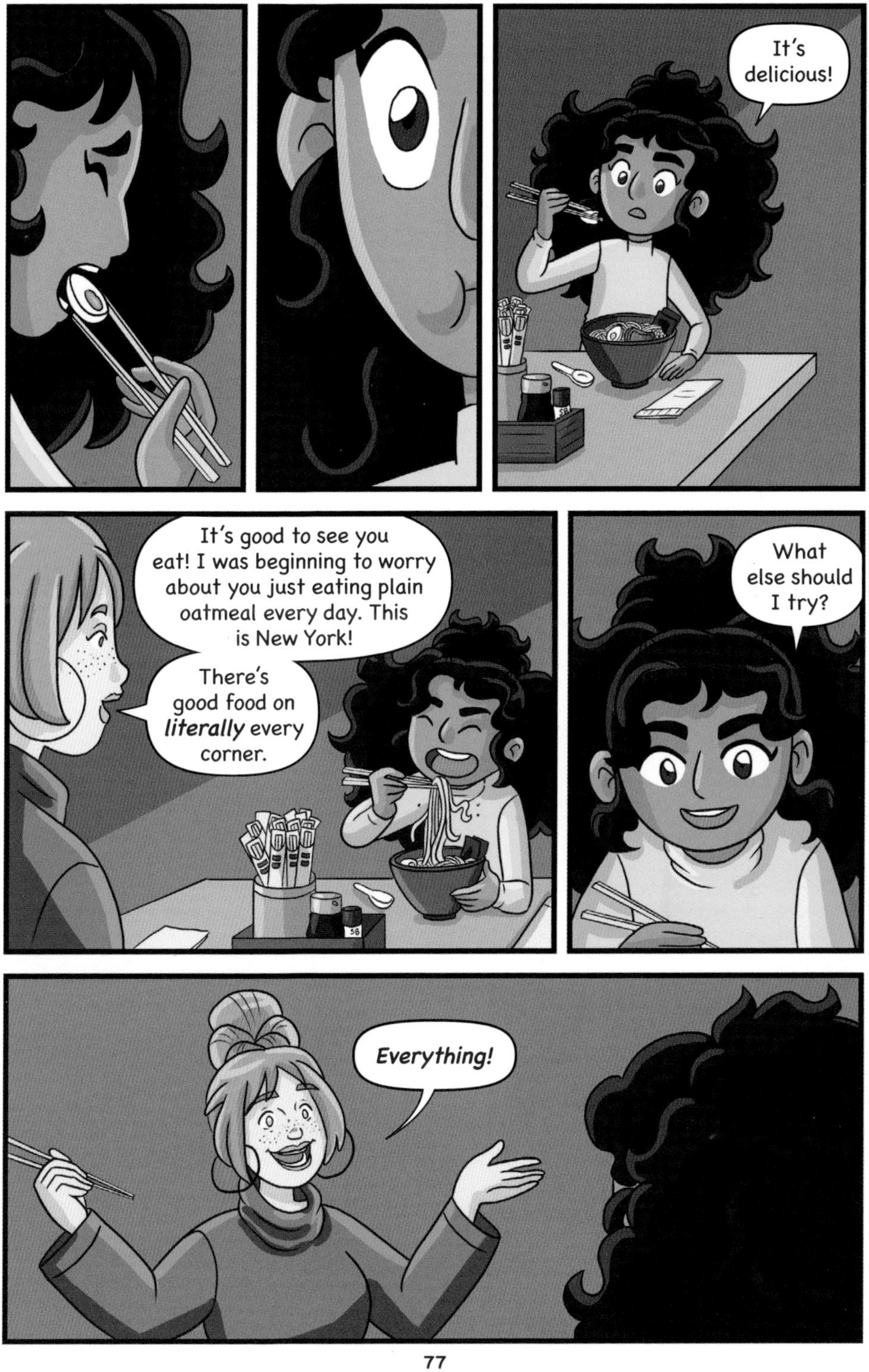
It's delicious!
It's good to see you eat! I was beginning to worry about you just eating plain oatmeal every day. This is New York!
There's good food on *literally* every corner.
What else should I try?
Everything!

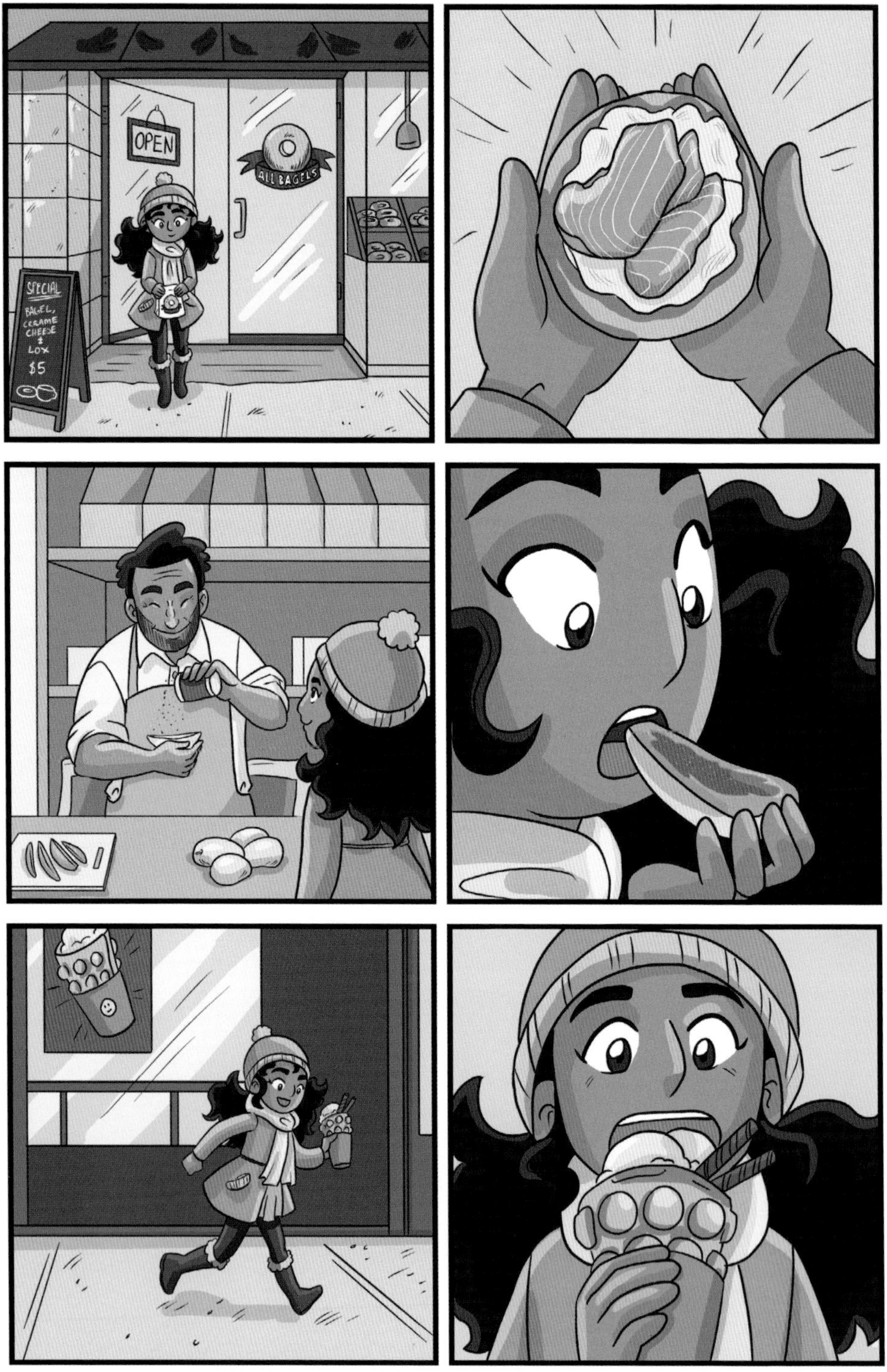
OPEN
ALL BAGELS
SPECIAL
BAGEL, CERAME CHEESE & LOX
$5

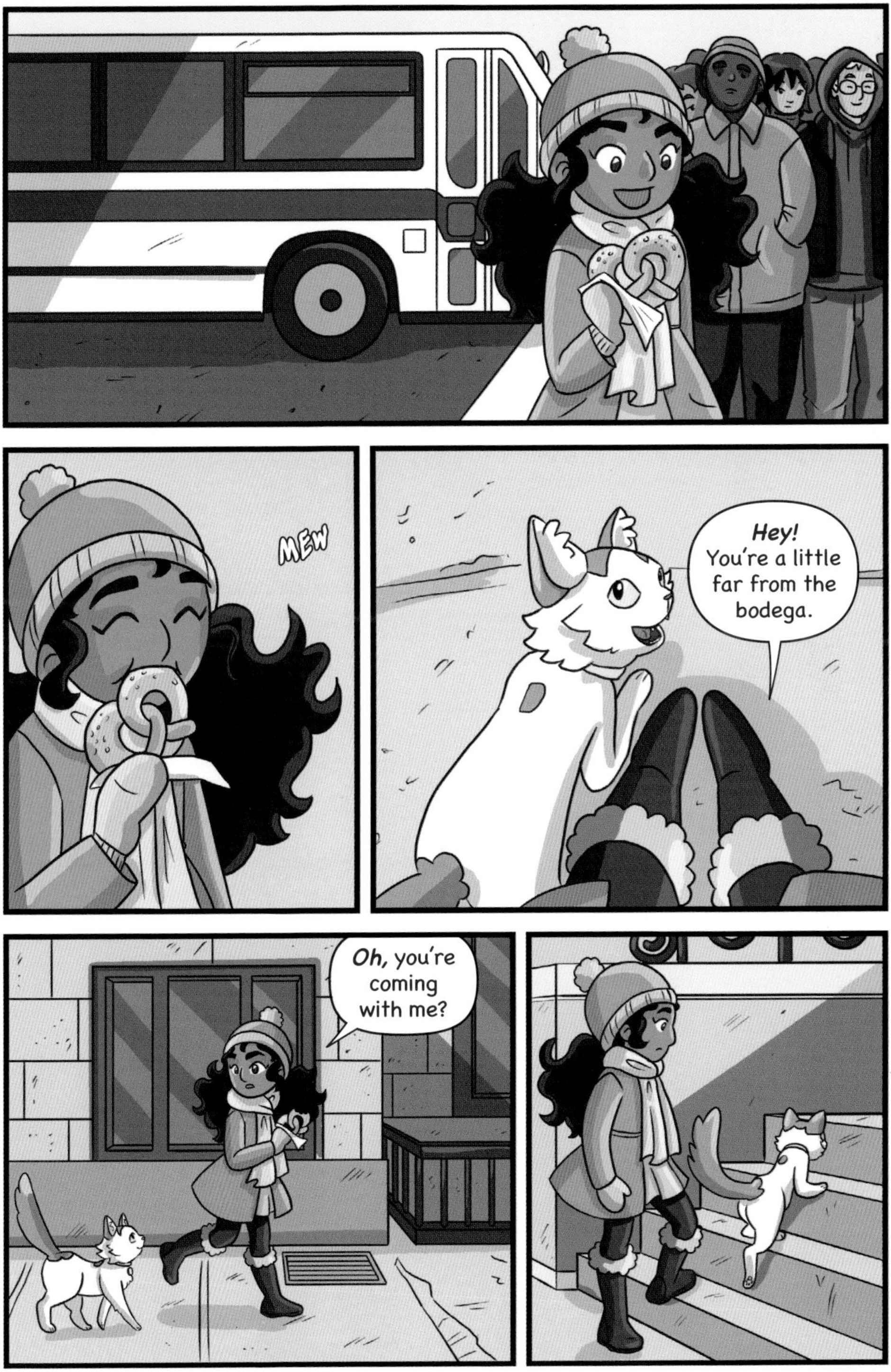
MEW
Hey! You're a little far from the bodega.
Oh, you're coming with me?

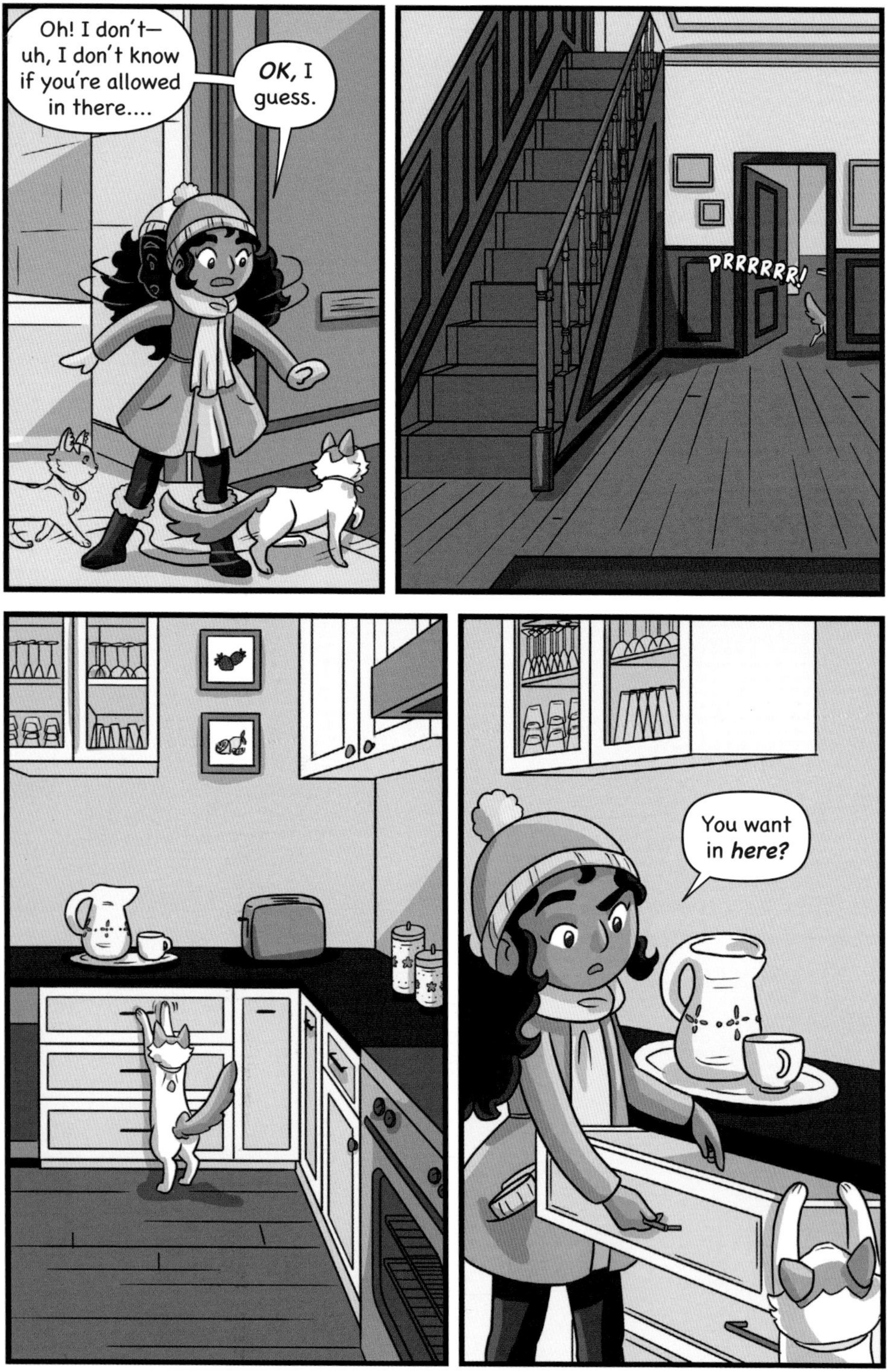
Oh! I don't—
uh, I don't know
if you're allowed
in there....
OK, I
guess.
PRRRRRR!
You want
in *here?*

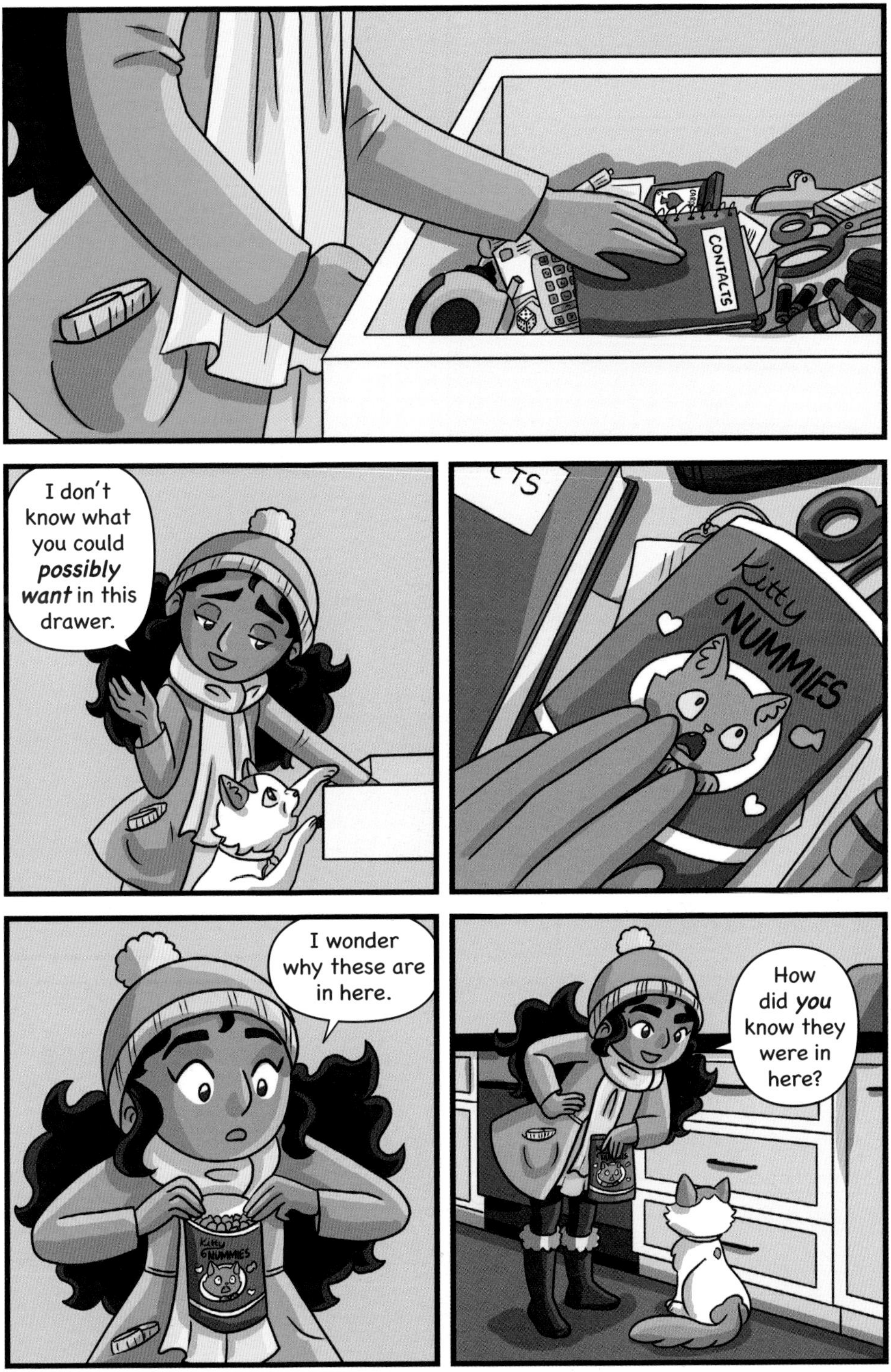
CONTACTS
I don't know what you could **possibly want** in this drawer.
CTS
Kitty NUMMIES
I wonder why these are in here.
Kitty NUMMIES
How did *you* know they were in here?

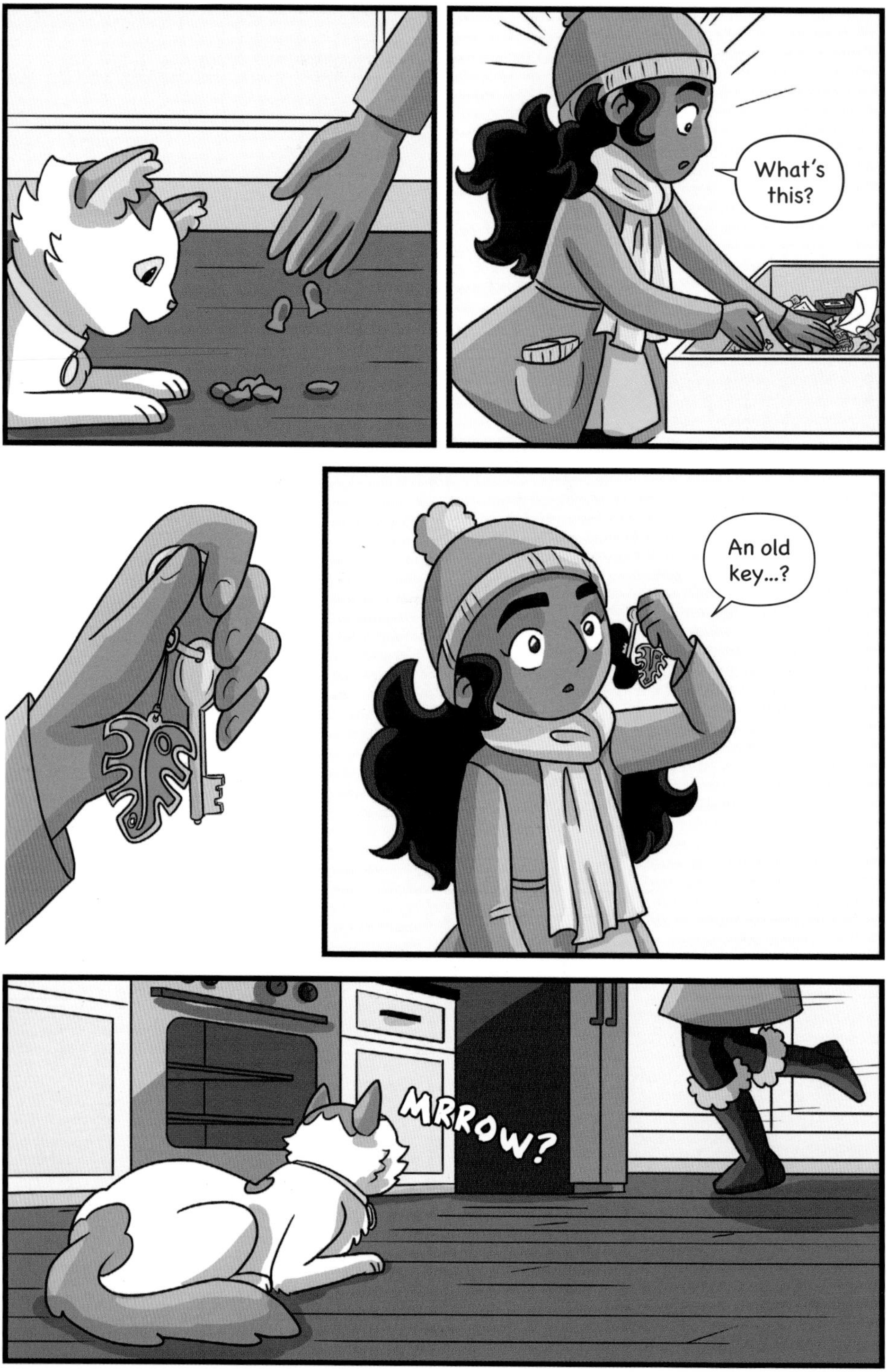
What's this?
An old key...?
MRROW?

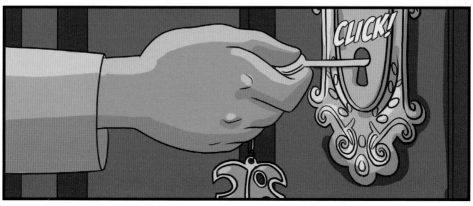

CLICK!

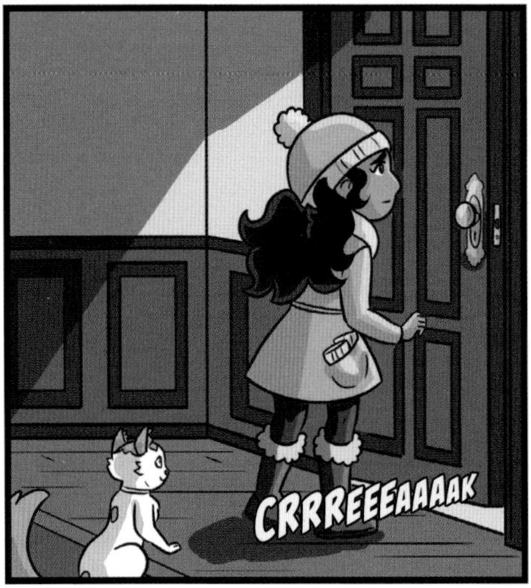
CRRREEEAAAAK

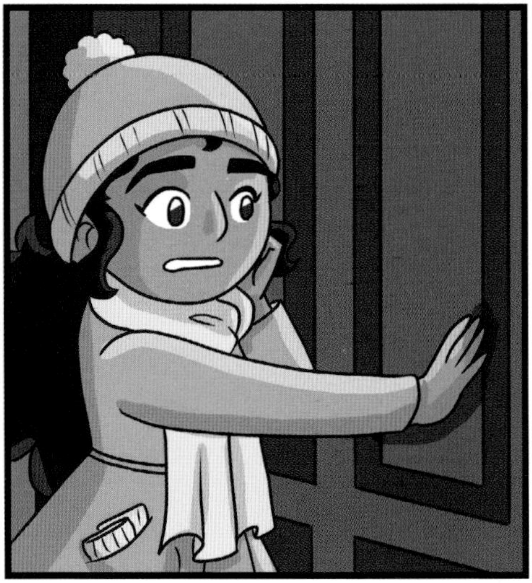

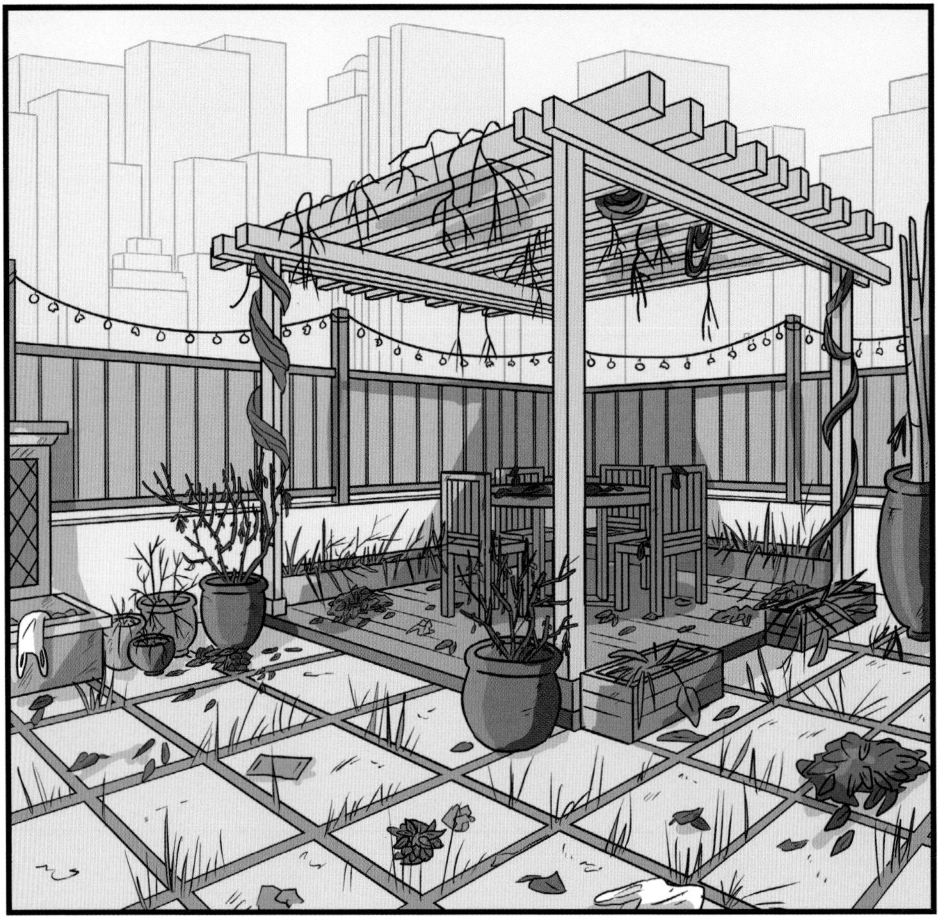

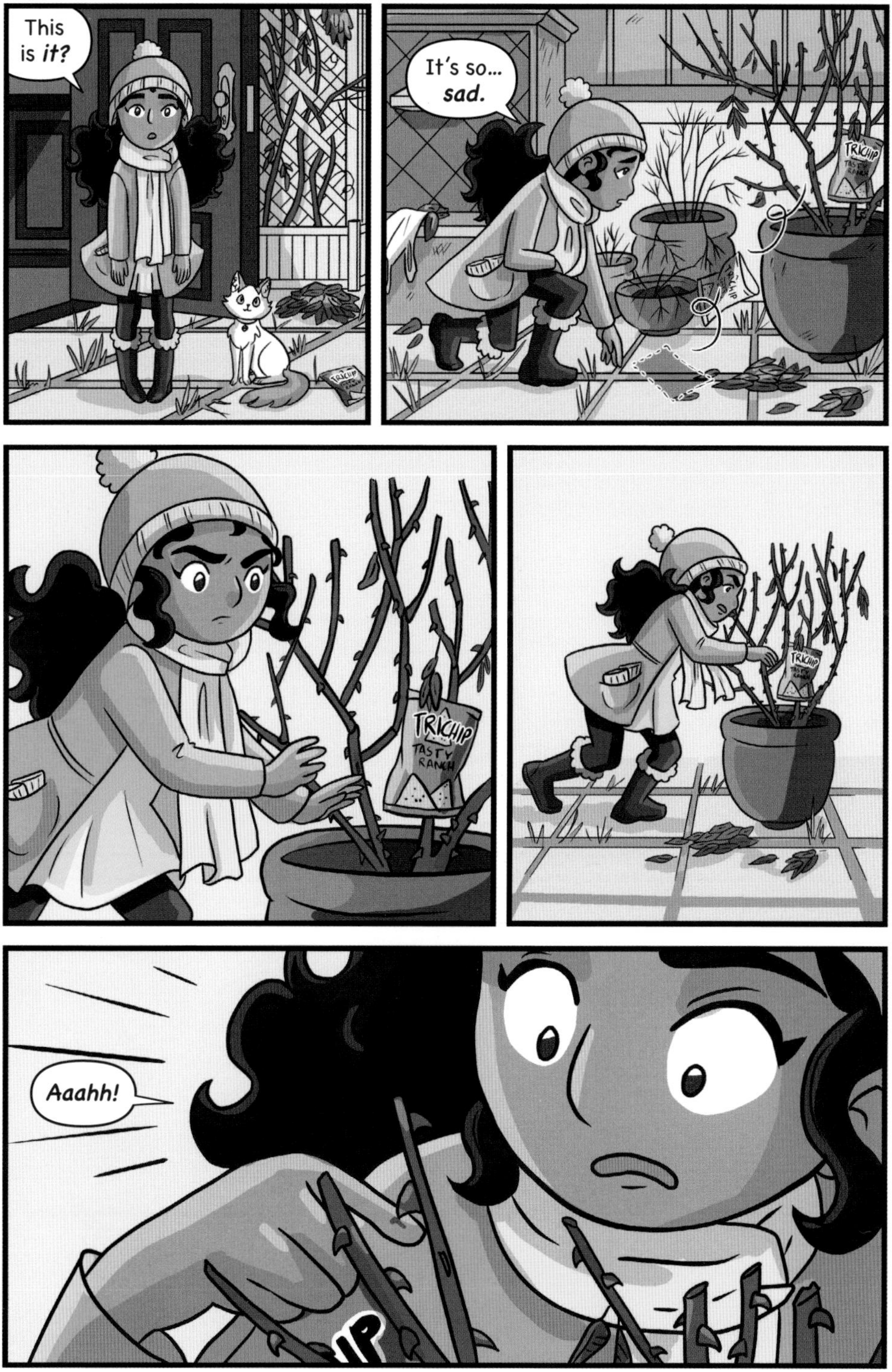
This is *it?*
TRICHIP
It's so... **sad.**
TRICHIP TASTY RANCH
TRICHIP TASTY RANCH
TRICHIP TASTY RANCH
Aaahh!

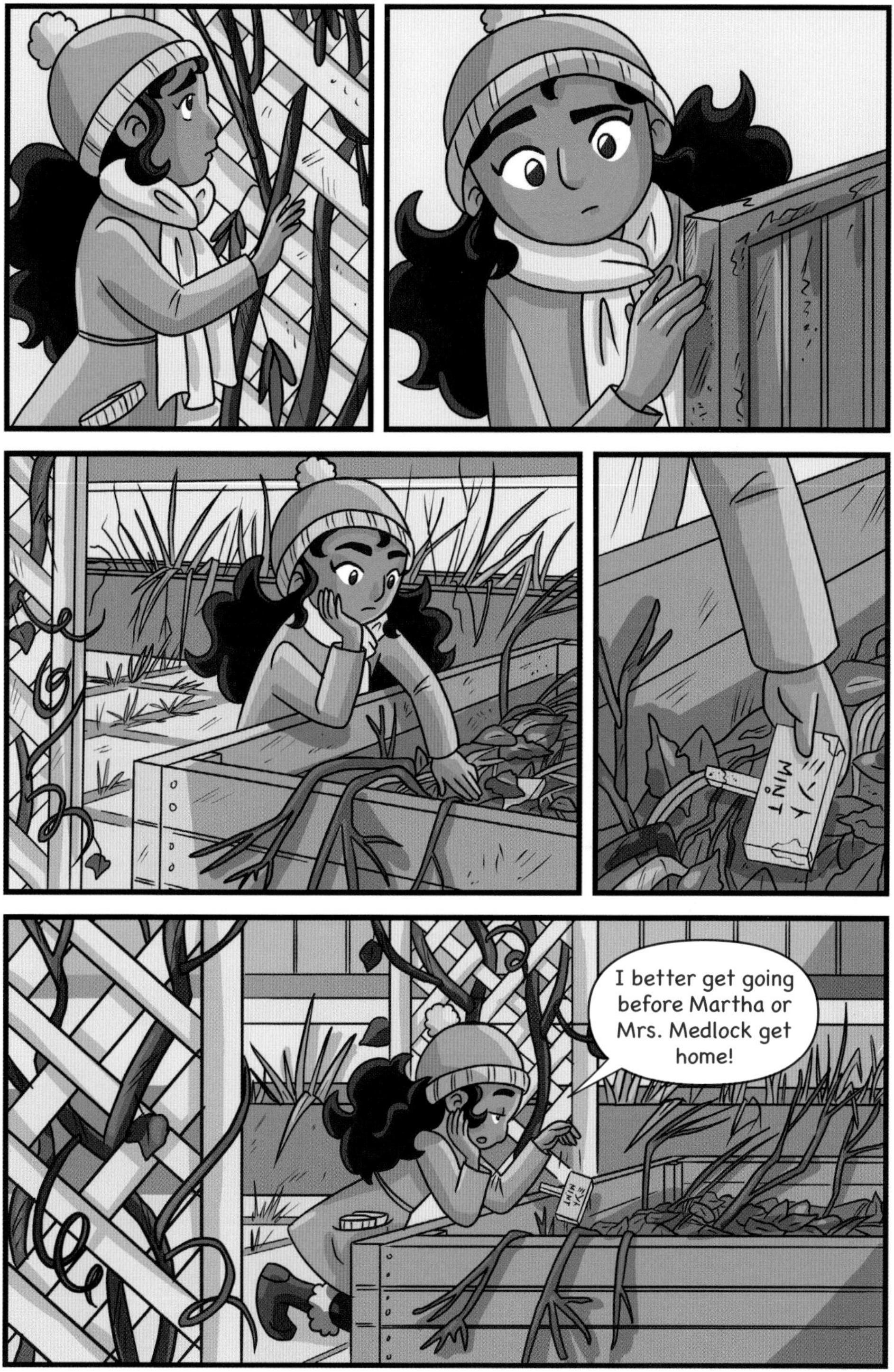
MINT
I better get going before Martha or Mrs. Medlock get home!

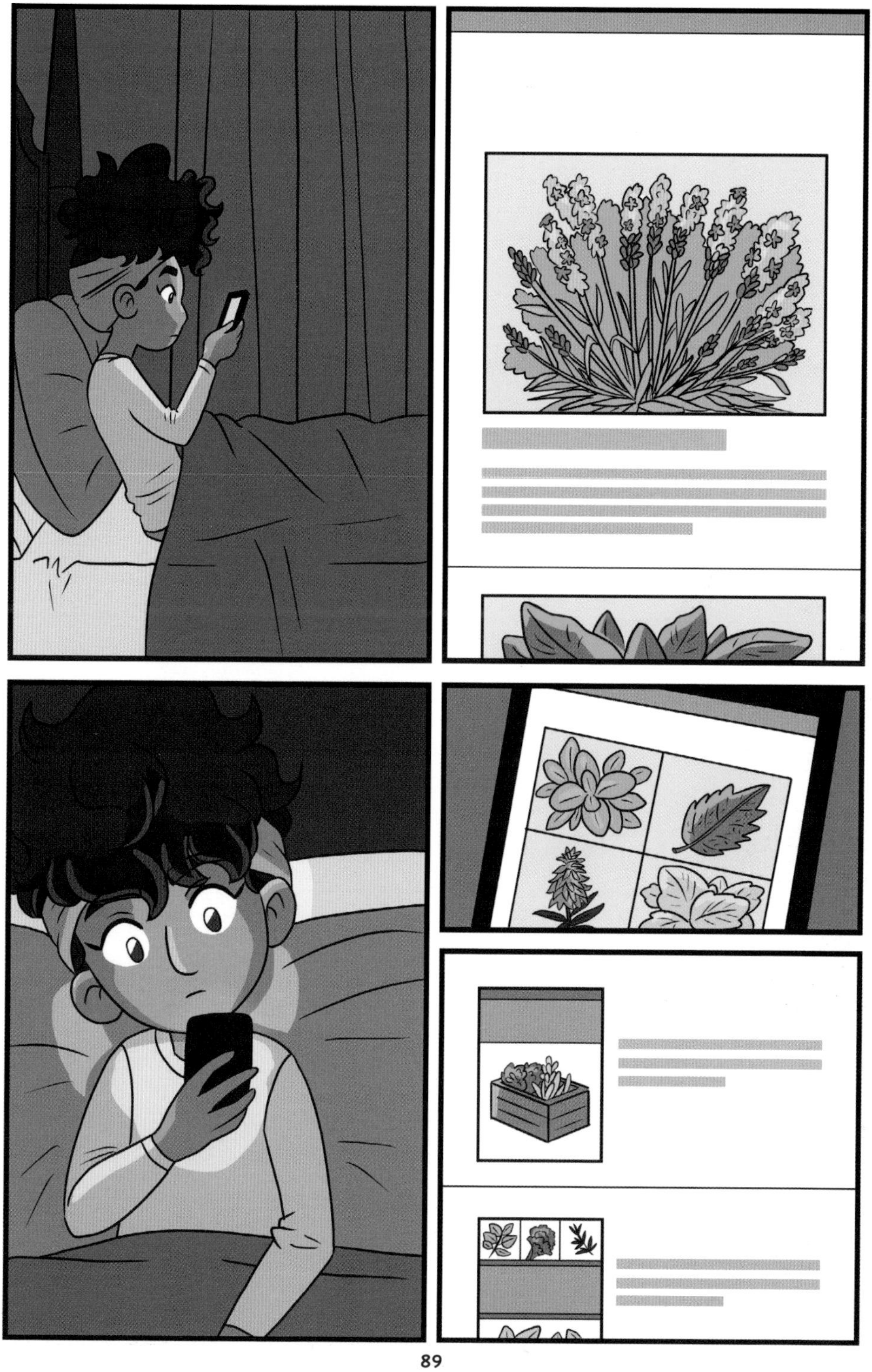

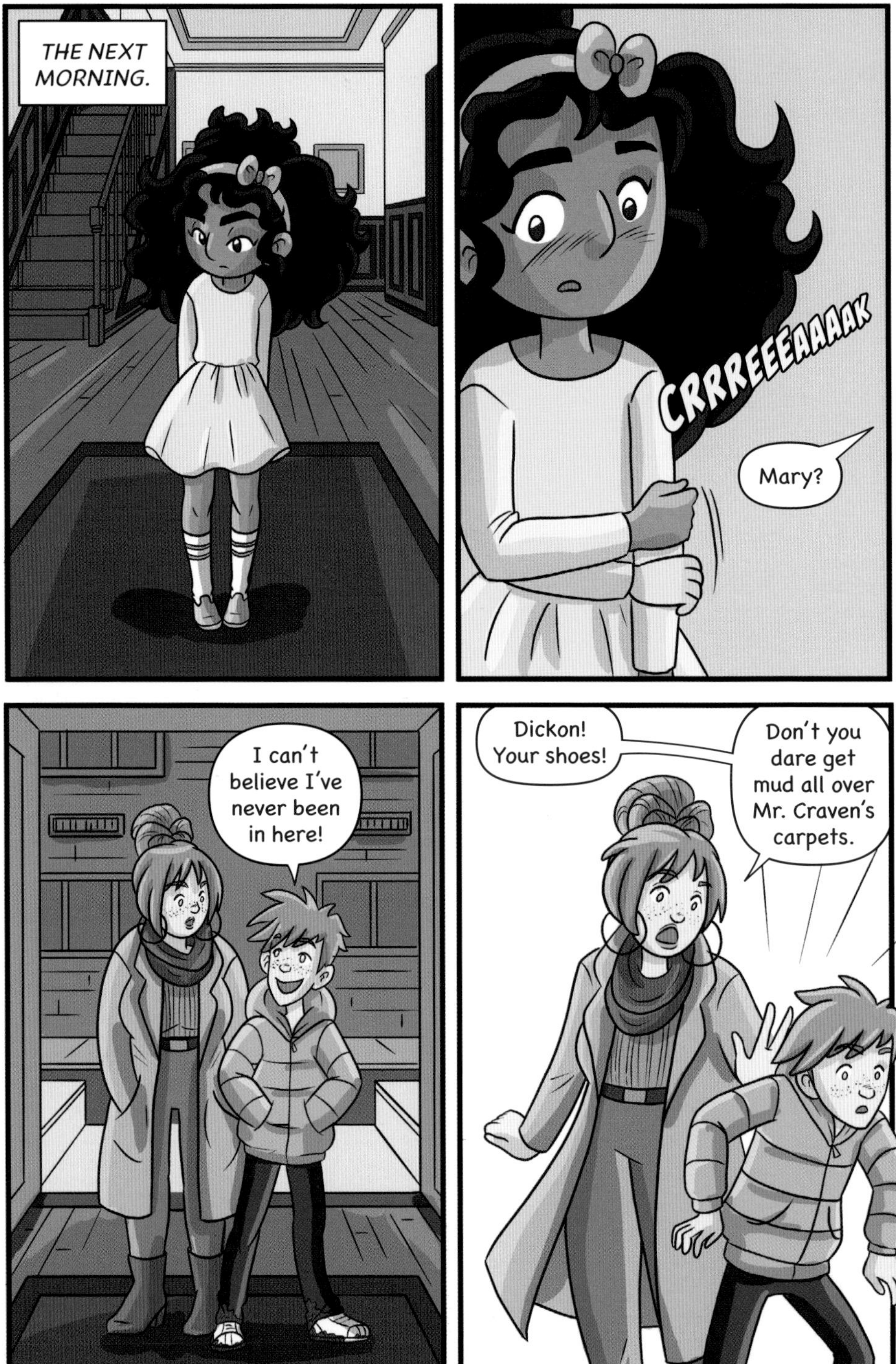
THE NEXT MORNING.
CRRREEEAAAAK
Mary?
I can't believe I've never been in here!
Dickon! Your shoes!
Don't you dare get mud all over Mr. Craven's carpets.

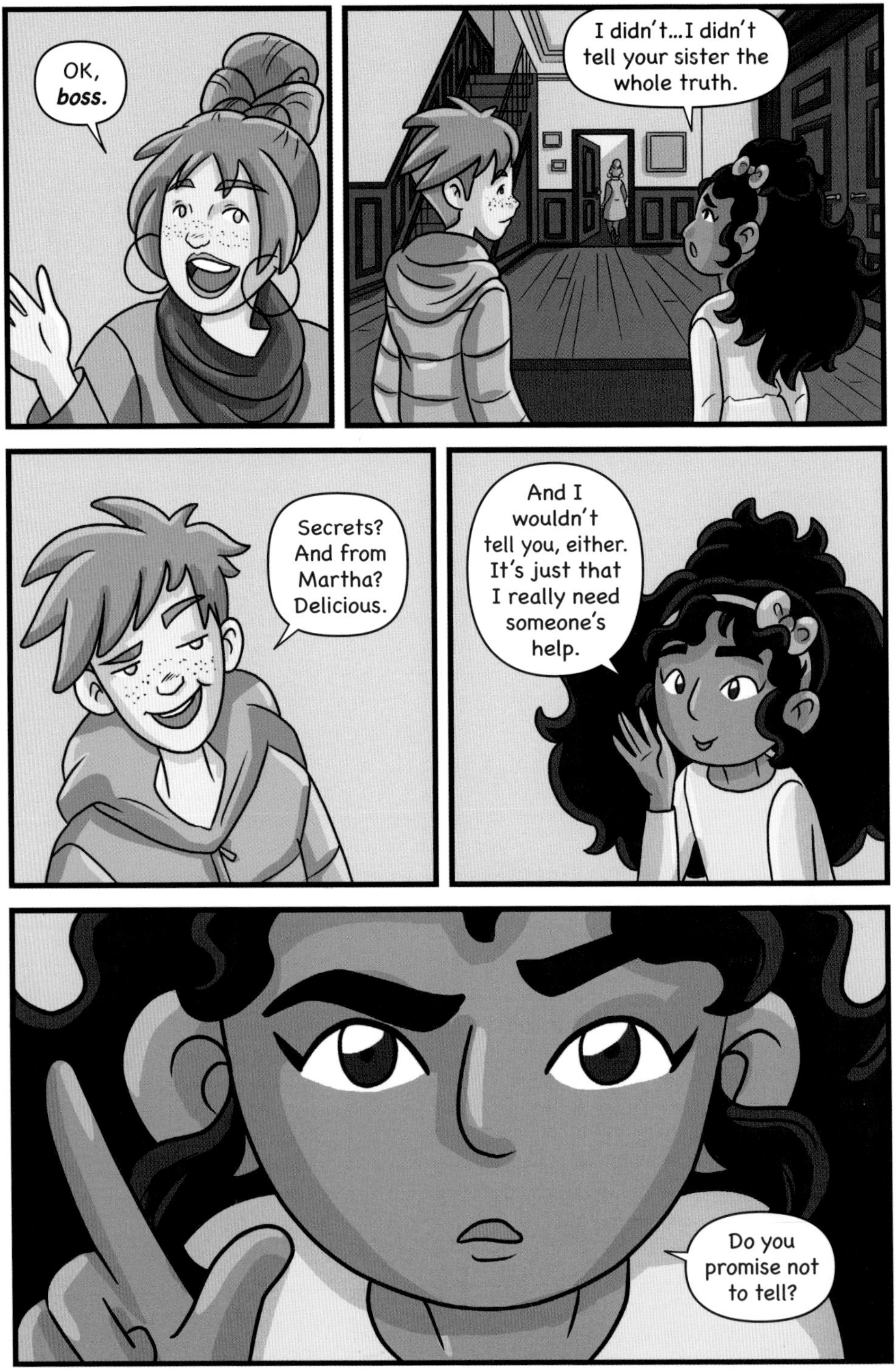
OK,
boss.
I didn't...I didn't tell your sister the whole truth.
Secrets? And from Martha? Delicious.
And I wouldn't tell you, either. It's just that I really need someone's help.
Do you promise not to tell?

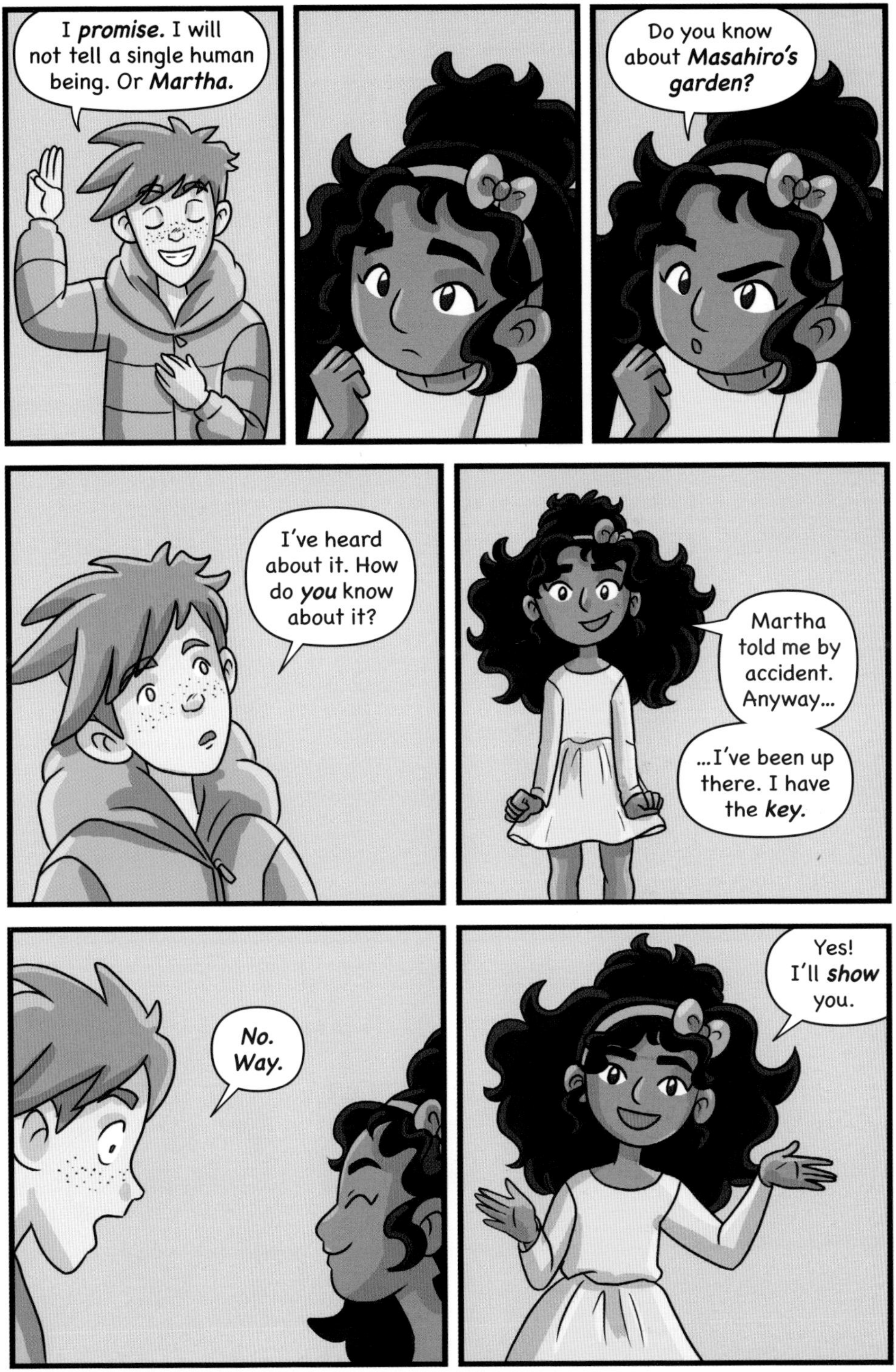
I *promise.* I will not tell a single human being. Or *Martha.*
Do you know about *Masahiro's garden?*
I've heard about it. How do *you* know about it?
Martha told me by accident. Anyway...
...I've been up there. I have the *key.*
No. Way.
Yes! I'll *show* you.

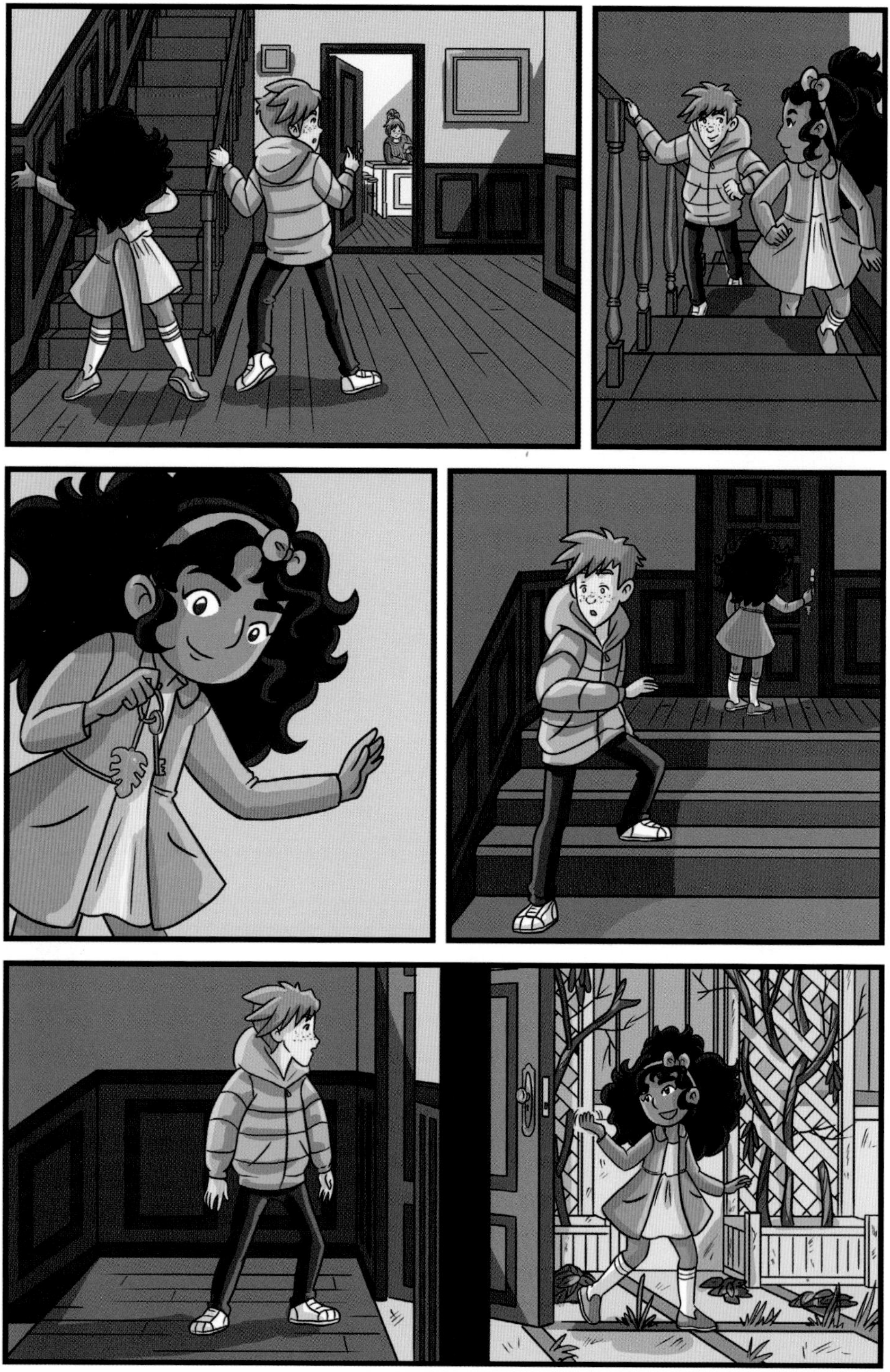

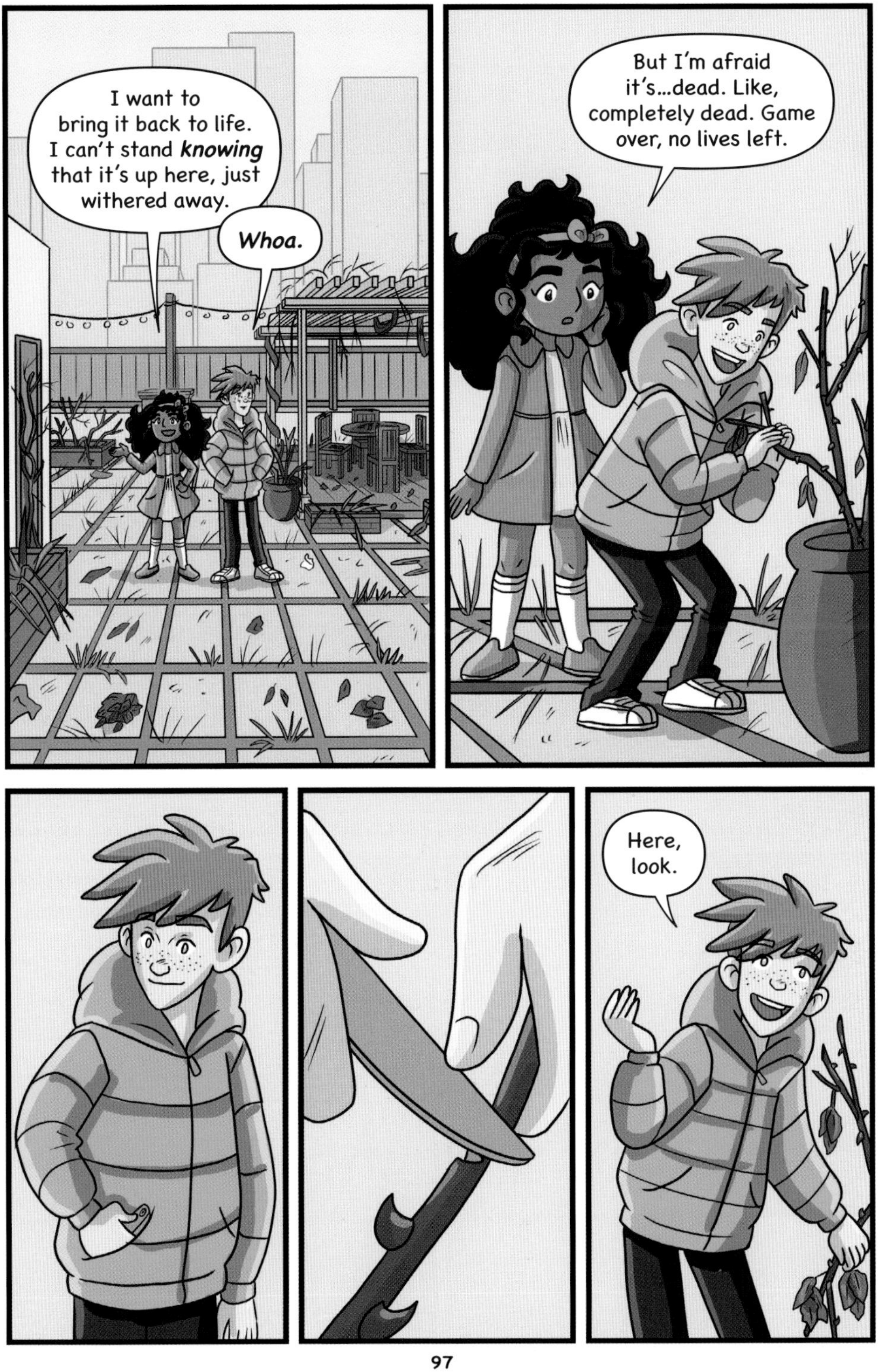

I want to bring it back to life. I can't stand *knowing* that it's up here, just withered away.
Whoa.
But I'm afraid it's…dead. Like, completely dead. Game over, no lives left.
Here, look.

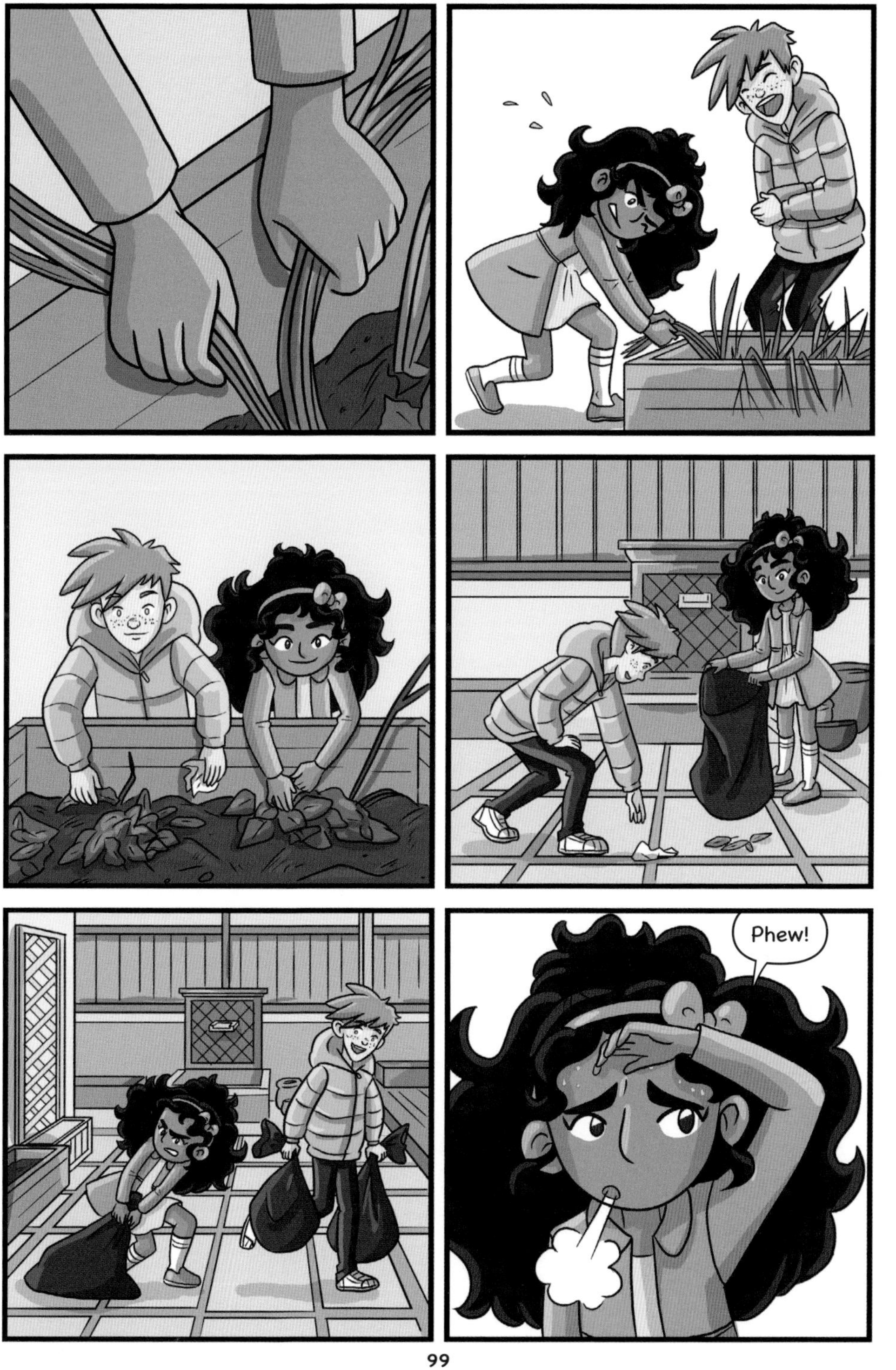
Phew!

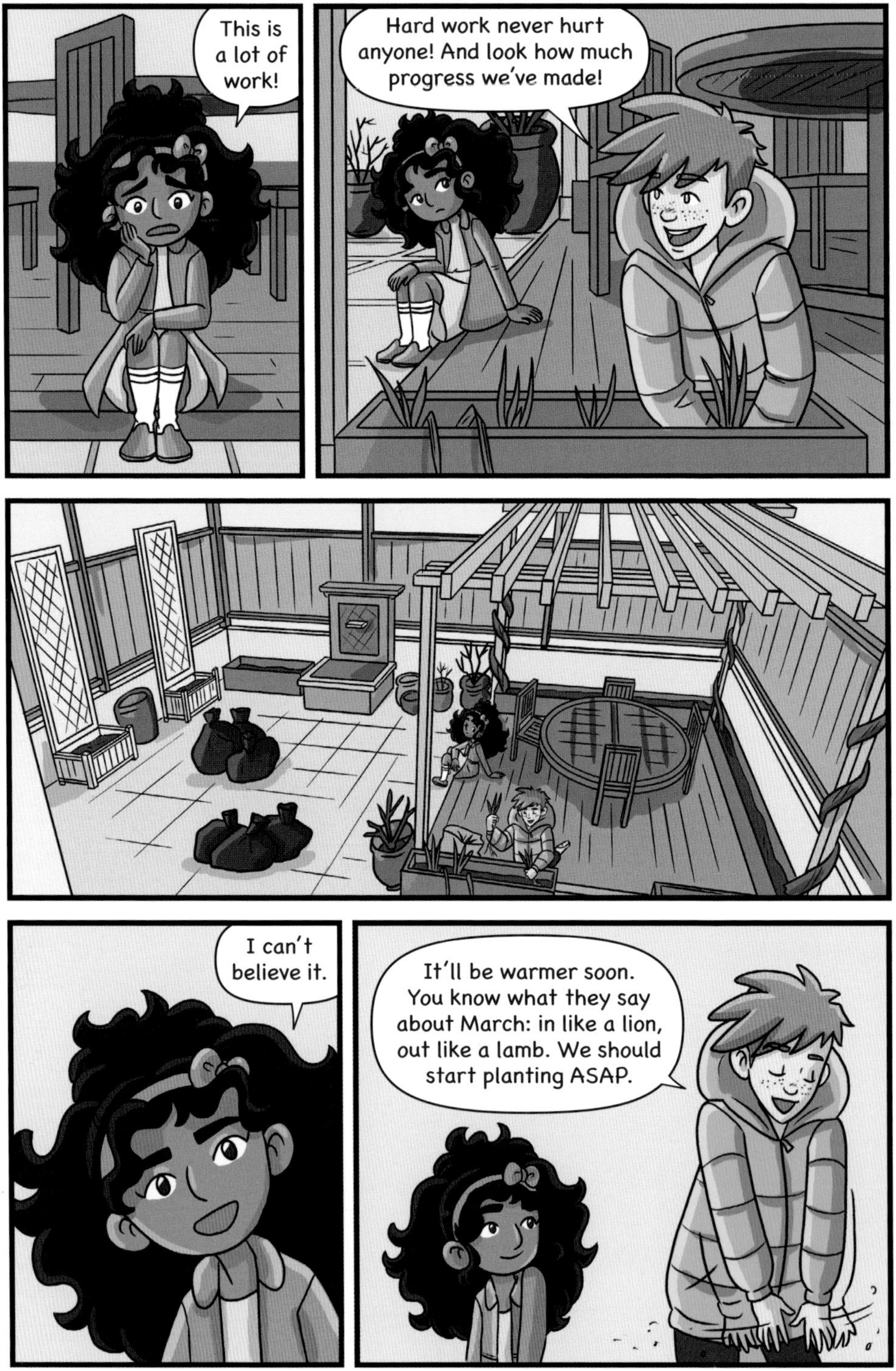
This is a lot of work!
Hard work never hurt anyone! And look how much progress we've made!
I can't believe it.
It'll be warmer soon. You know what they say about March: in like a lion, out like a lamb. We should start planting ASAP.

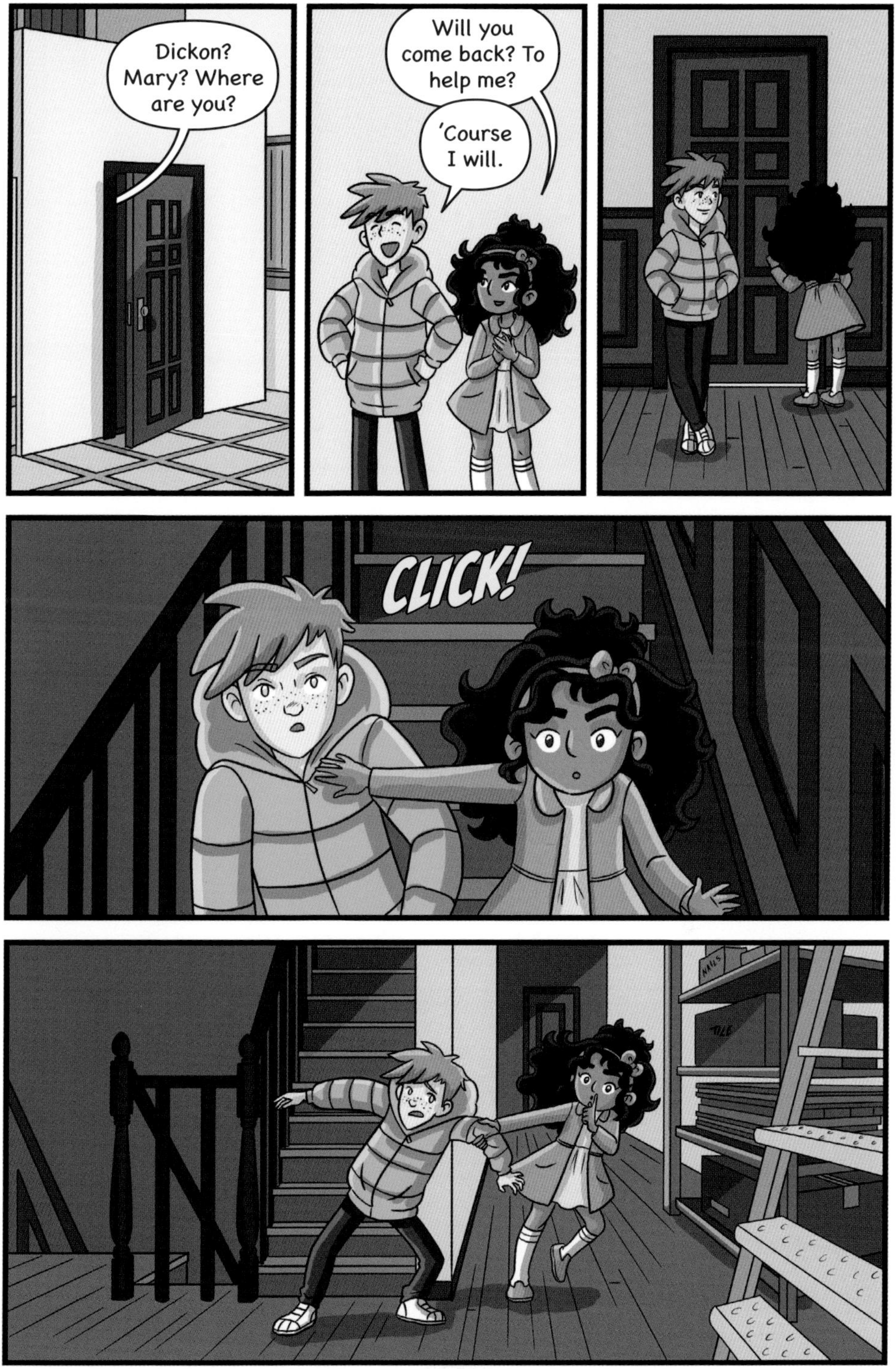
Dickon? Mary? Where are you?
Will you come back? To help me?
'Course I will.
CLICK!

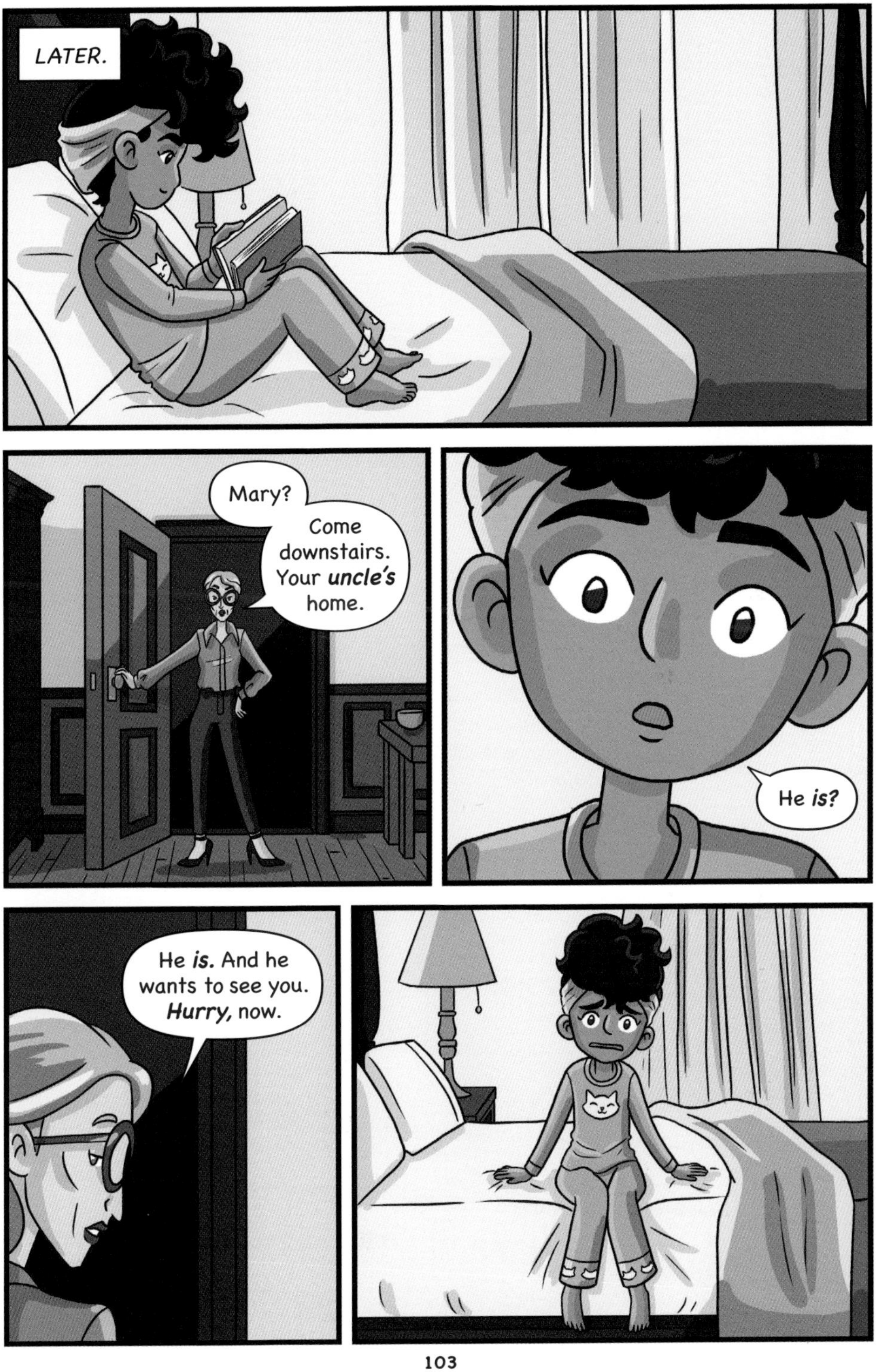
LATER.
Mary?
Come downstairs. Your uncle's home.
He is?
He is. And he wants to see you. Hurry, now.

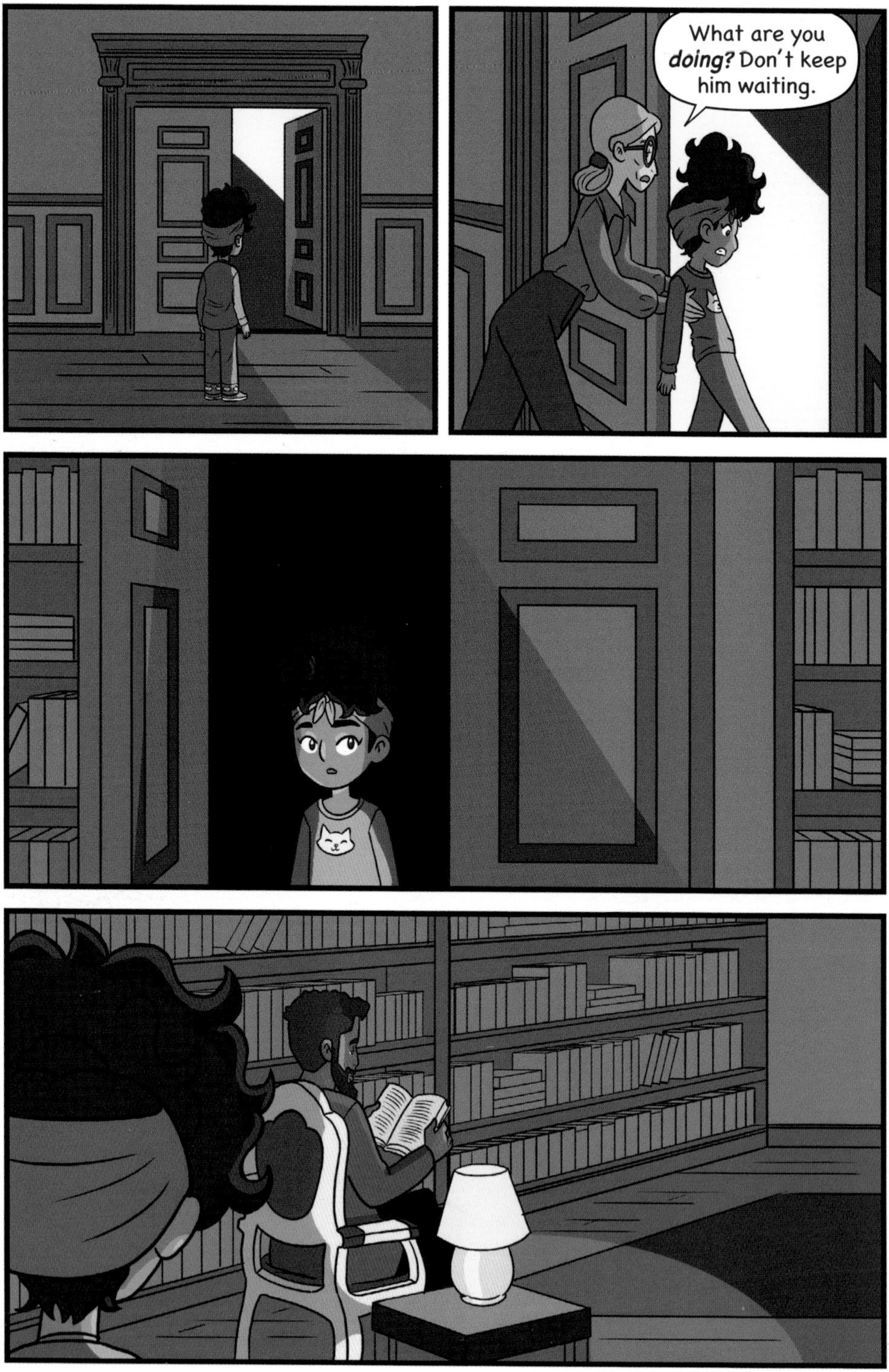
What are you *doing?* Don't keep him waiting.

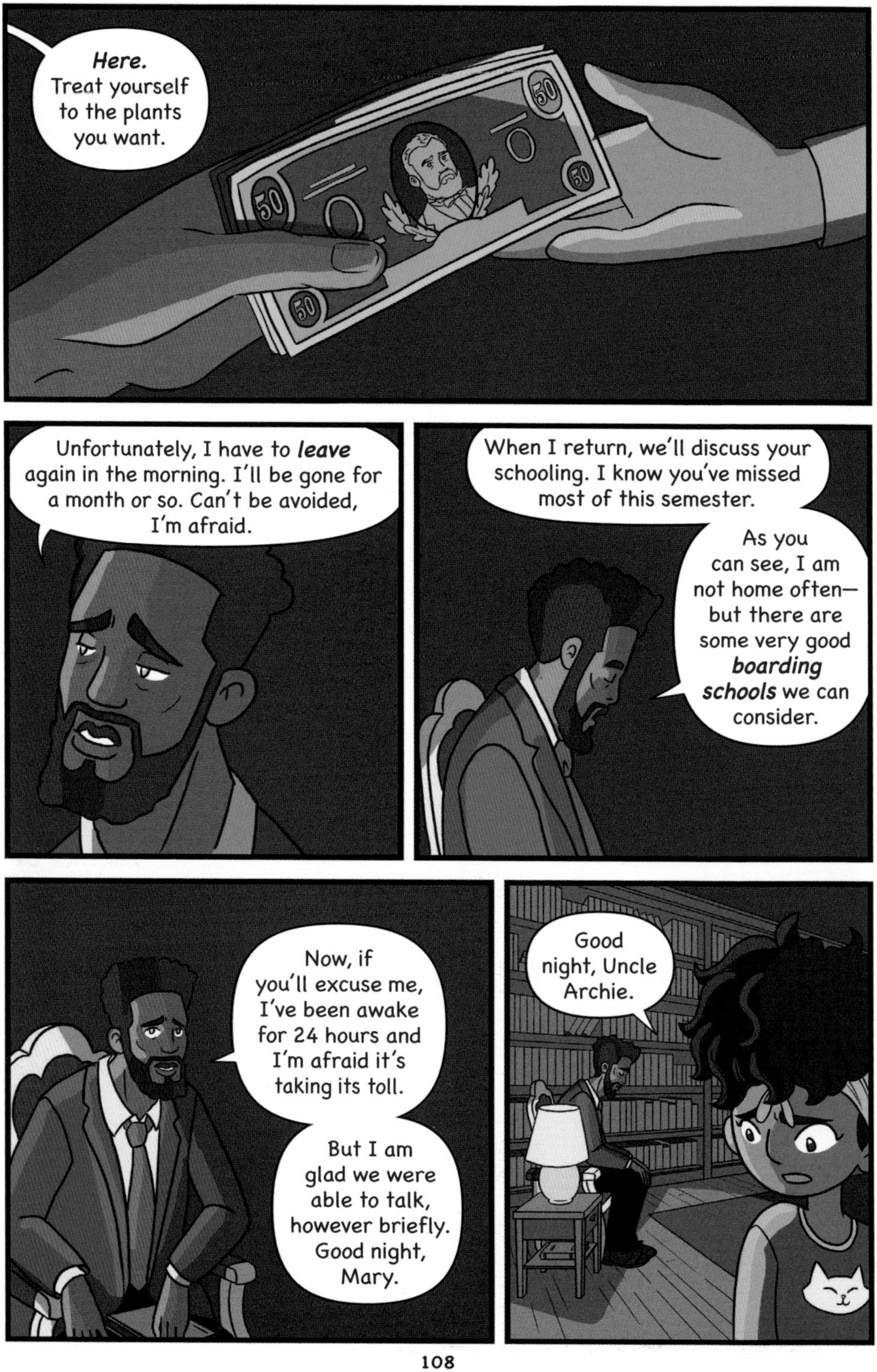
Here. Treat yourself to the plants you want.
Unfortunately, I have to *leave* again in the morning. I'll be gone for a month or so. Can't be avoided, I'm afraid.
When I return, we'll discuss your schooling. I know you've missed most of this semester.
As you can see, I am not home often— but there are some very good *boarding schools* we can consider.
Now, if you'll excuse me, I've been awake for 24 hours and I'm afraid it's taking its toll.
But I am glad we were able to talk, however briefly. Good night, Mary.
Good night, Uncle Archie.
50

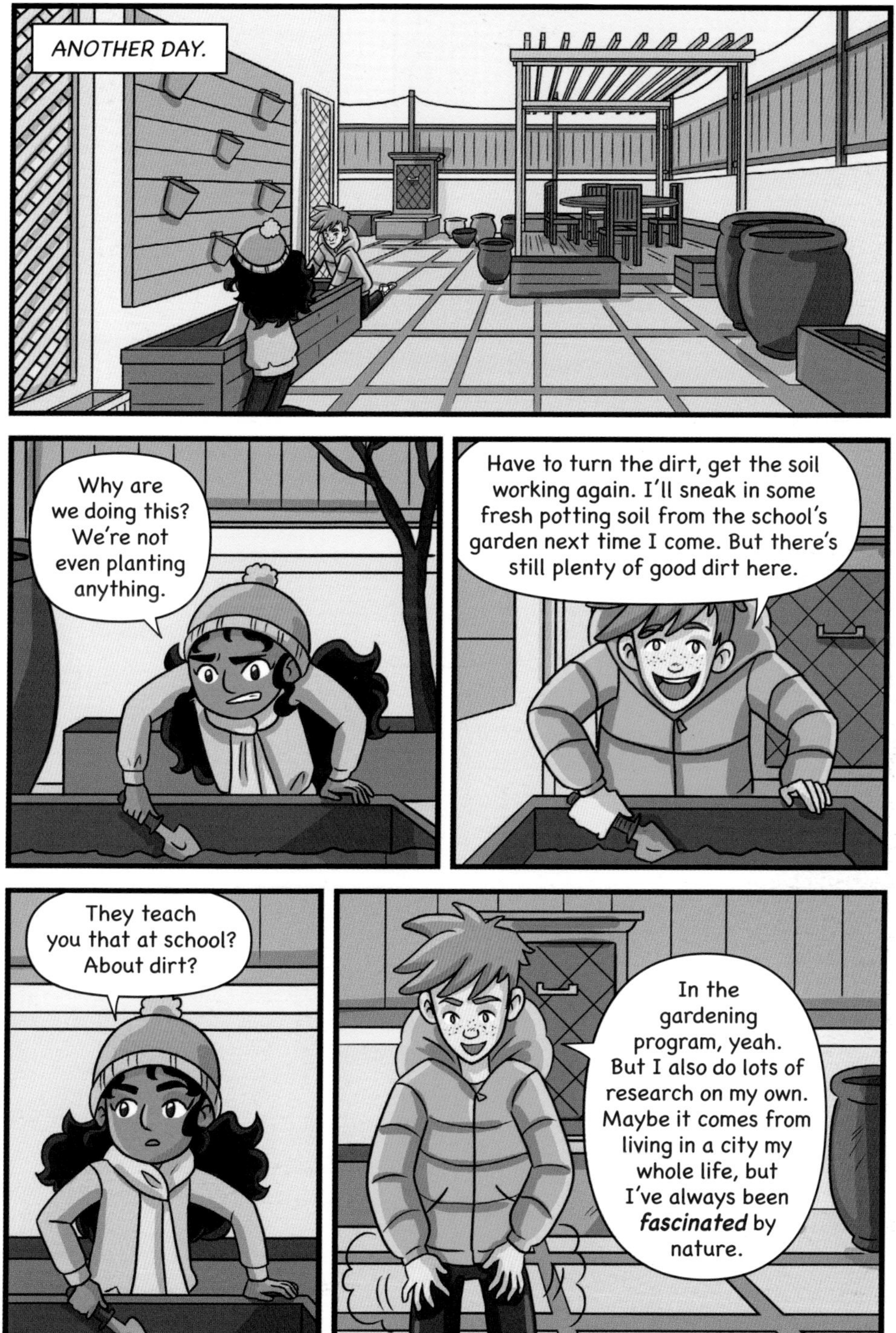
ANOTHER DAY.
Why are we doing this? We're not even planting anything.
Have to turn the dirt, get the soil working again. I'll sneak in some fresh potting soil from the school's garden next time I come. But there's still plenty of good dirt here.
They teach you that at school? About dirt?
In the gardening program, yeah. But I also do lots of research on my own. Maybe it comes from living in a city my whole life, but I've always been ***fascinated*** by nature.

The_Secret_Garden

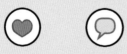

The_Secret_Garden Doesn't look like much yet…but just you wait!

The_Cultured_Cat

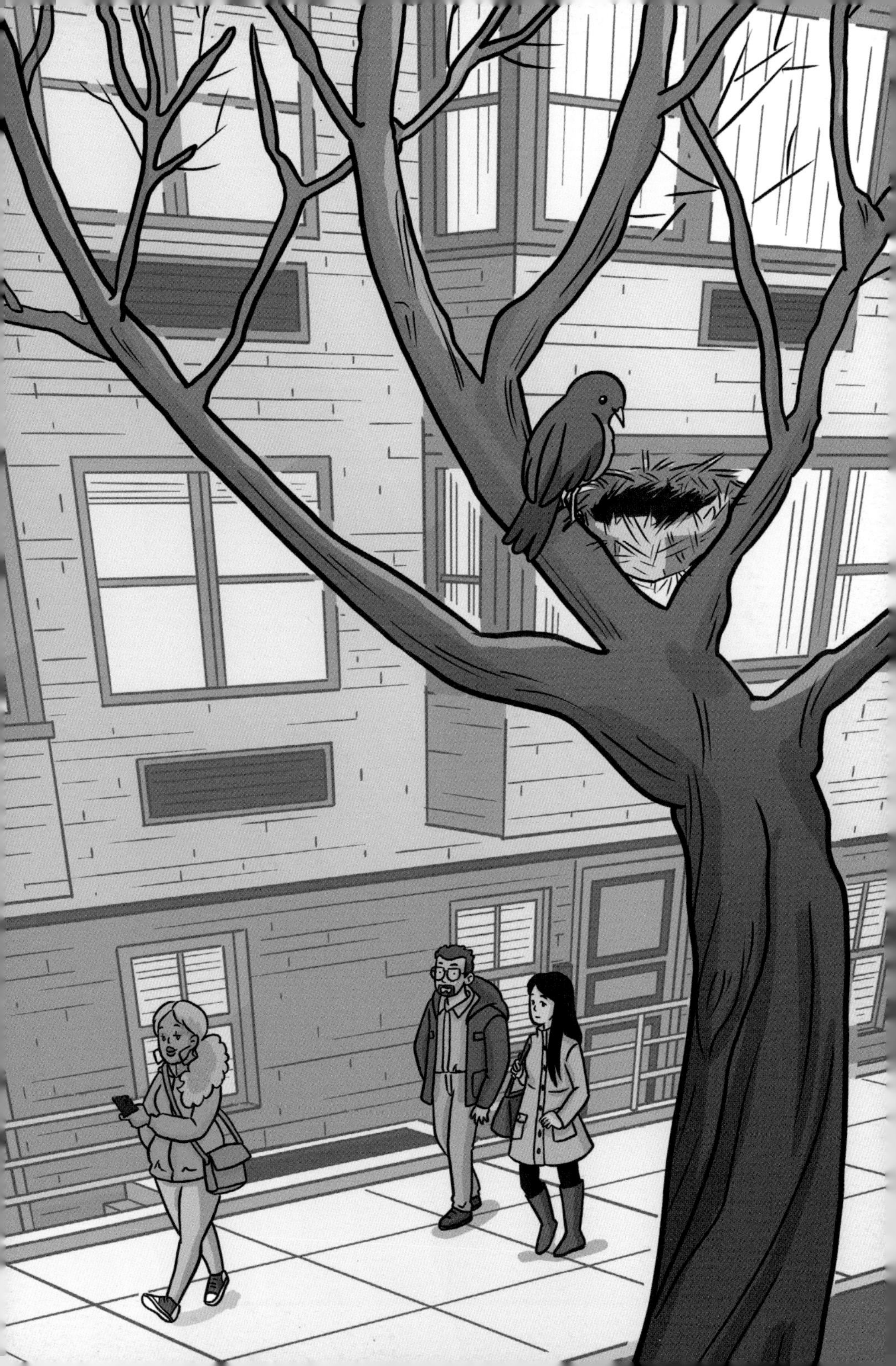

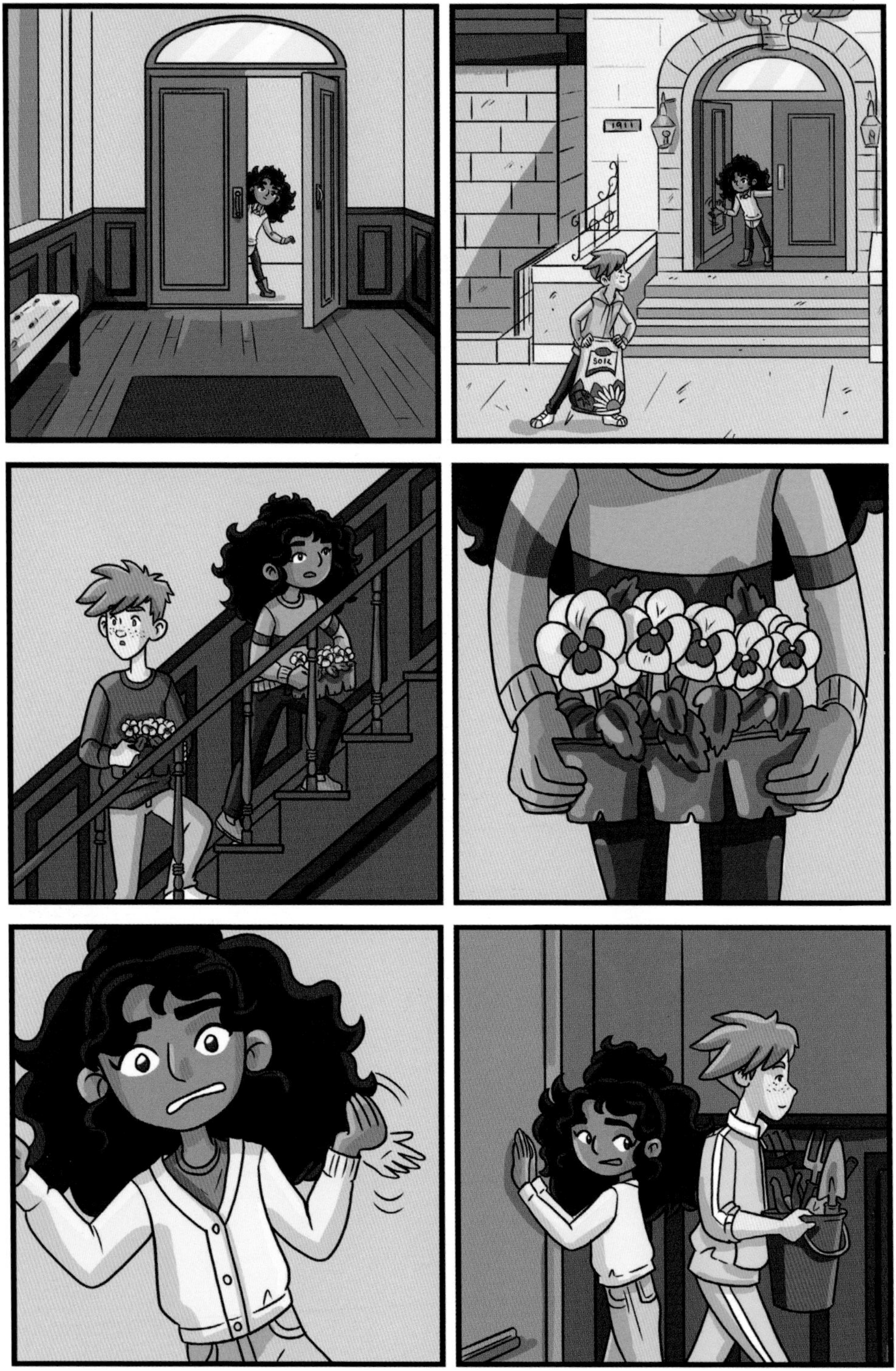
1911
SOIL

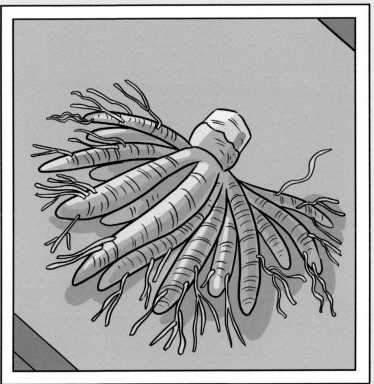

The_Secret_Garden Hard to believe it, but this ugly little thing turns into a beautiful lily! Once it sprouts, it needs plenty of hot sun. The flowers will be the most intense shade of yellow!

PrettyCoolDog

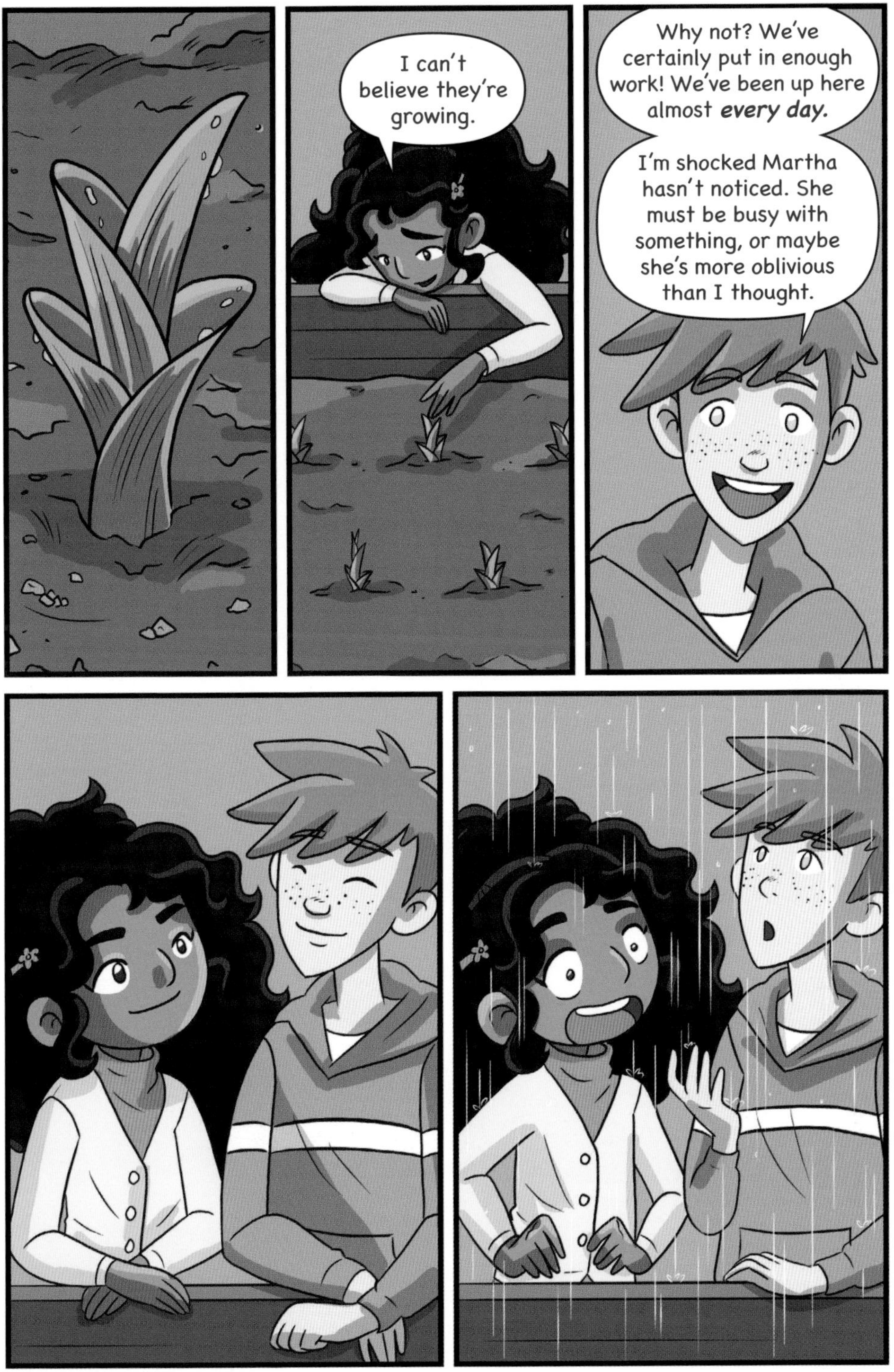
I can't believe they're growing.
Why not? We've certainly put in enough work! We've been up here almost ***every day.***
I'm shocked Martha hasn't noticed. She must be busy with something, or maybe she's more oblivious than I thought.

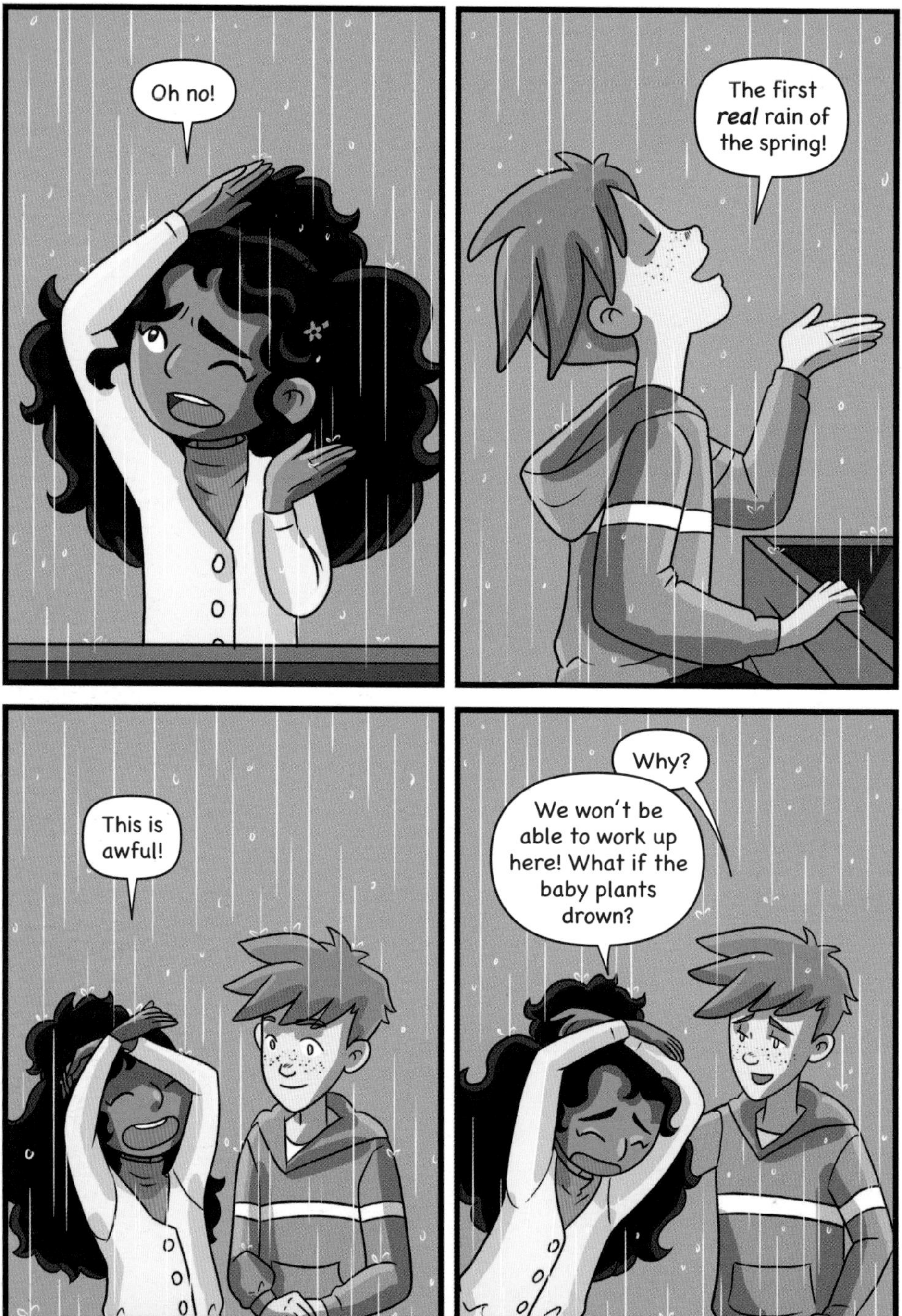
Oh no!
The first *real* rain of the spring!
This is awful!
Why?
We won't be able to work up here! What if the baby plants drown?

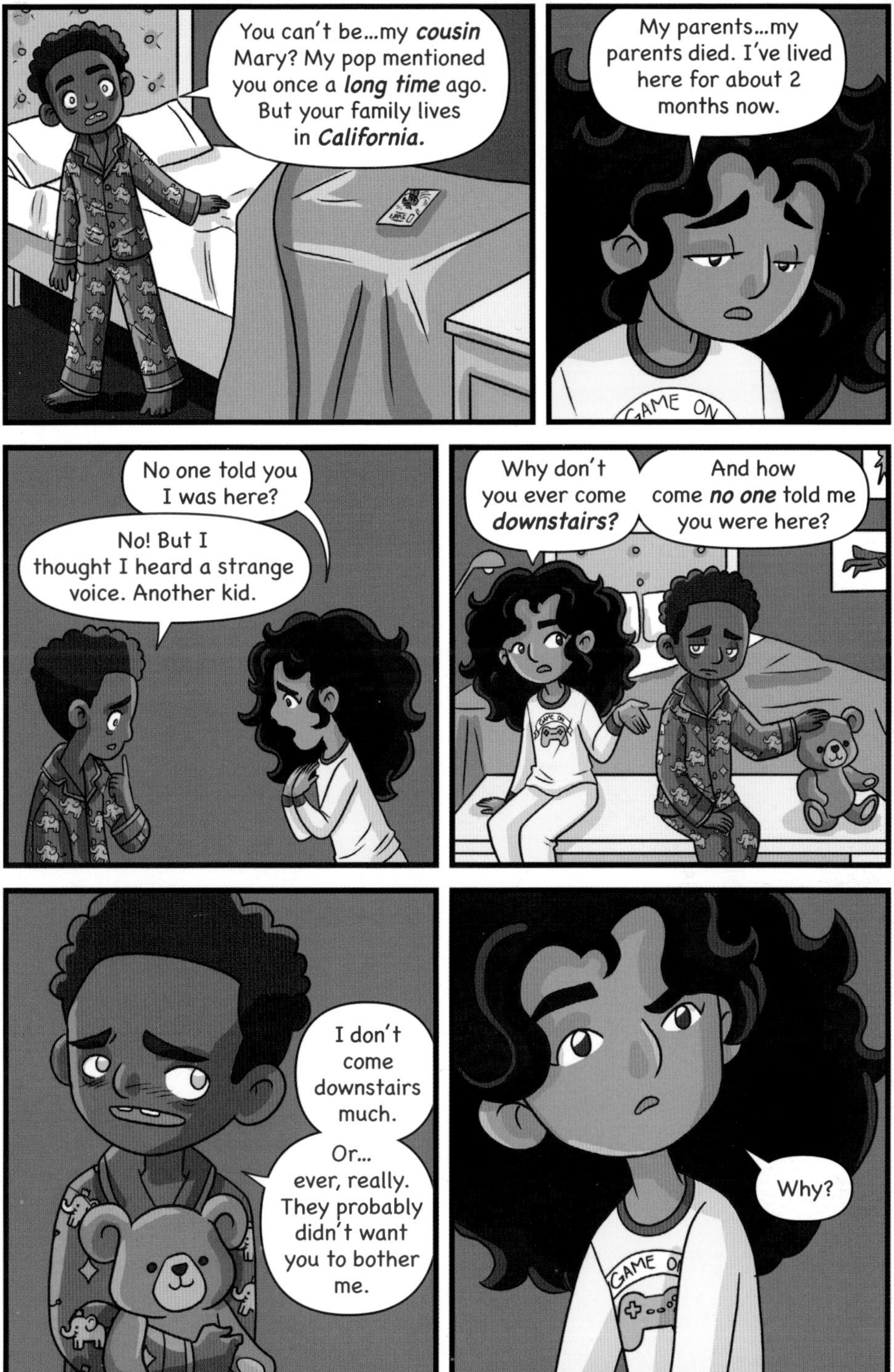
You can't be...my *cousin* Mary? My pop mentioned you once a *long time* ago. But your family lives in *California.*
My parents...my parents died. I've lived here for about 2 months now.
GAME ON
No one told you I was here?
No! But I thought I heard a strange voice. Another kid.
Why don't you ever come *downstairs?*
And how come *no one* told me you were here?
I don't come downstairs much.
Or... ever, really. They probably didn't want you to bother me.
Why?
GAME O

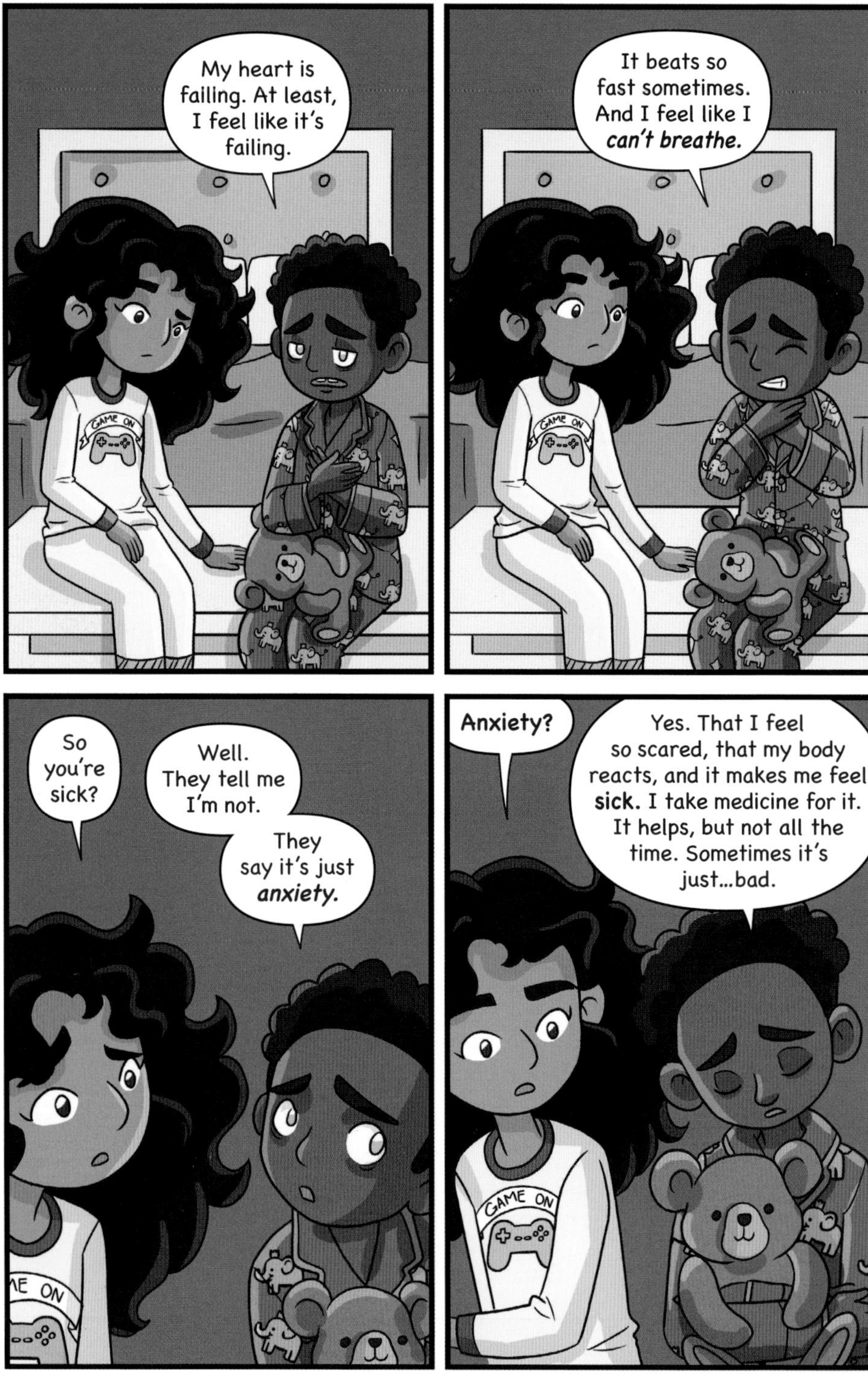
My heart is failing. At least, I feel like it's failing.
GAME ON
It beats so fast sometimes. And I feel like I *can't breathe.*
GAME ON
So you're sick?
Well. They tell me I'm not.
They say it's just *anxiety.*
ME ON
Anxiety?
Yes. That I feel so scared, that my body reacts, and it makes me feel **sick.** I take medicine for it. It helps, but not all the time. Sometimes it's just...bad.
GAME ON

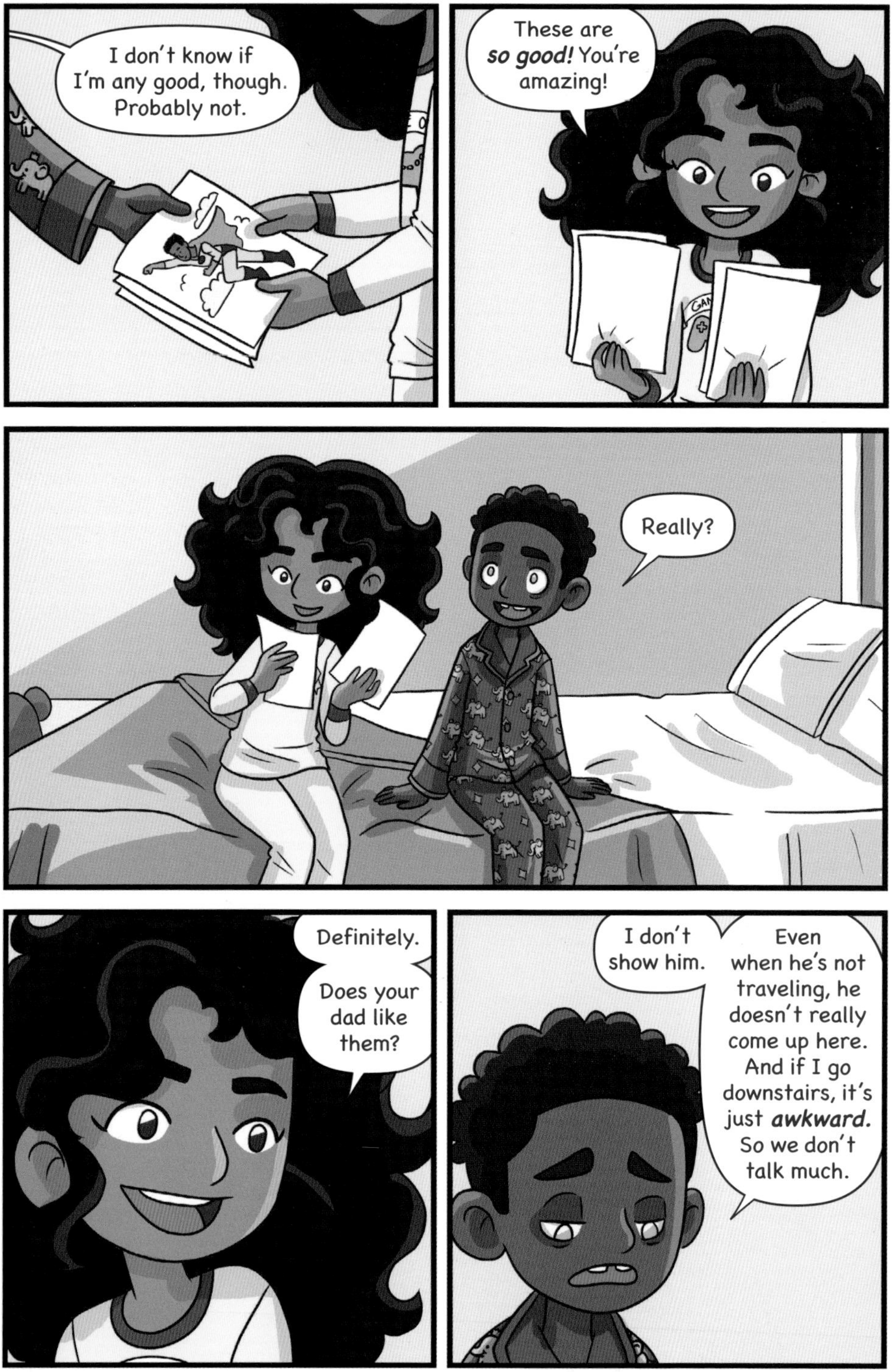
I don't know if I'm any good, though. Probably not.
These are *so good!* You're amazing!
Really?
Definitely.
Does your dad like them?
I don't show him.
Even when he's not traveling, he doesn't really come up here. And if I go downstairs, it's just ***awkward.*** So we don't talk much.

129

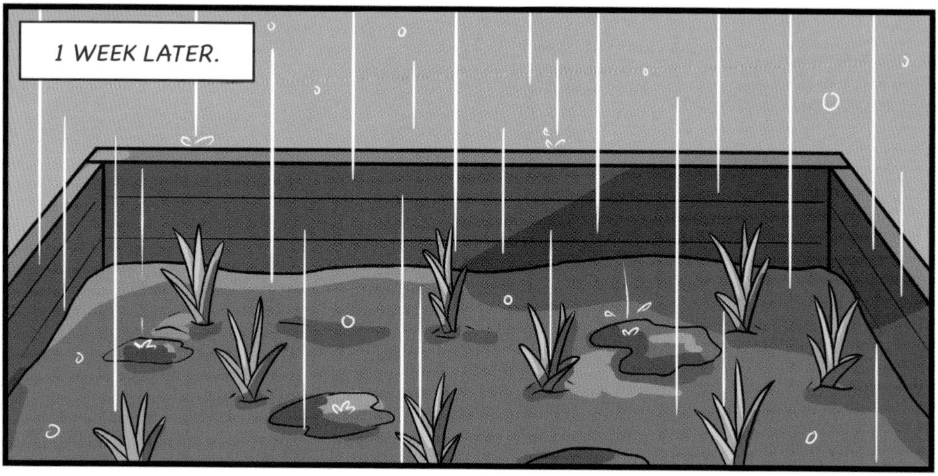
1 WEEK LATER.

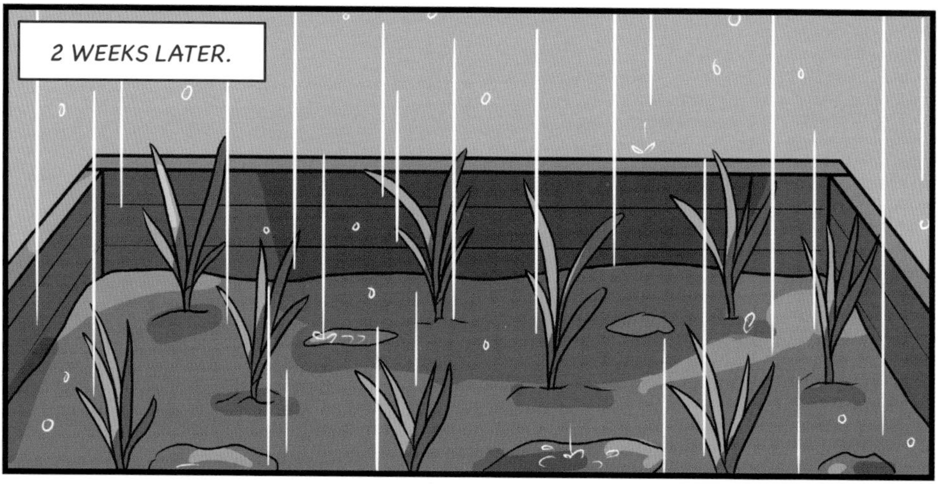
2 WEEKS LATER.

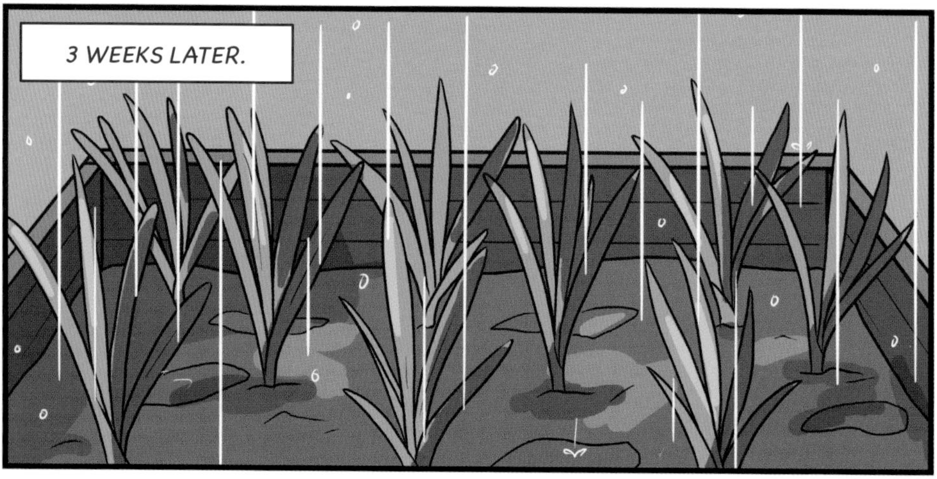
3 WEEKS LATER.

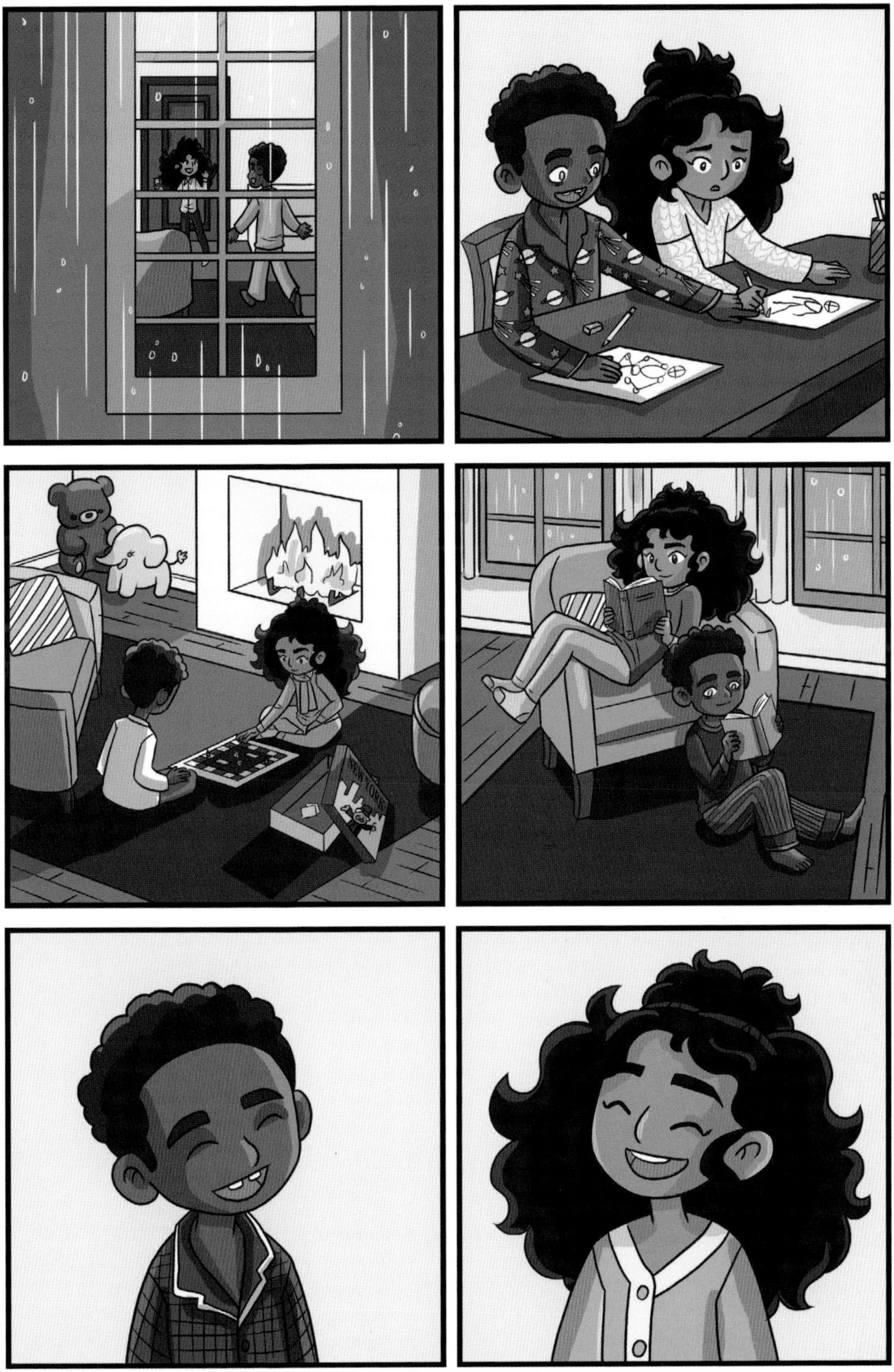
NEW YORK

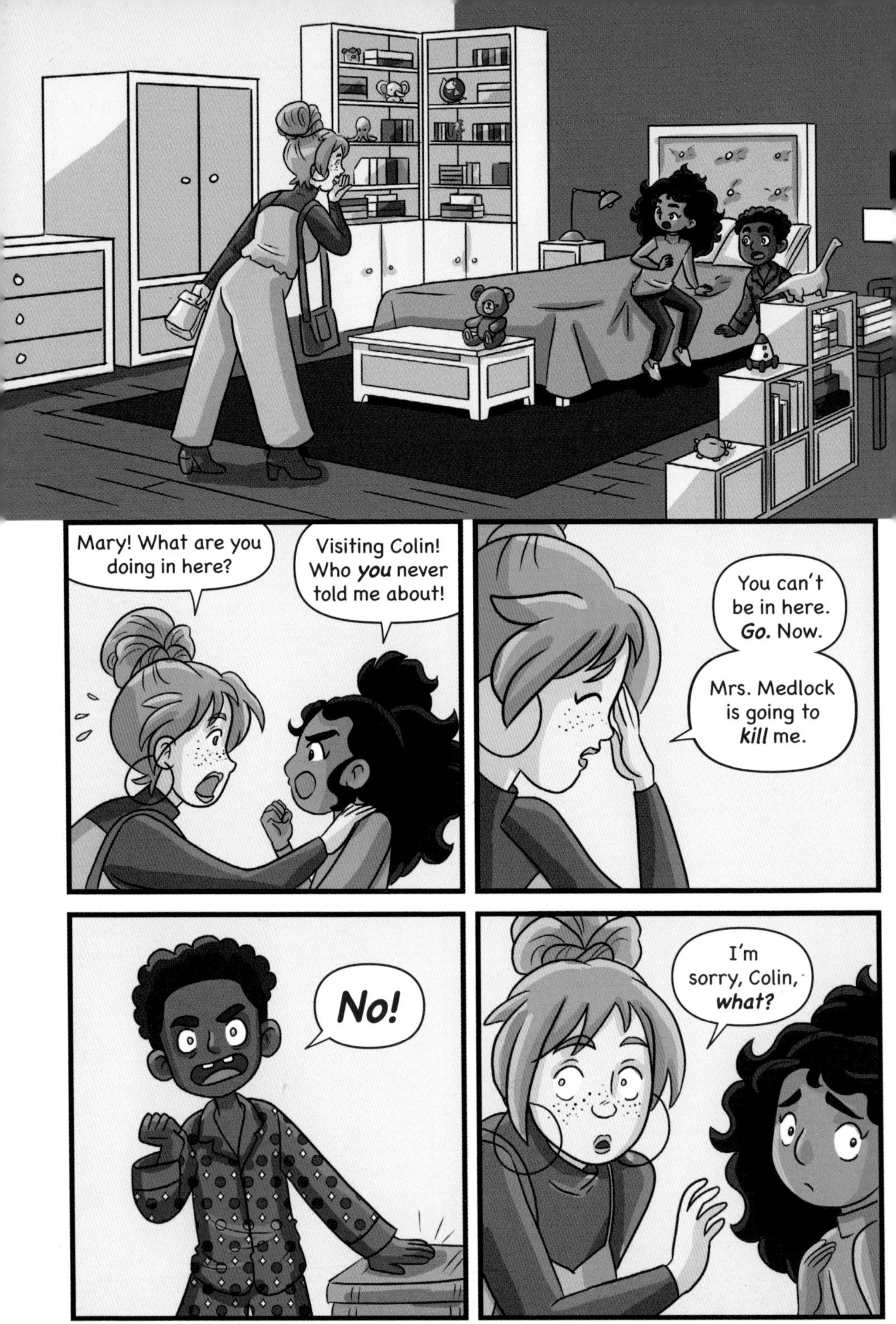

Mary! What are you doing in here?
Visiting Colin! Who *you* never told me about!
You can't be in here. ***Go.*** Now.
Mrs. Medlock is going to ***kill*** me.
No!
I'm sorry, Colin, ***what?***

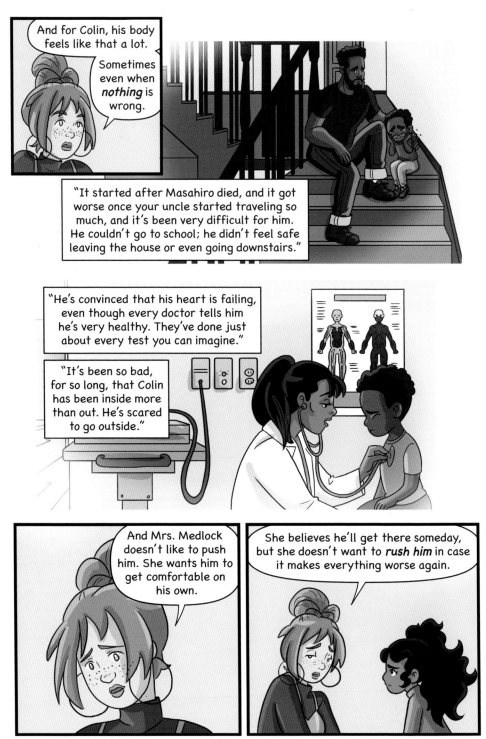

And for Colin, his body feels like that a lot.

Sometimes even when *nothing* is wrong.

"It started after Masahiro died, and it got worse once your uncle started traveling so much, and it's been very difficult for him. He couldn't go to school; he didn't feel safe leaving the house or even going downstairs."

"He's convinced that his heart is failing, even though every doctor tells him he's very healthy. They've done just about every test you can imagine."

"It's been so bad, for so long, that Colin has been inside more than out. He's scared to go outside."

And Mrs. Medlock doesn't like to push him. She wants him to get comfortable on his own.

She believes he'll get there someday, but she doesn't want to *rush him* in case it makes everything worse again.

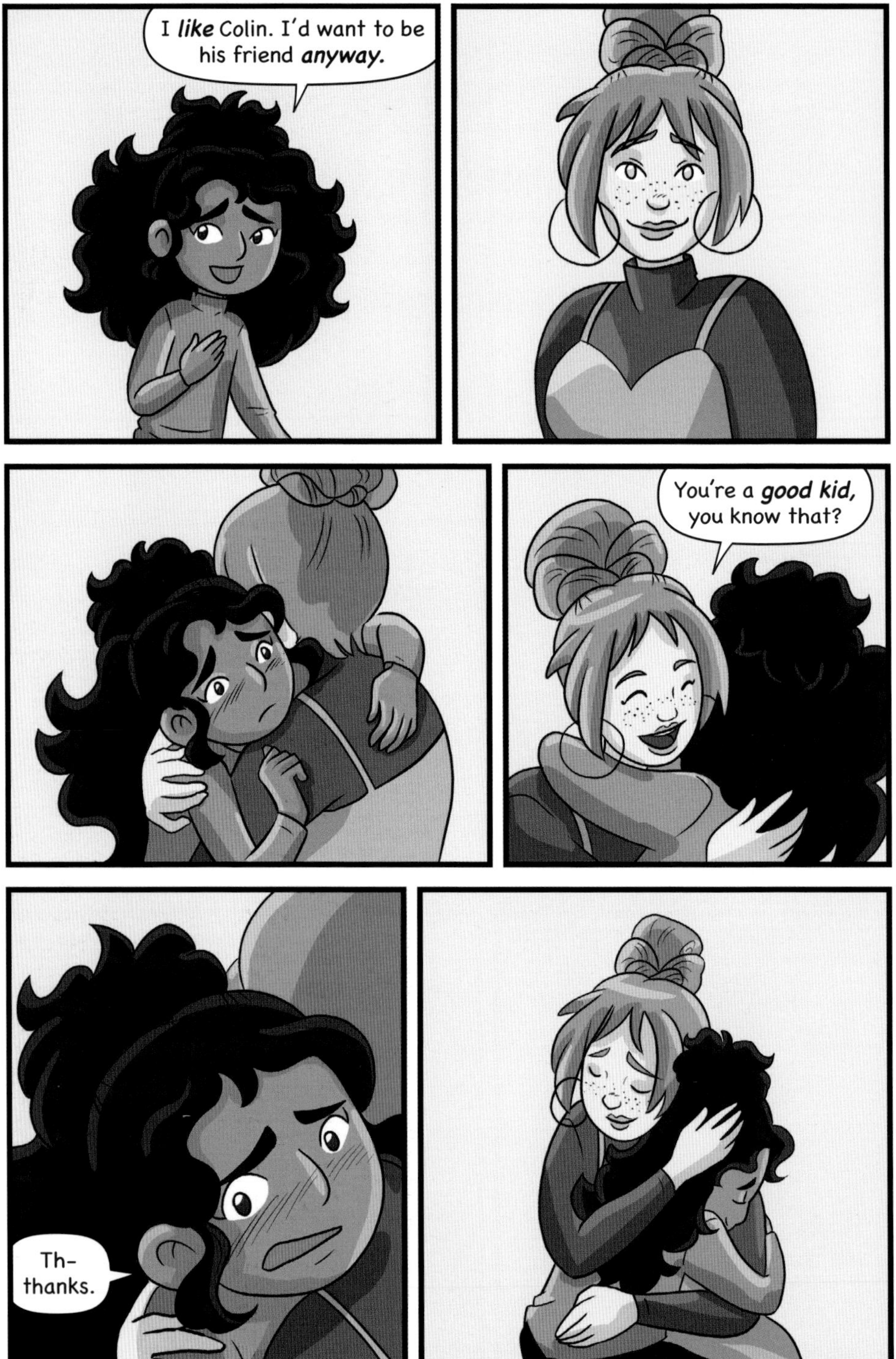
I *like* Colin. I'd want to be his friend ***anyway.***
You're a ***good kid,*** you know that?
Th- thanks.

146

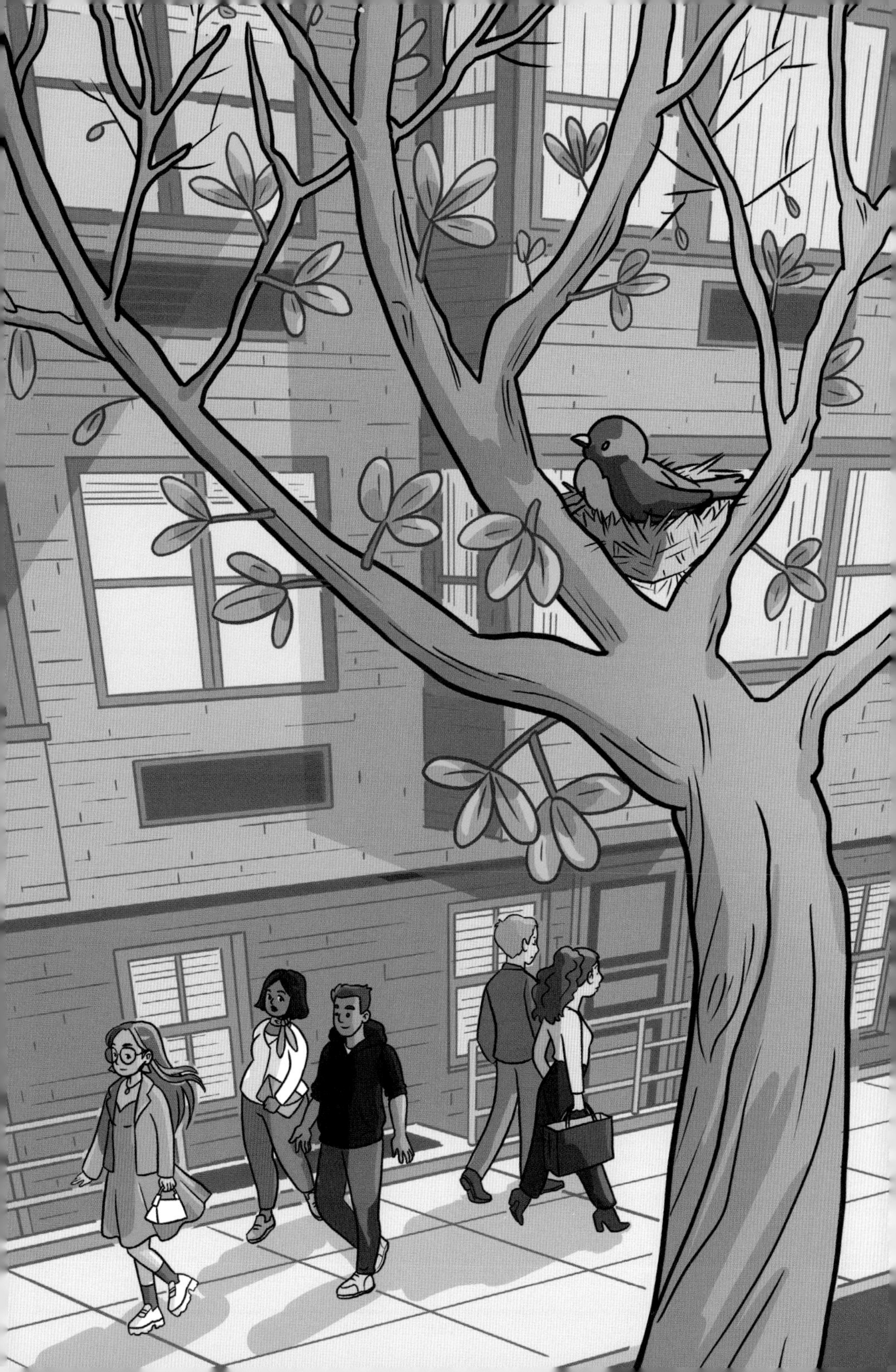

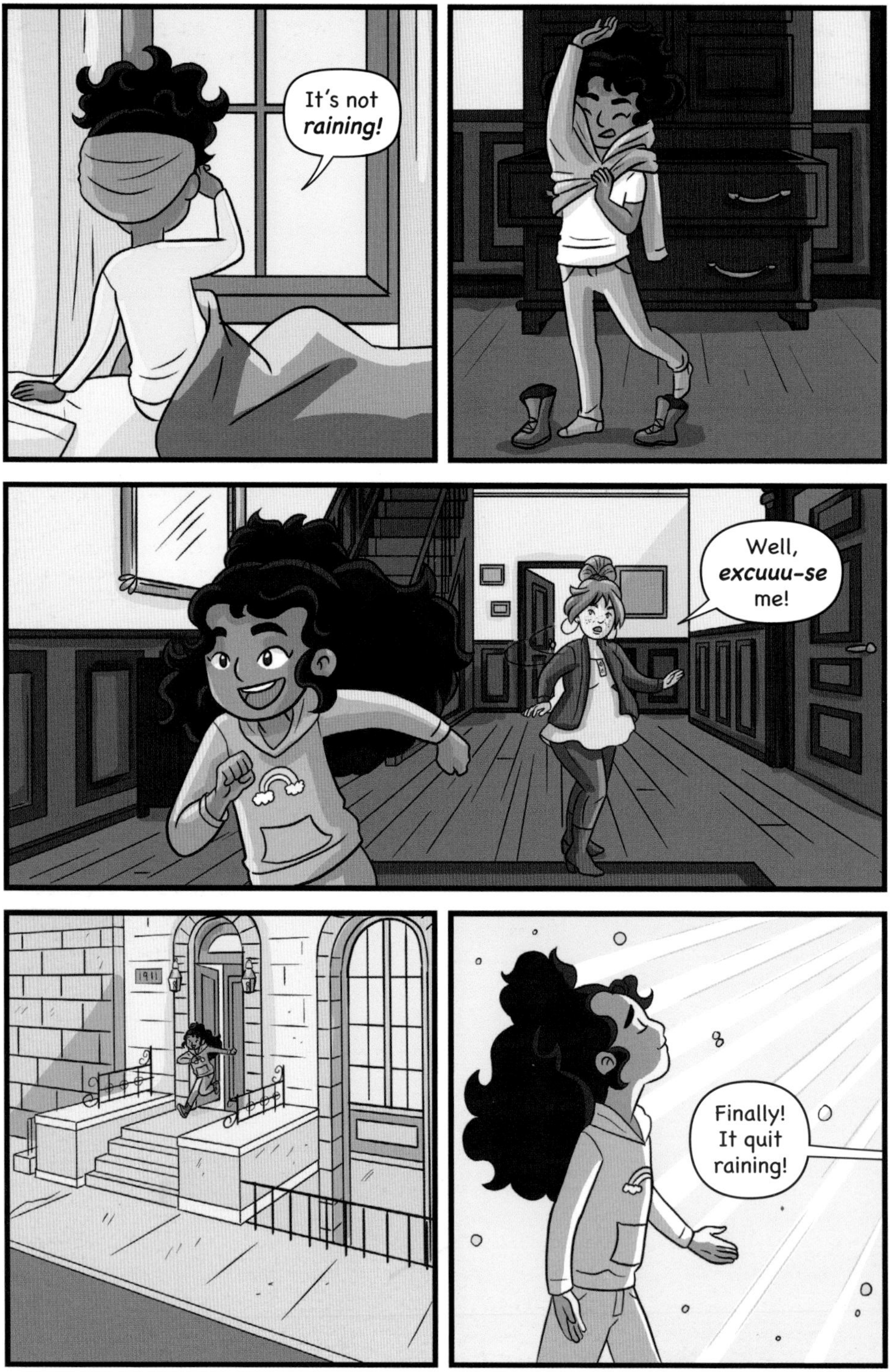
It's not *raining!*
Well, *excuuu-se* me!
1911
Finally! It quit raining!

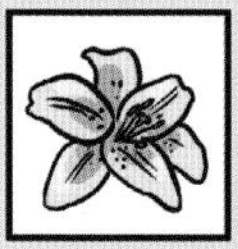

The_Secret_Garden

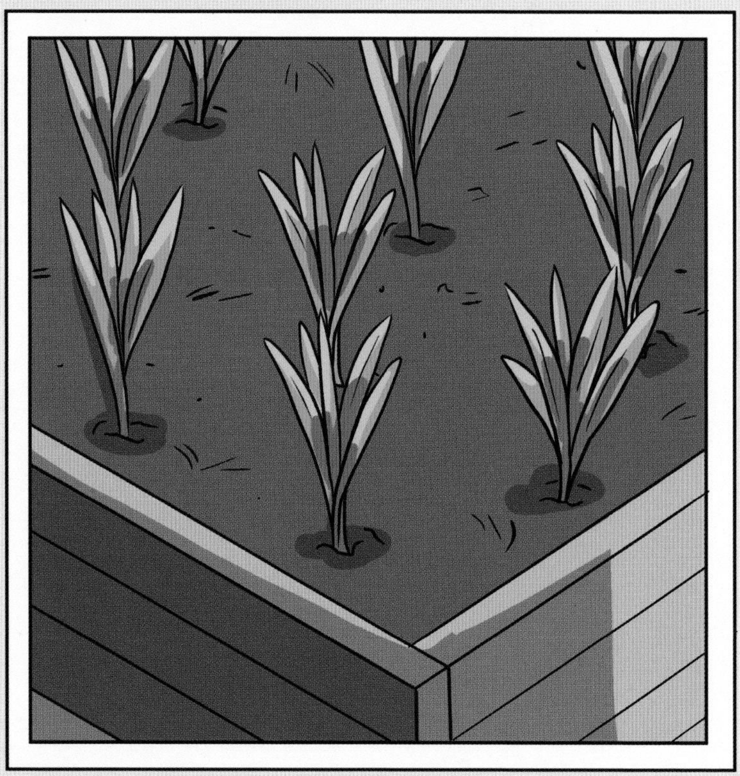

The_Secret_Garden Coming soon!!! 🌱🌱🌱🌱🌱🌱🌱🌱🌱

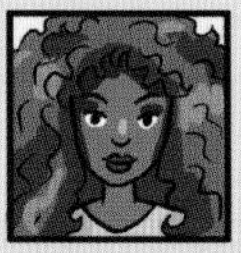

Pot_It_Like_Its_Hottt

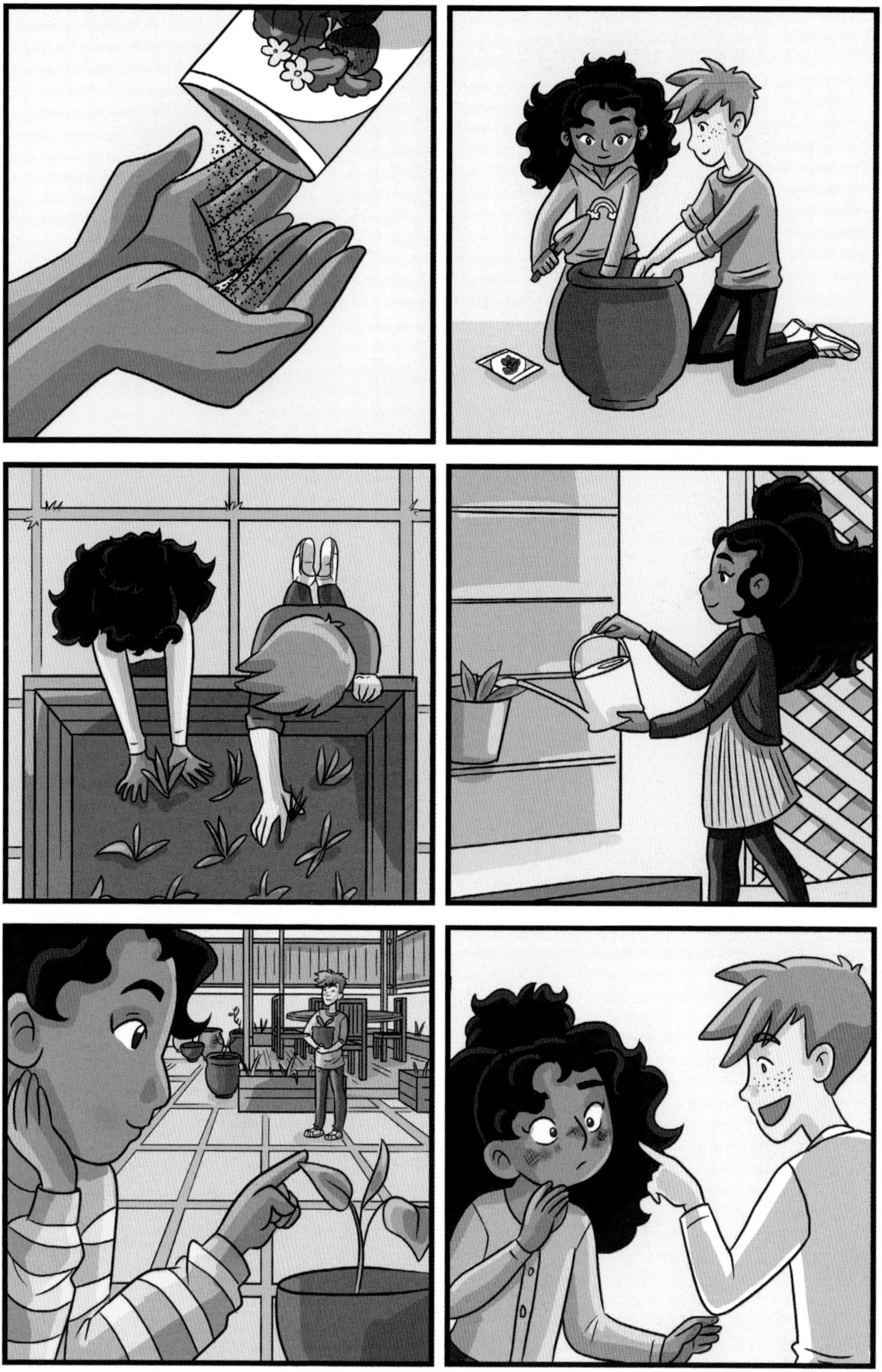

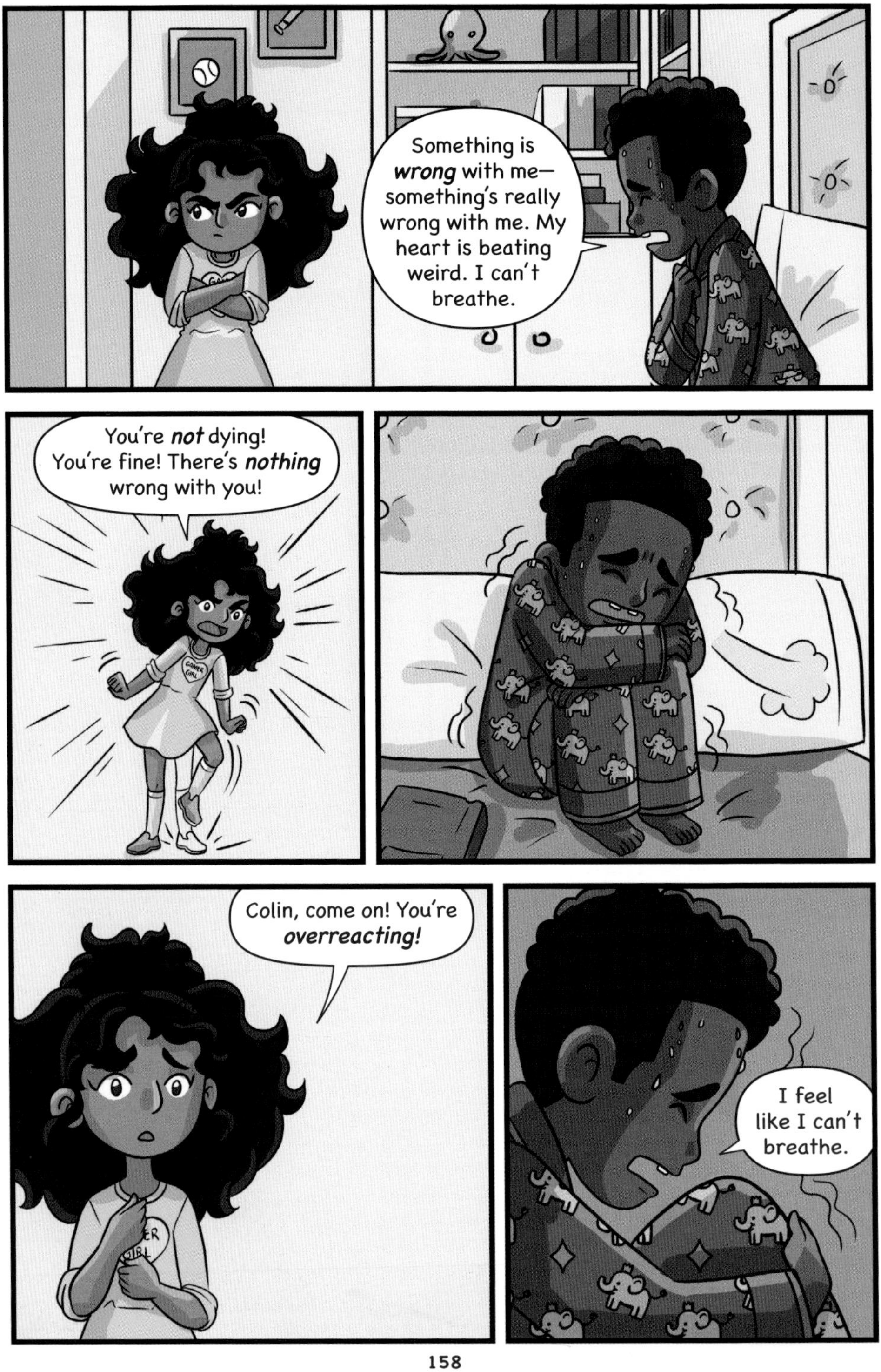
Something is *wrong* with me—something's really wrong with me. My heart is beating weird. I can't breathe.
You're *not* dying! You're fine! There's *nothing* wrong with you!
Colin, come on! You're *overreacting!*
I feel like I can't breathe.

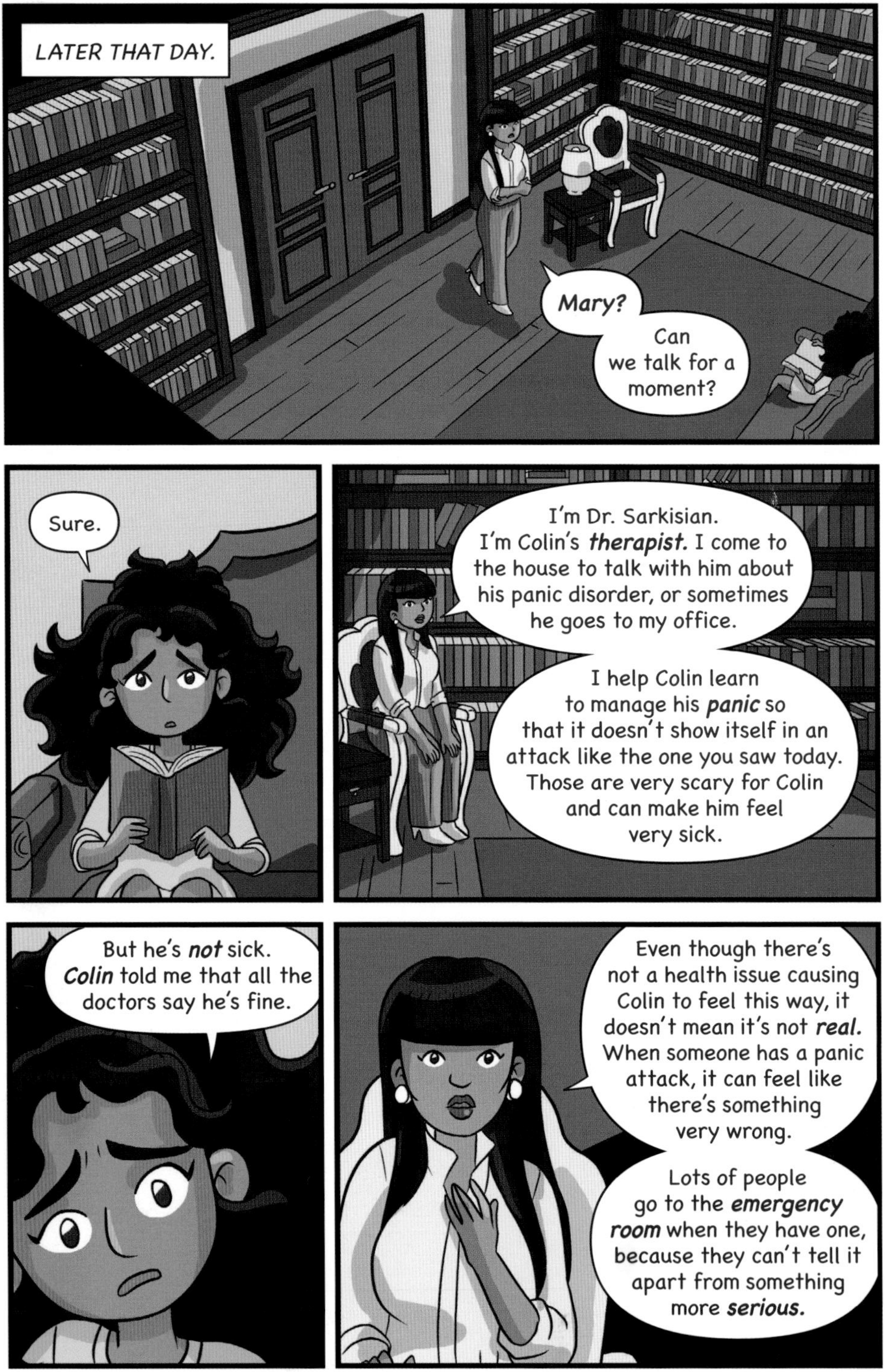
LATER THAT DAY.
Mary?
Can we talk for a moment?
Sure.
I'm Dr. Sarkisian. I'm Colin's *therapist.* I come to the house to talk with him about his panic disorder, or sometimes he goes to my office.
I help Colin learn to manage his *panic* so that it doesn't show itself in an attack like the one you saw today. Those are very scary for Colin and can make him feel very sick.
But he's *not* sick. *Colin* told me that all the doctors say he's fine.
Even though there's not a health issue causing Colin to feel this way, it doesn't mean it's not *real.* When someone has a panic attack, it can feel like there's something very wrong.
Lots of people go to the *emergency room* when they have one, because they can't tell it apart from something more *serious.*

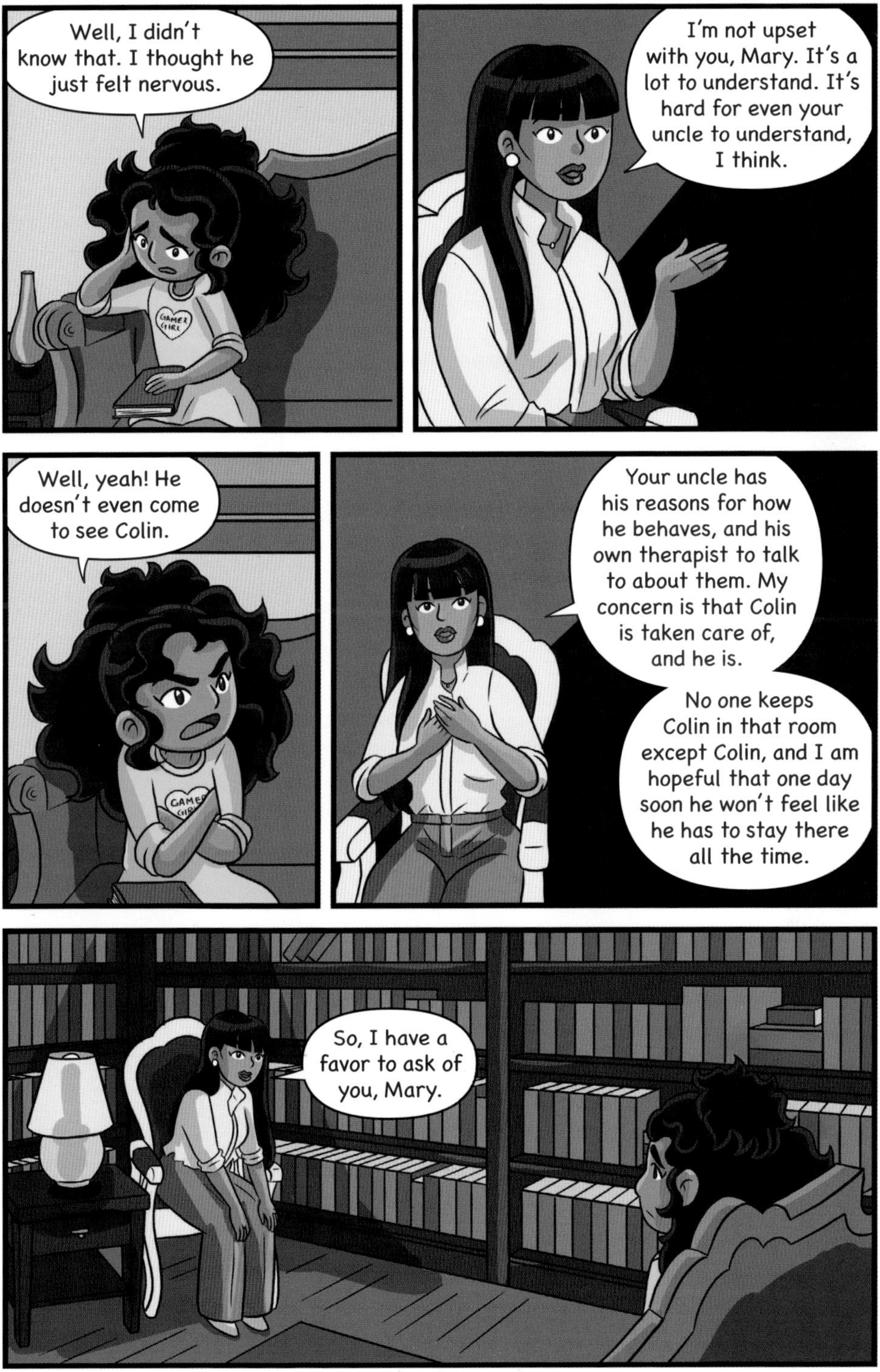

Well, I didn't know that. I thought he just felt nervous.
GAMER GIRL
I'm not upset with you, Mary. It's a lot to understand. It's hard for even your uncle to understand, I think.
Well, yeah! He doesn't even come to see Colin.
Your uncle has his reasons for how he behaves, and his own therapist to talk to about them. My concern is that Colin is taken care of, and he is.
No one keeps Colin in that room except Colin, and I am hopeful that one day soon he won't feel like he has to stay there all the time.
So, I have a favor to ask of you, Mary.

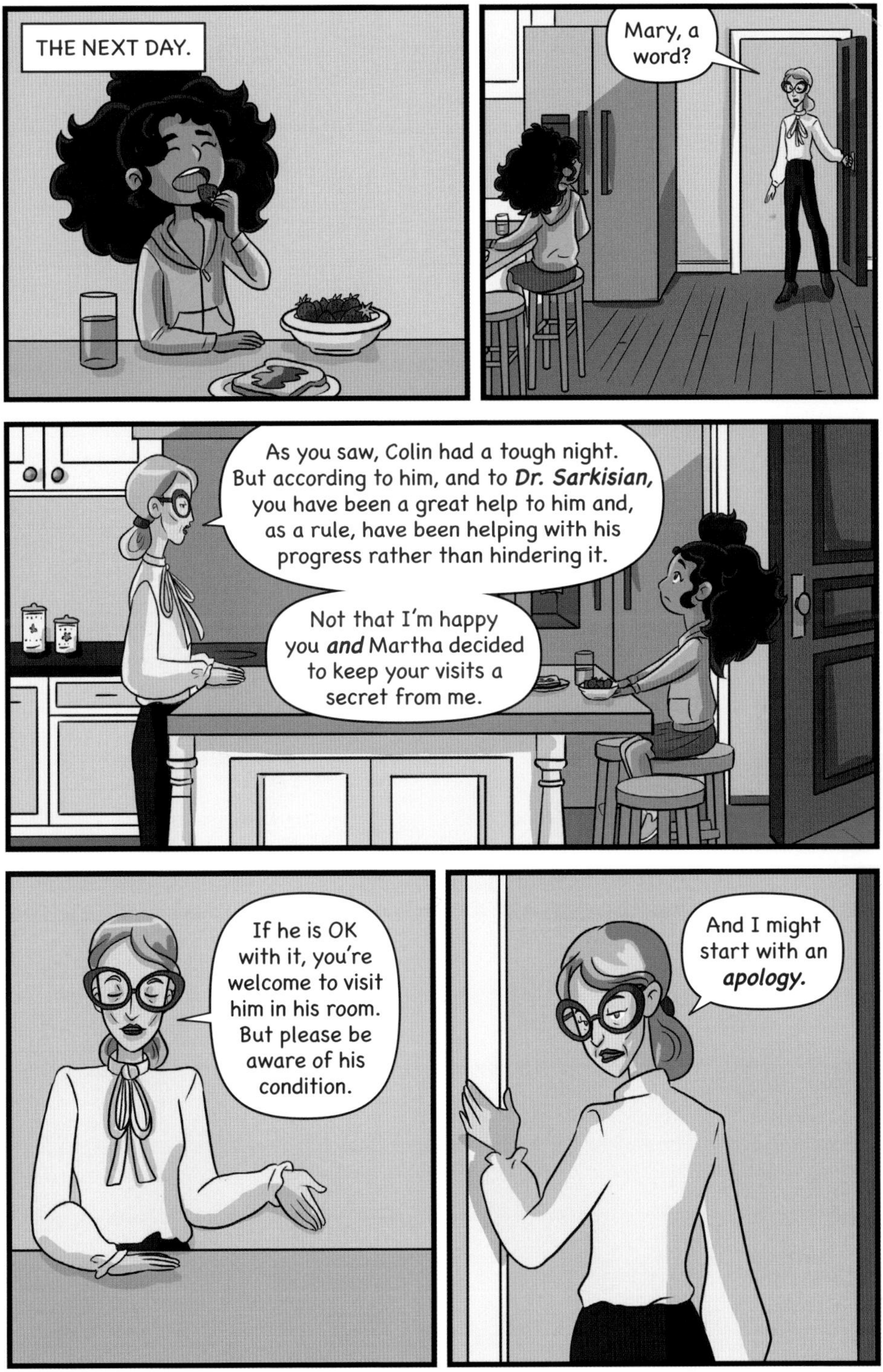
THE NEXT DAY.
Mary, a word?
As you saw, Colin had a tough night. But according to him, and to ***Dr. Sarkisian,*** you have been a great help to him and, as a rule, have been helping with his progress rather than hindering it.
Not that I'm happy you ***and*** Martha decided to keep your visits a secret from me.
If he is OK with it, you're welcome to visit him in his room. But please be aware of his condition.
And I might start with an ***apology.***

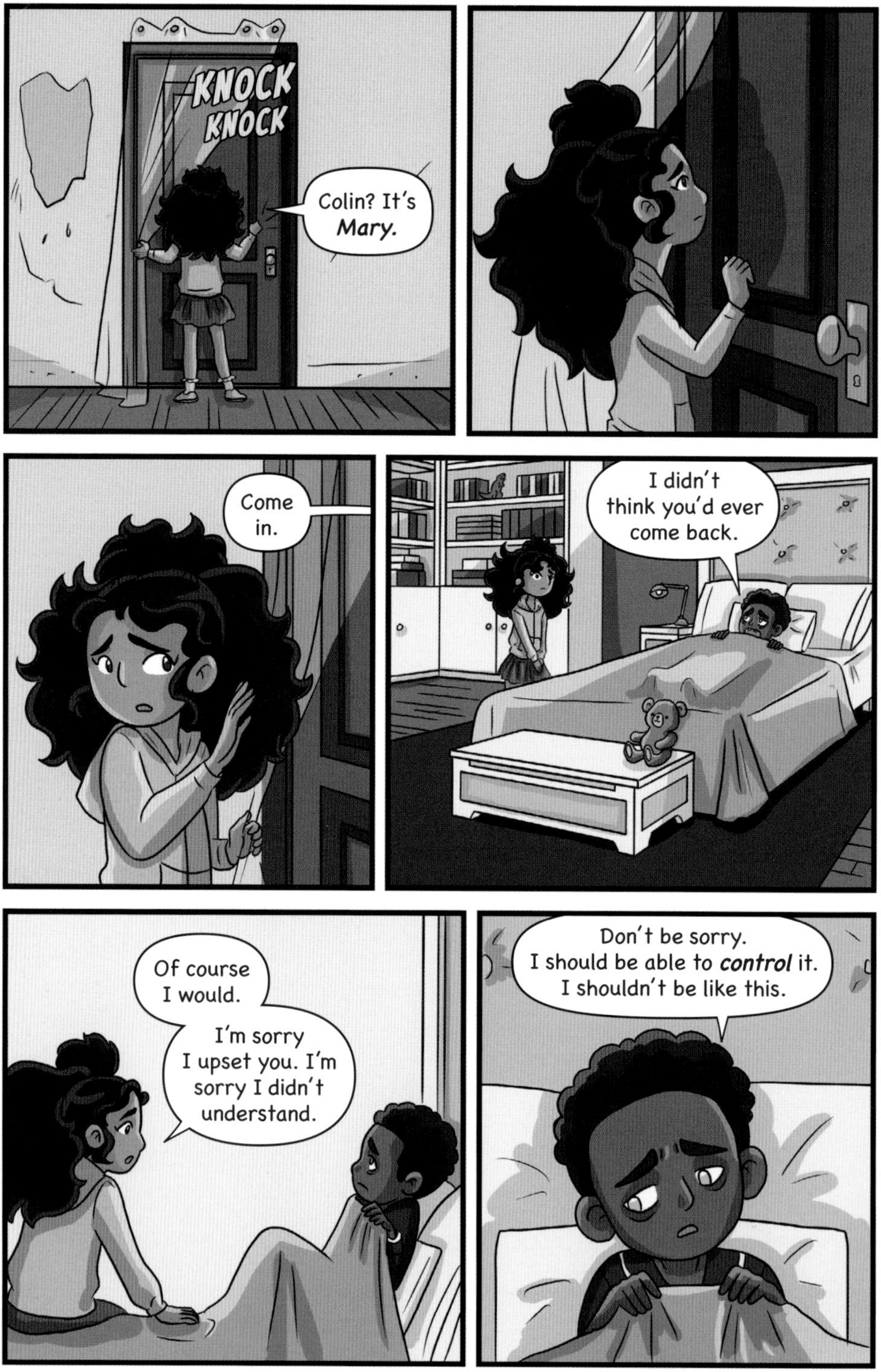
KNOCK KNOCK
Colin? It's *Mary.*
Come in.
I didn't think you'd ever come back.
Of course I would.
I'm sorry I upset you. I'm sorry I didn't understand.
Don't be sorry. I should be able to *control* it. I shouldn't be like this.

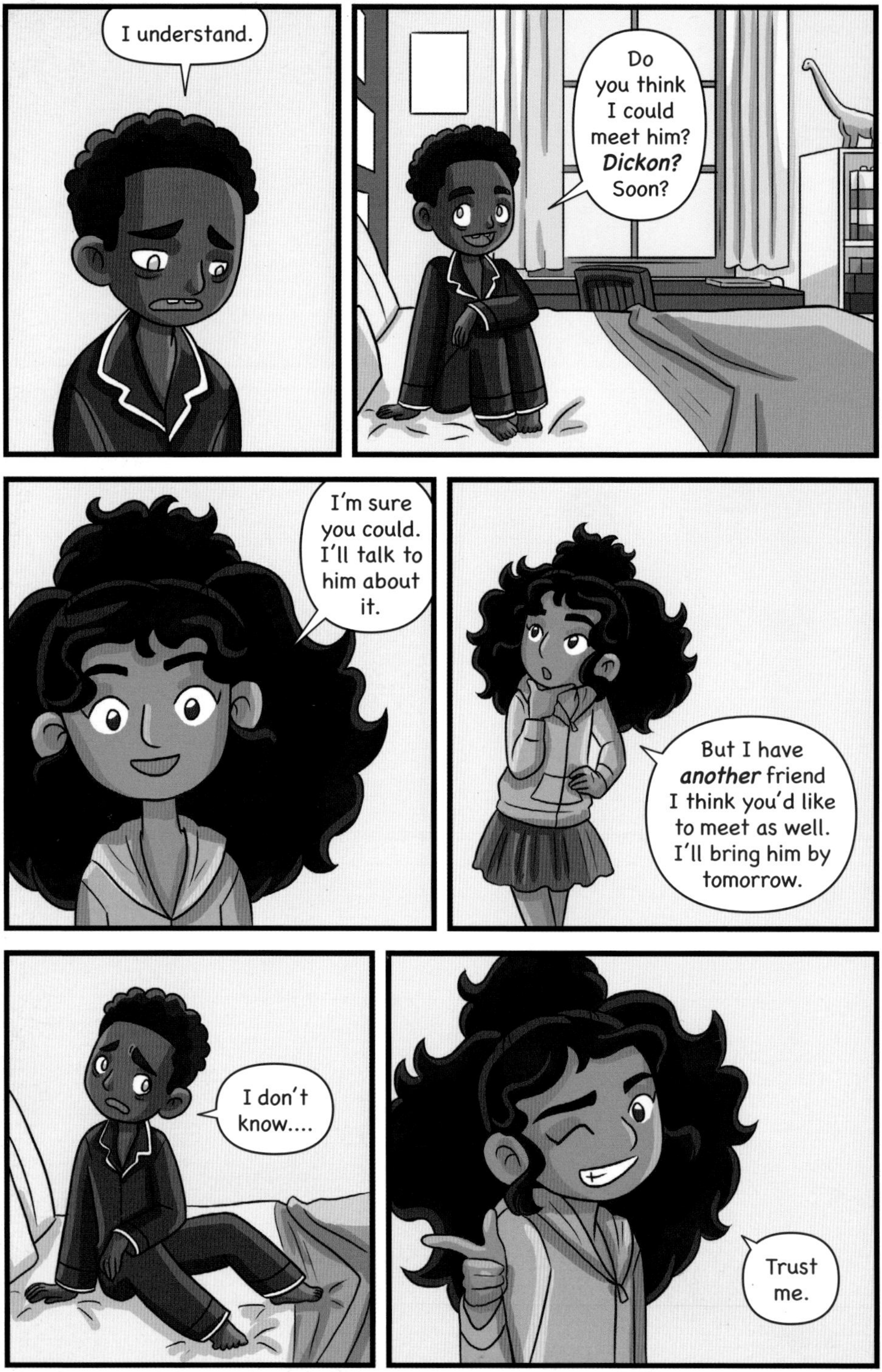
I understand.
Do you think I could meet him? *Dickon?* Soon?
I'm sure you could. I'll talk to him about it.
But I have *another* friend I think you'd like to meet as well. I'll bring him by tomorrow.
I don't know....
Trust me.

The_Secret_Garden

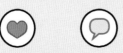

The_Secret_Garden Did you know that irises are one of the earliest flowers to bloom? We're sure happy to see them up here after all this gray weather. After they're done blooming, you can separate out the clumps, save them, and have even more irises next year!

UnicornBaker4Life

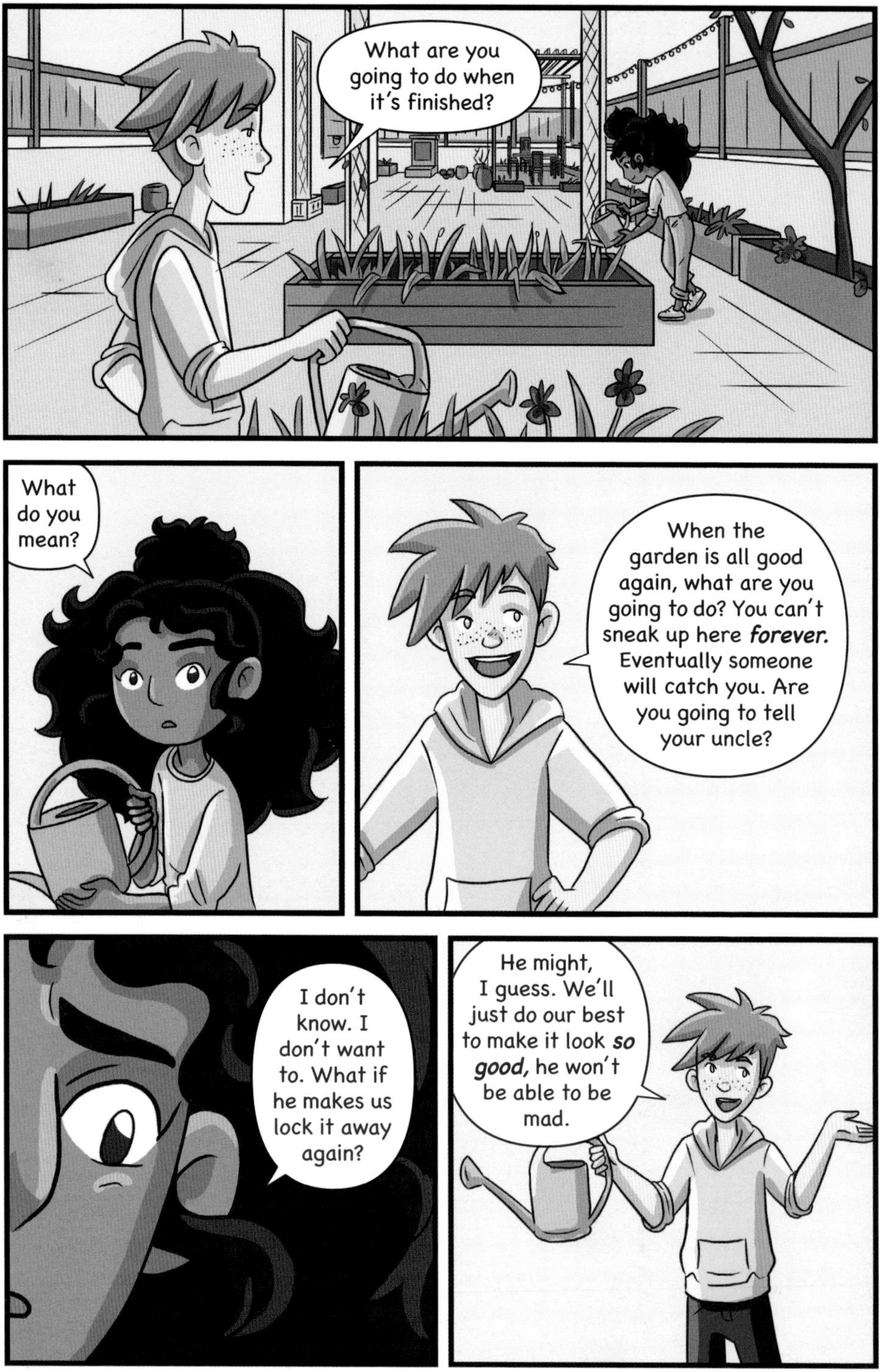
What are you going to do when it's finished?
What do you mean?
When the garden is all good again, what are you going to do? You can't sneak up here *forever.* Eventually someone will catch you. Are you going to tell your uncle?
I don't know. I don't want to. What if he makes us lock it away again?
He might, I guess. We'll just do our best to make it look *so good,* he won't be able to be mad.

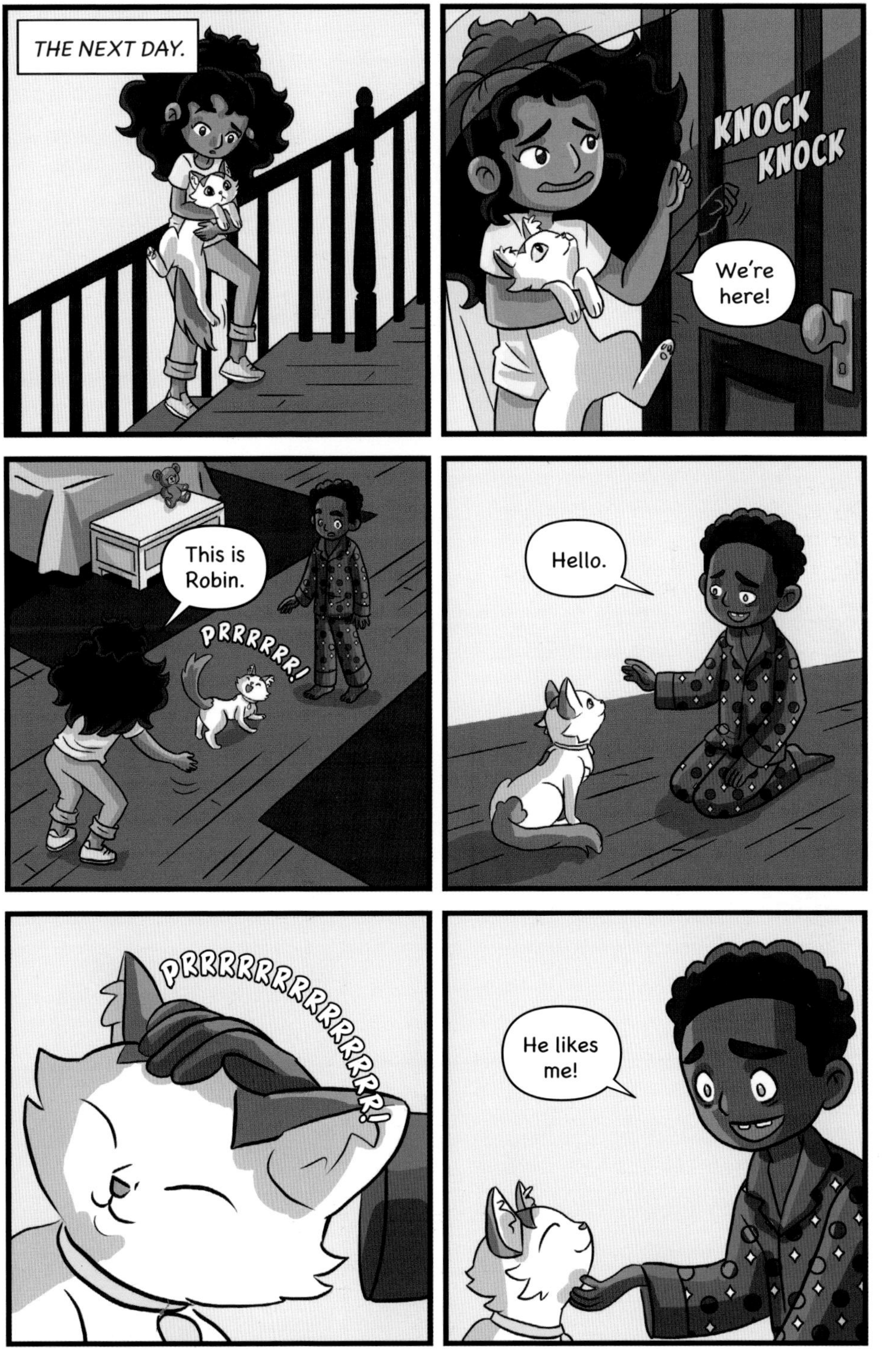
THE NEXT DAY.
KNOCK KNOCK
We're here!
This is Robin.
PRRRRRRR!
Hello.
PRRRRRRRRRRRRRRR!
He likes me!

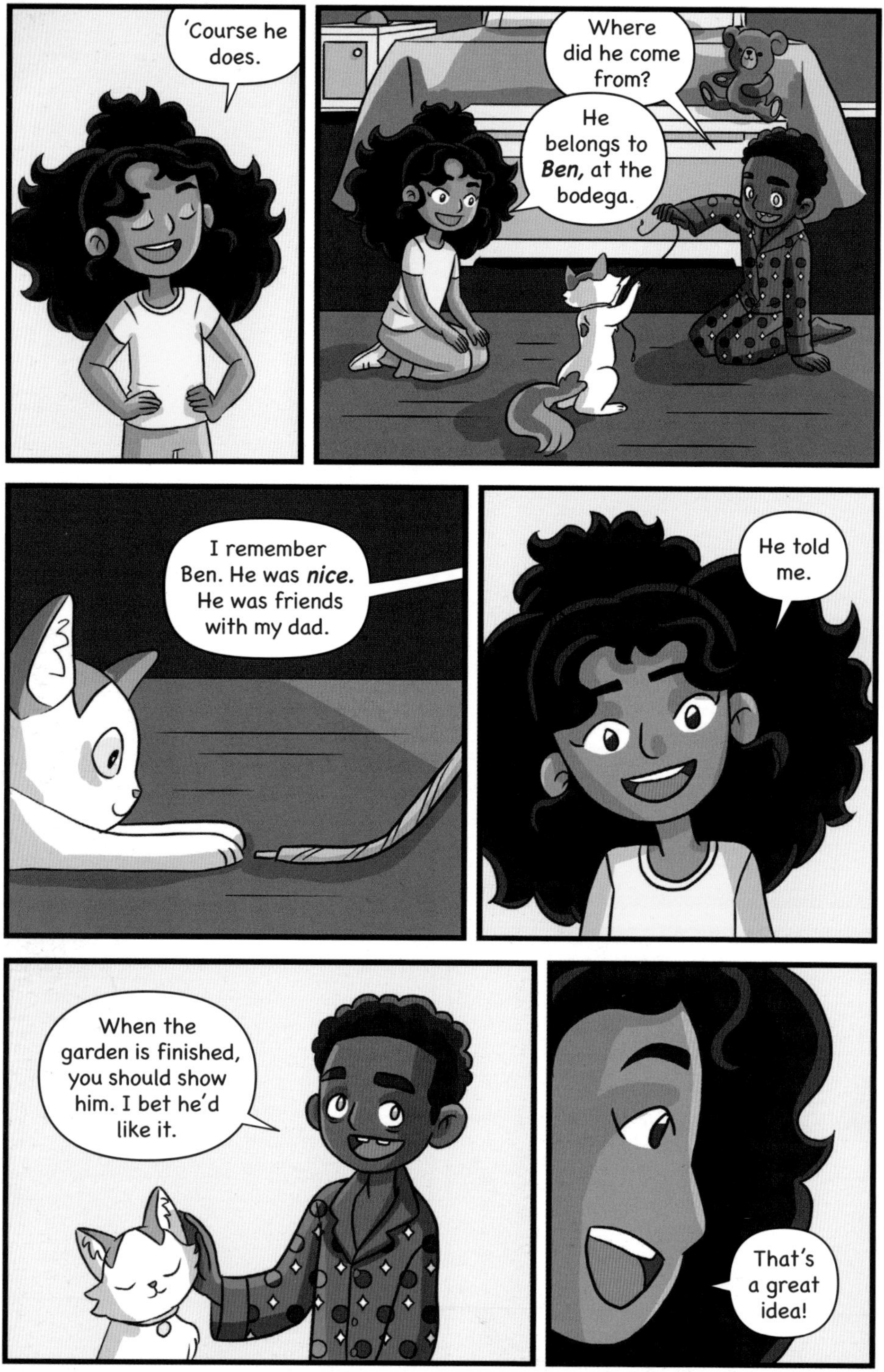
'Course he does.
Where did he come from?
He belongs to *Ben,* at the bodega.
I remember Ben. He was *nice.* He was friends with my dad.
He told me.
When the garden is finished, you should show him. I bet he'd like it.
That's a great idea!

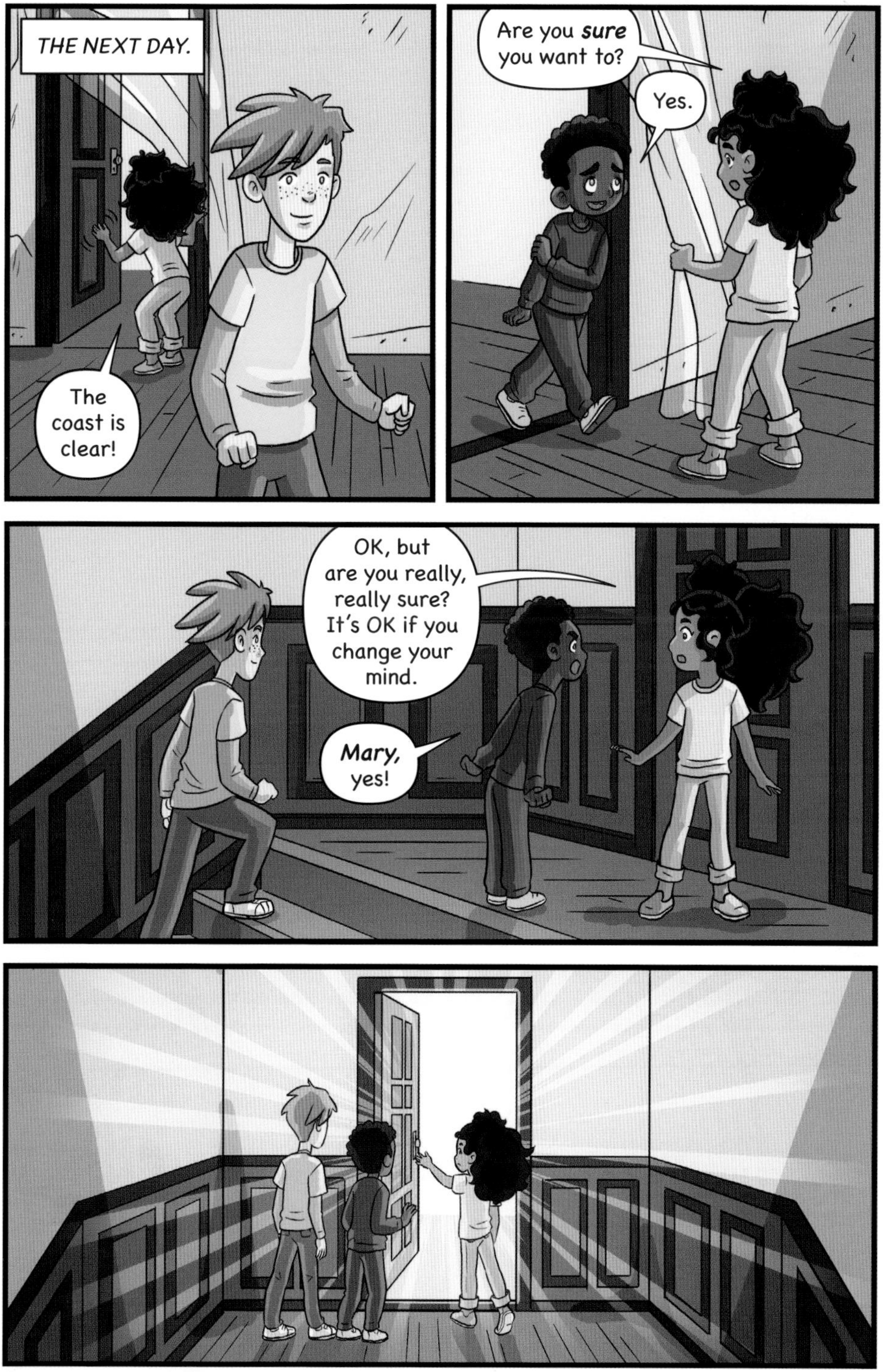
THE NEXT DAY.
The coast is clear!
Are you **sure** you want to?
Yes.
OK, but are you really, really sure? It's OK if you change your mind.
Mary, yes!

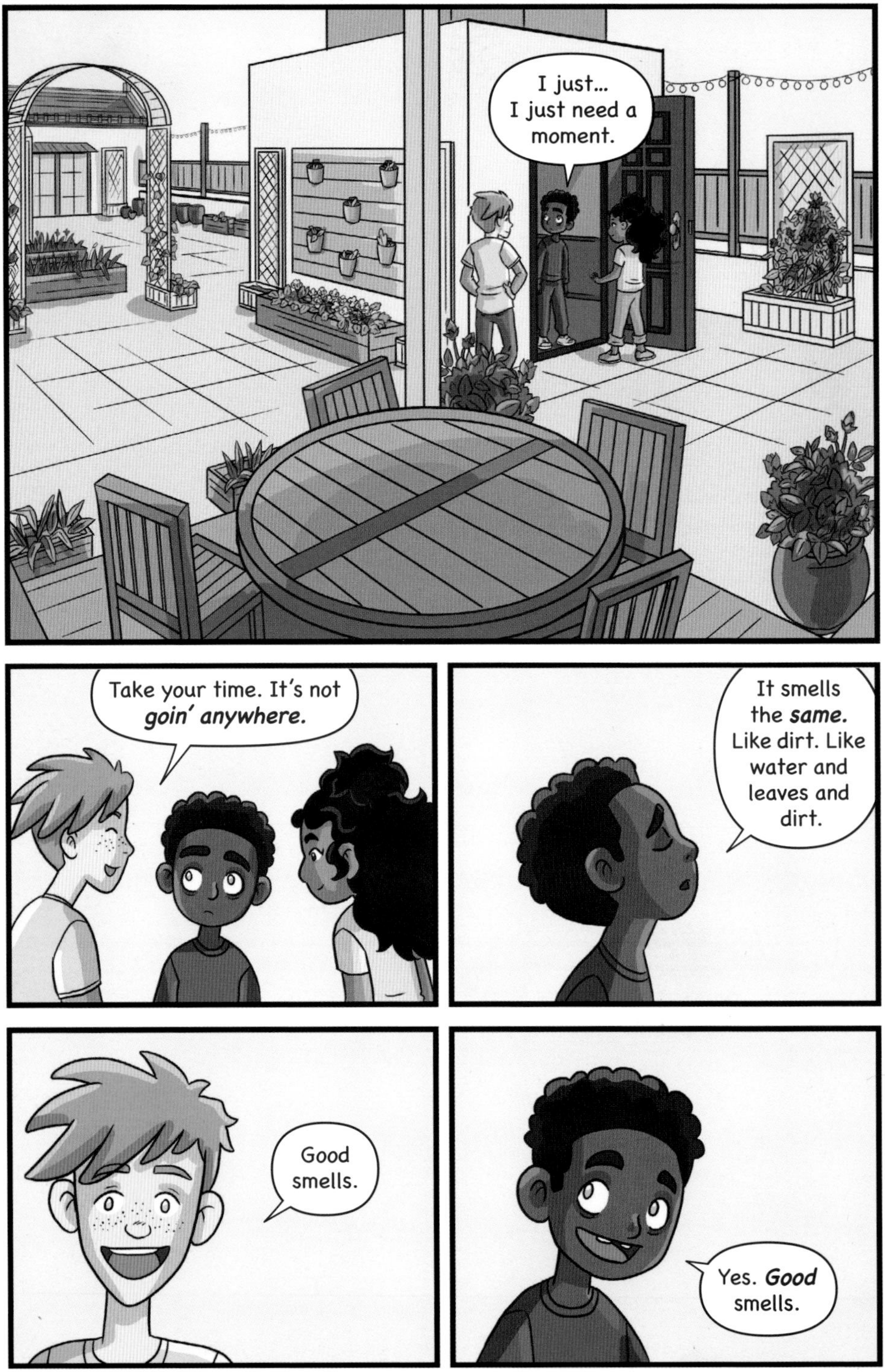
I just...
I just need a moment.
Take your time. It's not *goin' anywhere.*
It smells the ***same.*** Like dirt. Like water and leaves and dirt.
Good smells.
Yes. ***Good*** smells.

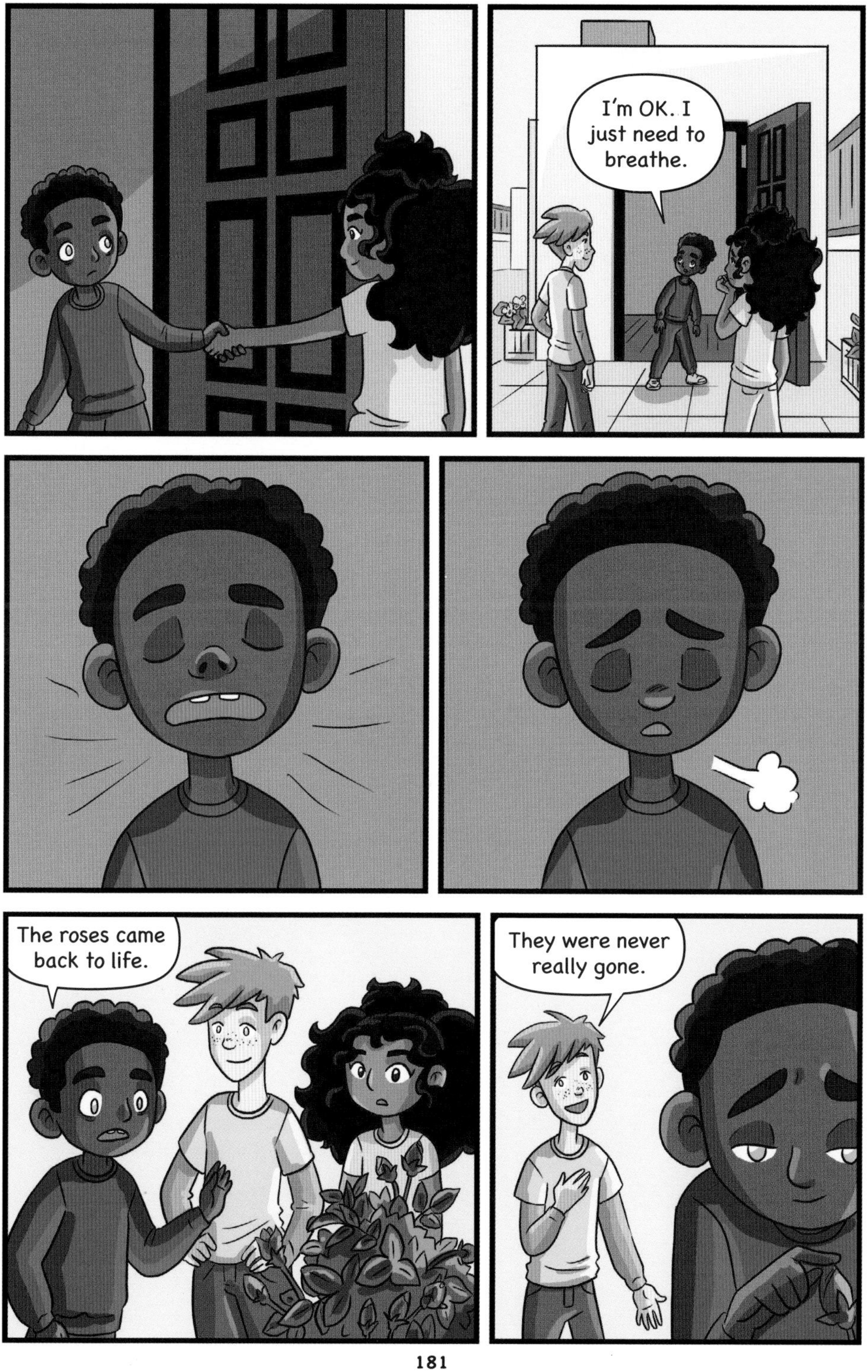
I'm OK. I just need to breathe.
The roses came back to life.
They were never really gone.

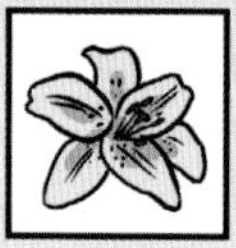

The_Secret_Garden

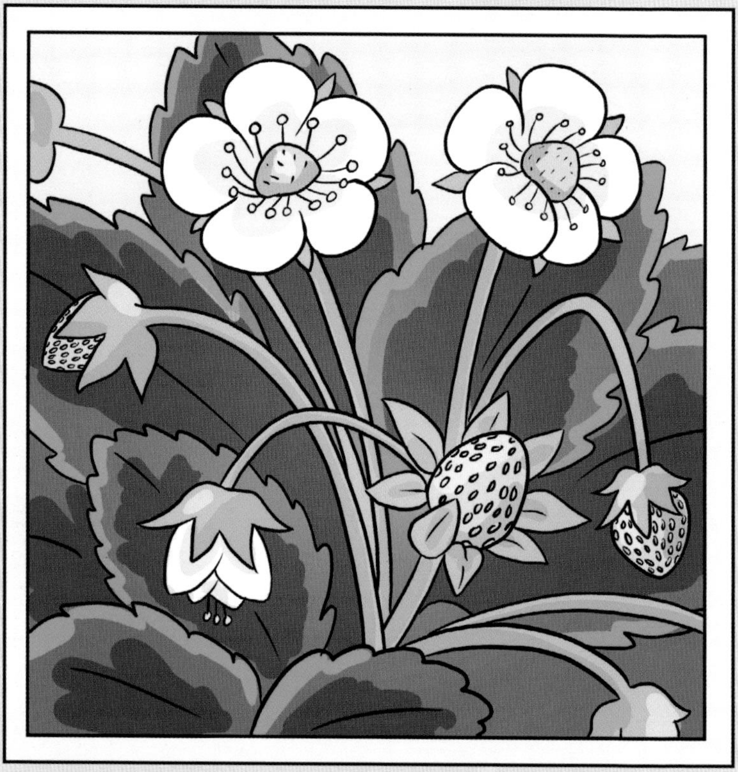

The_Secret_Garden These baby strawberries were just little white flowers a few days ago! They'll be super tasty soon... if the birds don't get them first. We're going to put up some mesh netting around them to help keep them safe! 🐦

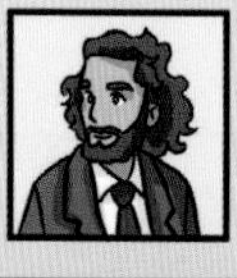

Plant_Prof

187

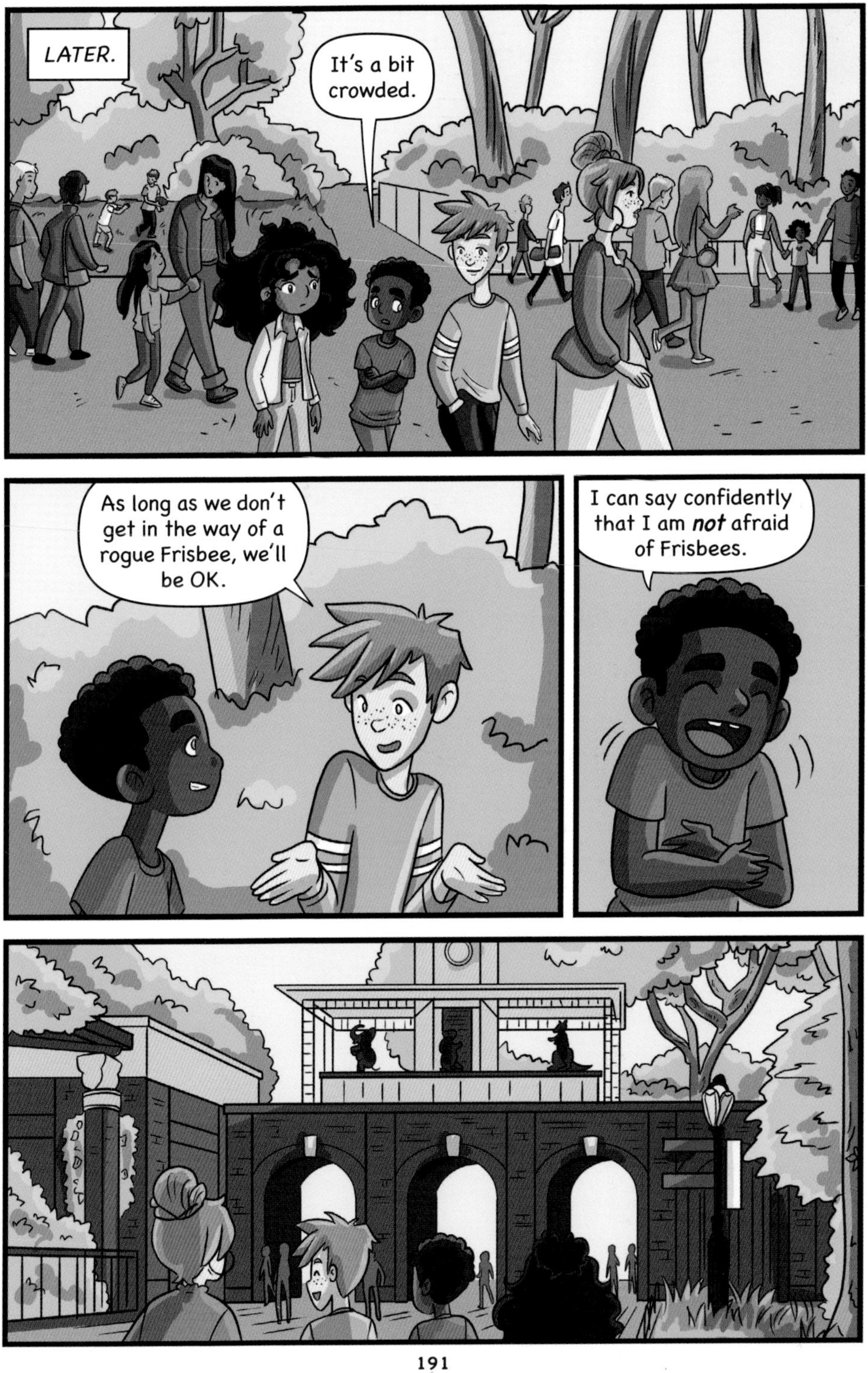
LATER.
It's a bit crowded.
As long as we don't get in the way of a rogue Frisbee, we'll be OK.
I can say confidently that I am *not* afraid of Frisbees.

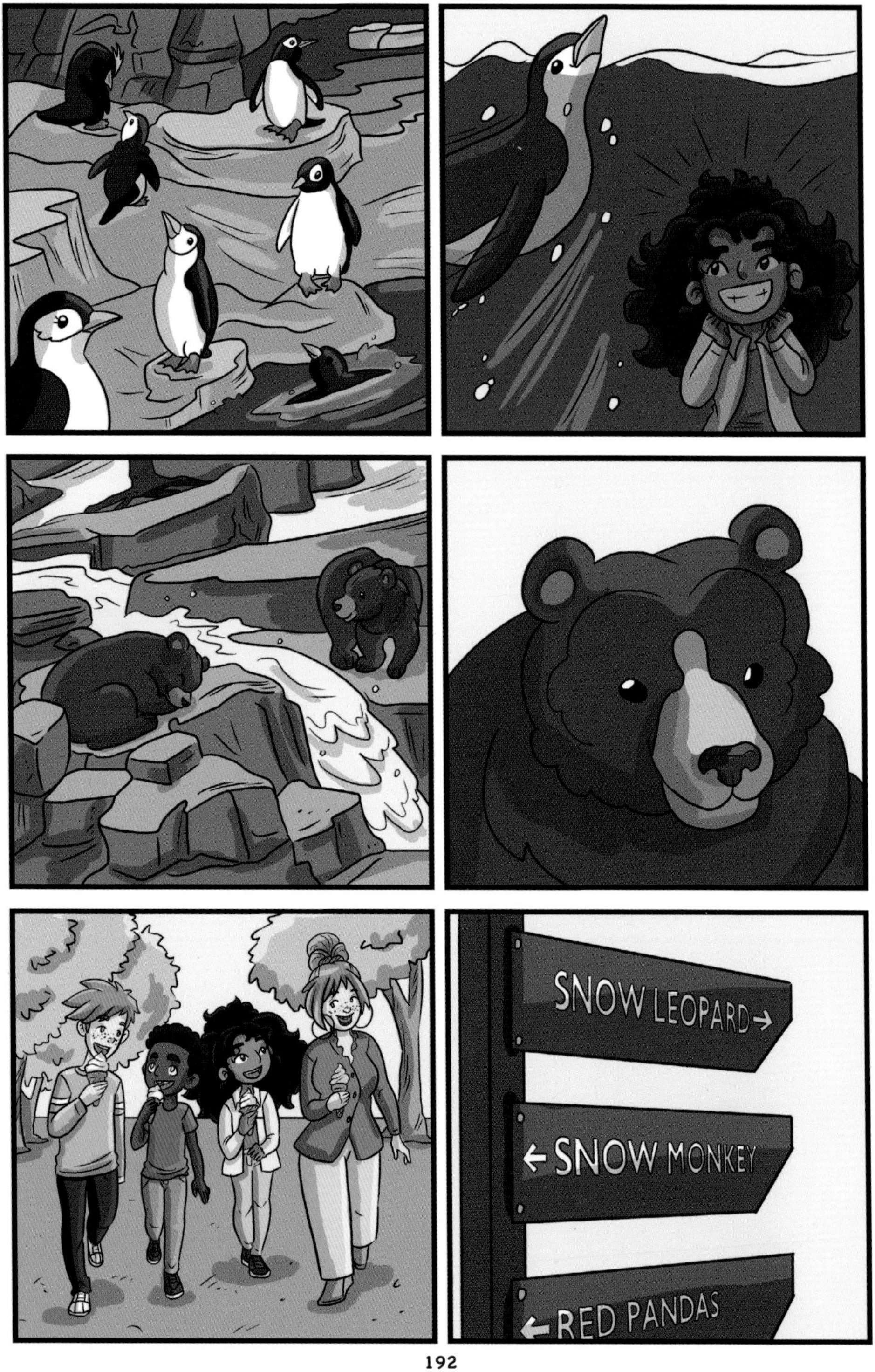
SNOW LEOPARD →
← SNOW MONKEY
← RED PANDAS

Martha

eMAIL

INBOX | Starred | Sent | Drafts | Spam

NEW MESSAGE

TO: archibald_craven@craveninc.com

FROM: martha_cravenhousehold@craveninc.com

SUBJECT: Mary Update

Mr. Craven,

I hope you're having a good time in Asia and not working too hard! Spring has finally truly sprung here in NYC and I wanted to just give you an update on the house. I've gotten to know Mary, and even though she started out a little prickly, she's turned out to be a great girl. She and Dickon have become fast friends! Colin is doing well, really well, in fact. He was asking about you just today. Maybe we can set up a time for you to have a video call with him? Just a thought.

Best,
Martha

SEND

Personal

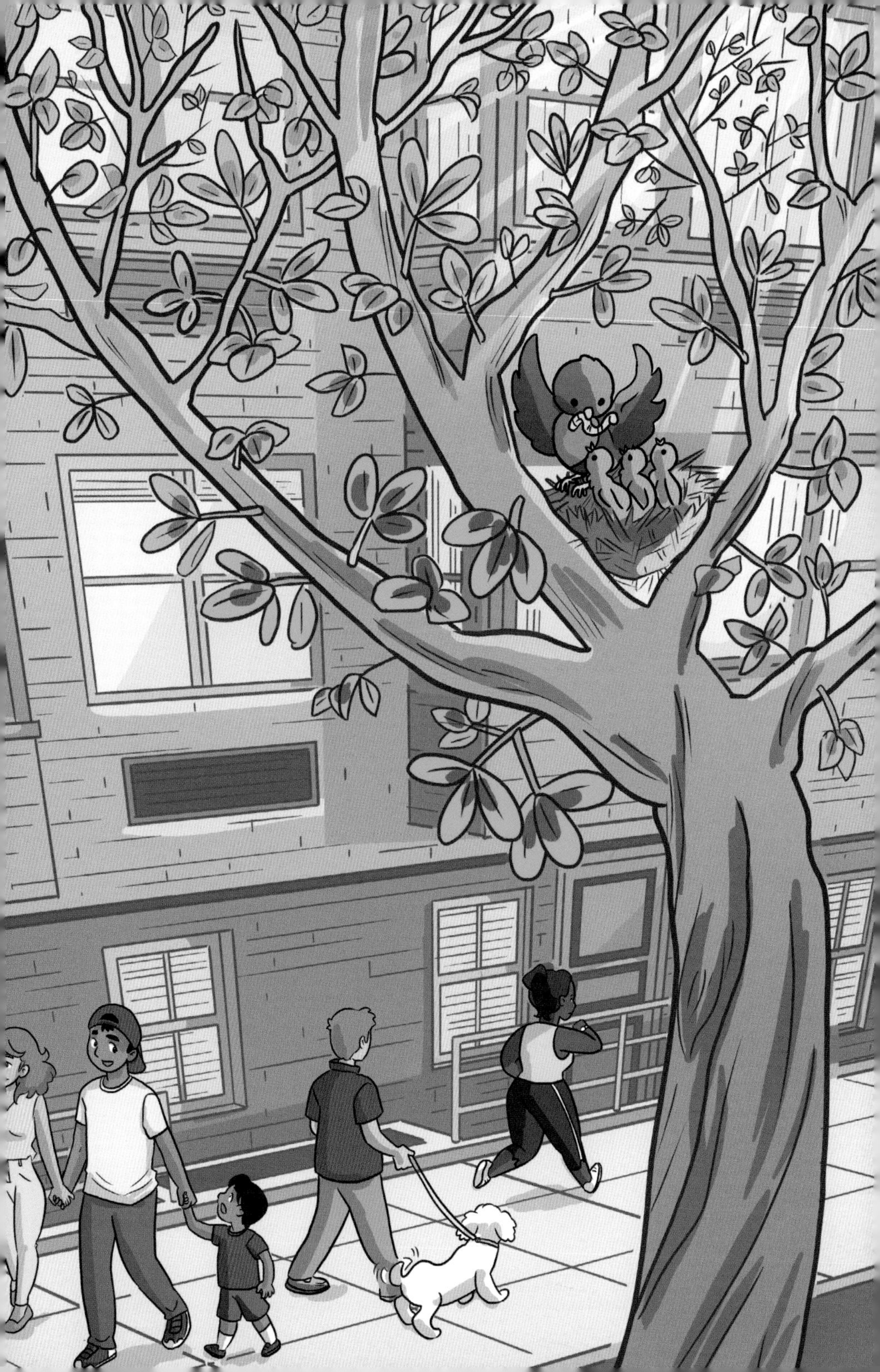

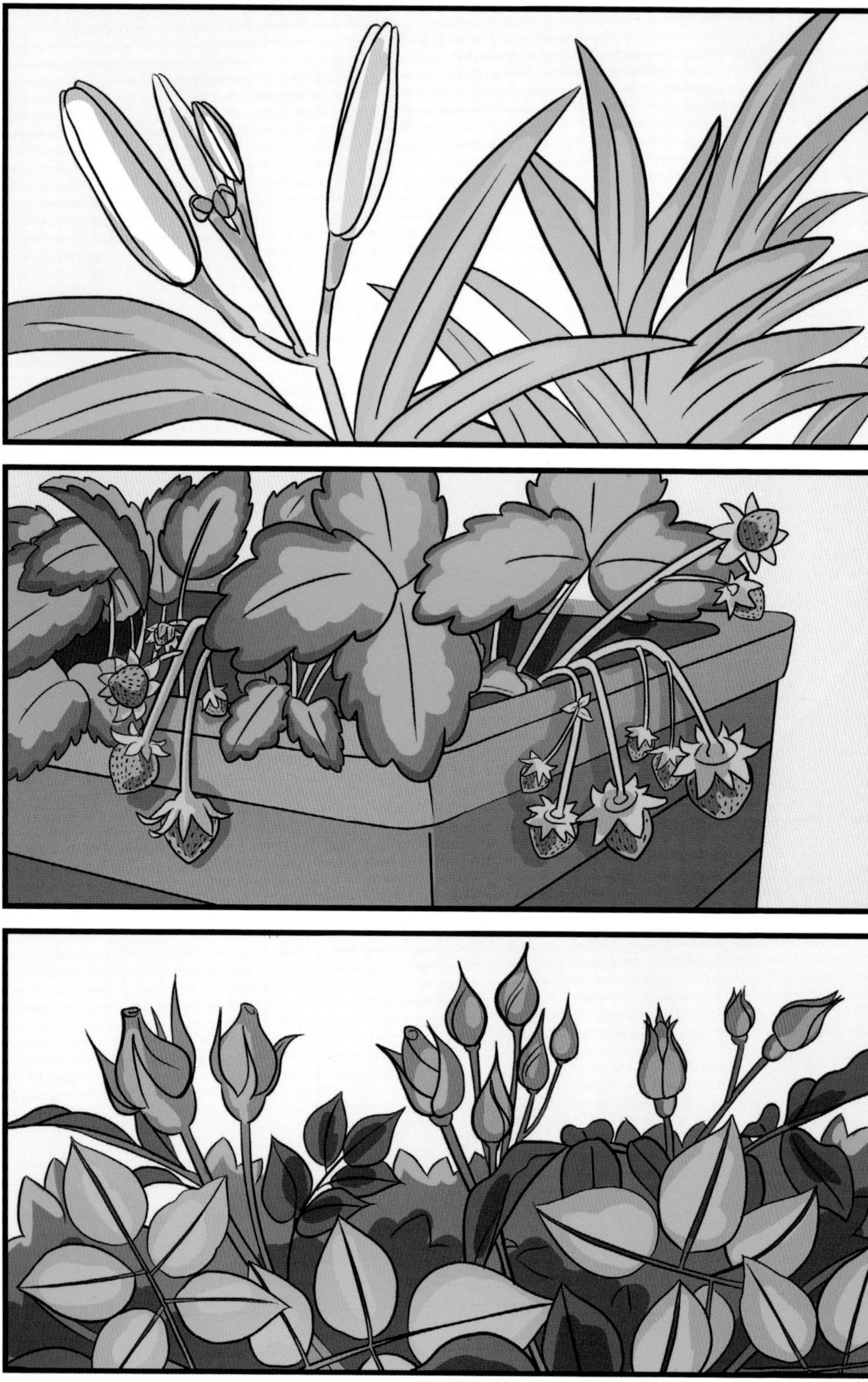

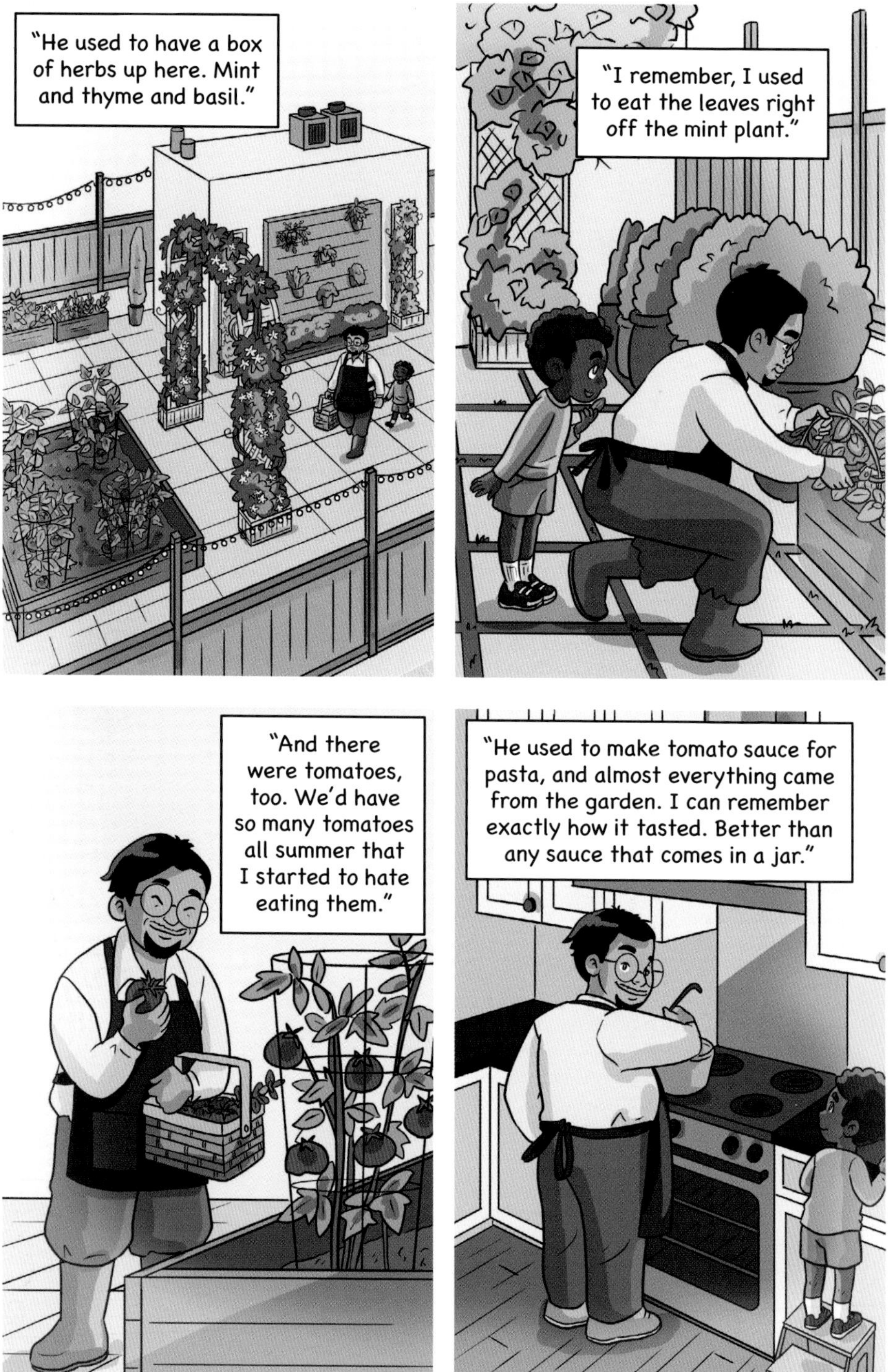
"He used to have a box of herbs up here. Mint and thyme and basil."
"I remember, I used to eat the leaves right off the mint plant."
"And there were tomatoes, too. We'd have so many tomatoes all summer that I started to hate eating them."
"He used to make tomato sauce for pasta, and almost everything came from the garden. I can remember exactly how it tasted. Better than any sauce that comes in a jar."

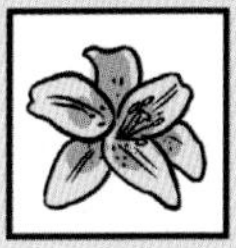

The_Secret_Garden

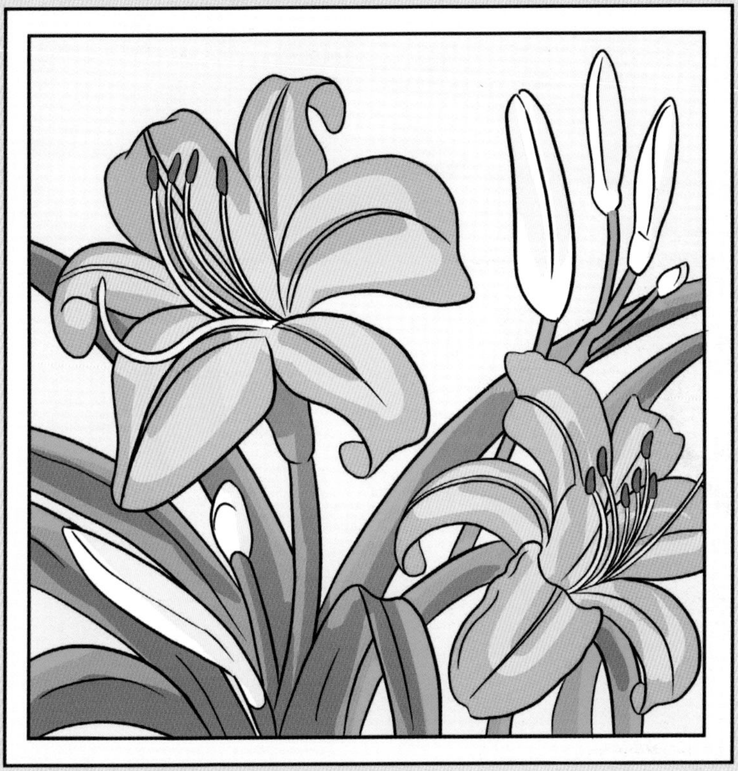

The_Secret_Garden Remember that ugly little bulb? It's a beautiful lily now! We were worried that it wouldn't grow in the raised beds, but now it's rocking this giant bloom. :) We also read online that daylily buds are edible—would you ever try one?

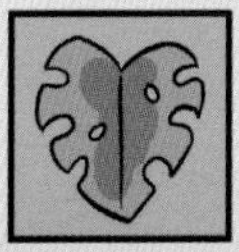

Plant-tasticPlants

The_Secret_Garden

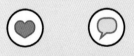

The_Secret_Garden Happy #Caturday! Did you know that both catnip plants and cats love a hot, sunny spot?

therealcupoftea

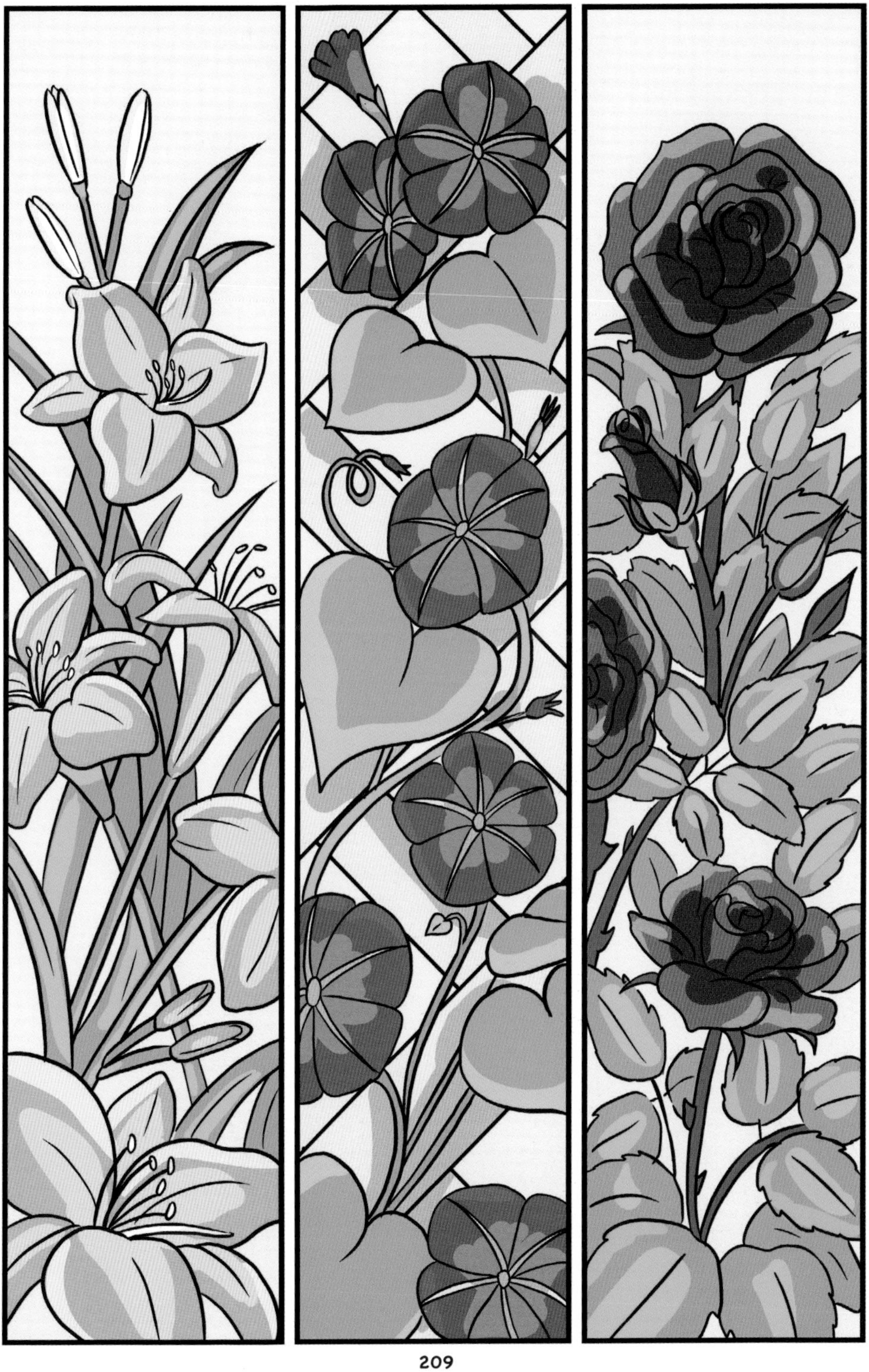

The_Secret_Garden

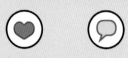

The_Secret_Garden We planted all the herbs where we'd brush past them while watering, pruning, and mulching…they smell amazing!

Bugs_And_Hugs

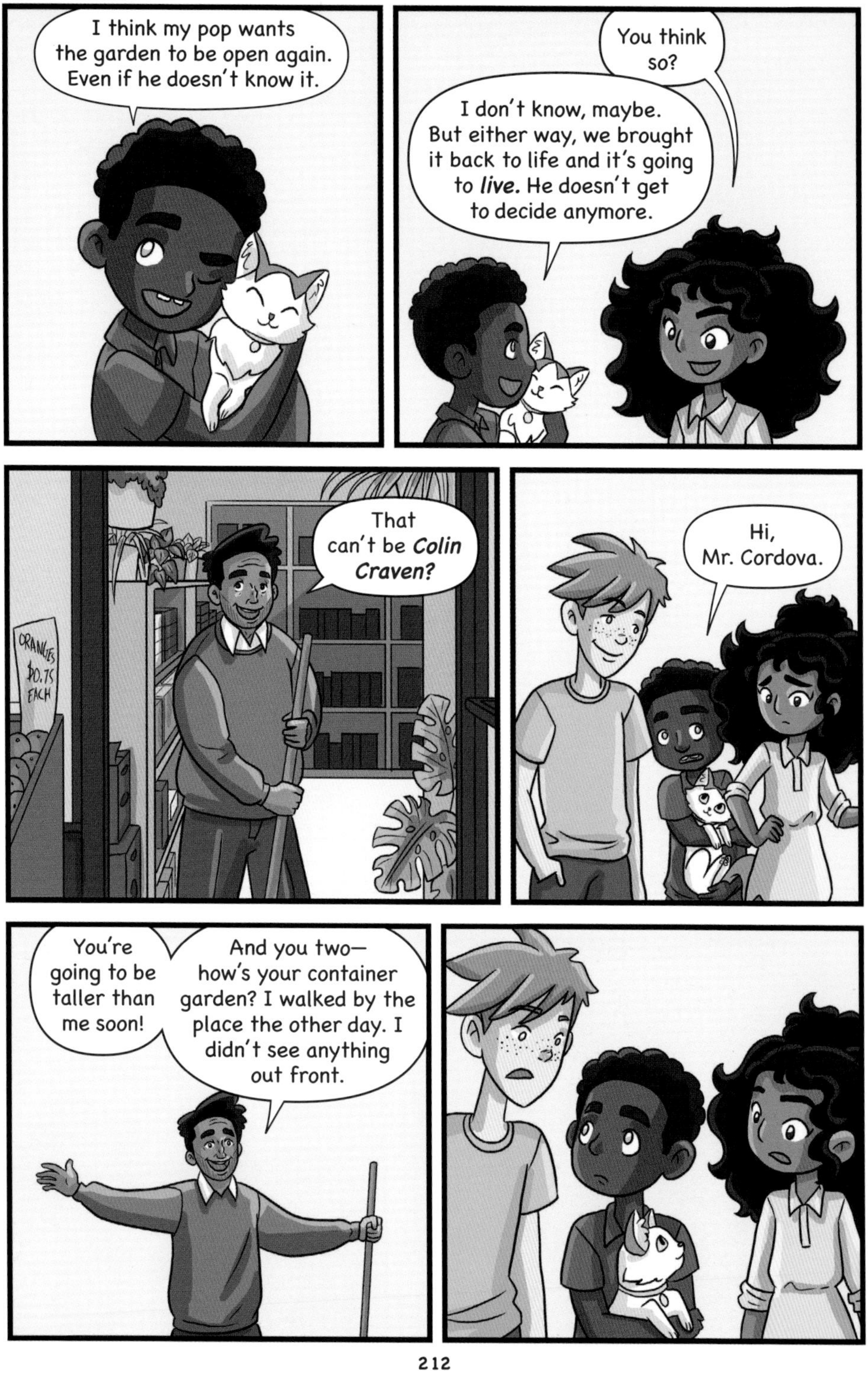
I think my pop wants the garden to be open again. Even if he doesn't know it.
You think so?
I don't know, maybe. But either way, we brought it back to life and it's going to *live.* He doesn't get to decide anymore.
That can't be *Colin Craven?*
ORANGES $0.75 EACH
Hi, Mr. Cordova.
You're going to be taller than me soon!
And you two— how's your container garden? I walked by the place the other day. I didn't see anything out front.

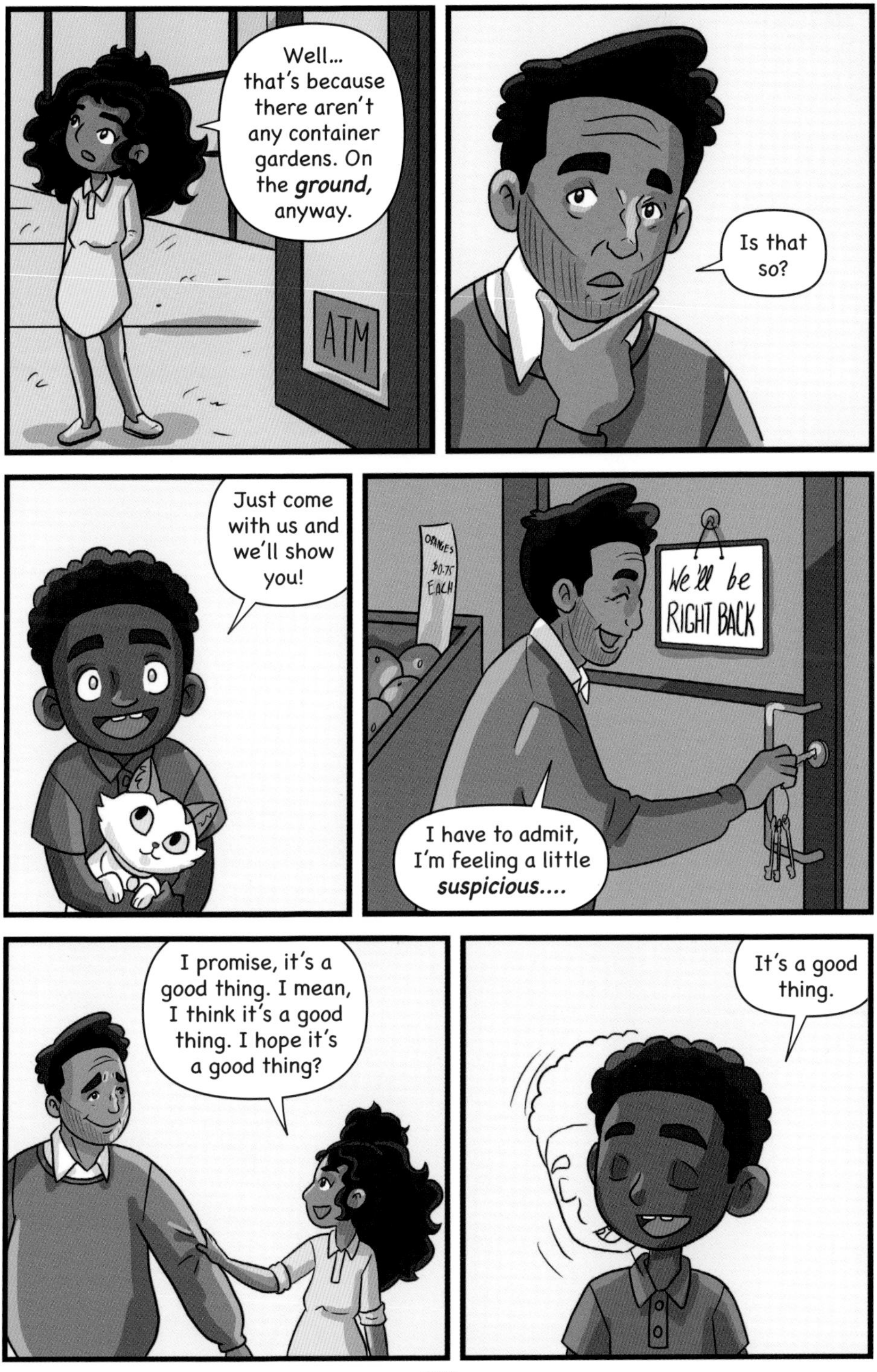
Well... that's because there aren't any container gardens. On the *ground,* anyway.
Is that so?
Just come with us and we'll show you!
ORANGES $0.75 EACH
We'll be RIGHT BACK
I have to admit, I'm feeling a little *suspicious....*
I promise, it's a good thing. I mean, I think it's a good thing. I hope it's a good thing?
It's a good thing.

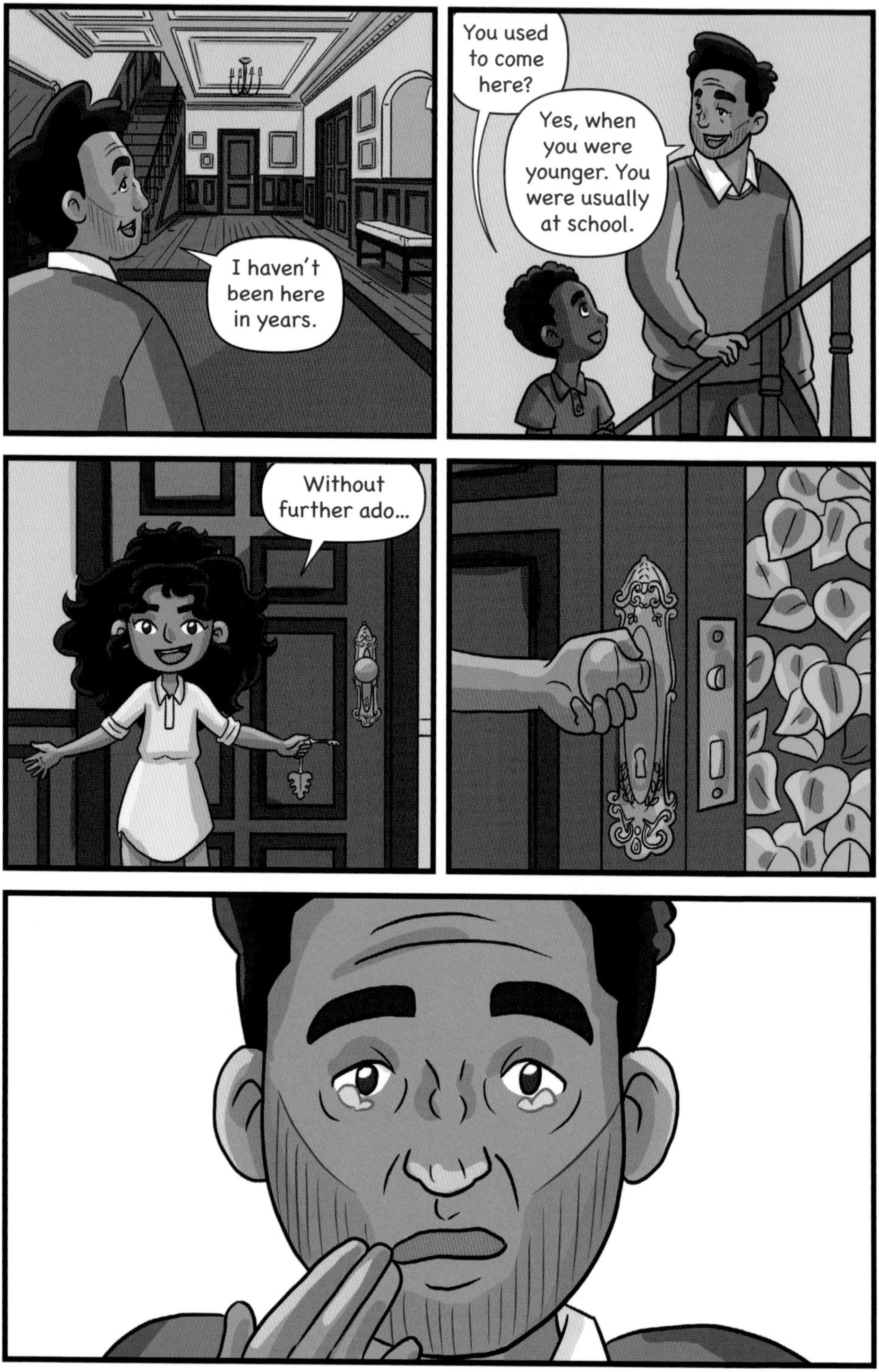
I haven't been here in years.
You used to come here?
Yes, when you were younger. You were usually at school.
Without further ado...

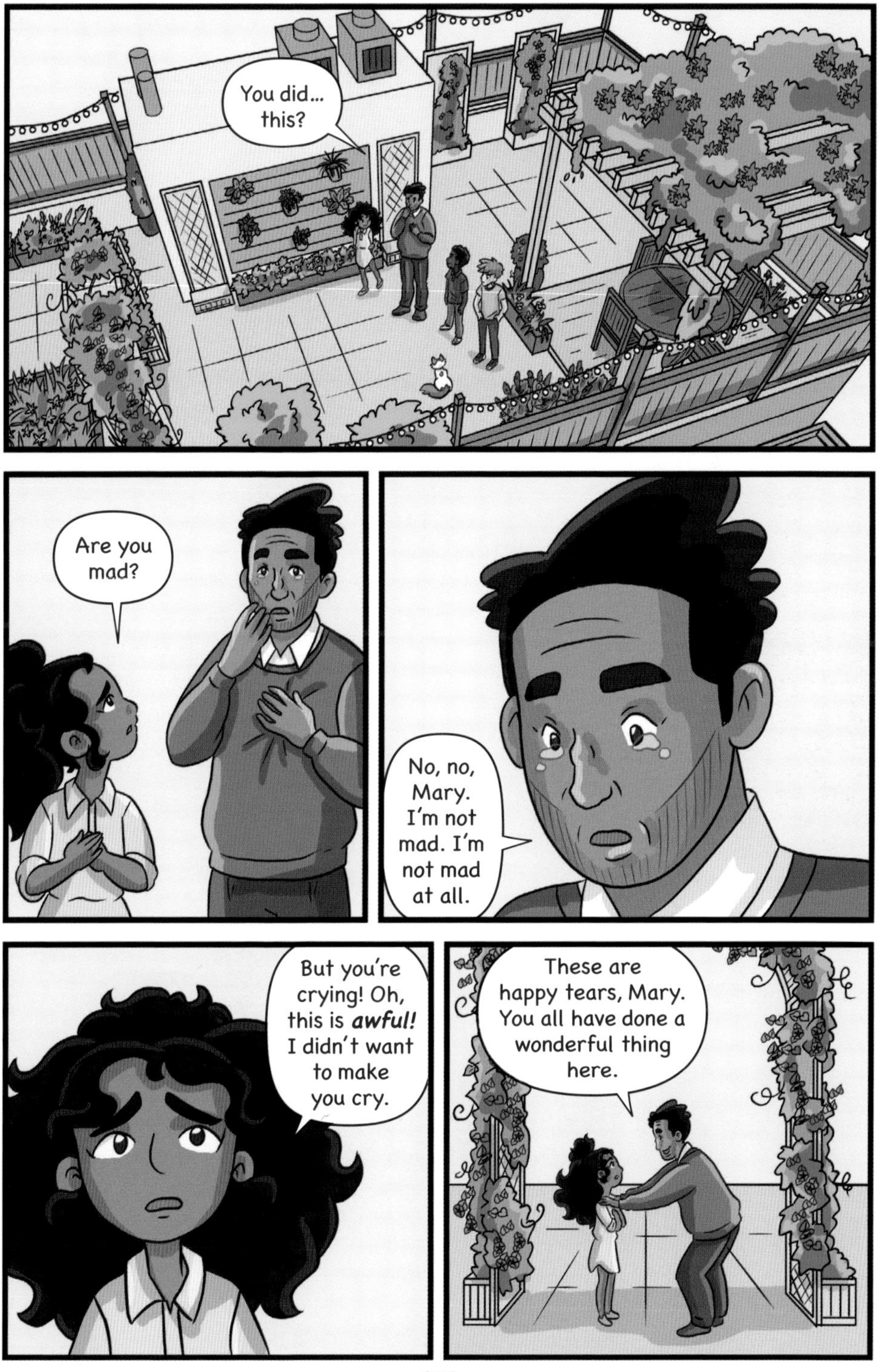
You did... this?
Are you mad?
No, no, Mary. I'm not mad. I'm not mad at all.
But you're crying! Oh, this is ***awful!*** I didn't want to make you cry.
These are happy tears, Mary. You all have done a wonderful thing here.

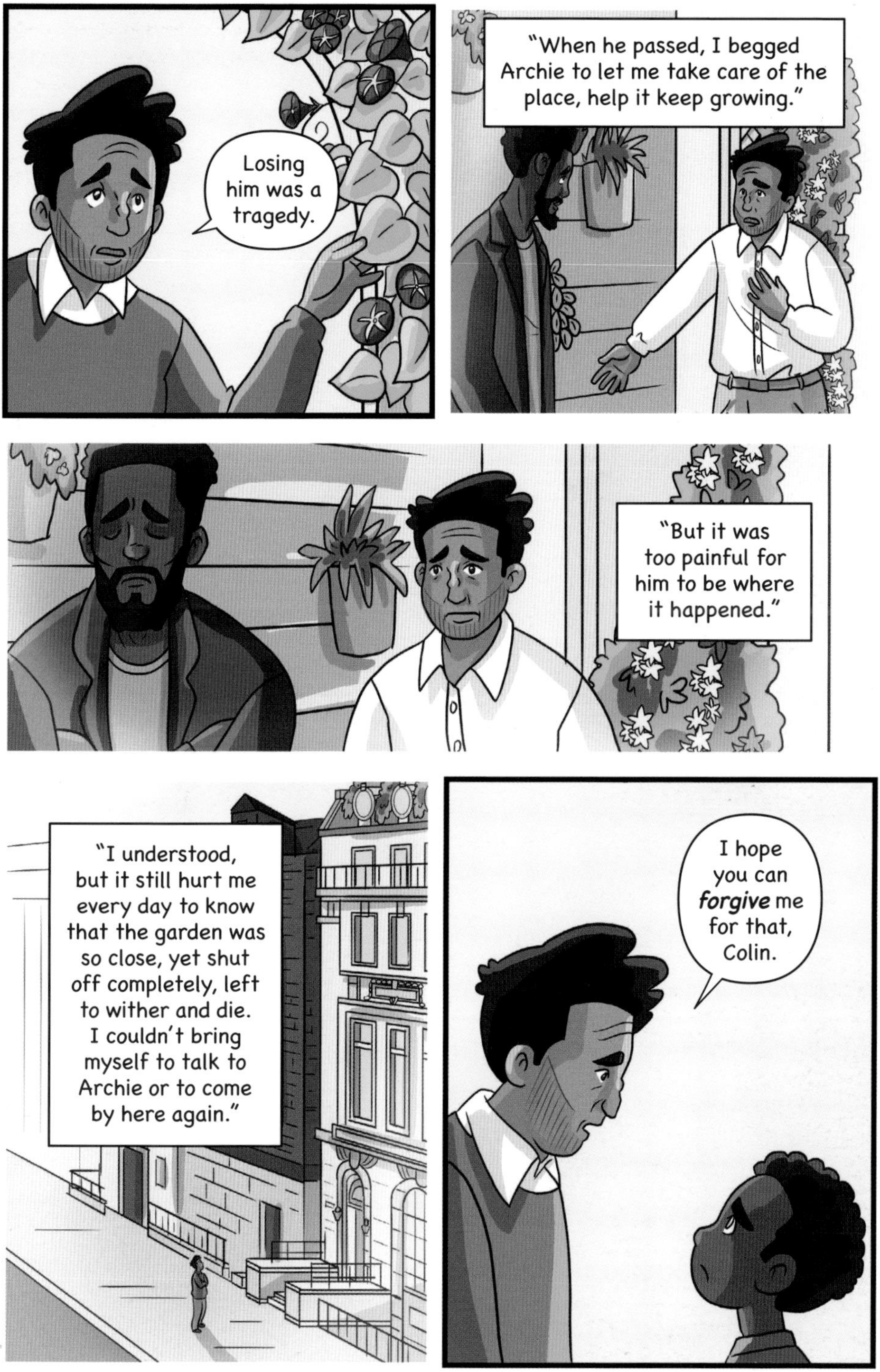
Losing him was a tragedy.
"When he passed, I begged Archie to let me take care of the place, help it keep growing."
"But it was too painful for him to be where it happened."
"I understood, but it still hurt me every day to know that the garden was so close, yet shut off completely, left to wither and die. I couldn't bring myself to talk to Archie or to come by here again."
I hope you can *forgive* me for that, Colin.

219

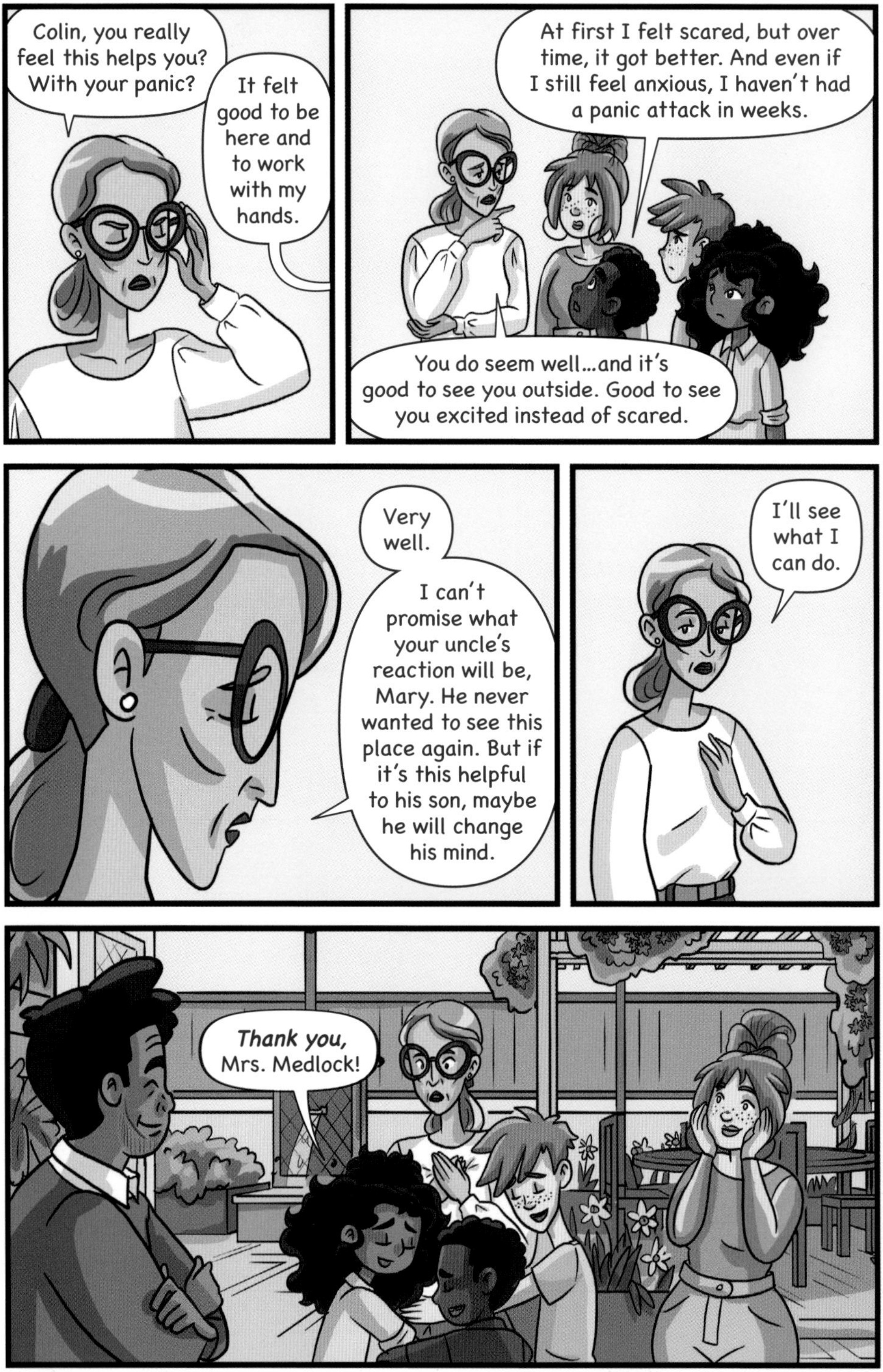
Colin, you really feel this helps you? With your panic?
It felt good to be here and to work with my hands.
At first I felt scared, but over time, it got better. And even if I still feel anxious, I haven't had a panic attack in weeks.
You do seem well...and it's good to see you outside. Good to see you excited instead of scared.
Very well.
I can't promise what your uncle's reaction will be, Mary. He never wanted to see this place again. But if it's this helpful to his son, maybe he will change his mind.
I'll see what I can do.
Thank you, Mrs. Medlock!

Medlock

eMAIL

INBOX | Starred | Sent | Drafts | Spam

NEW MESSAGE

TO: archibald_craven@craveninc.com

FROM: medlock_cravenhousehold@craveninc.com

SUBJECT: Colin

Archie,

I hope things are well in Hong Kong. The purpose of this letter concerns Colin. Don't worry, he is well—he is more than well. He and your niece have found each other and, despite my worries that the girl would be too much for him, they seem to have bonded quite quickly.

I know you had planned to stay in Asia an additional month. But I feel like now would be a good time for you and Colin to talk. I may be overstepping my role here, but I hope you will at least consider coming to see him.

Best wishes,
Constance

SEND

Household finance

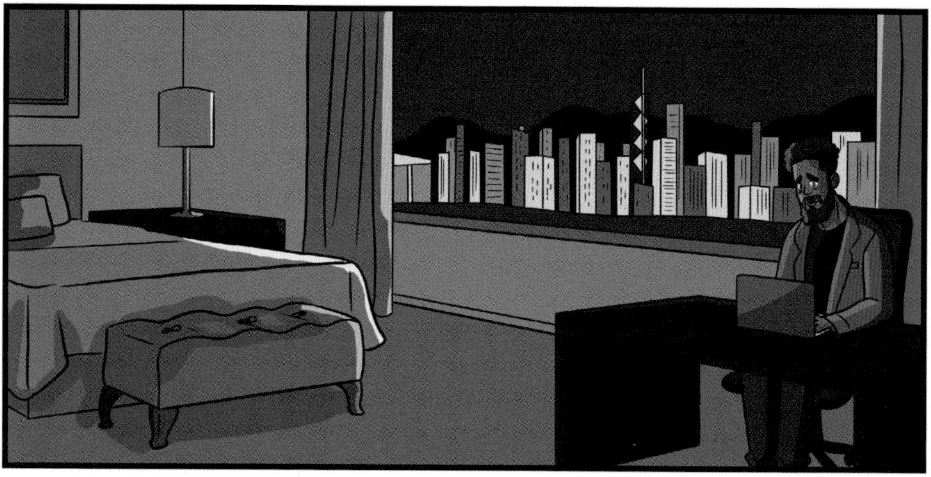

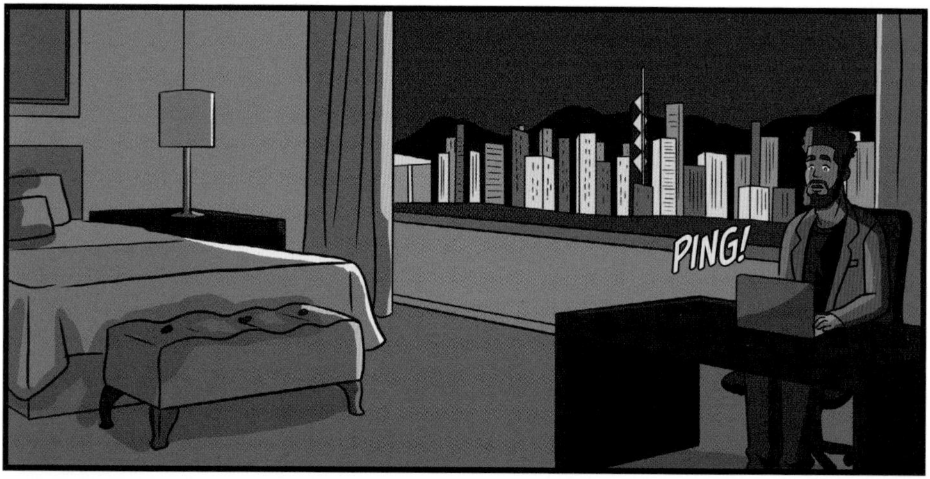
PING!

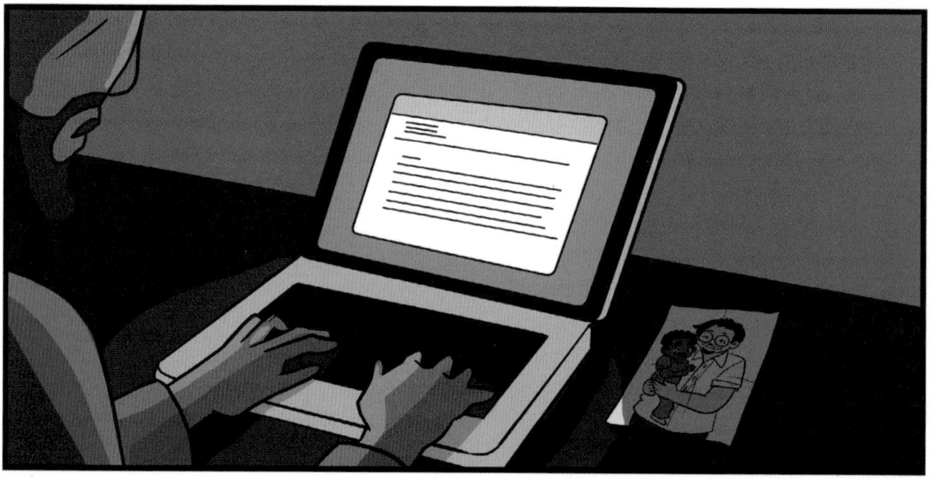

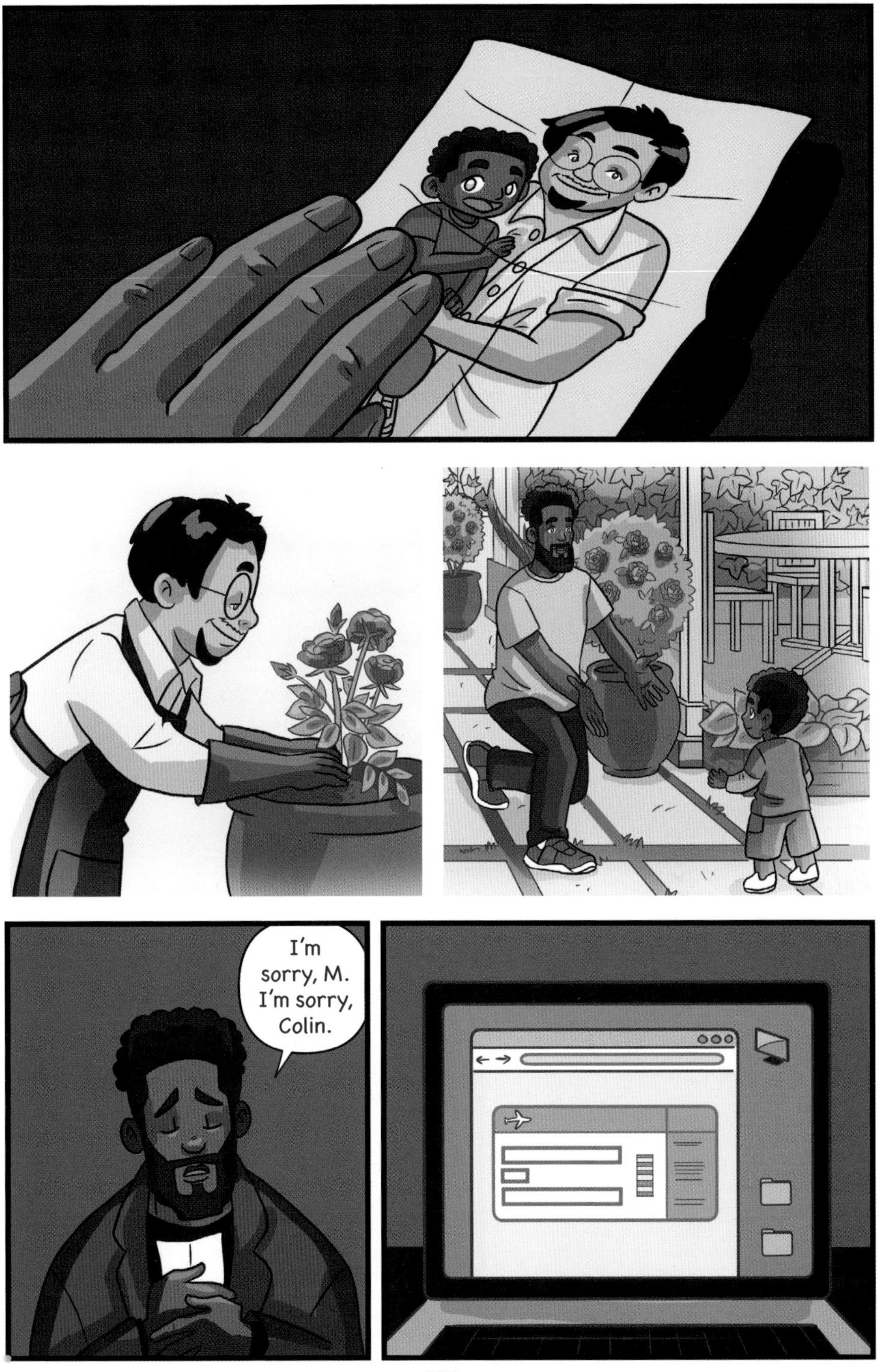
I'm sorry, M. I'm sorry, Colin.

228

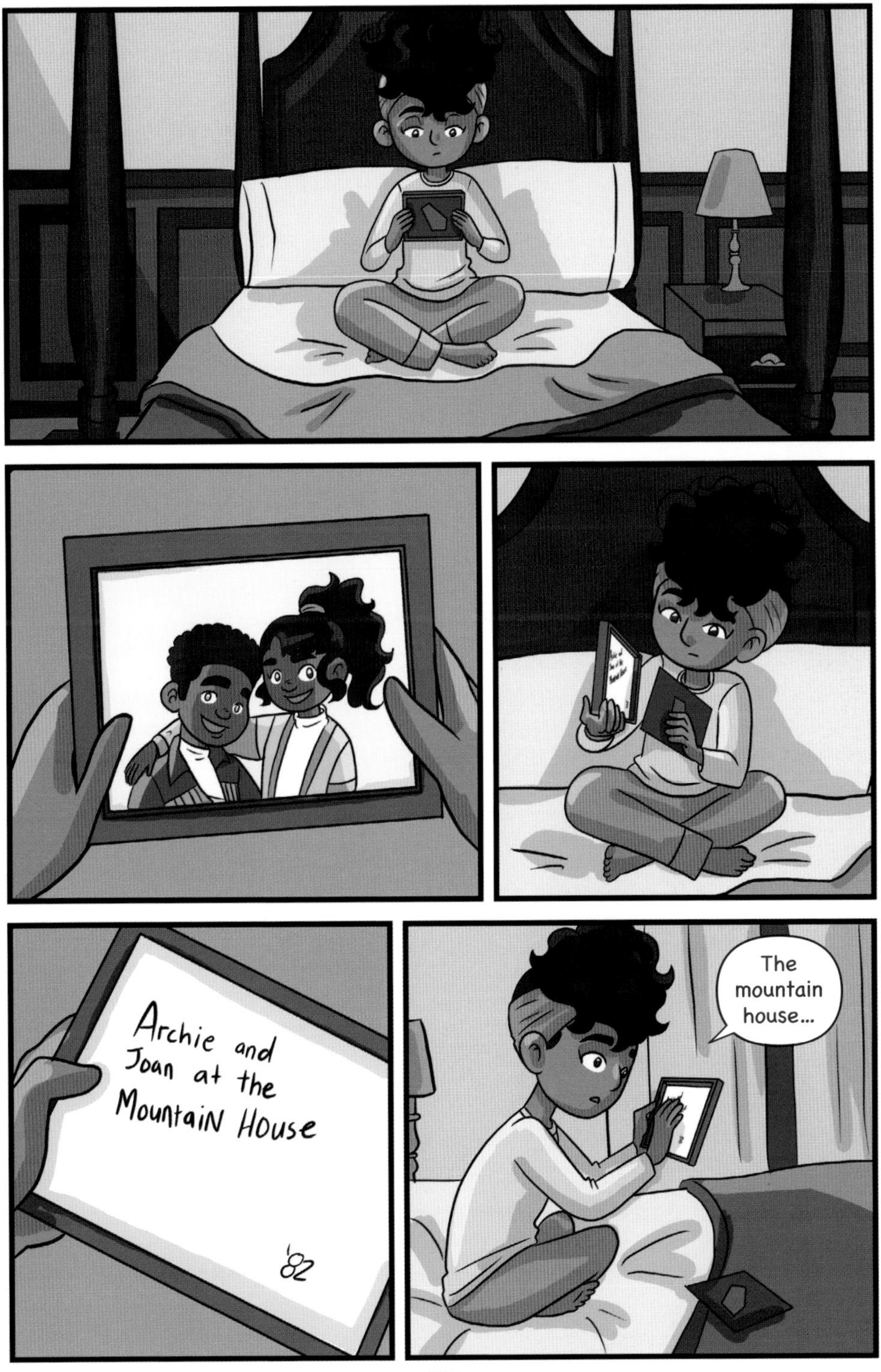
Archie and Joan at the Mountain House
'82
The mountain house...

230

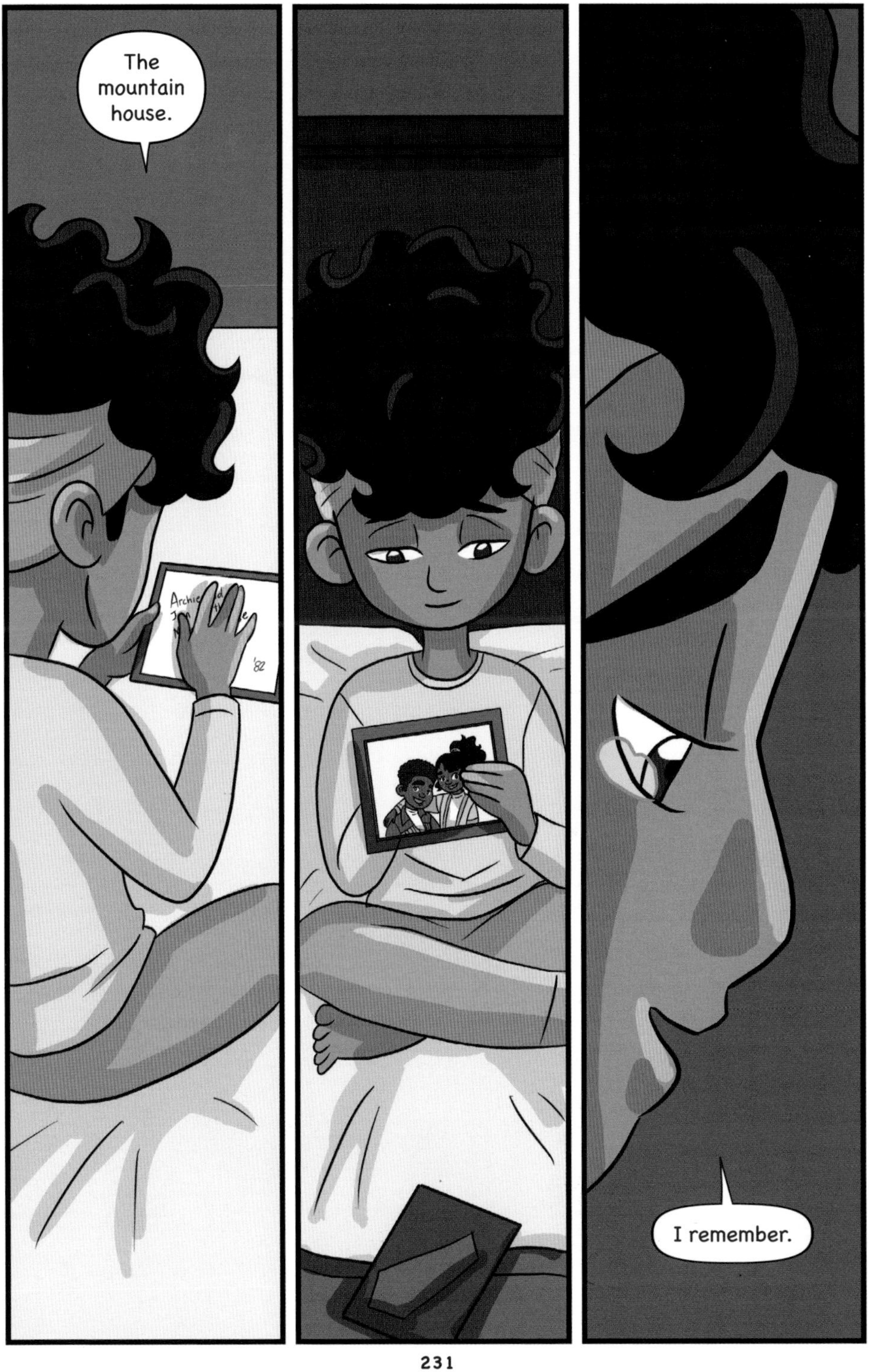
The mountain house.
I remember.

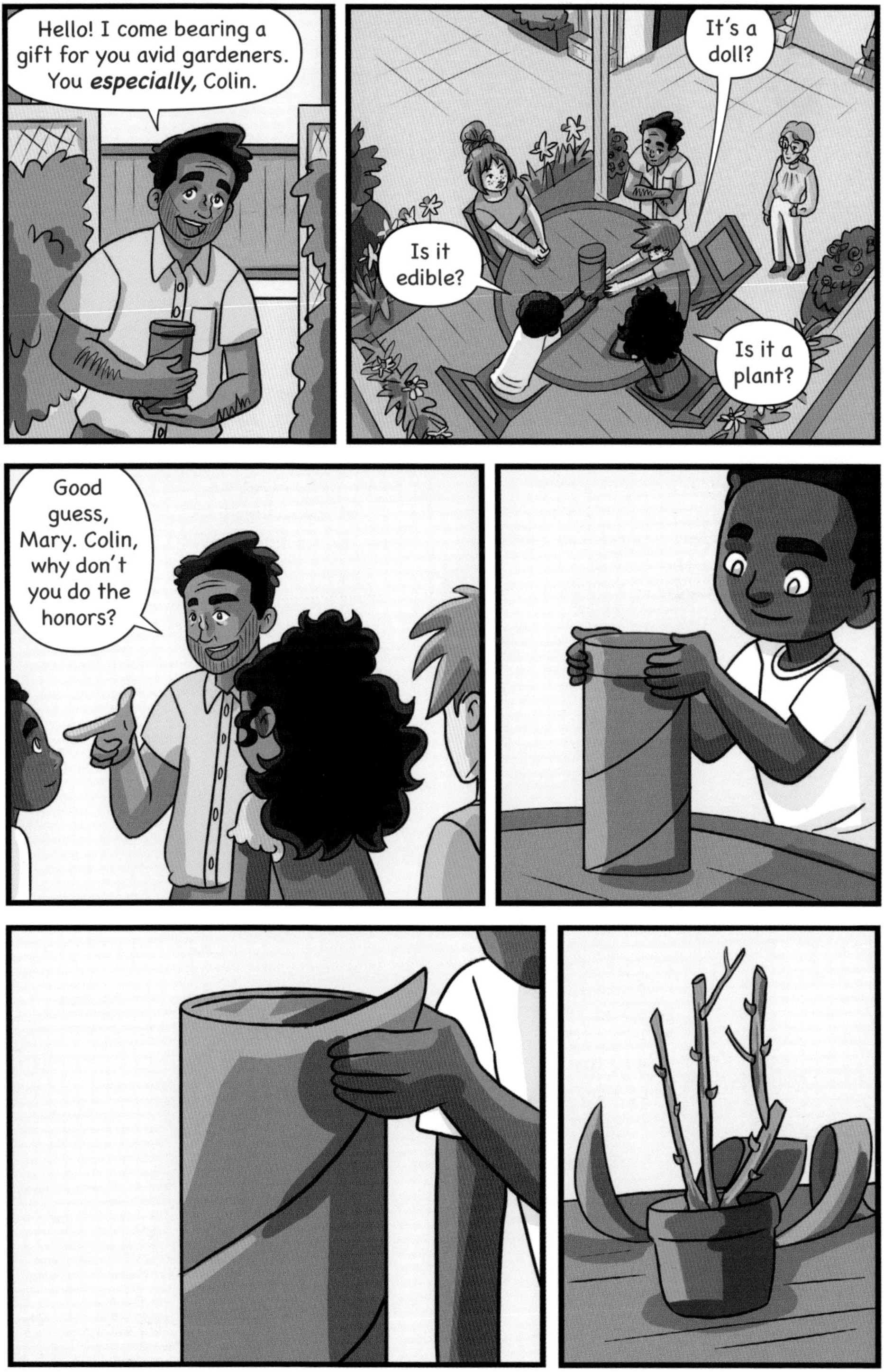

Hello! I come bearing a gift for you avid gardeners. You *especially,* Colin.
It's a doll?
Is it edible?
Is it a plant?
Good guess, Mary. Colin, why don't you do the honors?

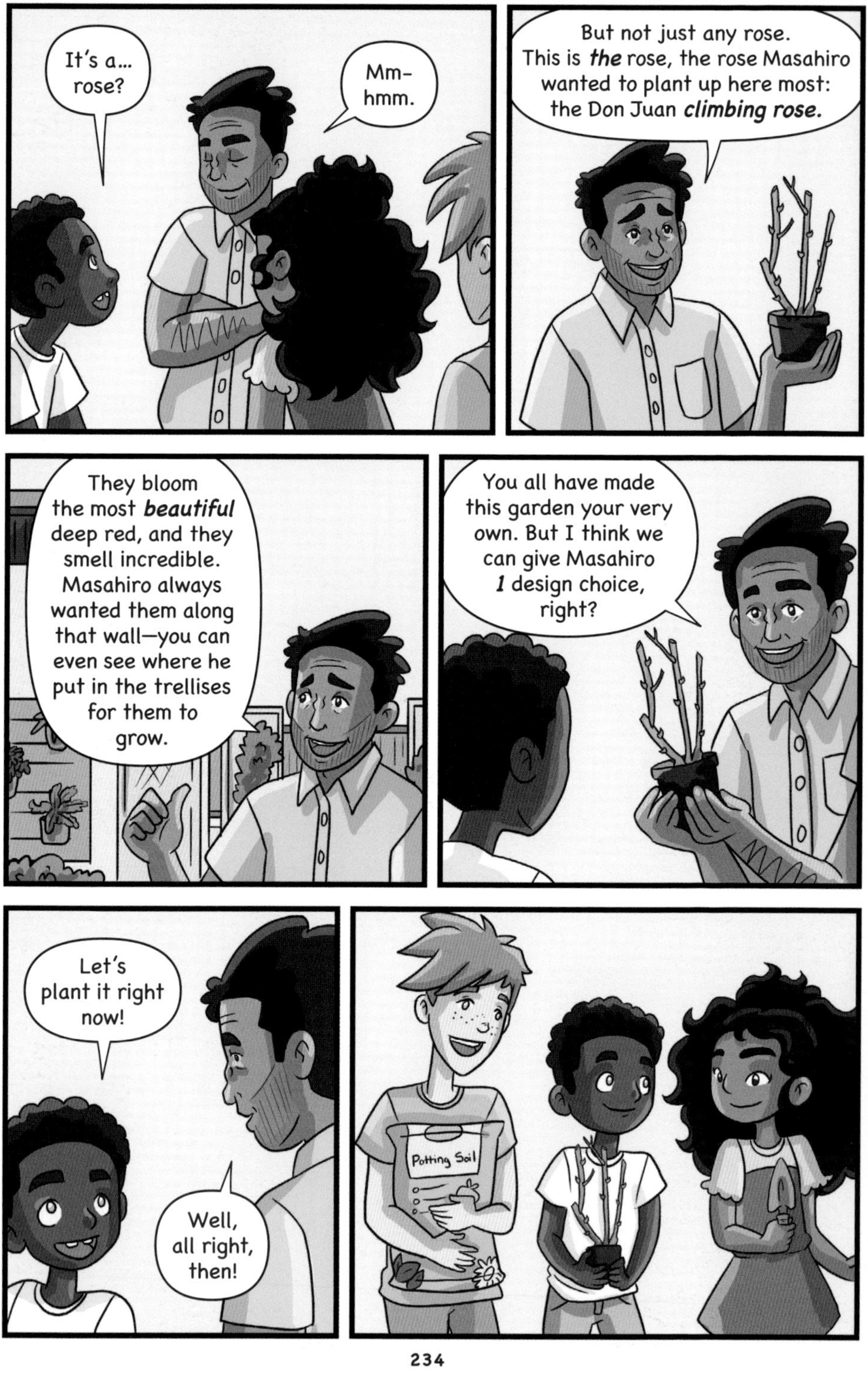

It's a... rose?
Mm-hmm.
But not just any rose. This is *the* rose, the rose Masahiro wanted to plant up here most: the Don Juan *climbing rose.*
They bloom the most *beautiful* deep red, and they smell incredible. Masahiro always wanted them along that wall—you can even see where he put in the trellises for them to grow.
You all have made this garden your very own. But I think we can give Masahiro *1* design choice, right?
Let's plant it right now!
Well, all right, then!
Potting Soil

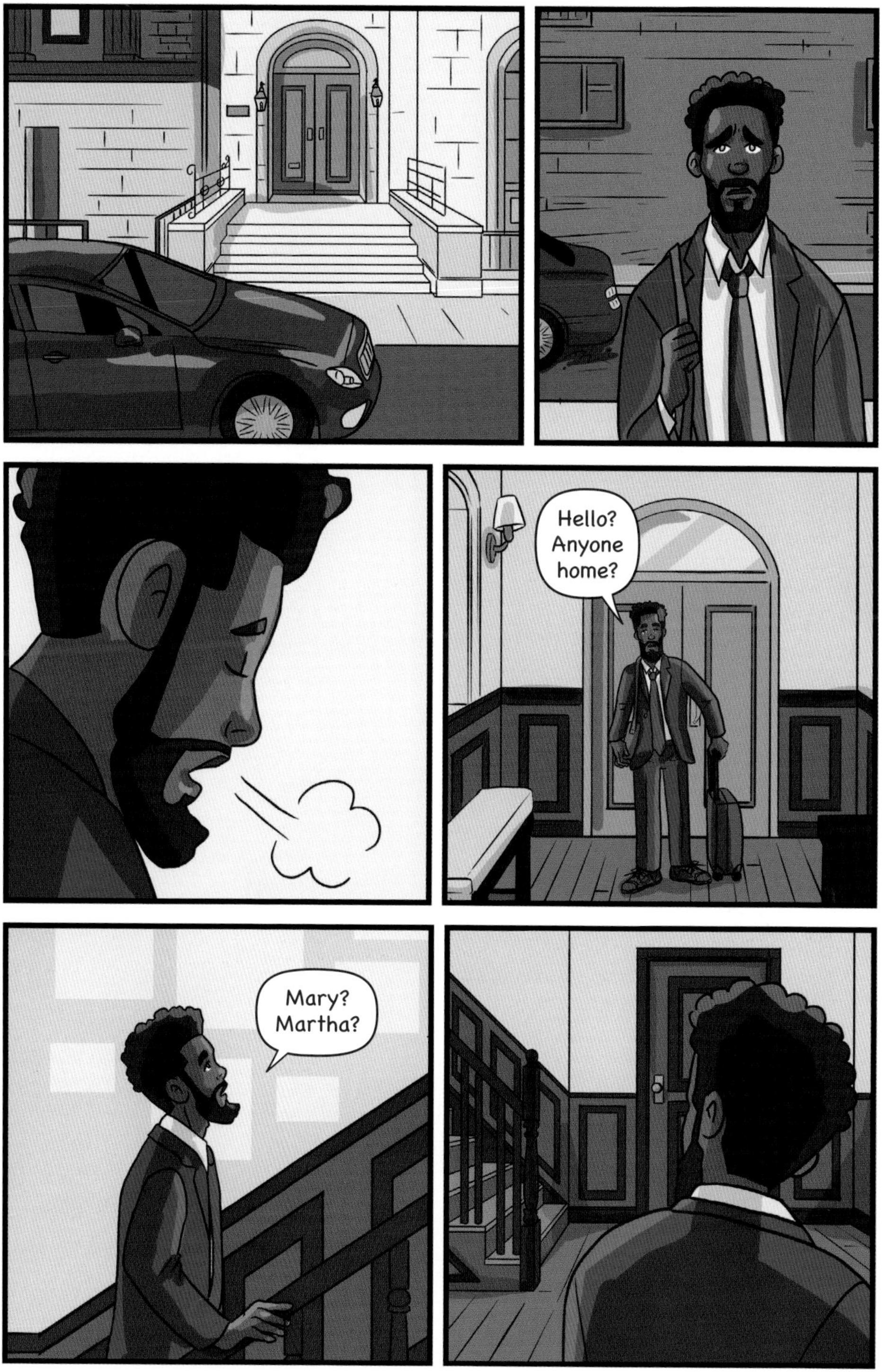
Hello?
Anyone
home?
Mary?
Martha?

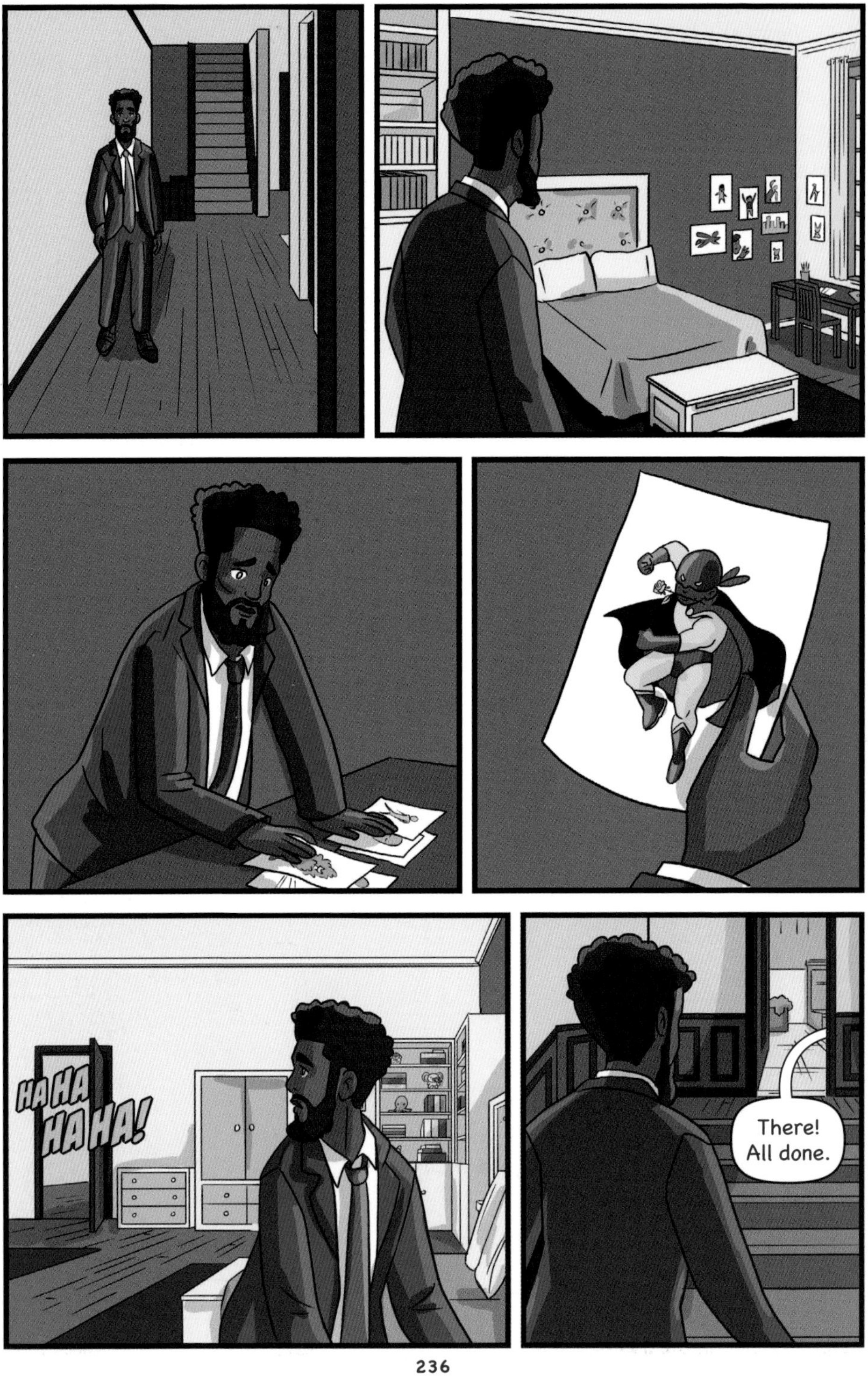
HA HA
HA HA!
There! All done.

P-pop...?

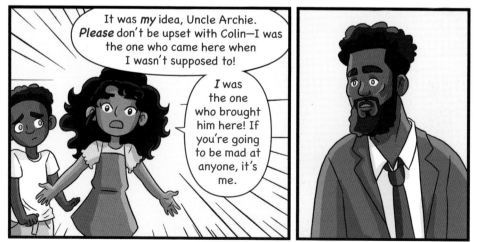

It was *my* idea, Uncle Archie. *Please* don't be upset with Colin—I was the one who came here when I wasn't supposed to!

I was the one who brought him here! If you're going to be mad at anyone, it's me.

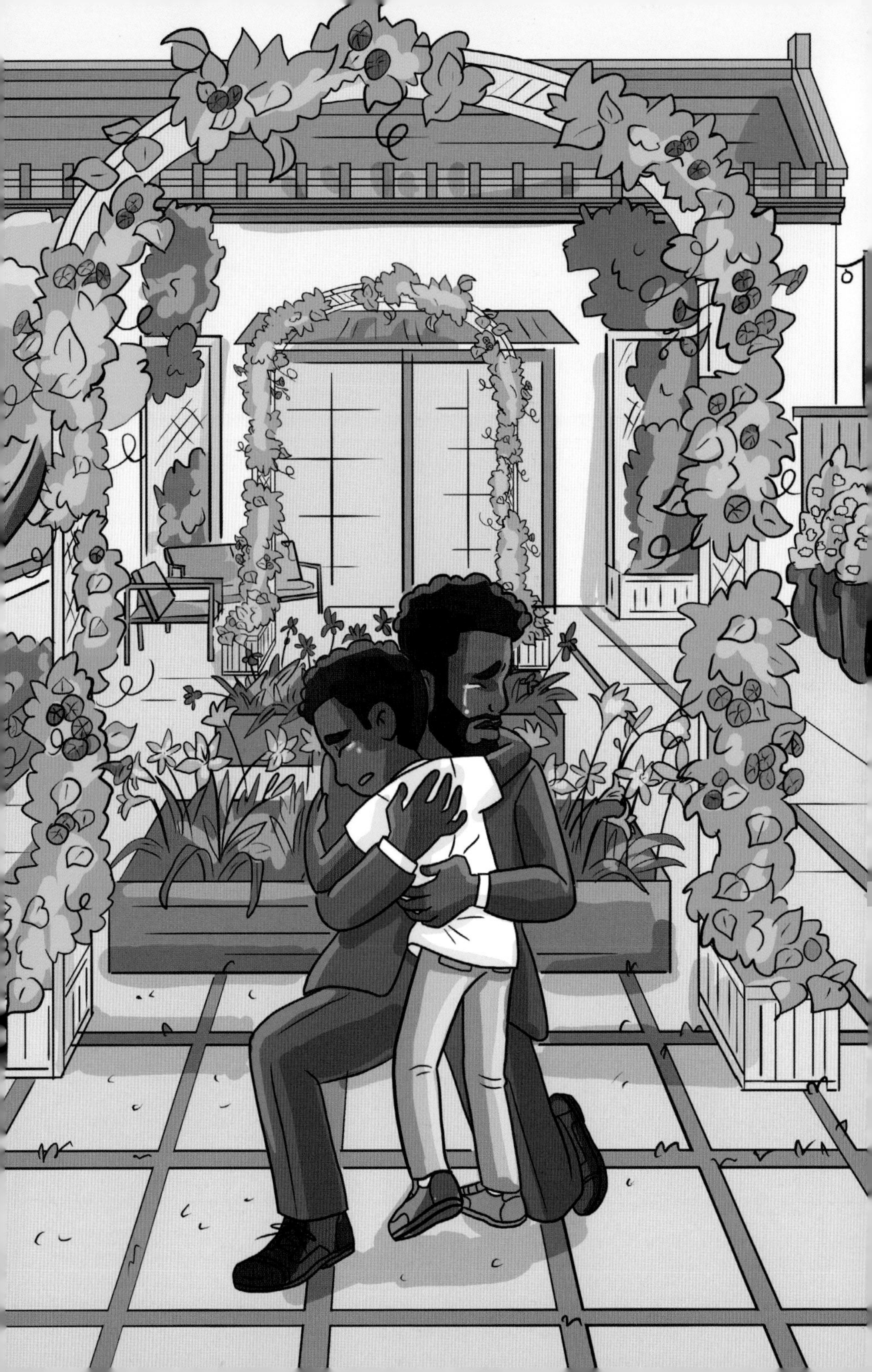

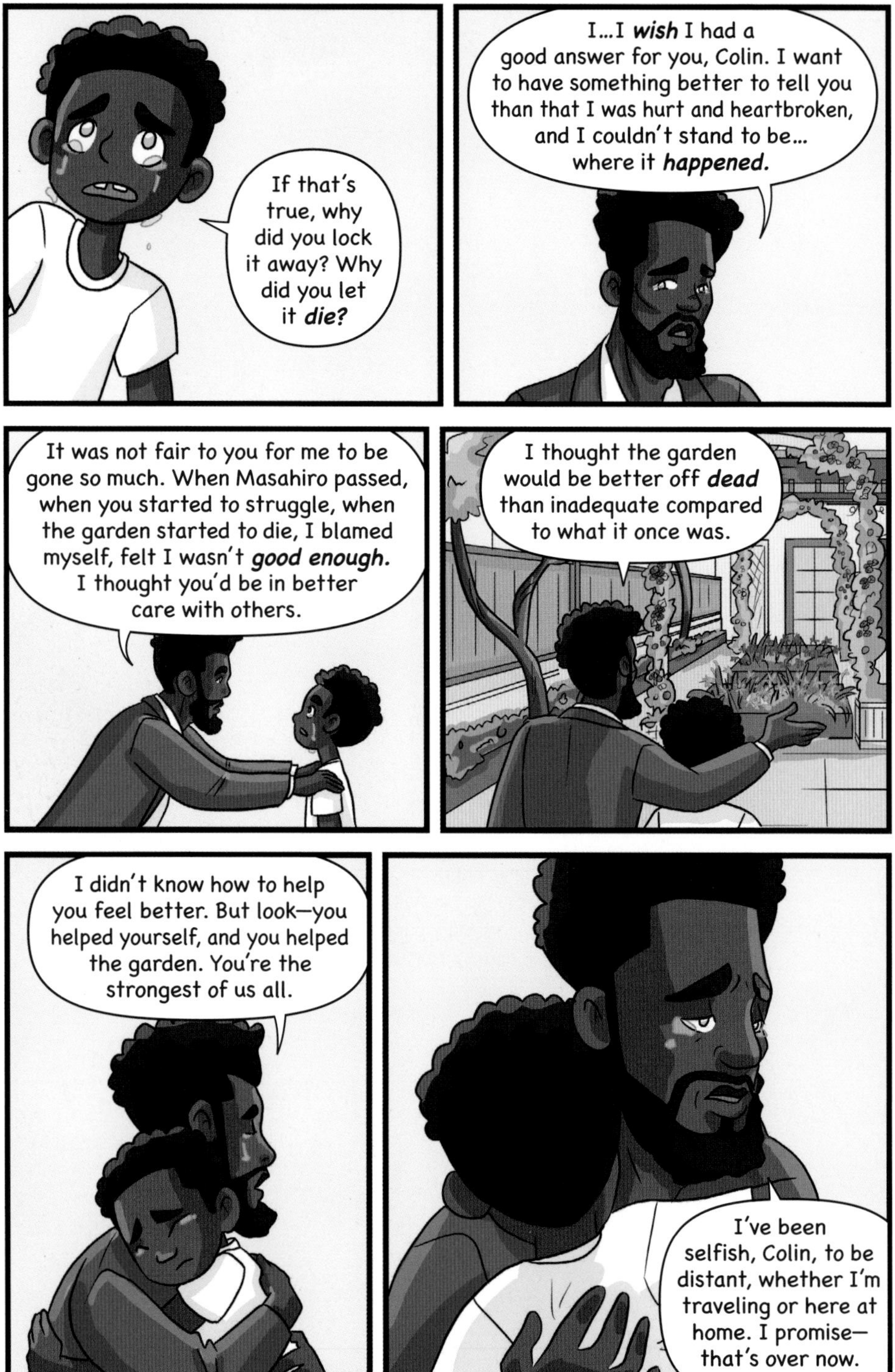
If that's true, why did you lock it away? Why did you let it *die?*
I…I *wish* I had a good answer for you, Colin. I want to have something better to tell you than that I was hurt and heartbroken, and I couldn't stand to be… where it *happened.*
It was not fair to you for me to be gone so much. When Masahiro passed, when you started to struggle, when the garden started to die, I blamed myself, felt I wasn't *good enough.* I thought you'd be in better care with others.
I thought the garden would be better off *dead* than inadequate compared to what it once was.
I didn't know how to help you feel better. But look—you helped yourself, and you helped the garden. You're the strongest of us all.
I've been selfish, Colin, to be distant, whether I'm traveling or here at home. I promise—that's over now.

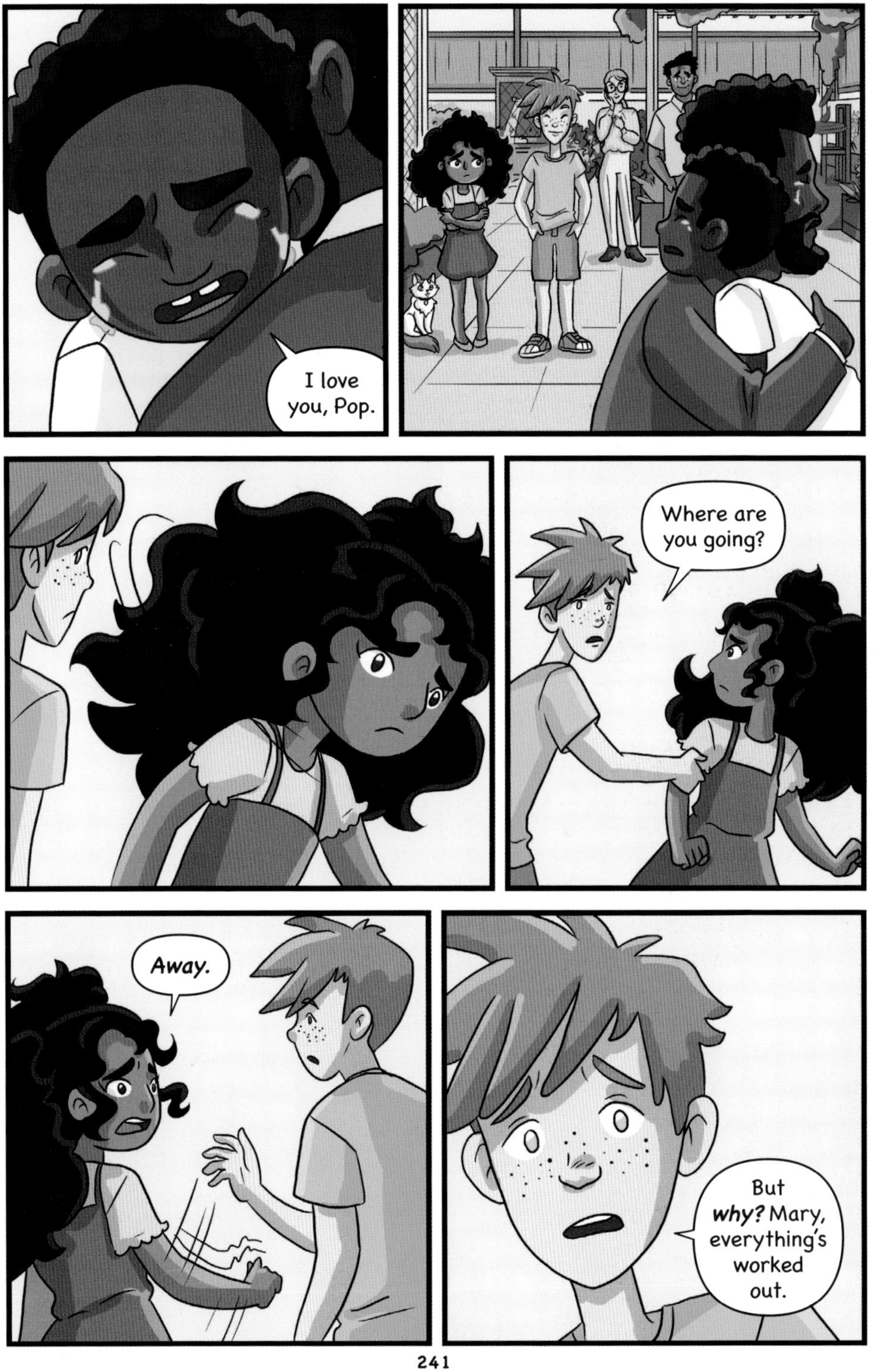
I love you, Pop.
Where are you going?
Away.
But *why?* Mary, everything's worked out.

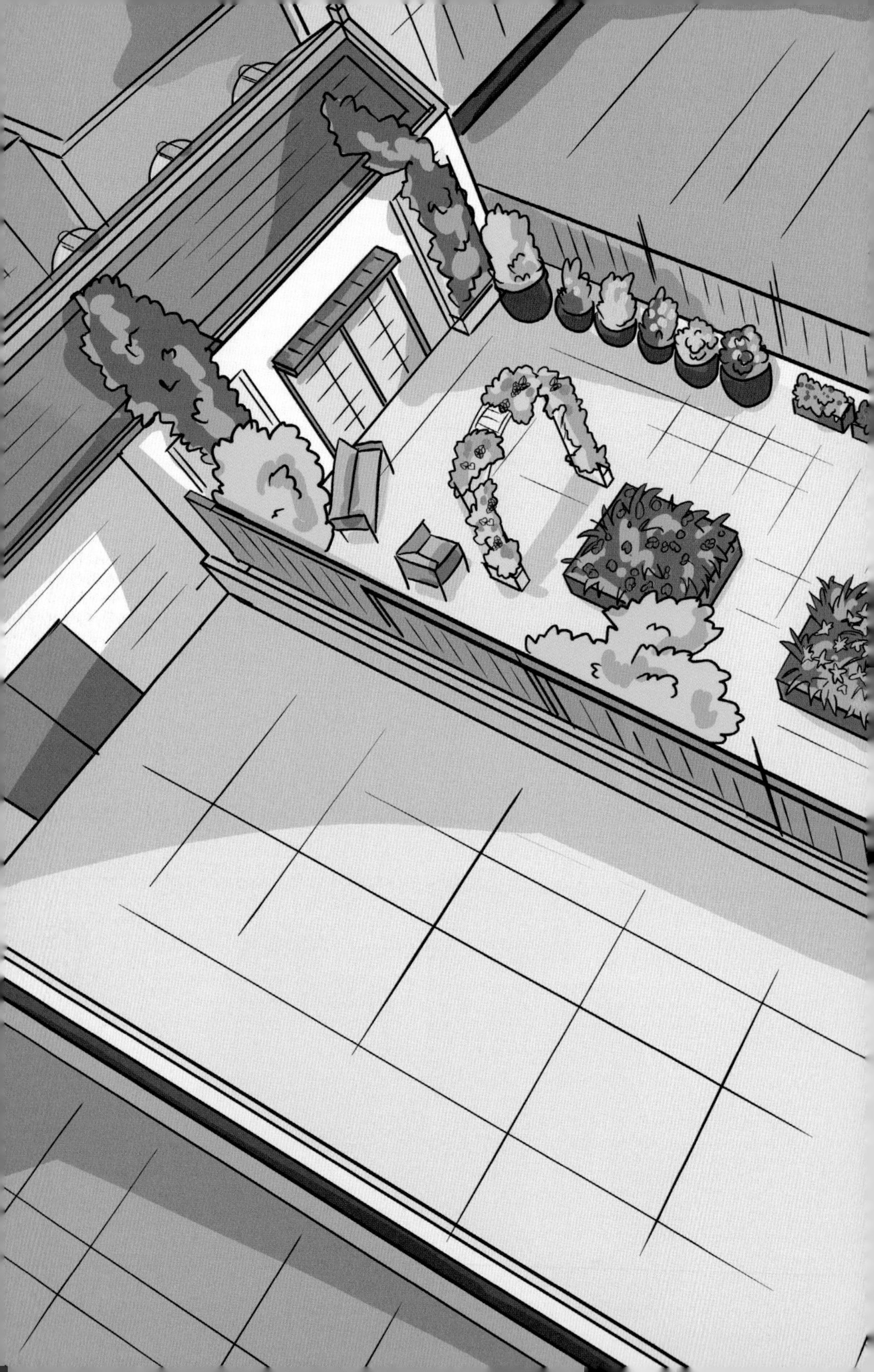

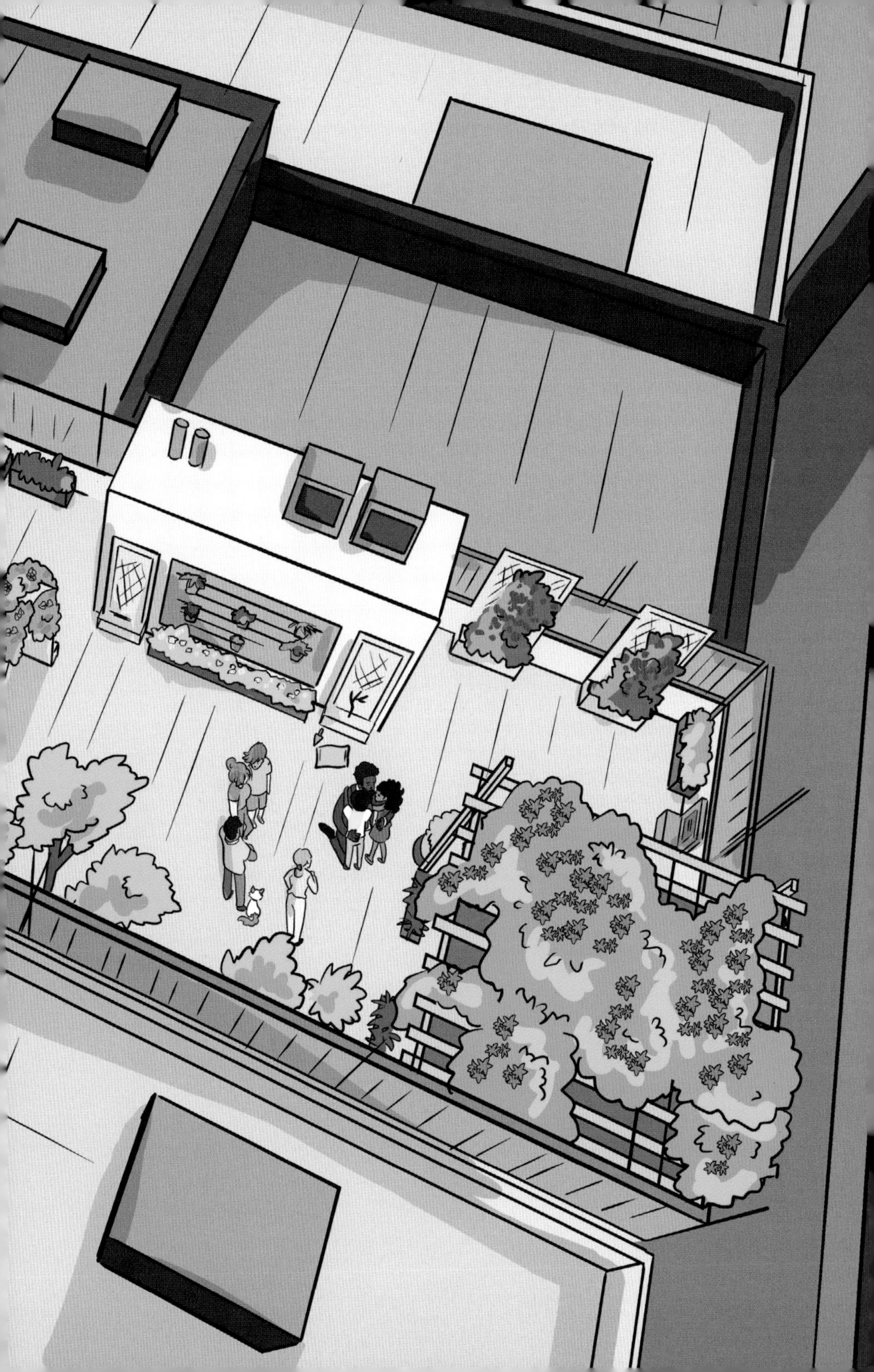

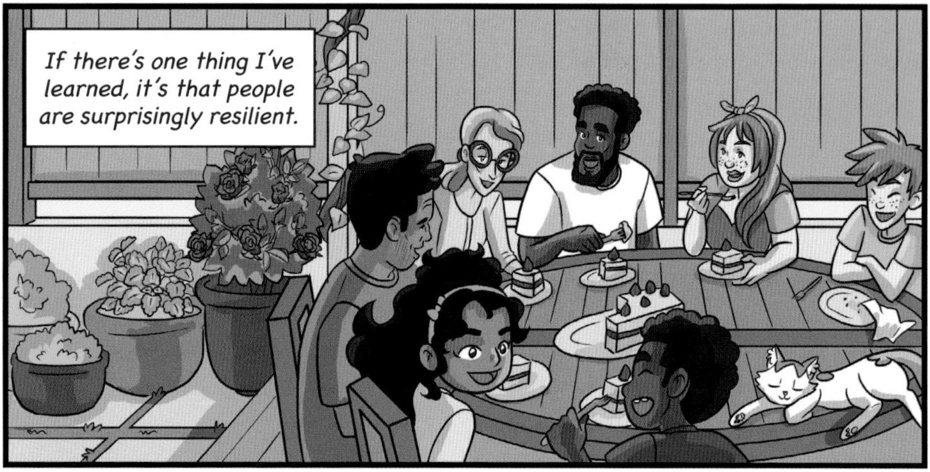
If there's one thing I've learned, it's that people are surprisingly resilient.

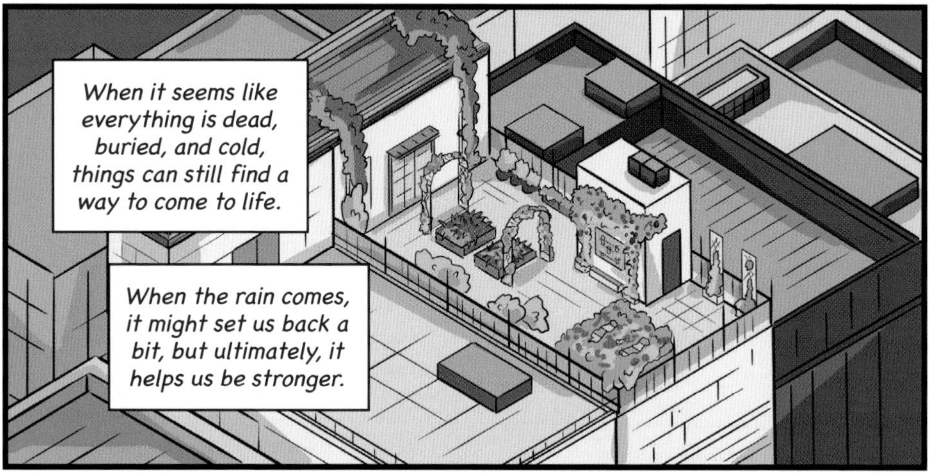
When it seems like everything is dead, buried, and cold, things can still find a way to come to life.
When the rain comes, it might set us back a bit, but ultimately, it helps us be stronger.

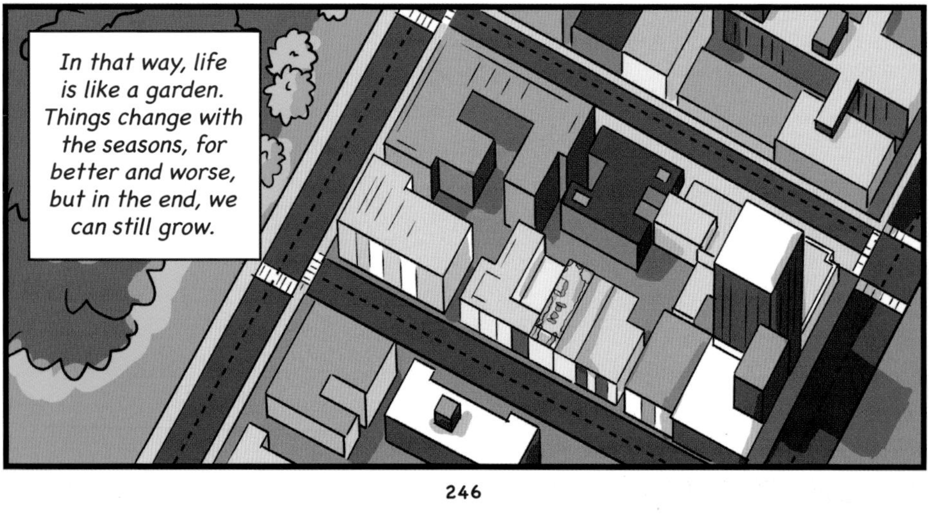
In that way, life is like a garden. Things change with the seasons, for better and worse, but in the end, we can still grow.

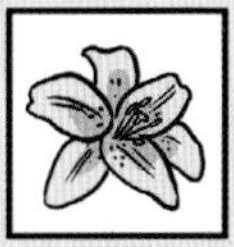

The_Secret_Garden

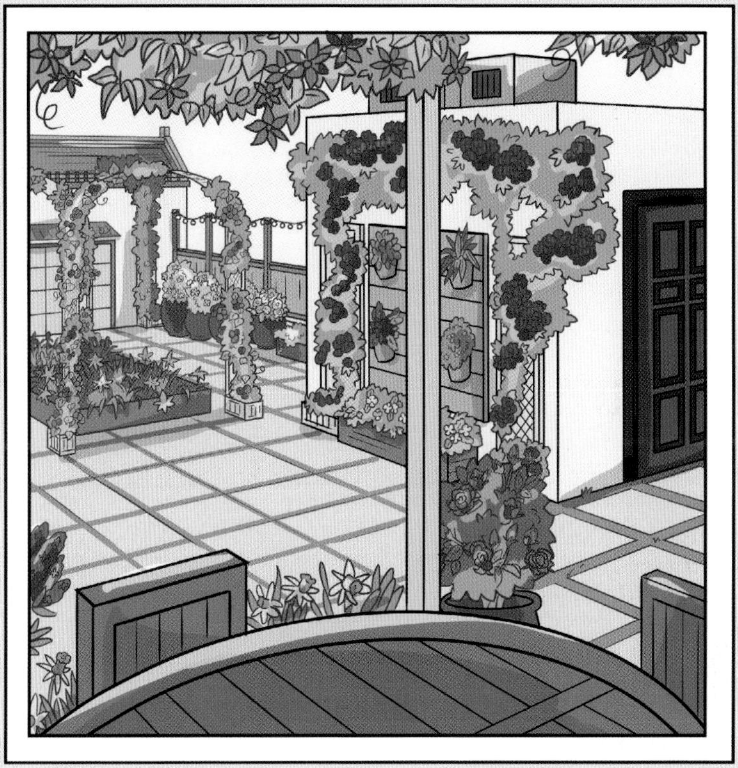

The_Secret_Garden Since the garden is in the sun all day, these plants are pretty much always thirsty. All this beauty means hours of watering!

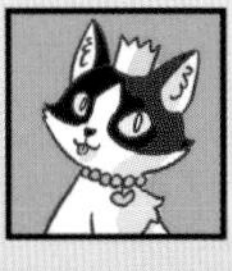

The_Cultured_Cat

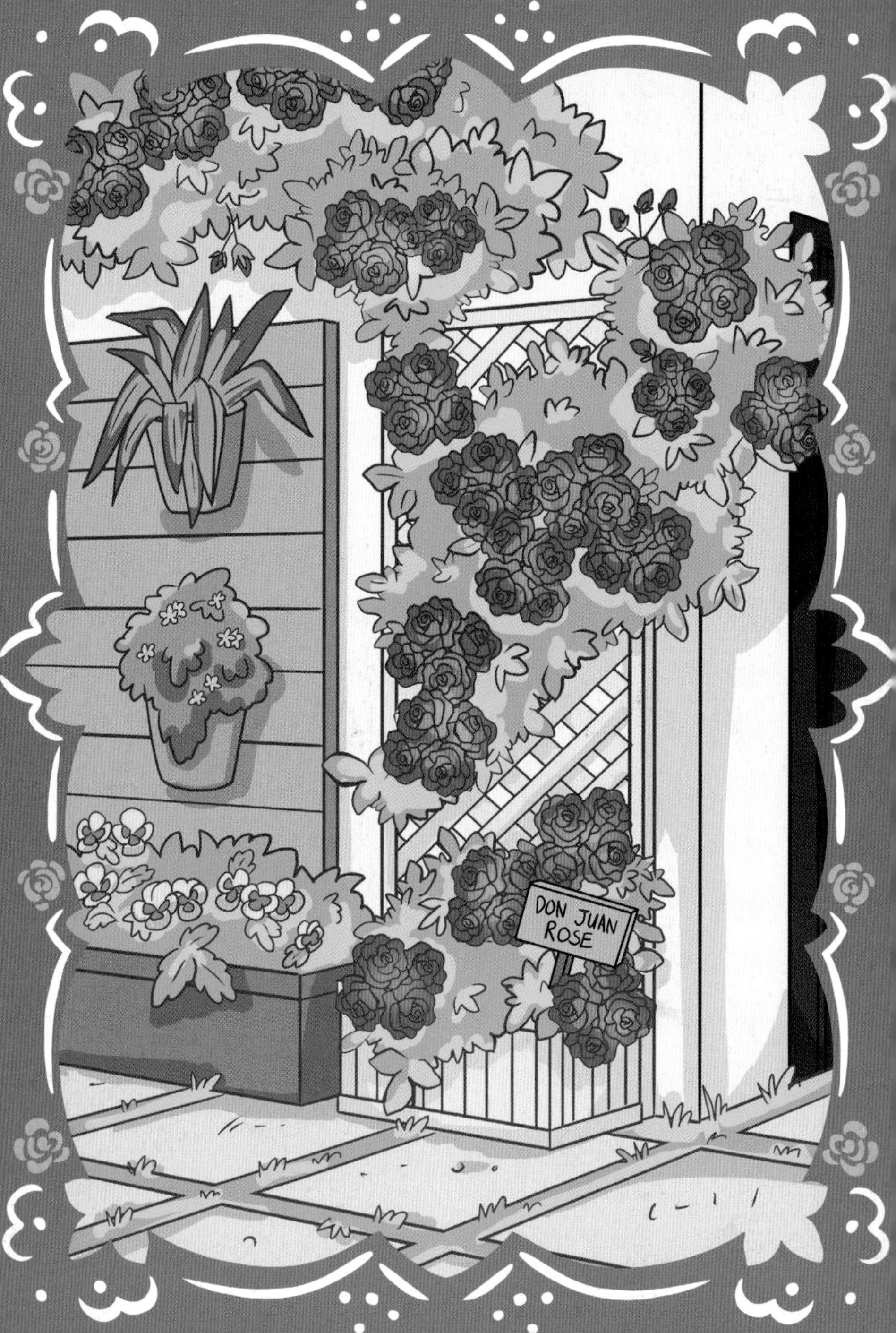
DON JUAN ROSE

Acknowledgments

Endless thanks to my agent, Anjali Singh, for her wisdom and guidance, and my editor, Rachel Poloski, for her insight, for her encouragement, and for the opportunity to tell Mary's story. Forever love to my husband, Eugene, for his support and his frozen-pizza-baking skills on deadline nights. Eternal gratitude to Steenz, my best friend, creative sounding board, and hype man. –Weir

Thank you to my husband, Ioannis, who did more than just support me while I ventured through the biggest project in my life thus far. Thank you to the BlamKatz, who gave me all the pointers, tips, and encouragement a newbie could ask for. Thank you to my family, who gave me unconditional support in my art aspirations so that I never doubted what was possible. Thank you to every art teacher, college professor, work colleague, and friend who knew I could do this. And lastly thanks to Nicky Rodriguez and K. Novack, who made sure I could get to that finish line. –Padilla

Ivy Noelle Weir

is a writer of comics and prose. She is the cocreator of the Dwayne McDuffie Award-winning graphic novel *Archival Quality*, and her writing has appeared in anthologies such as *Princeless: Girls Rock* and *Dead Beats*. She lives in the greater Boston area with her husband and their two tiny, weird dogs.

Eugene K. Ahn

Amber Padilla

is a cartoonist and illustrator based in Oakland, CA, and holds an MFA in Comics from California College of the Arts. *The Secret Garden on 81st Street* is Amber's debut graphic novel. Originally from Santa Ana, CA, she was raised on a healthy diet of animation, science fiction, soap operas, and Japanese anime and manga. When she's not drawing or crafting, she enjoys snuggling with her cat and spending time with her husband, family, and friends.

Amber Padilla